MW00592494

The Comedian Harmonists
The Last Great Jewish Performers In Nazi Germany

To Sandy + Warren
With best wish...

Douglas E. Friedman

HarmonySongs Publications – West Long Branch, New Jersey

Copyright © 2010 by Douglas E. Friedman.
Published by HarmonySongs Publications, West Long Branch, New Jersey

All rights reserved.

ISBN 978-0-9713979-1-0

Library of Congress Control Number: 2010934576

Reproduction or translation of any part of this work beyond that allowed by the United
States Copyright Act, without the written permission of the copyright holder, is not
permitted. Any requests for permission should be addressed to the publisher at
defriedman@harmonysongs.com.

Publisher Web Site: www.harmonysongs.com

Layout and back cover design by Gail McNeil. Front cover design by Benjamin Fong.

To my wife Linda with love and thanks.

CONTENTS

The Comedian Harmonists

CONTENTS

ACKNOWLEDGMENTS

This book has many co-authors – people without whom it could not have been written.

Although it is difficult to single out a few when so many helped, there are several people who have made major substantive contributions to this book. In Germany there were Theo Niemeyer and Jan Grübler. Theo is the archivist for the group and his permission was required to view the large archive of documents from the Biberti Estate that reside in the Staatsbibliothek in Berlin. He helped to guide me through the mysteries of the group and answered many questions. Many of the photographs and other illustrations that appear in the book were provided by Theo. He invited my wife and me into his house where he, his wife Sigrun and their daughter Lisa made us feel at home. Theo showed me what he called the "holy grail" of the Comedian Harmonists – the Frommermann scrapbooks – along with other rare memorabilia. He was also one of the fact-checkers and proofreaders of the book.

I came into contact with Jan Grübler after I returned from Germany. Jan has studied the Biberti Estate papers extensively and very generously shared his knowledge with me (translating into English most of what he provided). Jan would always ask, "What else can I do to help?" He was extremely helpful in unraveling the disputes within the Meistersextett. Much of the information in the Appendices came from Jan. But his help went way beyond that. His assistance and support were major factors in the writing of this book. He was another of the fact-checkers and proofreaders.

In the United States, there were Brita Schmitz (by way of Germany) and Pamela Rosen. Finding Brita was a real stroke of luck. I needed someone to do translating for me and I found her while she was teaching at Monmouth University, near my home. She not only became my translator, but her family and mine have become great friends. Pam, who is from California and has studied the group for many years, learned German to be able to read documents in their original language. She generously provided me with much insight and information and introduced me to Jan.

Josef Westner (unbelievably, a college student with remarkable knowledge for one of any age) supplied me with hard-to-find biographical information and music. Uwe Berger shared information and photos about the Leschnikoff family. Andreas Schmauder kindly allowed me to use his wonderful discography. Sebastian Semler helped guide me through the Staatsbibliothek in Berlin. Erwin Bootz' widow, Mrs. Helli Bootz, provided me with information and photos. Others in Germany who helped were Karsten Lehl and Andreas Wellen of Ensemble Six, Marina Seeger-Holle (who resides in the "founding apartment" and graciously invited my wife and me into her home), Roland Schmidt-Hensel and the staff at the Staatsbibliothek in Berlin, Elisabeth Trautwein-Heymann, daughter of the great composer Werner Richard Heymann, and Harry Frohman's stepson Eric von Späth and his wife, Beate. My wife and I spent an afternoon in the von Späths' house, where Harry Frohman lived the last years of his life.

Michael Hortig (from Austria) allowed me to use pages from the Mayreder diaries and Andrea Hollmann provided some photos.

Pam put me in contact with Carolyn Harcourt, who provided papers from the Cycowski Estate that were not available elsewhere. Erich Collin's grandchildren, Marc Alexander and Deborah Tint, were both generous with photos and information about their family. Belinda Cooper helped me in the very early days of my study of the group. The staff at the Goethe Institut in New York, Washington and Los Angeles were extremely helpful in my search for the English-subtitled version of the Fechner film. Mrs. Eleonore Kramer, widow of Comedy Harmonists' pianist, Fritz Kramer, shared some memories with me and Bob Scherr, longtime friend of the Cycowskis, gave me first-hand accounts. Ursula Elkan Bootz Hammil's daughter, Beryn Hammil, helped with information and photos of her mother.

Many people were good enough to write short articles and "favorite song" pieces for the book. They are: Marc Alexander, Peter Becker, Karsten Lehl, Jim Lowe, Theo Niemeyer, Andreas Schmauder, Carolyn Harcourt, Marv Goldberg, Jan Grübler, Josef Westner, Uwe Berger, Robert Scherr, Pamela Rosen, Elisabeth Trautwein-Heymann, Deborah Tint and Helli Bootz.

Several people read the book in draft form and provided helpful comments. They were Jan, Theo, Pam and my good friend, playwright Tevia Abrams.

Others who assisted along the way were Al Zager, Dale Daniels and my late friend Ronnie Italiano, who helped to show me the way to better vocal group harmony which made me more open to appreciating the Comedian Harmonists.

The primary editor was my brother Ken Friedman. His comments and especially his encouragement were, as always, invaluable. Finally, my wife, Linda Lashbrook, helped with the editing, proofreading, was my chief sounding board and never complained about the time I spent on this or about having to learn more about the Comedian Harmonists than she may have wanted to know.

T he Comedian Harmonists – their music and their story – have captivated people for generations. The German singing group was wildly successful in the early 1930s, but because three of the six members were either Jewish or considered Jewish under the Nazi decree defining non-Aryans, the German government forced them to disband in 1935 – at the height of their popularity. This aspect of the Holocaust – the dehumanization of Jews, in this case in the arts, in the early days of the Third Reich – has not been as widely written about as the stories of the camps and the individual survivors.

For many, the Comedian Harmonists' music is more than enough. Their sound is timeless and encompasses many genres – pop, jazz, folk, classical. Their music also went in an entirely new direction. At first, they were heavily influenced by an American group, the Revelers, and the new jazzier style the Revelers had introduced. But the Comedian Harmonists took it further, faster. They were not mere imitators; they were innovators – in the type of music they sang and in its presentation.

When I first heard the Comedian Harmonists, I could not (and did not want to) get the music out of my head. What I knew of their story was compelling, but I was frustrated by the difficulty in finding out more – in getting beyond the basics. I bought a copy of a film – *The Harmonists* – that more or less tells their story. I visited the largest web site on the group (http://www.comedian-harmonists.com) which fortunately is in both German and English. I still wanted to know more. I found a biography – *Comedian Harmonists, Ein Vokalensemble erobert die Welt* (The Comedian Harmonists, A Vocal Group Conquers The World) by Peter Czada and Günter Große – but the book was in German, which was not a language that I could read, so I arranged to have the book translated. I discovered a documentary and a book with transcripts of the interviews for the documentary; however, both the film and the book were in German. After months of searching, and with much help from the Goethe Institut, I found the only version of the documentary that included English subtitles and I also had the book of interviews translated.

But even after all that, I still thought that the Nazis' attacks on so-called "degenerate" art had not been presented fully or placed in a proper context. And, surprisingly, I could not find much discussion about the Comedian Harmonists' infectious music. Only after a lot of searching, days in an Archive at the Staatsbibliothek (State Library) in Berlin and much assistance from generous enthusiasts both in Germany and the United States, did I begin to feel that I had gained a true understanding of what had happened with the group and its members.

The story of the Comedian Harmonists sadly and vividly illustrates the effect of the Nazis' policies on Jews in the arts. The Comedian Harmonists are particularly interesting to study from this perspective because their ensemble contained not only Jews, but also Aryans and one member (Erich Collin) who was of one hundred percent Jewish heritage, but had been baptized and raised as a Christian. The National Socialists began to mount their attacks on so-called entartete Kunst (or degenerate art) in the early days of the Third Reich. The Reichskulturkammer (RKK or Federal Culture Chamber) – established in 1933 – effectively banned artists who were considered to be unsuitable by excluding them from membership in any of the RKK's Chambers, thereby denying these artists the right to practice their profession or to show or perform their work.

In the field of music, where the Reichsmusikkammer or Federal Chamber of Music reigned, some of the well-known people affected by these policies were classical artists Arnold Schoenberg, Otto Klemperer and Bruno Walter, the jazz group Weintraubs Syncopators, the great composer Werner Richard Heymann, and, of course, the Comedian Harmonists.

The Jüdischer Kulturbund or Jewish Cultural Association is also worth mentioning. After the RKK and its chambers began formal exclusion of Jews from the arts in 1933, the Kulturbund was created by Jews in order to give Jewish artists an opportunity to continue to perform. The Nazi government approved the organization – although for less than altruistic reasons – seeing it as a way to make the claim that they were not persecuting Jews. The Kulturbund had to be staffed solely by Jews and the members were only allowed to play to Jewish audiences at one theater in Berlin. In 1941, the government ordered the Kulturbund dissolved. Although the Comedian Harmonists were never involved in the Kulturbund, it is a part of the story of Jews in the arts under the Third Reich.

While the Comedian Harmonists performed longer than any of the other premier Jewish artists in Germany, they too were eventually caught in the Nazis' pernicious web. Many of those in the arts, including the Comedian Harmonists, managed to avoid the horrors of the concentration camps. Being legally unable to work as artists or musicians, they found their way to more hospitable countries during a time when leaving Germany was still an option. After the war, some returned to Germany, while others remained in their adopted homes.

In this book, for the first time in English, is the story of these musical innovators who had the misfortune to come together and succeed just at the time when the Nazis and their powerful and inescapable repression also began.

I have been a serious student of pre-1960 vocal groups and their history for many years and first came across the Comedian Harmonists in that connection. Their story triggered in me a continuing journey of discovery that combined my love of vocal group music with my Jewish heritage.

I could not have dreamed what would follow and how this subject would occupy so much of my time over the next few years – and still does. I also found out that I was not alone – there were other enthusiasts both in Europe and the U.S. who were studying the group and were involved in the search for information. Many of these people gave me substantial assistance in compiling the information necessary to write this book and are mentioned by name in the Acknowledgments.

I eventually learned about the existence of the Staatsbibliothek Archive and that it contained some of the papers of the group. After receiving special permission to view the contents from Theo Niemeyer (the Archivist), my wife and I traveled to Berlin in May 2007 for what turned out to be the experience of a lifetime. I spent a week in the Archive and even though I know only a few words in German, it is amazing what can be done with knowledge of proper nouns, cognates and important dates. I was able to identify many relevant documents to copy and brought these papers home to be translated. We also met with many people with some association with or relation to the Comedian Harmonists and we saw both the apartment where the group was founded and the house where Harry Frommermann, the founder, had died.

Some may wonder about the subtitle that I used for the book — "The Last Great Jewish Performers In Nazi Germany." After all, only three of the six members were Jewish. But the Nazis didn't care. That is the point. Even one Jew was enough to "contaminate" the group. To the Nazis, the Comedian Harmonists were Jewish and therefore they had to be banned.

During the time I was researching the book, I was asked to join the Board of Directors of the nationally recognized Holocaust, Genocide & Human Rights Education Center at Brookdale Community College in Lincroft, New Jersey, and accepted. The Center does invaluable work in providing education about the Holocaust and other genocide and human rights issues. Because of this, I made the decision to donate 100% of my profits from this book to the Center.

CHAPTER ONE

"Hoppla, jetzt komm' ich"[1]

(Okay, Here I Come)

Beginnings

The year is 1910. The boy, only four years old, would go with his father to rehearsals of the Philharmonic, where his father sang in the chorus. The boy sat, sometimes in the woodwind section, sometimes among the brass instruments. As a boy would do, he tried to imitate the sounds coming from the instruments. It probably never occurred to him that the talents he was developing would help propel him to fortune and fame. It can be said with great certainty that the boy never dreamed that the path on which he was headed would also lead to persecution, disillusionment and exile.

Fast-forward to the 1950s. The boy is now middle-aged. He has little money. He sits in a rented room, in a foreign country, trying to produce a 28-track tape recording in which he uses only his voice to create the sound of a complete vocal orchestra. After many years of exile, his journey will eventually bring him back to his home country, where he is facing serious illness and ultimately death, likely hastened by the stress of the life he has led.

Rewind to 1927. The same boy, now 21 years old, has recently lost both his parents. However, he still has a keen interest in music and wants to form a singing group modeled after the famous Americans, the Revelers.[2] To find the other members, he places an ad in a newspaper.

A young man wanting to form a vocal group is not an unusual story. But this story will be different because the place is Berlin and the young man – Harry Frommermann – is Jewish.

The story of Frommermann and the group he founded, the Comedian Harmonists, is one of aspiration, great musicality, enormous success, the Holocaust, war, betrayal, the pursuit of the American dream, and more. Some may question whether this is a Holocaust story – but there were many aspects to the Holocaust. Yad Vashem (Israel's Holocaust Martyrs' and Heroes' Remembrance Authority) defines the Holocaust as "the sum total of all anti-Jewish actions carried out by the Nazi regime between 1933 and 1945: from stripping the German Jews of their legal and economic status in the 1930s, to segregating and starving Jews in the various occupied countries, to the murder of close to six million Jews in Europe."[3] The Comedian Harmonists are one of the most prominent examples of how the National Socialists tried to erase all traces of Jewish

---

1   Recorded by the Comedian Harmonists in 1932.
2   In Germany, the spelling was Revellers.
3   http://www.yadvashem.org/ (accessed November 5, 2007)

civilization and culture from German society – as one writer called it, "the slow smothering of Jewish life."[4]

The Revelers

Harry Frommermann was immediately taken with the Revelers. Their style and technique were new and unique and Frommermann was "enthused about their weightlessness in voice-giving." He "started to write scores for a so far non-existent group – inspired by the popularity of the Revelers' records. The scores differed from the Revelers in that in them I tried to connect my talent to imitate musical instruments with the composition for a men's quartet."[5]

An extremely important and popular group in the 1920s and early 1930s, the Revelers advanced the vocal group music genre by using more voice separation and a less formal style than previous popular groups, as well as by pioneering in the use of their voices to imitate instruments.[6] They were also the group that began to build the bridge between the very formal vocal groups of the first two decades of the twentieth century (such as the American, Peerless and Haydn Quartets) and the musically freer

4   Grimes, William. *New York Times*, October 26, 2005, "The Radical Restructuring of a Germany Headed To War."

5   Frohman, Harry M. *The Story Of The Comedian (Comedy) Harmonists*, Comedian Harmonists Archive, Theo Niemeyer ("Frohman story"). Frommermann later changed his name to Frohman. This story was written by Frohman in English.

6   The Revelers started as the Shannon Four in 1917 and recorded on the Victor label. The members were Charles Hart, Harvey Hindermyer, Elliott Shaw and Wilfred Glenn. In 1918, Lewis James replaced Hindermyer. They became the Shannon Quartet in 1923, but Hart left and they had no fixed lead tenor. Soon after, they became the Revelers, with Franklyn Baur as first tenor, James (also as tenor), baritone Shaw, Glenn as the bass and Ed Smalle on piano. The Revelers had 13 hit records from 1926 to 1930 on the Victor label, with their biggest being "Dinah" in 1926. In those days, some groups would record simultaneously for various record companies and use a different name on each label: on Columbia, they were called the Singing Sophomores; on Brunswick, the Gaiety Musical Comedy Chorus and the Merrymakers

and jazzier groups that followed. In his book *Stardust Melodies*, Will Friedwald said of the Revelers: "This vocal quartet was harmonically quite innovative and was an important influence on such later groups as [Paul] Whiteman's own Rhythm Boys and the German Comedian Harmonists. Rhythmically, however, the Revelers were stiff beyond words and even the most rudimentary syncopation seems quite beyond them."[7] Another view of the Revelers – this from the other side of the Atlantic – comes from Comedian Harmonists biographers, Peter Czada and Günter Grosse [German: Große], in their book, *Comedian Harmonists, Ein Vokalensemble erobert die Welt* (*The Comedian Harmonists, A Vocal Group Conquers The World*): "Popular music in America started to experience a subtle change in the middle of the twenties, which would inspire [the Revelers'] Wilfred Glenn. He would later say that the character of the songs which the quartet would be requested to sing by the record companies at the beginning of 1925 increasingly displeased him…. [M]ore modern music was reserved for the instrumentalists. Glenn developed a new concept of arranging and presentation for his quartet at that time, supported by Franklyn Baur…. The result was a new, more relaxed style of singing, closer to jazz…"[8]

German vocal music before the Comedian Harmonists was stiff and lacking in rhythm. German quartets sang traditional songs, wore gloves, and held songbooks in front of them. Frommermann wanted to break with that tradition. The Revelers had not yet performed in Germany because they demanded more money for performances than German promoters could pay. This encouraged Frommermann; he believed that a similar, German group could make a lot of money because their fees would not be too high, but could be high enough to make them successful.

Frommermann was right. And although he may have been inspired by the Revelers, what he and the others created was no mere copy. The Comedian Harmonists

Berliner Lokal-Anzeiger, December 18, 1927

---

7   Friedwald, Will. *Stardust Melodies*. New York: Pantheon Books, 2002, p. 123

8   Czada, Peter and Günter Grosse. *Comedian Harmonists: Ein Vokalensemble erobert die Welt*. Berlin: Edition Hentrich, 1993, 1998 ("Czada"), p. 12. All references are to the 1998 edition.

were one of the best vocal groups of any era and had a unique sound that was and still is unmistakable.

Rare Opportunity

When Frommermann had completed 15 arrangements, he decided to put his plan into action.[9] He placed an ad in the Sunday, December 18, 1927, edition of the *Berliner Lokal-Anzeiger*, a daily newspaper, that read as follows: *Achtung. Selten. Tenor, Bass (Berufssänger, nicht über 25), sehr musikalisch, schönklingende Stimmen, für einzig dastehendes Ensemble unter Angabe der täglich verfügbaren Zeit gesucht. Ej. 25 Scherlfiliale, Friedrichstr. 136.* (Attention. Rare opportunity. Tenor, Bass (professional singer not over 25), musically talented, nice-sounding voices, for unique ensemble. Kindly give days and times when available [for rehearsals, etc.].) The ad, which included a reply address of a newspaper's branch office, cost 12.50 marks.[10]

At the time, the number one song in the U.S. was "My Blue Heaven" by vocalist Gene Austin. "My Blue Heaven" was the second best-selling non-holiday record of the entire pre-1955 period, selling more than 5,000,000 copies![11] The Revelers had already charted ten times by then, but competition was not that fierce in those days: If you had a contract with a major label, such as the Revelers had with Victor, charting was almost assured.[12]

The *Lokal-Anzeiger* was a full-sized paper and the small advertisement could easily have been overlooked. But, luckily for Frommermann, the ads were listed by category – in this case under "Musik u. Gesang" or "Music and Singing." The *Lokal-Anzeiger* advertisement gave the address of a mail drop on the other side of Berlin. Frommermann and Theodor Steiner wrote individually to the applicants inviting them to audition at Frommermann's apartment. (Steiner was a childhood friend of Harry's who played piano and was also to be the baritone voice for the group.) The response to the advertisement was overwhelming. Times were not good for singers and there were few jobs available. According to Frommermann, about 70 people showed up for the January 3, 1928, audition, lining the staircase to his fifth-floor apartment and spill-

---

9   Frohman story

10 Harry Frommermann, Radio Bremen Interview, Loretta Findeisen, January 13, 1973 ("Radio Bremen Frommermann Interview")

11 Whitburn, Joel. *Joel Whitburn's Pop Memories 1890-1954*. Menomonee Falls, Wisconsin: Record Research, Inc., 1986, p. 38. The number one seller of the period was "Near You" by Francis Craig & his Orchestra in 1917. Whitburn p. 627.

12 The Merry Macs had already formed in Minnesota, but would not get a recording contract until 1932. Bing Crosby and the Rhythm Boys joined Paul Whiteman's Orchestra in 1926 and the trio had made the charts, with Whiteman, on "Side By Side" in July and "I'm Coming Virginia" in September of 1927. The Boswell Sisters recorded as early as 1925 but would not chart until 1931. The Mills Brothers' first hit was in 1931. The Peerless Quartet had faded, with its last chart hit coming in early 1926. The American Quartet had disappeared even earlier (in 1924).

BERLINER GEDENKTAFEL

In einer Mansarde dieses Hauses
wurden zur Jahreswende 1927/28 auf Initiative
von HARRY FROMMERMANN mit
ROBERT BIBERTI, ERWIN BOOTZ, ERICH COLLIN,
ROMAN CYCOWSKI und ,ARI' LESCHNIKOFF die
»COMEDIAN HARMONISTS«
gegründet. Das weltberühmte Vokalensemble
wurde 1935 durch die erzwungene Emigration der
drei jüdischen Mitglieder getrennt.

The plaque on the wall at Stubenrauchstrasse 47, Berlin; it reads "In an attic of this house in the years 1927/1928 on the initiative of Harry Frommermann with Robert Biberti, Erwin Bootz, Erich Collin, Roman Cycowski and Ari Leschnikoff, the 'Comedian Harmonists' were founded. The world-famous vocal group was broken up in 1935 when the three Jewish members were forced to emigrate."

ing out onto the sidewalk below.[13] That number may be exaggerated; it seems a large number to invite to appear.

When I walked up those stairs and stood in that apartment on a May morning in 2007, it was difficult for me visualize the scene as it must have been 80 years earlier. The Stubenrauchstrasse neighborhood is a nice middle-class area, not a poor one, and it was hard to understand how Frommermann could afford to live there. Marina Seeger-Holle, whose family has owned the building since it was erected and who now lives in the famous top-floor apartment with her family, explained that the rooms were originally intended for storage and were not meant to be lived in. Because it was not a proper apartment, the rent was cheap.[14]

Frommermann told the story that one of the applicants, Robert Biberti, a "huge basso," shouldered his way past the others and was "the first and only choice among the seventy" who showed up. A letter found in the Biberti Estate Archive at the Staatsbibliothek (State Library) in Berlin, dated December 29, 1927, from Frommermann and Steiner to Biberti, invites Biberti to appear at their Berlin apartment at Stubenrauchstrasse 47 for an audition on January 3, 1928.[15]

---

13   Frohman story

14   Interview with Marina Seeger-Holle in Berlin on May 9, 2007

15   The book by Eberhard Fechner, *Die Comedian Harmonists: Sechs Lebensläufe*. Berlin: Quadriga Verlag, 1988 ("Fechner book") refers to an audition date of December 29, 1927, but the documents in the Archive contradict that date. See, Fechner book, pp. 156 and 163. (All references to the Fechner book are to the 1988 hardcover edition. There is also a paperback edition.)

Stubenrauchstrasse 47, Berlin

In his booming bass voice, Biberti made his case to Frommermann for inclusion in the group and demonstrated his not inconsiderable singing abilities. His audition number was the aria "O Isis and Osiris" from *The Magic Flute* by Mozart. Steiner accompanied him "a bit haltingly."[16]

Biberti could sight-read music, which was a big advantage, and he was also a fan of the Revelers. He was perfect for the group in one other respect – he was willing to rehearse without payment.[17] This was essential as Frommermann and Steiner did not have the means to pay anyone to rehearse; in fact, they barely had enough money for rent and food. Frommermann had to borrow money from his girlfriend, Jesta Nielsen (whose mother was Asta Nielsen, from Denmark, a famous stage actress in Scandinavia who became a silent film star in Germany) so that he could concentrate on music and not have to look for a job.[18] Two singers – Louis Kaliger and Victor Colani – had already been chosen; Biberti convinced Frommermann and Steiner that he could supply the other singers for the group and the remaining applicants were sent home.

Why was Biberti willing to work so hard, without pay? He put it this way: "What am I now? A zero, a zero in a chorus, a nobody. But if this works out, I suddenly am somebody. I am sure this was in all our heads, at that time, when there were so many

---

16   Biberti in Fechner film

17   Czada wrote that one of the applicants who impressed Frommermann, but was unwilling to rehearse without pay, was Johannes Heesters, a Dutch-born actor and singer, who went on to a very successful 85-year career in show business in Germany. As of 2008, at age 104, he was still performing. However, according to information obtained by Theo Niemeyer from Heester's wife, Heesters was not even in Berlin at that time.

18   Czada, p. 15.

6

unemployed people. And so every one of us tried to be disciplined and to conform oneself to the idea."[19]

Interior of Stubenrauchstrasse 47 in 2007

Present at the first rehearsal at the apartment on January 16, 1928, at three in the afternoon were Frommermann, Steiner, Biberti, Kaliger and Colani.[20] Kaliger and Colani were never part of the official group and they disappeared very quickly. They were replaced by Asparuch "Ari" Leschnikoff, who joined the group that January, and Walter Nussbaum [German: Nußbaum], two tenors Biberti had brought over from Berlin's Grosses [German: Großes] Schauspielhaus ("large playhouse"), a Berlin theater where they had been singing together.

The new group called themselves the "Melody Makers."[21] The English name was an obvious homage to the Revelers who, as mentioned above, used the name "Merrymakers" for some of their recordings on the Brunswick label. For reasons unknown, Steiner left the group in May 1928 and his place was taken by baritone Roman Cycowski, who shared a dressing room with Biberti and Leschnikoff at the Grosses Schauspielhaus.

As Steiner had been the group's pianist, they now also needed a new accompanist. Erwin Bootz, a young piano student, had a Bulgarian neighbor and the two frequented the Bei Kirow restaurant, where Leschnikoff was a waiter. Bootz became friendly with Ari. One morning while Bootz was still in bed after a late night, Leschnikoff burst into

---

19   Fechner book, p. 167

20   Fechner book, p. 166

21   The name appears in the documents spelled several different ways – Melodie Makers, Melodiemakers and Melody Makers. The last spelling is used in this book.

his room and told him about the group that was practicing at Asta Nielsen's apartment. At first, Bootz did not understand what was going on because Nielsen was a famous film star and he could not make the connection between her and the group. Ari urged him to get out of bed to prepare for an audition with the group. [22] Bootz went along the next day and was introduced to the group.

The final piece of the puzzle fell into place in March 1929, when Nussbaum left the group due to "confrontations" (according to Frommermann) [23] and was replaced briefly by Willi Steiner. Then Erich Collin (whom Bootz knew from the Hochschule für Musik[24] where they both studied) was recruited by Bootz to fill the second tenor slot.[25]

22   Fechner book, p. 129-130

23   http://www.comedian-harmonists.com/ (accessed December 5, 2007)

24   The State School for Music on Fasanenstrasse in Berlin.

25   Theo Niemeyer only recently discovered that Willi Steiner (no relation to Theodor Steiner), who was also a student at the Hochschule für Musik with Bootz and Collin, filled in as the second tenor between Nussbaum and Collin.

CHAPTER TWO

"Wie werde ich glücklich?"[26]

(How Can I Become Lucky?)

The Members

Although there are nine people who could legitimately claim to have been members of the Comedian Harmonists, only six were in the group for nearly its entire existence and they are universally considered to have been "the" members. In addition to Frommermann, they are Robert Biberti (bass), Ari Leschnikoff (first tenor), Roman Cycowski (baritone), Erwin Bootz (piano) and Erich Collin (second tenor).

Der Gründer: [27] *"The heart and soul of the Comedian Harmonists"* [28]

Harry Frommermann

Harry Maxim Frommermann was born in Berlin, Germany, on October 12, 1906. He was the true founder of the group and also its creative genius. His father, Alexander, was a native of Ukraine and a cantor who was 56 years old when Harry was born. Leonie, Harry's mother, was his father's second wife, and there were two much older sisters from his father's first marriage.

As a boy, Harry learned music theory from his father, who sang in the Berlin Philharmonic chorus and opened a school or Konservatorium for cantors called the Erste Internationale Kantoren-Schule zu Berlin. Harry also studied piano for a while.

Because Harry's father did not want him to go into the theater, when Harry left school he worked in a ladies clothing shop in Berlin. He was fired from that job after two years and never completed his apprenticeship. But by then, his father had died and his mother had converted the Konservatorium into a boarding house. Harry began to study acting at the Staatliche Schauspielschule, or National Theater School, under Leopold Jessner[29] and Carl Ebert.[30]

---

26 Recorded by the Comedian Harmonists in 1930

27 German for "The Founder."

28 Cycowski in Fechner book, p. 141

29 Jessner was a producer and director from Königsberg, Germany. He directed the German State Theatre in the early 1920s. When the Nazis came to power, Jessner, who was Jewish, emigrated to the U.S. See, http://www. usc.edu/libraries/archives/arc/findingaids/mierendorff/index.html (accessed December 5, 2007)

30 Ebert was a stage director in Berlin who moved over to directing operas, including at the Glyndebourne Festival. He emigrated from Germany in 1934 and ended up in the U.S., where he died at the age of 93. See, http://en.wikipedia.org/wiki/Carl_Ebert (accessed December 5, 2007)

Harry got a theater job with Erwin Piscator, the famed German director and producer who was one of the foremost exponents of epic theater, but earned only 60 marks a month – a pittance. While performing at the Berliner Volksbühne,[31] Harry met and became friendly with Alexander Granach, a well-known Jewish actor in Germany in the 1920s and early 1930s.[32] To thank Granach for befriending Harry, Leonie Frommermann would send samples of her Jewish cooking to the actor. In return, Granach gave her a gramophone and it was on this machine that Harry listened to his Revelers records.[33] However, Harry's first contact with the Revelers came at the apartment of his girlfriend, Jesta Nielsen. Of course, there was a gramophone in the Nielsen apartment and Jesta and Harry would listen to American jazz records, particularly those by the Revelers.[34]

Frommermann's Bar Mitzvah

Leonie died in a flu epidemic in early 1927. Harry sold what little property there was and rented the small apartment at Stubenrauchstrasse 47. He also gave up his job at the Volksbühne, and, at a loss as to what to do with his life, conceived the idea of forming a Revelers-type vocal group.

Although he did not at first sing with the group, Harry soon inserted himself as the third tenor. As a singer, he was not on the same level as the others, but he was able to capitalize on his childhood efforts and create many of the Comedian Harmonists' imitations of musical instruments.

Fans of the Comedian Harmonists are fortunate that Frommermann maintained scrapbooks on the group dating from their first engagement. Many of the photographs and documents from the early days of the group come from those scrapbooks.

Der Bass: "...that lovely, velvety, noble bass." [35]

Robert Edgar Biberti was born into a musical family on June 5, 1902, in Berlin. His father, Georg Robert Biberti, was an opera singer, originally from Vienna. His mother, known as Emilie, was born in Herbesthal in what was then Prussia and is now part of

31   Translated as People's Theatre. It opened in 1914 at the Bülowplatz (since 1947, Rosa-Luxemburg-Platz) and was destroyed in the Second World War. After the war it was rebuilt. See, http://www.volksbuehne-berlin.de/volksbuehne-berlin-cgi/vbbNav.pl?webtext=englisch (accessed December 5, 2007)

32   Granach emigrated to the U.S. and made many movies during the war years when German refugee actors were in demand. See, http://www.cyranos.ch/smgran-e.htm (accessed December 5, 2007)

33   Czada, p. 27

34   Fechner book, p. 153

35   Bootz in Fechner film.

The Frommermann Scrapbooks

Belgium. The original family name was Bibert, but it was changed to Biberti so as to sound Italian – an advantage in the opera world. The father formed a singing group called the Meistersänger-Quartett which made some recordings in 1898, shortly after the birth of the industry.

Biberti's father eventually lost his voice. In Eberhard Fechner's 1976 documentary on the Comedian Harmonists,[36] there is an interesting juxtaposition of comments where Biberti and Cycowski in turn explain what happened. Biberti says, "My father ... enjoyed astonishingly good health, but lost his voice and was dismissed by the director of the opera. That was a terrible blow for the family."[37] Cycowski says, "(Biberti's father) drank a lot and that ruined his voice."[38]

Robert Biberti

Georg Biberti turned to woodworking to try to support his family. Young Bob assisted his father in that business, but they continued to have severe financial problems. Biberti's mother, Emilie, was a pianist who played in movie theaters in the days of silent film. Biberti had an older brother, Leopold, known as Pelle, who would become a successful actor in Germany and Switzerland.

Although born in Berlin, Biberti seems to have been an Austrian citizen until the death of his father in 1925. His father had French documents; however, as late as 1926, Biberti's citizenship on his identity card was listed as "questionable." In 1926, Biberti applied for naturalization as a German citizen and the papers read: "The chorus singer Robert Edgar Biberti, born on June 5, 1902 in Berlin, acquired, on the date of handing over

---

36   *Die Comedian Harmonists – Sechs Lebensläufe*, Eberhard Fechner, Director. Norddeutscher Rundfunk. Germany 1976 ("Fechner film").
37   Biberti in Fechner film
38   Cycowski in Fechner film

this document, the citizenship in Prussia by naturalization and therewith he became a German."[39]

From 1908 to 1912, Biberti attended Primary School No. 19 in Berlin. He then went to Kaiser-Friedrich Secondary School, transferring in 1914 to the Hindenburg-Realschule. Biberti's grades were not particularly good. Even in singing his marks ranged from "good" to "sufficient" to "deficient." His teachers wrote that he was not conscientious and not good about his attendance: he did not participate in class and his advancement in school was "not assured." Despite all this, at age nine, he was serving as an extra in productions at the Royal Playhouse. Undoubtedly, his father had something to do with this arrangement. When Bob left school, his leaving certificate said that he was going to pursue a career in singing.[40]

Biberti's father wanted him to become a woodworker, but Emilie and young Bob decided on a singing career. Bob appears to have had no formal music education. One close relationship that helped Bob shape his development was the one with his brother Leopold. They corresponded frequently after Leopold went to Switzerland. In later years, the brothers traveled together. It was Leopold who gave his younger brother his first camera and photography would become one of Bob's main interests outside of music.

In 1921, after having auditioned at the Theater am Nollendorfplatz (with a mark of "good"), Biberti became a member of the German Chorus Singer and Ballet Association and found whatever singing work he could.[41] For a time in 1926 he also took on day jobs; for example, as a bobbin coiler for Siemens. He looked for work in opera and found work in several choruses. In 1927, he secured a temporary job at the Grosses Schauspielhaus in Berlin where he met Cycowski and Leschnikoff. His first salary was 165 marks per month which rose to 180 marks for a production in late 1927. At the same time, he began rehearsals with the Melody Makers. To help get by, Biberti sang in a trio that would go around to backyards and sing for money. If the people liked what they heard, they would throw money from their windows.[42] The Comedian Harmonists' song, "Hof-Serenade" (or "Hofsänger-Serenade") from 1931, is about groups such as this. The word "hof" in German means "yard" or "courtyard" and many apartment buildings in Berlin had these courtyards.

Like his father, Biberti was always trying to be the funny guy – both on stage and off. Marion Kiss (Frommermann's first wife, who later changed her first name from Erna to Marion and married a man whose last name was Kiss) said, "He was funny and I was

---

39   Email from Jan Grübler, September 11, 2007. Jan Grübler is a Comedian Harmonists enthusiast who has studied the Biberti Estate documents.

40   All from email from Jan Grübler, September 11, 2007

41   Email from Jan Grübler, September 14, 2007

42   Early street corner harmony?

his best audience. I sometimes shed tears laughing about him."[43]

When the famous ad appeared in the *Berliner Lokal-Anzeiger*, it was not Biberti who noticed it but his mother. She answered the ad – without telling him – and then showed him the response from Frommermann inviting Bob for the audition.

Die goldene Nachtigall: [44] *A voice of "rare beauty."* [45]

Asparuch "Ari" David Leschnikoff, the oldest group member, was born on July 16, 1897, in Haskovo, Bulgaria, near Sofia.[46] Ari's father, Dimiter, was the head of the Haskovo post office. Leschnikoff said that his mother, Anna, had a beautiful voice and that he likely inherited his talent from her.[47] As a child Ari sang in the church choir.

Leschnikoff attended the Military Academy in Sofia from 1916 to 1918.[48] As a cadet, he used to sing in the park. One day his commander heard him and said, "You won't stay an officer; you'll be a singer."[49] Ari served in the Bulgarian army at the end of WWI. He went to the front and rose to the rank of Lieutenant.

Georgi Atanasov, a Bulgarian opera composer, and Alois Mazak, a military bandleader, recommended that Leschnikoff study with Ivan Vulpe, an opera singer and teacher who was one of the co-founders of the Bulgarian Opera Society. Leschnikoff studied with Vulpe for two years in Sofia, and then, in 1922, went to Berlin for further music study. As he said, "I wanted to learn culture, German culture."[50] In Berlin, he lived in a Bulgarian student hostel.

Leschnikoff auditioned for a scholarship at the Sternsches Konservatorium, where he was one of only four successful applicants out of 180.[51] Then, in 1926, he received a contract as a chorus singer at the Grosses Schauspielhaus. The pay was meager, but it was there that he met Biberti and was recruited to be in the Melody Makers.

Ari Leschnikoff

---

43   Marion Kiss in Fechner book, p. 92

44   The Golden Nightingale

45   Biberti in Fechner book, p. 111.

46   Some records in Bulgaria list other birth dates, but July 16, 1897, appears to be the one Leschnikoff used.

47   Leschnikoff in Fechner film

48   At the Academy Leschnikoff met Christo Smirnenski, a poet who was the lyricist on several songs that Leschnikoff later sang as a solo artist.

49   Leschnikoff in Fechner film

50   Leschnikoff in Fechner book, p. 36

51   Czada, p. 31

To supplement his income, Leschnikoff worked as a waiter at "Bei Kirow," a Bulgarian student restaurant. Although not hired to be a singing waiter, Ari would occasionally sing for the patrons. One evening, after Ari sang an aria from Eugene Onegin, a woman stood up and hugged and kissed him. She was Olga Tschechowa, a Russian-born actress who gained great fame in German films in the 1930s.[52]

One day, Ari returned to the student hostel where he lived and found "a postcard from Biberti, saying that somebody wants to form a quartet and is looking for good voices. The next day he [Biberti] takes me to Harry Frommermann. Cycowski was also there and we founded the Comedian Harmonists."[53] As Marion Kiss said, "When Leschnikoff was introduced to someone, even a complete stranger, he always said, 'Leschnikoff, Comedian Harmonists.' It was the most important thing in his life."[54]

Ari had an unusually high voice, capable of reaching "E" or "F" above high C without having to go into falsetto.[55] Leschnikoff recalled meeting boxer Max Schmeling in Frankfurt. Schmeling, a German, became the heavyweight boxing champion of the world when he knocked out American Joe Louis in 1936. Louis beat him in the 1938 rematch, disposing of Schmeling in only 124 seconds. Schmeling signed an autograph for Leschnikoff that read, "To my little golden nightingale. Max Schmeling."[56]

Marion/Erna said, "Ari was the first tenor. He had a sweet sexy voice; it really was so (sweet), that the people in the audience shouted 'Ari!!' – just like with Sinatra later. Women had a soft spot for him. He was small and slender and really ugly – but interestingly ugly. He had such a little black beard and then this incredible voice."[57] Bootz added, "Within the ensemble Ari was unsurpassed as a consumer of female humans of various kinds."[58]

Der Bariton: "He captivated through his voice."[59]

Baritone Josef Roman Cycowski was the other non-German in the group (besides Leschnikoff). He was born in Tuszyn, Poland, near Lodz, on January 24, 1901, into an Orthodox Jewish family that included many rabbis. His father owned a small spinning mill near Lodz.

Cycowski tells a story in the Fechner film about how, as a young boy, he learned anti-Russian songs at a time when the Poles were rebelling against the Russians and

---

52   http://www.answers.com/topic/olga-tschechowa (accessed December 5, 2007)

53   Fechner book, p. 38. Leschnikoff's memory is faulty here. Cycowski did not join the group until May 1928, several months after Leschnikoff.

54   Kiss in Fechner film

55   Bootz in Fechner book, p. 29

56   Fechner film

57   Kiss in Fechner book, p. 30

58   Bootz in Fechner book, p. 30

59   Bootz in Fechner book, p. 65.

Roman Cycowski

their occupation of Poland. In this battle, the Jews sided with the Poles who had promised "liberties" if the Jews helped with the revolution. One day, while on his way to see his grandmother, the five-year-old Cycowski was stopped by some Polish boys who demanded that he sing for them or take a beating. Roman sang one of the revolutionary songs that he had learned and the Poles kissed his hand and let him pass. Cycowski said that from that day on he wanted to become a singer.[60]

Cycowski began to study with the cantor at the synagogue and attended the Talmud school as well. A permit was needed to run a school and Roman's community could not afford the fee. To get around this, they established secret schools on the upper floors of some houses, and Roman attended one of these schools. One day, his teacher left the school briefly to buy cigarettes. On his way to the store, the teacher could hear Cycowski singing all the way down on the street. The teacher ran back upstairs to quiet the young man for fear the school would be discovered by the authorities.[61]

Cycowski's father's spinning mill was burned down in the First World War during a German offensive against the Russians. The Poles were caught in the middle between the Germans and the Russians. Cycowski said that the Poles would say to the Jews, "Yours are the Prussians and ours are the Russians." Polish Jews favored the Germans in the war because the Jews were oppressed under the Poles and the Russians. Cycowski said, "The Jews prayed in the synagogues that the Germans would win the war and free them from the Russians and the Poles. We still wish today that the Kaiser had won the war – then there never would have been a Hitler government. The Jews had many advantages under the Germans. Education – the children could go to school; it was a completely different life."[62]

When Roman decided to leave Poland, his father told him to go to Germany because there was culture there.[63] But Cycowski was 19 and at draft age and could not leave Poland legally. So he used the papers of a dead cousin who would have been 24.[64] Cycowski left in 1920 and went to Beuthen, Germany, in former Upper Silesia[65] where he sang in the temple choir. There were about 3500 Jews in Beuthen at the time.[66]

---

60   Cycowski in Fechner film
61   Cycowski in Fechner book, p. 70
62   Cycowski in Fechner film
63   Cycowski in Fechner film
64   Fechner book, p. 75
65   Beuthen is now part of Poland and called Bytom.
66   http://www.jewishgen.org/databases/Holocaust/0098_Beuthen.html (accessed December 5, 2007

The president of the synagogue owned a large hardware store and offered Cycowski a job that he accepted. While Roman worked, he would sing. A young woman heard him and suggested that he audition at the Municipal Theater where her sister worked. Director Hans Knapp and the Conductor, Salzmann, were present at the audition. Roman didn't know any German songs, so he sang one in Hebrew. When he was finished, they asked him what language it was and, being afraid to say "Hebrew," he thought quickly and said "Oriental." They then asked him to sight-read a piece from *The Gypsy Baron*, which he did. [67] Salzmann turned to Knapp and said, "I've got to have that man," and they hired him on the spot.[68] Roman spent the next five years traveling all over Germany singing in various provincial towns, including Cottbus, Danzig, Rostock, Stralsund and Bad Oeynhausen. At first, Roman sang in the chorus, but he soon moved on to some solo parts. In 1926, he went to Berlin for further music study. One of the things he had to work on was getting rid of his Jewish accent.

At the age of 24, Cycowski fell in love for the first time – with Fräulein von Karlstadt, a noblewoman. He was a self-described "late developer" in the area of romance. The relationship ended when she asked him to give up his career in the theater and he refused. [69]

In 1926, Cycowski went to the Polish Consulate for a passport and they informed him that he would have to perform his military service. He declined and they took away his Polish citizenship. Biberti said, "He deserted the Polish army and that is why he could never return to Poland later on."[70] Cycowski explained it more as a matter of his choice, rather than desertion, with the consequence being the loss of Polish citizenship.

Cycowski ended up performing in the same Grosses Schauspielhaus chorus as Biberti, who then brought him into the Melody Makers. Roman was reluctant at first because he wanted to be an opera singer, but Biberti convinced him that he could make enough money so that he could leave the group after a few years and pursue a career in opera.

Cycowski and Leschnikoff were quite friendly since they were both foreigners who knew a little Russian and didn't speak German very well.[71] Leschnikoff said of Cycowski, "He was my best friend in the Comedian Harmonists. We understood each other, in every way, because he had something Slav about him. He was a very cultivated person and I loved him."[72]

Biberti said, "An irreproachable character, exceptionally human, never rude, never abusive, always reasonable, always calming. That was Roman Cycowski – I love him until today."[73]

---

67   An operetta by Johann Strauss, Jr., called "Der Zigeunerbaron"; it had its premiere in 1885.

68   Cycowski in Fechner film

69   Fechner book, p. 79-80.

70   Fechner book, p. 64

71   Cycowski in Fechner film

72   Leschnikoff in Fechner book, p. 64

73   Robert Biberti in Fechner book, p. 64

Der Pianist: "A pianist of special talent." [74]

"We realized very quickly what we had in Bootz when he started improvising on the piano."[75] The youngest of the six Comedian Harmonists, pianist Erwin Werner Wilhelm Bootz was born in what was Stettin, Germany on June 30, 1907.[76] The family owned a music store. Erwin's father, August Bootz, would travel around the countryside on a moped, with a gramophone strapped on the back, trying to sell the new machine. Erwin said that people were often suspicious. At one pub, where his father was showing the gramophone, a man said, "Don't let the ventriloquist fool you." His father then went outside to prove that it was the gramophone and not ventriloquism. The problem was that everyone followed him outside, not wanting to be left inside with the "infernal machine."[77]

Erwin Bootz

Bootz' mother, Martha, helped to manage the music store. Cycowski thought she was "a little anti-Semitic…. One can feel these things. One cannot say it for sure, but one feels it."[78]

Bootz began playing piano when he was four and by the age of ten, he was studying at the Loewe Conservatory in Stettin. His major influence was Eugene d'Albert[79] and he had also read the biographies of Franz Liszt and Frederic Chopin.[80] Dissatisfied with his instruction and bored with piano exercises, he discontinued formal lessons and began to teach himself by listening to gramophone records and trying to copy what he heard. It worked well enough for him to have a successful audition at the Conservatory and to perform there when he was only 13.

In 1924 Bootz went to Berlin where he attended the Hochschule für Musik. Of his early days in Berlin, Bootz said, "I have to confess I was mostly attracted by the wonderful Berlin cabarets, where the current time was mirrored in naughty speeches and where the questions of the day were addressed with humor and ready wit…. And a big longing developed within me to belong to these people, who knew a lot about everything, and I fulfilled my wish later on and went to the cabaret. It was a wonderful

---

74 Marion Kiss in Fechner book, p. 117

75 Biberti in Fechner book, p. 117

76 Now Szcezcin, Poland

77 Bootz in Fechner film

78 Cycowski in Fechner book, p. 116

79 Eugene Francis Charles D'Albert was a Scottish pianist and composer and a student of Franz Liszt. He moved to Berlin and became a German citizen. See, http://www.picturehistory.com/ (accessed December 5, 2007)

80 Fechner book, p. 125

17

time. But I found out in between that the people there did not really know that much and that a good joke is not the answer to a difficult problem."[81]

Unlike most of the others, Bootz came from a fairly well-to-do family. Frommermann later said that although Bootz had studied to be a concert pianist, he "had a weakness for jazz that charmed him to the point of participating in [the] enterprise."[82]

Der zweite Tenor: [83] "His musical talent was great" [84] "He was exactly what we needed" [85]

Erich Collin

Erich Collin, the second tenor, was born Erich Abraham in Berlin on August 26, 1899. He was the son of Paul Abraham, a prominent pediatrician. Although Collin was baptized, as his sister, Anne-Marie, put it, "Erich and I were both full-blooded Jews."[86] Both parents had been born into Jewish families. His mother was Elsbeth Collin, whose father was a publisher and bookseller. Elsbeth had converted to Christianity and their father listed himself as "unaffiliated."[87] Collin's parents divorced when he was four years old and he took his mother's last name. Erich, Anne-Marie and their older sister, Charlotte, had a Swiss governess named Sello who taught them French songs. It was from her that Erich learned French. Anne-Marie told the story that one day Erich announced that he had kissed Sello and the governess was sent back to Switzerland.[88]

Everyone in Collin's family was musical. His mother and Anne-Marie both played piano and his mother also sang. In high school, Erich sang and played violin. His father was also a violinist and on visits they would play together. Occasionally his father's friend – Albert Einstein – would join them. Erich also took singing lessons. Anne-Marie told another story from their childhood: "Once we went to Bavaria with Mother during vacation. We sat in the garden of a coffee house. And on the stage was a group of singers and they sang the old Bavarian folk songs. Every now and then they took a break and the stage was empty. And my brother went up there with me and started to sing French

---

81   Radio Bremen Interview ("Radio Bremen Bootz Interview")

82   Frohman story

83   The Second Tenor

84   Marion Kiss in Fechner book, p. 47

85   Bootz in Fechner film

86   Anne-Marie Collin in Fechner film

87   Interview on September 14, 2005 with Marc Alexander, grandson of Erich Collin.

88   Anne-Marie Collin in Fechner film

Erich, Dr. Paul Abraham and Anne-Marie (1910)

songs and I had to accompany him at the piano. We got a lot of applause. I was a little musical myself. And then my mother came and got us from the stage. She was upset that we did this. But from that day, when we sang our French songs in Bavaria, simply and unselfconsciously, Erich decided to study music."[89]

Although Collin wanted to study music or art, his father was against it. So, after serving in the army in the First World War, Erich began to study medicine. After several years he quit and again said that he wanted to study music. Once more, his father intervened, urging Erich to learn a practical occupation. Collin acquiesced and worked in a bank for about a year.

It was a time of tremendous inflation in Germany and the Collin-Abraham family was hit hard: "Our whole assets vanished within a few days," said Anne-Marie. She was hired by a music publisher to give English language lessons to his employees. After each lesson, Anne-Marie would get paid. So, she would teach early in the morning and then immediately take the money that she had earned and buy food for that evening. If she waited any longer, the money would lose much of its value.[90] Mrs. Collin and the children moved to a smaller apartment and then the father died. Nevertheless, Erich began to attend the Hochschule für Musik in 1924. His mother called it "unprofitable arts" and opposed his decision.[91] But it was at the music school that Erich met Erwin Bootz.

---

89   Anne-Marie Collin in Fechner book, p. 56
90   Anne-Marie Collin in Fechner book, p. 58
91   Anne-Marie Collin in Fechner film

In March 1929, Collin was recruited by Bootz to replace Walter Nussbaum (think of Nussbaum as the Pete Best of the Comedian Harmonists).[92] Bootz said that Collin's voice was not very resonant, "but it was exactly what we needed, because we did not want two timbres struggling for supremacy."[93] In addition to singing, Collin initially served as the group's secretary, accountant and travel agent.

Anne-Marie portrayed Erich as "a noble, old-fashioned character and a day-dreamer. We called him scatterbrained, because he forgot everything and was always very occupied with himself, with his own world, and everything else did not exist for him.... The world he lived in was all colors, shapes and music."[94] Bootz said, "He was a gentleman, a really well-bred gentleman with a good education. One from the Bendlerstrasse, as one used to say in Berlin in earlier times, and that meant a very good family."[95] Cycowski described Collin as "a gentleman through and through. I would have entrusted a million dollars to him, uncounted. He was honest by nature."[96]

Once the membership was firmly established, they were a group of six young men, diverse as to religion – two Jews, three non-Jews and one of Jewish heritage, but who had not been raised in the religion – and diverse as to nationality – four Germans, a Pole and a Bulgarian, who came together in Berlin, the cultural center of that part of the world, to form a singing ensemble that would become the toast of Europe.

Other Members:

There were three other people who were official members of the Comedian Harmonists, each only for a short time – Theodor Steiner, Walter Nussbaum and Walter Joseph.

Theodor Steiner

Theodor Steiner, Frommermann's childhood friend, and co-founder of the Melody Makers, became a director of radio plays in Germany, including the play *Zauberei* in 1962, and also worked in vocational education.[97] He lived in Frankfurt after the war and then in Bad Homburg. He died in the early 1970s.

Hochschule für Musik Yearbook

---

92   Pete Best was the original drummer for the Beatles who left them in 1962, just before they hit it big. He was replaced by Richard Starkey, better known as Ringo Starr. Willi Steiner was the first replacement for Nussbaum for a brief time before Collin joined the group.

93   Bootz in Fechner film

94   Anne-Marie Collin in Fechner book, p. 51

95   Bootz in Fechner book, p. 45

96   Cycowski in Fechner book, p. 46

97   http://de.wikipedia.org/wiki/Theodor_Steiner (accessed January 12, 2008)

Walter Nussbaum

Not much is known about Walter Nussbaum, but it is clear that he was brought into the group by Biberti, so probably he was also at the Grosses Schauspielhaus, where Biberti found the other members. In any event, Nussbaum appears in early photos and on early recordings. Nussbaum left the group on February 28, 1929, and there was a formal termination letter on March 1, 1929.

Walter Joseph

Walter Joseph, a pianist, joined the Comedian Harmonists in December 1930, when Bootz briefly left the group. He had been appearing at the Nelson-Revue, where he and Rudolph Nelson accompanied the performers on two grand pianos.[98] Joseph left the Comedian Harmonists in July 1931. He later showed up as the piano player in a combo that backed Edith Piaf on a song recorded in 1936.[99] He also backed up German actress/singer Annemarie Hase on several recordings from that era.[100]

Others

There were three others who either sang with or practiced with the group but were never taken on as full members – Willi Steiner, Victor Colani and Louis Kaliger.

Willi Steiner

Although not mentioned in either the Czada or Fechner books, Willi Steiner sang second tenor with the Comedian Harmonists between the time Nussbaum left and Collin arrived. Proof of this includes a photo of the group from March 1929 that was originally thought to have included Nussbaum, but has the following inscription written on the back, "with Steiner, Hamburg

Walter Nussbaum   *Willi Steiner*

---

98   Czada, p. 55
99   Django Reinhardt was the guitarist in the group.
100 http://www.br-online.de/bayern4/programm/tag/b4_tp20041201.shtml (accessed December 5, 2007)

March 1929."[101] Willi Steiner had been at the Hochschule für Musik with Bootz (and Collin). A comparison of the individual in that photo with others that are known, by their date, to include Nussbaum, clearly shows two different people. This, along with other proofs, has led some experts to conclude that the Hamburg photo shows Willi Steiner.[102] It is fairly clear that this was not a return of Theodor Steiner since two letters from Biberti to his mother in March 1929 (long after Theodor Steiner had left) refer to, "our new singer, Steiner, is not good ... he has to leave."[103]

It does not appear that Willi Steiner ever became a full member and we know that he was not in any of the partnership agreements. He also never sang on any of their recordings.

Victor Max Colani

Colani was at the first few rehearsals of the group but never became an official member. He was born in Zittau, Germany in 1895 and died in The Hague in 1957. Appearing in at least 30 films, he had a fairly successful career as an actor and singer until 1929. After that, all that is known is that he appeared in a Dutch film in 1952.

Louis Kaliger

Kaliger, a German actor, was in a similar position with the group as Colani. By letter from Frommermann and Steiner of March 1, 1928, his participation in the Melody Makers was terminated. Interestingly, the reason they gave him was that they planned to reduce the singing part of the group to a quartet.[104] Kaliger appeared in several films in the mid-1930s and died in 1944.

MY FAVORITE COMEDIAN HARMONISTS SONG

Regarding favorite recordings by the Comedian Harmonists, there are so many that I hardly know where to begin. However, I think the film clip of the group singing "Veronika" is very special, because it opens a window and allows one to see their performance style – a combination of suave sophistication and playfulness. Also, that film clip takes me to a very privileged place, for I can see my grandfather "come alive" when he was younger than I am today.

~ *Marc Alexander, Erich Collin's grandson. (The short film referred to here is "Kreuzworträtsel" from 1931. The film includes the Comedian Harmonists performing "Veronika, der Lenz ist da.")*

---

101   Photo in Comedian Harmonists Archive, Theo Niemeyer
102   Email from Theo Niemeyer, June 11, 2007
103   Estate of Biberti, Staatsbibliothek, Berlin ("Biberti Estate")
104   Biberti Estate

CHAPTER THREE

"Einmal schafft's jeder" [105]

(Everyone Can Finally Make It)

"A Four-Part Chord Was Floating In The Air" [106]

Rehearsals and Auditions

Even before Harry Frommermann placed his ad seeking singers, he had written, without the aid of a piano, all the parts for each member of the group that he envisioned: He could hear each one of the five voices in his head, from the bass to the first tenor.[107] These arrangements would later be hailed as masterpieces, significantly more complex than anything that had come before (or after) and, at the same time, sounding uncomplicated. In these arrangements, the voices provided the orchestral accompaniment, sometimes imitating instruments, but more often simply replacing them.

The group began a period of intense practice sessions. Frommermann had to persuade the others to work for hours a day for several months with no pay. They used the Revelers' recordings to steer them, but they were also trying to create something original. Harry said he "included himself as a partaking member of the group-to-be by adding to the set for a modern male-quartet his own voice for special antics and his gift of imitating instruments vocally." He wanted to give "the future ensemble a style of its own, not wanting to start with a copy of any other group existing."[108] There was often despair because the sound they were seeking did not come easily, but they persevered. Frommermann said that they "trained themselves endlessly to gain that important easiness, known to hide the hard work."[109] The voices had to work together to achieve one sound.

As noted, Theodor Steiner left the group in May 1928 and was replaced by Cycowski. The Melody Makers sent a letter to Odeon informing them that Steiner was no longer authorized to handle the business affairs of the group and that Bootz (who had already joined at this time) was the new business manager.[110] Letters to others indicated that either Biberti or Frommermann was the new business manager. Nussbaum also handled some of those duties. It appears that each handled a different aspect of the management duties. Bootz also worked on shortening Frommermann's musical arrangements – they

---

105   Recorded by the Comedian Harmonists in 1932.

106   Czada, p. 17

107   Erika von Späth (Frommermann's companion during the last years of his life) in Fechner book, p. 155

108   Frohman story

109   Frohman story

110   Biberti Estate, letter dated May 17, 1928

were each about twelve minutes long and had to be cut back to about three minutes.[111]

To keep discipline, the members initiated a system of escalating fines for being late for practice. The fines were either one, two or three marks, depending on how late you were. Leschnikoff, the poorest, was always on time. Bootz, who was given an allowance by his family and was the only one who did not have to work to support himself, was often late. Bootz said, "I got 200 marks a month and could have lived well if I hadn't spent it all by the 15th." Every three months Bootz's mother would visit Berlin and pay off his debts.[112] Once, Harry arrived for rehearsal in a taxi (normally an extravagance), still in pajamas. Apparently, the taxi fare was less costly than the fine.

On May 10, 1928, the Melody Makers entered the recording studio for the first time and made test recordings of "Ninon, du süsse Frau" (Ninon, You Sweet Lady)[113] and Duke Ellington's "Jig Walk,"[114] for Deutsche Grammophon. The recordings were never issued. They were raw efforts and far below the standard they desired. Fortunately, Biberti saved these test recordings, which, when compared to their later recordings, illustrate vividly the group's tremendous progress.

They needed a place to practice where people would not complain about the noise. Harry was still seeing Jesta Nielsen, and when her film-star mother went on an extended vacation in the summer of 1928, Nielsen offered the use of her apartment.[115] The neighbors did not complain: The apartment had thick carpets and drapes and the tenant in the apartment below was rarely at home.[116] They practiced very late at night and into the morning hours – after Biberti, Leschnikoff and Cycowski finished their performances at the Grosses Schauspielhaus. However, when Harry started seeing Erna Eggstein, they had to find a new place to rehearse.

Biberti said that they would get depressed when listening to the Revelers because what the Melody Makers were doing was "far from what [was] on those records."[117] Cycowski said, "Most important were the Comedian Harmonists, not the individuals. And we all agreed on that. We harmonized as human beings. We got on well together. Of course, there were occasional arguments; but that was positive and useful for our development."[118] Bootz said, "The Comedian Harmonists had something that doesn't exist anymore today. They had achieved a degree of perfection that is no longer aimed

---

111   Bootz in Fechner film

112   Bootz in Fechner film.

113   "Ninon" was put out by Odeon after being re-recorded on August 18, 1928. It is the German version of the American song, "So Blue."

114   Ellington recorded this song in 1926 for Paramount.

115   Jesta Nielsen committed suicide in 1964.

116   Coincidentally, that neighbor was Hermann Haller of the Hermann-Haller Revue, a vaudeville-type entertainment extravaganza in Berlin in the 1920s.

117   Czada p. 17

118   Cycowski in Fechner film

Bootz, Frommermann and Leschnikoff

at today."[119] Leschnikoff, the so-called uncomplicated one, summed it up years later: "The old group would have conquered the whole world."[120]

Auditions

The group managed to get an audition at the Scala club.[121] The audition was a disaster: Marx, the director, said that they were better suited for an undertaker's establishment.[122] That made them even more determined, and a period of even more intense rehearsals followed. Biberti was particularly helpful in keeping the group together during this difficult time.

Frommermann said that one of their biggest problems was trying to get the individuals to sing as a group. To do that, the members who were not singing lead had to hold back on their volume: "That's why at the beginning of each rehearsal I would admonish everybody, 'Children, you all have wonderful voices, you don't have to convince anybody of that by being loud! Try to use your voice to nearly whisper.' And this is how we built the first chord, which I had them hold for a while and listen to it carefully. What an exciting experience! They weren't Mister A, B, C and D trying to impress me

---

119   Bootz in Fechner film

120   Leschnikoff in Fechner film

121   The Scala, a Jewish-owned vaudeville-type nightclub in Berlin, opened in 1920 and was very successful. When the Nazis came to power, they took over the Scala and the nightclub continued to do well until Joseph Goebbels, Nazi Propaganda Minister, declared that only wartime presentations would be permitted.

122   Bootz in Fechner film

or show off with their voices anymore, but a four-part chord was floating in the air." [123]

Cycowski had difficulty because he was the only one with a big voice and had to try to restrain himself. Leschnikoff had a beautiful voice, but it was thin. When Ari sang so softly, Roman had to sing even more softly. [124]

Bootz said, somewhat disdainfully, that Leschnikoff "could sing high C far higher than Caruso" – meaning that Ari was off-key. [125] It was only through practice that Leschnikoff learned to sing in tune. Biberti said, "Instruments are flexible, but the human voice is inflexible and first has to be taught to act as part of an orchestral mechanism." [126]

The group finally got an audition with Kurt Robitschek, a Viennese Jew who ran the famous Kabarett der Komiker (Comedian's Cabaret), also known as KaDeKo. It was the largest cabaret in Berlin, located at Lehniner Platz on the Kurfürstendamm: "The biggest names in kabarett appeared in the KADEKO offering everything from comic operas to critical sketches." [127]

The audition was successful, but the scheduled engagement never took place. In August 1928, Frommermann contacted a distant relative named Bruno Levy, who was an agent. Levy came to hear the Melody Makers at Biberti's apartment at Knesebeckstrasse, 88. Frommermann said, "[Levy] listened to us and he sat there with a fat cigar and we sang our whole repertoire and he sat without moving a muscle in his face, sat there and said [he imitates a person's voice and the sound of someone smoking], 'and what else do you have?' And we sang another song and we were sweating – it was August and it was very hot and suddenly he said: 'Do you have a phone here?' – 'Yes, sure we do.' And he dialed a number and said, 'Please connect me with Mr. Charell, this is Bruno Levy' . . . We all pricked our ears, still sweaty from singing and we shivered with tension. 'Hello, Mister Charell, this is Bruno Levy. I just listened to a vocal group. Better than the Revellers. Yes, all Germans." Charell agreed to see them immediately. [128]

Levy told them not to say a word during the negotiation that would inevitably take place: "You have no knowledge of such things, a wrong word at the wrong moment could be of damage to you, because Charell certainly has a lot more experience than you." [129] They went to the Grosses Schauspielhaus near Friedrichstrasse (where some of them were still singing in the chorus!) and sang for Charell. He offered the Melody Makers a contract on the spot. Levy told Charell that the amount was not enough and sent the group off to a pub while he

123 Czada, p.17

124 Fechner book, p. 178

125 Bootz in Fechner film

126 Biberti in Fechner film.

127 Munz, Lori. *Cabaret Berlin: Revue, Kabarett and Film Music between the Wars*. Hamburg: edel Classics GmbH, 2005, p. 10

128 Radio Bremen Frommermann interview. Eric Charell was a prominent impresario in Berlin, who produced musical revues.

129 Czada p. 21

pursued the negotiation. Levy joined them a little later and took them to the Haller Revue in the Admiralspalast. While they were waiting to be heard, a messenger arrived with a letter from Charell that said, "I offer double the salary, but if you sign with Haller, I will make you look impossible in the whole business." Frommermann said, "So we did not sing for Haller, went back to Charell, signed the contract and on September 5, 1928 we had our first stage appearance in the Grosses Schauspielhaus with the revue *Casanova*."[130] The contract paid them 120 marks per night, a lot for an unknown group. Biberti, Leschnikoff and Cycowski had been earning 180 marks per month and Frommermann only 60, so this represented a substantial increase for all of them.

Charell did not like the Melody Makers name. Frommermann said: "One morning, while we were rehearsing the Italian intermezzo, Charell came into our room with Schanzer and Welisch, the two authors [of *Casanova*]. They had been thinking about our name. Charell thought it too tame. He said: 'No, no, children, 'Melody-Makers' – that sounds too matter-of-fact. It should be something that underlines your comic and your melodic in one name. How about 'Comedian Harmonists?' That sounds funny and harmonious; that sounds like comedy and harmony, like harmonious singing.' We did not say no, and that is how the name Comedian Harmonists came to be."[131] An English name was essential if you wanted to convey that you were a modern group.

MY FAVORITE COMEDIAN HARMONISTS SONG

My favorite song of the Comedian Harmonists is "In der Bar zum Krokodil,"* for its funny and frivolous lyrics. Maybe musically not their best recording but to me it is the best fun!! As a jazz enthusiast I like their version of "Creole Love Call" very much as well.

~Andreas Schmauder is an internationally known collector and seller of recordings. He owns the only known complete collection of all the original Comedian Harmonists' recordings. See www. phonopassion.de.

* Recorded by the Comedian Harmonists in 1934.

---

130   Radio Bremen Frommermann Interview. Czada, at page 22, puts the appearance at September 28, 1928, but records in the Biberti Estate show a start date of September 3, 1928.
131   Fechner book, p. 181

*"Sündig und süss"** (Sinful and Sweet)*

The Comedian Harmonists:
The First Successful Crossover Recording Group

by Peter Becker

The Comedian Harmonists' founding year, 1927, was an exciting time in technological innovation. Solo transatlantic flight, "talking" motion pictures, amplified home radio reception and even early television were only a few. But the invention of the first practical microphone for recording studio use would have a great effect on the "sound" of the new group.

Although initially influenced by the popular American vocal quartet, the Revelers, the then "Deutschen Revellers" (as the Comedian Harmonists were often called in Germany) were soon to evolve a sound far superior to the "Horn-and-Diaphragm" recordings of their model. This industry standard device had a limited range of recording frequency and favored primarily the mid-range acoustical spectrum. This was not flattering to the soprano and bass voice – the former sounded thin and shrill, the latter reedy and not resonant. Because of this, many fine vocal artists were excluded from the lucrative recording field, for their voices simply did not "take."

One has only to listen to the group's earliest recordings to experience this. These were made on a curious device with three "horns" jutting out in various directions – one for the pianist and the remaining two to be shared among the singers. The result was a mostly blocky, percussive piano part and bright, edgy vocals, very much in the popular American Jazz-Dance idiom.

The deployment of a new recording microphone technology (an example was the 1927 Neumann CMV3 condenser type) surely had more than a little influence on the "new" sound of the Comedian Harmonists, for it made possible the recording of far more intricate and nuanced arrangements. This innovation increased the dynamic range of recorded sound from 250-2,500 cycles to 50-6,000 cycles and resulted in a much greater clarity of dynamic extremes. Technological limitations that had once defined recorded material were no more, and hitherto unimaginable subtleties were mass marketed to an eager public.

This combination of new technology, superb vocal blend and deft arrangements that often parodied either current "hits" or classical pieces made the Comedian Harmonists an irresistible package. Odeon was the envy of other recording companies, and although a number of rival groups were formed and marketed, the Harmonists were "oft kopiert, nicht erreicht" (often copied, never duplicated). In fact none of these other groups even came close, for the almost other-worldly blend of five voices with Bootz's "katzenpfötchen" (cat's paw) piano (the sixth voice of the group) defied imitation.

The ensuing years yielded a large number of widely popular and best-selling recordings. The majority of them eschewed the swing, jazz element of American dance music and instead featured arrangements in their trademark classical style. The result ennobled the often banal melodies and sentiments of the day in a comic and parodic manner, and Bootz's sudden and often luscious key changes surely factored in this. Their easy mastery of all this was difficult to hear in live performance, for they appeared without amplification, often in very large venues. There are contemporary accounts of large audiences barely daring to breathe, let alone cough, for fear of not being able to hear the group.

The Comedian Harmonists' successful evolution of a classical "take" on popular music is then in no small part due to the serendipitous combination of superb voices adapted to the wonderful new recording medium of the day, and all within the glorious architecture of Erwin Bootz's and Harry Frommermann's arrangements and compositions. But the fruits of success held seeds of a bitter harvest. The blurred barrier between Classical and Popular, Art and "Entartete" [degenerate] and later, Jew and Gentile, became repugnant to the musical "apartheid" in German Culture – as hijacked by the National Socialists – and the golden age of the Comedian Harmonists came to an end.

~Peter Becker is the baritone for Hudson Shad, an American vocal group that has an amazingly large repertoire, including songs of the Comedian Harmonists.

*Recorded by the Comedian Harmonists in 1928.

CHAPTER FOUR

"Komm im Traum"[132]

(Come Into My Dream)

Early Successes and the Beginning of Their Recording Career

While awaiting the start of their revue performances with Charell, the group launched their recording career. On August 18, 1928, they recorded "Ein biss-chen Seligkeit" (A Little Bliss) for Odeon.[133] They also recorded the song in English on September 13, 1928 – it was called "Souvenirs" and is the American song, "Among My Souvenirs."[134] This was their first recording to be released and is a pretty raw effort.[135] Leschnikoff's beautiful high tenor can be heard slightly above the group, but not in a pure solo. There is a nice part near the end where the group sings a chorus without words that gives a hint of what was to come. That same day, they also recorded "Ich hab ein Zimmer, goldige Frau" (I Have A Room, Cute Lady), which opens with instrument imitation and is very much in the Revelers' style. The recording features a short solo by Biberti in which his voice is more operatic than pop. The name that appeared on the label was "Comedian Harmonists – gen. die deutschen Revellers."[136] Apparently, Odeon believed that they had to tell the public what type of group was on the recording. So well-known were the Revelers that a simple reference to them would suffice.

The German-language version of "Souvenirs" marked the first appearance of Fritz Rotter as the lyricist on a Comedian Harmonists song – but far from the last. Rotter, who was Jewish, was born in Austria and, as with so many others in the arts at that time, went to Berlin where he wrote for cabarets and film. In 1933 Rotter left Germany and returned to Austria. Like the Comedian Harmonists, after the Nazis took over Austria, Rotter went to England and then on to the United States. After the war, Rotter returned to Europe. Among his many hit songs was "Veronika, der Lenz ist da," (Veronica, Spring Is Here) one of the Comedian Harmonists' signature tunes.

---

132 Recorded by the Comedian Harmonists in 1934

133 All recording information is taken from *Irgendwo auf der Welt - Die Schallplatten der Comedian Harmonists und ihrer Nachfolgegruppen* by Andreas Schmauder, published in 1999. See the discography in Appendix C, also courtesy of Andreas Schmauder.

134 This song was introduced by Paul Whiteman and reached number one on the charts in February 1928. The Revelers also charted with it the next month, reaching the number ten position. *Joel Whitburn's Pop Memories 1890-1954.*

135 As mentioned previously, they had done two test recordings while still the Melody Makers, but the sides were not released.

136 This means, "Comedian Harmonists, called the German Revelers." The German word "genannt" is ab-breviated as "gen."

*Clockwise from upper right: Cycowski, Nussbaum, Leschnikoff,
Bootz, Biberti and Frommermann*

Four other songs were recorded that day, including the Comedian Harmonists' first piece with music by Bootz, "Du hast mich betrogen" (You Have Betrayed Me), with lyrics by Rotter. Cycowski and Leschnikoff both soloed on the new version of "Ninon, du süsse Frau." Their ability to perform as soloists was, in the beginning, somewhat limited by their poor German, but as their German-language skills improved, that situation changed. On the following Wednesday they recorded two *intermezzi* from the revue *Casanova* (in which they were about to appear) on the Electrola label.

On September 3, 1928, they debuted in *Casanova* under the Comedian Harmonists name. They appeared dressed as Bohemian, Italian and Spanish singers. Because they were late additions to the show, they performed only the *intermezzi* between other acts. Most of them were happy with their performances, but Bootz, who was always a perfectionist, recalled, "I remember that we sang appalling at Charell's because Leschnikoff skidded off upwards."[137] The audience did not seem to notice. Biberti described it: "We earned a lot of applause. Backstage we jumped for joy."[138] The famous conductor, Bruno Walter, was in the audience and "applauded them after each piece with a broad smile. Afterwards he congratulated them in person."[139]

Because their contract with Charell at the Grosses Schauspielhaus was not exclusive, they were allowed to perform in other venues, and they appeared in nightclubs

---

137 Bootz in Fechner film
138 Biberti in Fechner film
139 Frohman story

and in the KaDeKo where they earned 90 marks per show. A review in the *Deutsche Tageszeitung* read: "An exquisite specialty are the Comedian Harmonists, a group of humming and whispering singers, who can imitate musical instruments in a jazz orchestra amazingly well."[140]

The group also appeared at the Barberina, a nightclub that Biberti did not like at all: "There we stood in the middle of the floor, which was unpleasant. We were surrounded by boozing and guzzling people and they didn't keep quiet as we would have liked. We took ourselves very seriously. It was most unpleasant. But we got 20 marks a day and that was quite good."[141]

The Berlin of the 1920s and early 1930s, "was a city of possibilities, of myriad outcomes, glowing with promise as well as threat.... [T]he first all-night city, the city without shame."[142] "The years of so-called 'relative stabilization' (1924-1929), between the end of the German inflation and the beginning of the global depression, were the golden age of the Weimar revue."[143] Charell was one of the big three of the revues – the other two being staged by Herman Haller (featuring the Tiller Girls) and James Klein. The average person was preoccupied with economic hardships such as high unemployment and extremely high inflation. However, there was another side to the city that was recalled, for example, in "Glitter and Doom: German Portraits from the 1920s," an exhibition at New York City's Metropolitan Museum of Art in late 2006 and early 2007. It showed Berlin's café society with erotic shows and sexual freedom that were unrivaled

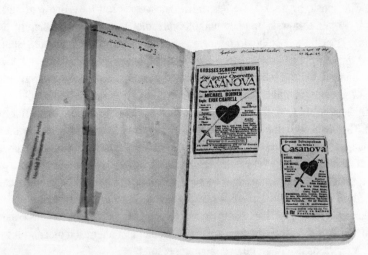

First page of Frommermann scrapbook

140   Czada, p. 24
141   Biberti in Fechner film
142   Ross, Alex. *The Rest Is Noise. Listening To The Twentieth Century.* New York: Farrar, Strauss and Giroux, 2007, pp. 178-179
143   Jelavich, Peter. *Berlin Cabaret.* Cambridge: Harvard University Press, 1996, p. 165

in the world at the time. As author Rudolf Lorenzen described it: "It goes without saying today that the 'golden' twenties only deserve their decorative description within limits – it far too much glorifies that time, whose gold also had a backside: there were terrific bankruptcies next to glamorous careers, eccentricity next to the fight for existence, and the amusement fever at that time was often rooted in fear."[144]

Grosses Schauspielhaus, Berlin. People called it the "stalactite cavern."

The Comedian Harmonists were entertainers and they had their "groupies" – just like rock stars a few decades later. But while their music was sometimes risqué (Veronika, for example), much of it was either lighthearted without sexual overtones ("Ich hab' für Dich 'nen Blumentopf bestellt" – I Ordered A Flowerpot For You or "Mein kleiner grüner Kaktus" – My Little Green Cactus) or serious (their classical pieces or ballads such as "Liebling, mein Herz lässt Dich grüssen" – Darling, My Heart Greets You, by Werner Richard Heymann).

Each member performed a function within the group in addition to his singing role. Frommermann and Bootz arranged songs, and Bootz, whom Frommermann called a "highly gifted" arranger, also served as musical director.[145] Leschnikoff was in charge of making sure that their wardrobe was ready for each show. Collin (after he joined) planned their tours and handled all correspondence. Collin, and to a lesser extent Biberti, negotiated the payments for their performances.

The group remained with the Charell Revue until February 1929. In the meantime, they were back with Odeon to record "Ich küsse Ihre Hand, Madame" (I Kiss

---

144 Rudolf Lorenzen (1922-) is a German author. Two undated short stories ("Lorenzen Stories") by him about the Comedian Harmonists were found in the Biberti Estate papers in the Staatsbibliothek. He also wrote articles about the Comedian Harmonists in newspapers and magazines; produced two short films with Biberti as an actor, and wrote the liner notes for an Electrola double LP of Comedian Harmonists songs released in 1974.

145 Frohman story

Your Hand, Madame), on September 14, 1928. The recording featured Leschnikoff and showed significant improvement over their previous efforts. Nussbaum also had a solo part.[146] They closed out 1928 with a very nice version of "Mein blauer Himmel" (My Blue Heaven) on November 6, together with "Süsses Baby" (Sweet Baby), and on December 6, "Toselli Serenade" and "Legende d'Amour," with a beautiful sweet ending to the latter.

Cycowski said of these early efforts, "We made records because we badly needed money." They received a percentage of the selling price for all records sold and made as many records as they could. Cycowski and Bootz later said that they were not ready – what they were doing was not up to concert standard – and that making so many records so early in their development was a mistake (although they did not know it at the time).[147] Nevertheless, the November and December efforts were an improvement over those of August and September.

The group was still handling its own business matters and had set up shop in Biberti's Knesebeckstrasse apartment in the Charlottenburg section of Berlin.[148] Biberti described the scene: "From time to time we would get phone calls from agents presenting themselves, or once in a while from a variete-manager, who inquired about the rates of the group. We were always concerned to make our office ... sound very loud and lively in order to show the importance of our existence. So, when we received a phone call, we would all talk at the same time. One would use the typewriter without really writing anything, just so that it made a lot of noise. The caller must really have thought he was connected with the shipping office or the human resources office in a steel plant."[149]

The recording frenzy continued into 1929. The boys were back in the studio on January 22, 1929. That session brought four new releases on Odeon – "Anno dazumal" (Years Ago), Parts One and Two, and "Hallo, hallo, hier Wien" (Hello, Hello, This Is Vienna), Parts One and Two. Although all four, adapted by Camillo Morena, are somber-sounding, the latter featured a warbling bird call as well as a whistling part. February 21, 1929, saw four recordings on which an orchestra is heard, although usually not simultaneously with their singing – "Baby, Du hast Dich verändert" (Baby, You Have Changed), "Ich habe Ihnen viel zu sagen, sehr verehrte gnädige Frau" (I Have A Lot To Tell You, Dear Lady), "Eilali, Eilali, Eilala" and "Ol' Man River." The orchestra was led by Russian-born Dajos Bela.

---

146 A recording contract with Carl Lindström, AG (Odeon) dated October 22, 1928, is signed by all members, including Nussbaum.

147 All from Fechner film

148 Charlottenburg, a section of Berlin located just north of Kurfürstendamm, is best known for its castle, Schloss Charlottenburg. The area also has many bookshops, bars and restaurants. In his later years, Biberti's favorite bar/restaurant in that area was Diener's, today an unprepossessing-looking place. He could be found there virtually every evening, holding court.

149 Czada, p. 38

The Knesebeckstrasse building in 2007

Each recording brought them 200 marks plus 50 marks for their appearance. The recording process was much different in those days. There were no separate tracks and no way to listen to what you had just recorded. It took a few days to press the record and only then could you tell if it was up to the standard required to go into production. If not, you had to go back into the studio and try again.[150]

In the first part of 1929, the group continued to perform around Berlin. They had their first small concerts outside of Berlin, in Hamburg at the Hansa Theatre[151] and in Cologne where they were billed as "Komedian Harmonists vom Grossen Schauspielhaus Berlin" so that the audience would know they would be seeing a premier act. At these shows, Frommermann said, "They had a conférencier,[152] [and] a gifted young girl as a dancer and well-known diseuse,[153] sometimes Blandine Ebinger, sometimes Lina Carstens and usually the Harmonists reserving the second part of the show for themselves."[154]

---

150 Czada, p. 40

151 They were there for the month of March and received a fee of 4595 marks. It was probably their only appearance with Willi Steiner in the group.

152 Wikipedia defines conférencier as "the proper term for the master of ceremonies appearing in European cabaret. The term appeared in the 1920s and became synonymous with these persons who not only emceed cabarets, but were well known for their political and social commentary. They became controversial in the eye of the Nazi regime, which eventually cracked down and banned such commentary, keeping a watchful eye over these conférenciers." See: http://en.wikipedia.org/wiki/Conferencier (accessed December 27, 2007).

153 A diseuse is woman who introduces entertainment acts and also sings. See, http://dictionary.reference.com/browse/diseuse (accessed January 12, 2008)

154 Frohman story

During this time Walter Nussbaum left the group and Willi Steiner filled in for one month. However, Nussbaum did not go quietly. A letter from Frommermann to Biberti in 1975 says that Nussbaum "was ... made to leave,"[155] and there is a cryptic comment from Frommermann that the departure was due to "confrontations."[156] Biberti also said that Nussbaum "did not have the right character for such a collective, in which one had to work together by hook or by crook for months, if not for years. As I said, he was a whiner, as it turned out later."[157] Nussbaum consulted an attorney and sent formal letters to the group asking to be informed of the dates of rehearsals and recordings – even though he had been dismissed from the group.[158] Nussbaum claimed that they had told him he was being dismissed because he did not fit into the ensemble artistically. Nussbaum alleged that was a pretext "in order to disguise a personal conflict." [159]

Bootz cited musical reasons, saying that Nussbaum's voice was not reliable. The second tenor was "not so much a solo part, but contributes very much with his voice to accentuate the blend, the harmonies. And for that it needs a special musical sensitivity."[160] A letter was received from the Scala club stating that Nussbaum was seeking fulfillment of his contract and complaining that the club had not been informed

Willi Steiner (at far left), Cycowski, Bootz, Biberti, Leschnikoff and Frommermann

---

155   Czada, p. 34
156   http://www.comedian-harmonists.com/ (accessed December 5, 2007)
157   Fechner book, p. 166
158   Biberti Estate, letter dated July 4, 1929
159   Biberti Estate, document dated May 23, 1929
160   Fechner book, p. 190

of the change in membership in the group. Letters were exchanged between lawyers for the group and Nussbaum and a lawsuit was threatened. Eventually, they reached a settlement.

Bootz, Leschnikoff and Frommermann (upper row); Cycowski,
Biberti and Nussbaum (lower row)

When Nussbaum and then Willi Steiner left, the group had to take a break in order to incorporate the new voice, Erich Collin, into the ensemble. Their next performances took place in May 1929. One reviewer in Cologne (for the *Kölner Mittag)* wrote, "The main attraction of the evening is the Comedian Harmonists," while the *Kölner Tageblatt's* reviewer talked about their "super number, next to which everybody else has a tough time" and said that "they have something for everybody, and even those people who usually make fun of dance songs with Negroid structure."[161] The *Kölner Anzeiger* called their performance, "Jazz singing at its finest."[162] When the group returned to Berlin, they appeared in various venues, including the famous Der blaue Vogel cabaret in July.

The rave reviews meant that they would not stay unknown for long. The Scala, where they had failed so miserably in their first audition in 1928, now wanted them. Their first appearance at the Scala came in June 1929, but was not without incident. As they went to the dressing room to change for the show, they discovered that their tail coats had been stolen, and there was no way to replace the suits on such short notice.

---

161 Czada, p. 39
162 Fechner book, p. 198

They solved the problem by borrowing clothes from the waiters, even though the outfits were not all the same color.

Postcard of the Scala

In August, their heroes, the Revelers, came to Berlin for a series of performances at the Scala. The two groups met at a cabaret and their encounter was described this way: "The Revelers, who are currently giving guest performances at the Scala, sat at a table next to the Comedian Harmonists, known as the German Revellers. One group nonchalant in light suits, the other solemn in elegant tail coats. Glances were exchanged this way and that way. Everybody was anxiously waiting to see how this game between the rival brothers would develop. Much to the rapture of the audience it developed into an improvised singing duel. The German Revellers opened with 'Ol' Man River' and the American Revellers answered with 'In A Little Spanish Town.' It remains to be said that the German and American Revellers became friends that night. It remains further to be said that the performances of the two groups are equally good, that the 'true' and 'copied' groups can hardly be distinguished, except optically – the Americans are five, the Germans six likeable lads."[163]

On September 5, 1929, the Comedian Harmonists appeared in a revue at the Berliner Theater with Marlene Dietrich. The show, *Zwei Krawatten* (Two Bow Ties), was directed by Forster-Larrinaga, composed by Mischa Spoliansky with Georg Kaiser as the librettist. In his biography of Dietrich, Steven Bach said of the Comedian Harmonists' appearance that it was "not unlike having the Beatles in the chorus."[164] Newspaper

163   Czada, page 40
164   Bach, Steven. *Marlene Dietrich: Life And Legend.* New York: William Morrow, 2000.

reports at the time said that "the biggest applause of the evening was for the Comedian Harmonists."[165] They earned 150 marks per night for this show. In December, the show traveled to Leipzig's Schauspielhaus. Biberti said, *"Zwei Krawatten* became one of the memorable theater productions in Berlin. We, the Comedian Harmonists, saw, heard and learned a lot with this, particularly through the musical direction of Mischa Spoliansky."[166]

Despite the critical acclaim that the group had received, Odeon cancelled its contract with the Comedian Harmonists effective on October 22, 1929. Electrola was only too happy to take them on and a contract was signed on October 31, 1929. The pay per record was the same as with Odeon, but with Electrola the group also received a percentage of the profits, which at first was 5 percent but later increased to 7.5 percent. This agreement would prove to be quite lucrative for the Comedian Harmonists.

Their first release on Electrola came from a recording session on November 11, 1929, that produced two classics, "Puppenhochzeit" (an American song called "Wedding Of The Painted Doll") and "Musketiermarsch" (Musketeer March – this song is also known as "Drei Musketiere" or Three Musketeers, from the revue *Drei Musketiere*). In all, the group had 23 releases in 1929 – 17 on Odeon and six on Electrola. In October of 1929, they made their first radio appearance, on Funk-Stunde AG, and received 450 marks.

MY FAVORITE COMEDIAN HARMONISTS SONG

"Holzhackerlied"* (The Woodcutter's Song) is among my favorites. The guys get going pretty good on this one, not only featuring their usual vocal effects, but also tossing in some yodeling and whistling. When my wife and I visited with German friends in Berlin some years ago, they pooh-poohed this sort of thing as "children's songs." Apparently, old popular songs sung in a language that I can't even understand have an irresistible appeal to me that isn't necessarily evident to all the local folks. This tune is also so joyous. In public performance, it must have presented quite a contrast to the darkness of the times.

~ Jim Lowe is a retired attorney and popular culture enthusiast. He maintains Comedian Harmonists web pages within his "Popular Culture Excavation Site" at http://www.yodaslair.com/ dumboozle/eurojazz/eurodex.html.

*Recorded by the Comedian Harmonists in 1935.

---

165   Fechner book, p. 197
166   Biberti Estate, Biberti notes for 1963 radio broadcast

"Wir Flüstern"* (We Whisper)

by Karsten Lehl

For decades, several generations of singers have more or less successfully tried to emulate the sound of the Comedian Harmonists. This is no easy task, and even modern ensembles of highly trained professional singers more often than not seem to lack something in comparison. The secret of the Harmonists' sound seems to be rooted elsewhere. After several years of analysis my personal thesis, which anybody may feel free to contest, is: The continuing appeal of their recordings lies in an altogether unorthodox mixture of voices and artistic approach to their songs.

It may be a good idea to individually examine the voices that after a lengthy trial period of almost 18 months formed the definite line-up of the group:

Ari Leschnikoff's tenor is obviously well schooled, but not of great volume. This enables him to sing with an open and unrestricted voice, without overpowering his fellow musicians.

The full voice of Erich Collin is a rather dark-timbred tenor (his last concerts in the 1940s actually were as a baritone) of more power than Leschnikoff's. Thus he mainly uses his head voice or the mixed "voix blanche" register that not only enables him to sing considerably more softly, but also robs his voice of most of its personal characteristics – not advisable for a soloist in classical music, but perfect for a supporting voice that is supposed to blend with the others almost to the point of inaudibility.

Harry Frommermann can only be heard occasionally with his little vocal jokes and instrumental imitations. As his voice is untrained, most of the time he doubles the voice of Ari Leschnikoff, and his amazing musicianship is obvious in the fact that most of the time the listener will not be aware of this fact. He more or less disappears, but his contribution adds a little extra punch to Leschnikoff's tutti part, not to mention a few extra consonants that the Bulgarian tenor needs.

Roman Cycowski's baritone not only has great flexibility, it also combines some of the greatest virtues of the Polish cantorial tradition with first-class Italian schooling. Of all the singers, he is the most "classical" one, and his guidance in questions of vocal production was crucial to the group's success.

Robert Biberti has a warm and beautifully colored bass, but seems to lack any but the most basic knowledge of voice training. This fact is not necessarily a disadvantage, as his voice might otherwise have gained a lot of unwanted volume and lost some of its warmth.

The first recordings of the group for the Odeon label plainly show the shortcomings of the individual singers, but after months of hard work they developed a way to use even some of these faults to their advantage. For example, in the earliest recordings of the group, Leschnikoff frequently is too high with his top notes. In some later arrangements, Frommermann and Bootz seem to counter these problems by writing bass lines for Biberti in a way that encourages his tendency to sing flat, so that the two singers by listening to each other actually end up in tune. Or listen to the way Collin uses his artificially restrained voice to achieve comic pseudo-female effects or, on the other hand, moments of shy, almost adolescent lyricism such as the middle part of "Heute Nacht oder nie."

Using their records as rehearsal guidance (and later even buying a home recording machine), over a period of roughly three years the group considerably reduced its volume and by doing so achieved an even more homogeneous sound. In Erwin Bootz they were lucky to have found a pianist who was able to provide a backbone but with the required softness.

Another important factor in the excellence of the ensemble can be found in the varying musical tastes of its members: Leschnikoff and Collin had a soft spot for sentimental ballads, Frommermann and Biberti were more interested in jazz and music hall numbers, whereas Cycowski and Bootz were at first strictly classical in their preferences. Additionally, Frommermann and Biberti had complementary kinds of humor to add: While Frommermann had a great sense for intelligent wit and the comic possibilities music itself can present, Biberti's idea of fun was more (to put it mildly) folkloristic. On more or less every style the group touched in their repertoire, they had an expert. On the other hand, the peril of overdoing things could always be avoided by other members not hooked on the genre in the same degree.

Because of this disposition, nothing the group ever did was stylistically pure. Every American hit song always had a classical element; torch songs were infused with a touch of cabaret; classical numbers were refreshed by an ensemble that also featured untrained voices. It is this mixture that enabled the Comedian Harmonists to produce great music even at a point when they were hardly on speaking terms anymore, and it is this unique blend that makes it so difficult for other groups to even come close to this standard.

~Karsten Lehl is the baritone for Ensemble Six, a contemporary German vocal group that is devoted to the old treasures of vocal cabaret and revue of the 1920s and 1930s, including those of the Comedian Harmonists. See: www.ensemblesix.de

*Recorded by the Comedian Harmonists in 1928.

CHAPTER FIVE

"Mein blauer Himmel" [167]

(My Blue Heaven)

They Become the Most Popular Group in Europe –
Romances Enter the Picture

The Comedian Harmonists' first concert on their own, and not in a revue, was in Stettin, Bootz' home town, on January 20, 1930, and they performed 15 songs. By then, their fees had increased considerably and they received 950 marks for this appearance.

On January 26, 1930, they did a concert at the Leipziger Schauspielhaus and received a tremendous reception. Leschnikoff said, "The first time – how they applauded, how they raged, these shouts from the audience – not a word! Only tears! I cried as if I had lost my best friend."[168] The review in the *Leipziger Neueste Nachrichten* raved, "The Schauspielhaus will not be able to invite the Comedian Harmonists... too often, or the house will be stamped to pieces. This time the visitors in the orchestra already had stucco falling on their heads, so much did the audience rage and stamp; it came in masses despite the early hour [11:30 a.m.]."

The *Neue Leipziger Zeitung* said: "If you asked yourself why this style of singing, already known through records by the Revellers, has not been imitated earlier in Germany, there is only one answer to give you – this kind of singing requires the highest demands in musicality and intelligence of the performers. The Comedian Harmonists completely fulfill these requirements. They gave us back – in the area of light music – what was known to the church singers of former centuries: the art of musical improvisation. They entwine the melody with harmonious vocal twists, have funny interruptions, instrument-imitations, divide themselves in counterpoint-groups, in solos and colorful accompanying voices, and come up with all kinds of metric and rhythmical variations of the melody. And they do all of this with an astonishing confidence in their intonations and their performance...."[169]

Cycowski said of Ari's performance that night, "Leschnikoff was wonderful.... [T]he music was so lovely, so tender, so wonderful – it put me in a very special mood. I loved that music very much because to me it was art."[170]

A review of a May 1, 1930, concert in Baden-Baden, in the *Badische Volkszeitung* said: "Records coming to life is what it sounded like to our ears. Voices of the finest

---

167 Recorded by the Comedian Harmonists in 1928
168 Czada, p. 46
169 Biberti Estate
170 Cycowski in Fechner film

42

Biberti, Collin, Bootz, Cycowski, Frommermann and Leschnikoff

quality, sound variations known to us only from very difficult jazz instruments. These Comedian Harmonists are voice artists, of nearly virtuosic refinement – they are not only first class vocal artists, but they also can imitate jazz instruments with amazing precision."[171]

These reviews ensured further bookings and the Comedian Harmonists were in great demand. Czada described their performances: "It really meant a lot not only to hear them, but also to see them singing their songs…. No critic forgot to mention the comic gestures of their style of performing." The comic part of their performances was improvised, although they knew generally where the comic parts would be placed and what type of gestures would fit.

Czada continued: "They managed to produce the right balance between the seriousness of their musical demands and the sometimes very funny or even silly titles of their songs, which they interpreted very correctly dressed and with lots of movements and well placed 'gags.' And all that without any help from microphones or an amplifier – which means that with all their jokes, they still had to sing precisely and articulately in order to be heard even in the last rows of big concert halls. The mixture of serious vocal ability and funny performances amazed (the audience) and became a hit. It very much corresponded to the nature of the ensemble members, all of them trained in the 'classical' repertoire, but having two quite different comic talents in Frommermann and Biberti."[172]

Managing the business aspects of the group's career was time-consuming and was handled mostly by Collin with some assistance from the others (except for Leschnikoff

---

171   Biberti Estate
172   Czada, p. 59

and Cycowski). In 1929, Fred A. Colman was hired by the group as its first manager.[173] Colman's name was actually Helmut Jaretzki or Colman-Jaretzki, called "Jaro," and he was given power of attorney to make commitments for the group. That arrangement lasted for about six months and was dissolved amicably.[174]

The recording session of May 23, 1930, featured the classic comedy piece "Ich hab' für Dich 'nen Blumentopf bestellt" (I Ordered A Flowerpot For You), co-written by Bootz. This song was born when Bootz moved into new lodgings at Passauer Strasse 27/28 in the spring of 1930. His landlady, Frau Else Karlick, had a son, Gerd, who wrote poems. One of those poems concerned a flowerpot and Bootz put the poem to music. The result was one of the Comedian Harmonists' most enduring numbers.[175]

The "Blumentopf" lyrics are hardly memorable, for example:

I have ordered a flowerpot for you
A flowerpot for you
And I hope you like the flowerpot
The flowerpot
It is the nicest flowerpot
The nicest in the world
So water my flowerpot
So that it will keep long.

Despite the inane lyrics, "Blumentopf" featured, at different points, the entire vocal orchestra: the pizzicato strings in the introduction; percussion, horns, cello and woodwinds; the pizzicato strings again near the end; and then the winds at the very end – not necessarily trying to imitate the instruments, but doing vocally what instruments would otherwise do. It is typical of the greatness of the Comedian Harmonists that they brought a complex arrangement to such a simple song. The balance in the group is amazing, with no one trying to monopolize the sound. Biberti said: "This 'flower pot' and the Comedian Harmonists became two inseparable words.... [T]he easy light-heartedness of this little song amused us a lot.... "[176]

In May 1930, the Revelers had their last chart hit, rising to number 18 with "A Cottage For Sale." That summer, the Comedian Harmonists appeared in their first movie, *Die Drei von der Tankstelle* (Three Good Friends or The Three From The Gasoline

---

173   Earlier, there were some discussions with Heinz Baruch (also known as Heinz Barger) about representing the group. A draft contract was prepared but never signed. Baruch sued and the case was resolved amicably. He later served as manager of the famous instrumental band, Weintraubs Syncopators. Email from Theo Niemeyer dated November 9, 2007.

174   Colman showed up in Chicago as late as 1964 but it is not known what became of him.

175   Gerd Karlick was also the lyricist or co-lyricist on "Bei der Feuerwehr" (At The Fire Brigade) (1930), "Guten Tag, gnädige Frau" (Good Day, Dear Madam) (1930), "Schöne Isabella aus Kastilien" (Pretty Isabella From Castille) (1932), "Wenn die Sonja russisch tanzt" (When Sonya Does The Russian Dance) (1934), "Du bist mein Baby" (You Are My Baby), recorded by the Comedy Harmonists in 1937 and several others. IMDB.com also lists seven movies for which Karlick was the lyricist.

176   Biberti Estate, Biberti notes for 1963 radio broadcast

Station). The film was shot at the Universum-Film A.G. (Ufa) studios in Potsdam-Babelsberg.[177] Strangely, although the group was paid well for its appearances, they were rarely in the foreground in the movies in which they performed. They were in the background as bartenders in both *Tankstelle* and *Der ungetreue Eckehart* (The Unfaithful Eckehart) and as chefs in *Ihre Hoheit befiehlt* (Her Highness Commands), and sometimes only their voices could be heard, as in *Bomben auf Monte Carlo* (Monte Carlo Madness) and *Gassenhauer*.[178] One exception was a poorly lit scene in *Tankstelle* where the group was very much in the foreground as chefs, singing backup for Leo Monosson, who does the lead on "Liebling, mein Herz lässt Dich grüssen."[179]

The group's appearance in *Tankstelle* brought another substantial benefit. This was their first pairing with Werner Richard Heymann, the composer, who was born in Königsberg in 1896,[180] but also found his way to Berlin. Heymann composed classical music (he had a piece performed by the Vienna Philharmonic when he was only 22 years old), but then switched over to popular music and began writing for films and serving as a musical director for cabarets. This film introduced two timeless songs: "Ein Freund, ein guter Freund" (A Friend, A Good Friend) and "Liebling, mein Herz lässt Dich grüssen." A few of Heymann's other evergreens (as standards are called in Germany) were the phenomenally successful "Das ist die Liebe der Matrosen" (This Is The Love Of The Sailors), "Hoppla, jetzt komm ich!" (Okay, Here I Come), and the poignant "Irgendwo auf der Welt" (Somewhere in the World).[181]

What an incredible day it must have been at the studio on August 22, 1930, when four extraordinary numbers were recorded in a one-day session, including what has become the signature song of the Comedian Harmonists – "Veronika, der Lenz ist da" – and another masterpiece, "Wochenend und Sonnenschein" (Weekend and Sunshine, known in the English speaking world as "Happy Days Are Here Again"[182]). Biberti said

---

177   A German film conglomerate founded in 1917 and taken over by the Nazis in 1937.

178   Gassenhauer originally meant songs that were sung in the lanes or Gassen and backyards. The term has come to be used for German hit songs from the 1930s and 1940s and earlier.

179   Monosson was a singer/actor, born in Moscow in 1897, who, as did so many artists of the day, went to Berlin and appeared in about ten films in the early 1930s. He also sang with the Paul Goodwin and Marek Weber Orchestras. He died in 1967 in Jamaica.

180   Königsberg, then in East Prussia, is now Kaliningrad, Russia.

181   Heymann was Jewish and left Germany in 1933 for Paris, having seen what was coming, at least in the arts. He returned to Germany after the war and married for the fourth time, this time to actress Elisabeth Millberg. Their daughter, also named Elisabeth, recalls a meeting between her father and Biberti in Ascona, Switzerland, where they reminisced about old times. "My father died in 1961, he was very ill, life was not too nice to him. Through his music, he stays alive forever!" Email from Elisabeth Trautwein-Heymann dated December 11, 2006.

182   Written by Jack Yellen & Milton Ager (Ager's daughter was political commentator, Shana Alexander), the song became FDR's campaign theme song in 1932. Benny Meroff & His Orchestra hit Number One on the U.S. charts with this song in February, 1930. One month later, Ben Selvin also reached the top spot with the same song. Leo Reisman must have felt like a failure when he "only" topped out at Number Three, also in February, 1930.

Bootz, Leschnikoff, Collin, Frommermann, Cycowski and Biberti

that when the group performed, "The first song had to be a hit, and when we sang 'Veronika, der Lenz ist da' or 'Wochenend und Sonnenschein,' we had captured the audience and after that we could sing whatever we wanted."[183] The other two songs they recorded that day were "Ein Freund, ein guter Freund" and "Liebling, mein Herz lässt Dich grüssen." They made 16 recordings in 1930, all for Electrola.

Their last performance in a revue took place in September 1930 in Leipzig. Erna Eggstein-Frommermann, who would become Harry's wife (more about her later), was listed among the cast. The revue, *Wie werde ich reich und glücklich?* (How Can I Become Rich and Happy?), was written by Mischa Spoliansky and Felix Joachimson and produced the song, "Auf Wiederseh'n" (this is a different song from the much more famous, "Auf Wiedersehen, my Dear"). The group received about 500 marks per night for this show and had to sing only three songs.

The Comedian Harmonists' repertoire had increased to the point where they had enough arrangements to do a full concert by themselves, without any other acts. A solo performance required about 25 to 30 songs and extensive rehearsal time was needed to reach that number.[184] (Electrola also had been urging them to try concerts that were not part of the revue setting. At that time, there were only three acts that could sell out concert halls on their own: the Berlin Philharmonic, the Don Cossacks, and the Comedian Harmonists.)[185]

---

183   Fechner book, p. 201

184   At the time of the dissolution of the group in 1935, they had over 200 songs in their repertory.

185   Fechner book, pp. 224-225. The Don Cossacks were a Russian male choir formed by soldiers from the Don region of Russia while interned in Turkey in 1920 during the Russian civil war. In 1921, the Cossack regiments were moved to the Greek island of Lemnos [http://home.hetnet.nl/~kozakken/choirs.htm (accessed December 5, 2007)]. The choir members were among them and they continued to sing. By 1923, they had migrated to Bulgaria and gave a well-received public performance. Vienna was next and then on to great fame. They were featured in *Time* magazine in 1931. Over the years, they would give more than 9,000 concerts.

Biberti described how they set up their programs: "The most important thing was the program arrangement. If six men stand on the stage, just like that, and have to entertain their audience for two hours, then the choice and the order of the things matters. That has to be done very artfully so that a high point is reached again and again. Each evening was to have four parts. The first part had our so-called sparklers including a great encore. The second part was more reflective, with lyrical things, with folk songs and character pieces by Brahms, Rossini or Kreisler among others. By the way, when we sang those character pieces such as "Die Liebe kommt, die Liebe geht" (Love Comes, Love Goes), it hit the audience totally by surprise and was a big success, because this type of music requires great perfection, voices, taste, arrangements, movement, appearance – everything had to harmonize. And in this respect, we were pretty successful."[186]

Cycowski liked the German folk songs the best: "I loved Mozart, Brahms, and especially 'In einem kühlen Grunde' (In A Cool Dell) and 'Guter Mond du gehst so stille' (Good Moon, You Go So Quietly). Nobody could sing it the way we did. The music was so beautiful, so tender – wonderful. It made me feel that this was art. Nobody could do this, not even the Revellers – nobody."

Cycowski told how they chose the numbers that they performed: "The choice of songs was by the criteria of beauty, likeability and success. We got together and talked about what we wanted to pick. Everybody made their suggestions and then we voted – should we do this song or this? Some songs were so popular, there was no doubt about it, but sometimes we had big discussions. And often Biberti's mother would come and restore peace. She was wonderful with that. And when we had decided, the next question was, who was to arrange it, Harry or Bootz? Of course, Bootz always picked the best things, because he was the musical director, and Harry got whatever Bootz did not want to do, the thankless pieces, the ones where we did not know in advance whether they would be successful or not."[187]

The Comedian Harmonists' first verifiable appearance outside of Germany took place in November, 1930, with a concert in Amsterdam at the Cabaret La Gaité. The extent of their popularity can be shown by what occurred on a trip to Copenhagen for a concert. On arriving they noticed that there were no posters advertising the concert. This had never happened before and caused them to wonder if they had their dates mixed up. Biberti telephoned the booking agency to inquire, and they told him, "It's sold out. Why should we advertise a concert that's already sold out?"[188]

In 1930, the inclusion of the subtitle, "The German Revellers," gradually disappeared from their billings. In 1931, they made 23 recordings for Electrola, including several songs that were done in three different languages. One, their best-selling song "Das ist die Liebe der Matrosen," they did in an English version: "The Way With Every

---

186   Fechner book, p. 201-202. The song is sometimes known as just "Liebesleid."

187   Fechner book, p. 202

188   Bootz in Fechner film. This was a change as an earlier concert in Copenhagen had been poorly attended.

Sailor," and in French: "Les Gars de la Marine." The latter sold 200,000 copies in France alone – a remarkable accomplishment for the 1930s. Biberti later said: "'Das ist die Liebe der Matrosen' – the same song was then recorded in English and French. Especially in France, this record, sung in a Marseille dialect, became such a success, that it was declared the so-called national record in the year 1932. During our concerts in France we were never able to leave the stage without having sung 'Liebe der Matrosen – Les Gars de la Marine' once."[189]

Bootz tried a solo career from December 1930 to July 1931. He had been offered the opportunity to write the music for and appear in the movie, *Abschied* (*Goodbye*); during that time, he also served as the music director at the Kabarett der Komiker. It is not clear whether Bootz left to further his musical development or, as is more likely, for financial reasons. He was always in debt, and he could make more money at the KaDeKo – but that would soon change. Bootz was replaced by Walter Joseph. Fried Walter, later a composer and conductor of the RIAS[190] orchestra, was supposed to replace Bootz, but Joseph was selected instead after Walter completed a trial period, apparently unsuccessfully. Bootz was not easy to replace because so much of what he did was improvised, making it difficult to keep the sound of the group the same with a new pianist. Czada provides the text of an interesting letter written by Walter to Bootz many years later:

Dear Erwin Bootz!

I wanted to write to you for a long time. You don't know what role you have played in my life! It was 1930 and I was still a student of Arnold Schoenberg at the Akademie der Künste in Berlin. But I had immediately rejected the atonal twelve-tone music, when I noticed that Schoenberg could not whistle one of his themes by heart, and I simply did not attend class from then on.

I got to be a part of your famous group by chance, reluctantly and initially for a six-week trial period at Knesebeckstrasse 88. Eventually I was to become your successor. You have retrained me from serious music to entertainment music.

I often was at Harry Frommermann's for lunch and he taught me very patiently how to play the dezimen [tenths – an octave, plus two] on the piano with my left hand.

But unforgettable to me are the hours spent in your apartment, where you played not only Liszt and Chopin so wonderfully, but most importantly, you showed me how to magically play harmonious and cultivated hits on the piano. At the end of my trial period you gave me your worn socks and tie as a parting gift. . . .[191]

---

189 Biberti Estate, Biberti notes for 1963 radio broadcast

190 RIAS stood for Radio in the American Sector in post-war Berlin and is covered more thoroughly in Chapter Nine. Walter's real name was Walter Schmidt.

191 Czada, pp. 51 and 55. Letter dated October 23, 1982.

MY FAVORITE COMEDIAN HARMONISTS SONG

The songs that I prefer hearing change from time to time, but my favorite has really always remained "Ein Lied geht um die Welt" (A Song Goes Out To The World)*. It is my earliest favorite from the first Comedian Harmonists CD I found when I started listening to the group. Why? Well it is a song that just makes me happy while listening, with the typical Comedian Harmonists sound, the magic blend of their voices, as well as the solo voices (especially Leschnikoff). Also, it also remains a symbol for the success of the ensemble nearly all over the world, whose time might be gone forever, but whose music is everlasting.

~Theo Niemeyer lives outside of Hamburg, Germany. He has studied the Comedian Harmonists extensively and is the official Archivist for the Comedian Harmonists.

* Recorded by The Comedian Harmonists in 1933.

Joseph was asked to leave the group and Bootz returned. Joseph was not happy and wrote to Electrola blaming them for his departure from the Comedian Harmonists – they had commented unfavorably on his playing. Joseph questioned whether they had the expertise to level this criticism. Electrola responded (interestingly, Electrola's letter was signed by Rudolph Fischer-Maretzki, who would later become the manager of the Comedian Harmonists) explaining that Electrola had an interest in the quality of the recordings made by the Comedian Harmonists and saying that the company had the right to present constructive criticism. Fischer-Maretzki confirmed that several executives at Electrola had expressed their views and then said, "Your way of playing piano was especially challenging for our recording technician, as the sound of the piano was out of tune with the sound of the voices, or rather, as we say in the language of recording, a dynamic balance could only rarely be achieved." The letter went on to state that Electrola had other concerns, but that they had never said that they would refuse to make further recordings if Joseph were in the group.[192]

From 1930 to 1933, the group enjoyed their biggest artistic and commercial success, giving 150 concerts a year. They appeared in all the larger cities of Germany, made concert-tours throughout Europe, recorded over 100 songs, made radio appearances, more films, and became wealthy from high record royalties and sold-out performances. As an article in *Constanze* magazine from 1957 said, "'Comedian Harmonists' was once written in letters in flashing colors on the walls of the world's varieties."[193]

The members were all big spenders, except for Ari, whose only extravagance was a new car, a Hudson Cabriolet: Ari's driver's license photo shows him dressed in white tie and tails while holding a cigarette. They ate in the finest restaurants, except for Ari, who would pose as a student and go to university canteens where he could buy inexpensive meals.[194]

---

192   Biberti Estate, letter dated August 27, 1931

193   *Constanze Magazine*, 1957

194   Kiss in Fechner film

"Ich küsse Ihre Hand, Madame" [195]
(I Kiss Your Hand, Madame)

Soon, they all had wives or girlfriends

As mentioned earlier, Harry had met an aspiring actress named Marie Erna Eggstein, whom the others called "Mausi"[196] (and who would become his wife), at a birthday party in 1929 in the building where Bootz lived. "Little Frommermann" (as she called him) propositioned her, but she rejected him because she was just coming out of a very complicated relationship that had not ended well. She next ran into Harry on the street during the time when the group was inactive due to the switch from Nussbaum

Erna Frommermann

to Collin: "We went into a cheap café and I noticed that he did not smoke anymore. I knew that he had been a strong smoker, and offered him a cigarette, but he declined, saying that he had stopped smoking. I later learned that he had to quit because he did not have any money for cigarettes. And when I found out just how badly he was doing I lent him money for a little while. He gave everything back to me later on. And from that moment on we were really good friends – and more than that."[197]

Cycowski said of Erna, "She wanted to become an actress; she'd done a bit of singing. She's an intelligent woman and was sometimes too domineering for Harry."[198] Leschnikoff lamented, "Oh dear, Harry and his wife Mausi." Erna was not very thrifty: "We were all very young at the time. And it all rather went to our heads."[199] She married Frommermann on May 15, 1931. (As mentioned earlier, a program from a September 1930 revue lists her as Erna Eggstein-Frommermann, but they were not married yet. This taking liberty with names was not uncommon in Berlin at the time.) Because Erna was Protestant and Harry Jewish, they were married in a civil ceremony. Their honeymoon consisted of touring with the group. Of the difference in their religions, Erna later said, "By the way, when I say now that my husband was Jewish, I was not really thinking about it then. I only really realized it later, well, when the Nazis came. Prior to that nobody thought anything about it."[200]

Leschnikoff's first love was a woman named Ella from Danzig whom he met when she stopped him to ask for directions. Ella was studying piano at the conservatory.

---

195   Recorded by the Comedian Harmonists in 1928
196   "Maus" is the German word for "mouse."
197   Fechner book, p. 190
198   Cycowski in Fechner film
199   Kiss in Fechner film
200   Fechner book, p. 227

Heiratsregister Nr. *415* des Jahres 1 *931* H

Heiratsſchein.

Vornamen und Familiennamen des Mannes *Klaus*
Georg Frommermann
Stand: *Tonkünstler*
aus **Berlin-Wilmersdorf**
geboren am *12* ten *Oktober* 1 *906.*
in *Berlin*
Vornamen der Frau; *Marie Erna*
geb. Linn
geborene *Eggstein*
aus **Berlin-Wilmersdorf**
geboren am *20* ten *Juni* 1 *905*
in *Linden - Hannover*
Eheſchließung am *12* ten *Mai* 19 *31*
in **Berlin-Wilmersdorf**

Berlin-Wilmersdorf, am *12. Mai* 19 *31*

Der Standesbeamte

Ehemann: Geburtsregister Nr. *1809*
des Standesamtes *II Berlin*
Ehefrau: Geburtsregister Nr. *1041*
des Standesamtes *IV Hannover.*

4

Comedian Harmonists Archiv
Theo Niemeyer

Marriage Certificate of Harry and Erna

Ari wanted to marry Ella, but her parents objected to her marrying a foreigner. Ari then met Delphine David, a member of the Tiller Girls, a world-renowned English dance troupe formed by John Tiller in Manchester, England in 1890.[201] Leschnikoff first saw Delphine in 1932 in Leipzig where the group was making a guest appearance. Ari sent her his card but received no encouragement. A short time later, back in Berlin, Ari was driving to the recording studio when he happened to see Delphine at the British Embassy. After the recording session, he went to the Embassy and she came out. Ari said, "She looked at me, blushed and I said, 'We know each other mademoiselle.' She replied, 'I don't speak German very well.' 'That doesn't matter, neither do I," answered Ari. He continued, "I thought she was French, but she came from England. The father was French, the mother Irish. Her name was Delphine. We met at the Hotel Eden for five o'clock tea. She came with her cousin, and Harry and Mausi came with me. That's how we met. We talked and danced and a month later she was my wife."[202]

Marion Kiss (Erna) described her: "Yes, Delphine was English, a petite dancer who performed with the Tiller Girls. Very pretty, with long, red curls, an enchanting face, a sweet little thing and she had real red hair. A delightful girl who couldn't speak a word of German…. Poor girl. She said, 'If Ari's unfaithful to me it'll kill me.' And Ari was constantly unfaithful to her."[203] Ari and Delphine had a son, Simeon, in 1934.

Collin met Fernande Holzamer in an artists' bar in Frankfurt in April 1930.

---

201 Two of the more famous ex-Tiller Girls are Diana Vreeland, former Editor of *Vogue Magazine,* and Betty Boothroyd, Speaker of the British House of Commons from 1992-2000. See, http://en.wikipedia.org/wiki/Tiller_Girls (accessed December 5, 2007)

202 Fechner book, p. 228

203 Kiss in Fechner film

Ari and Delphine 1932

Fernande attended the group's concert the next evening with a date. After her date took her home, she went back to the concert and saw Erich. Fernande obviously impressed Erich because as the group continued its tour, he wrote to her. But he misspelled her last name and she was offended.[204] When the Comedian Harmonists returned to Frankfurt in May 1931, they saw each other again and were married later that year. Fernande called it love at first sight.[205] She was part French – her mother was French and her father was German – and was born in Paris in 1909. Biberti described Fernande as "a real beauty."[206] When Leschnikoff was asked about her in the documentary, he smiled and simply said "Oh, Fernande" in a wistful way.[207] Collin and Fernande had a daughter, Suzanne, who was born in Berlin in 1932. Marion Kiss described Fernande cryptically: "There are people whom one does not like to talk about. We always said, 'Silent waters are deep.' I don't want to say more."[208]

Erich and Fernande went to Paris for a brief honeymoon, and then caught up with the others in Scheveningen, a Dutch seaside resort near The Hague. Collin was the forgetful type, as illustrated by this story told by Fernande: "They had a first rehearsal in the hotel and I stayed downstairs in the hall and waited for Erich to pick me up. And after the rehearsal all of them came downstairs, I sat there and read, and they went past me outside without paying attention to me, even Erich. He totally ignored me. Of course I was very upset. I

Delphine and Simeon

204   Interview with Deborah Tint, September 23 and 26, 2007
205   Fernande (Collin) Currie in Fechner film
206   Biberti in Fechner film
207   Leschnikoff in Fechner film
208   Fechner book, p. 230

Fernande Holzamer

Ursula Elkan

was still very young and I thought this was the end. So I walked through Scheveningen for hours. Erich had meanwhile returned to the hotel, remembering that he had a wife, but I was not there. I think they then called the police and they were all very upset, until I finally decided to return. But Erich's forgetfulness made me suffer my whole life."[209]

Bootz also met Ursula Elkan in the same Frankfurt artists' bar and they were married in 1933. Ursula was Jewish, and her father, Benno Elkan, was a famous sculptor, best known for creating the giant menorah that stands outside the Knesset in Jerusalem.[210] Given that Bootz' mother was anti-Semitic (according to Cycowski), she was not happy with the match, but the marriage took place nonetheless.

Cycowski met Mary Panzram in Cologne in May 1929, at a party given by the family of his former girlfriend. Collin showed some interest in Mary, but after seeing her dance with Cycowski, Erich told him, "She means you."[211] Mary moved to Berlin, took an apartment and began studying fashion. In 1931, Roman bought her a candy store to operate but it was not successful and it closed.

Cycowski wanted to marry Mary, but she was not Jewish. Roman asked her if she would consider converting. She said she would have to think about it because as she said, "I'll do it properly or not at all."[212] Two weeks later Mary agreed. As she later related, "My mother used to say, 'Your God's there where you find him." This was 1933 and under the law in Germany, they were not permitted to marry – so they waited. The couple stayed together and finally were married in 1937.

209 Fechner book, p. 230-231
210 The piece was commissioned by members of the British Parliament and donated by them to Israel in 1956. See, http://www.jewishvirtuallibrary.org/jsource/History/knessmen.html (accessed December 6, 2007)
211 Fechner book, p. 195
212 Cycowski in Fechner film

Ursula Elkan and Erwin Bootz on their wedding day.

Biberti met actress Hildegard (Hilde) Liesbeth Longino in 1932 at the Babelsberg film studio where she was an extra in a film. She would become his long-time companion and eventually, his wife. Said Biberti, "At that time she was a bit player and was standing charmingly dressed for a Hungarian film in the canteen of the old Ufa studios in Babelsberg. She looked enchanting and made a tremendous impression on me." [213] Biberti married her after a ten-year relationship.

Conflicts Arise Among the Members

All was not rosy, however – things are never easy for a group and the Comedian Harmonists were no exception. Frommermann felt tyrannized by Biberti and Bootz. There was a rivalry between Biberti and Frommermann because they were both trying to be the funny guy on stage. Biberti saw it this way: "Frommermann tended rather to crave for admiration, with the result that during performances he played the role of the buffoon." Cycowski said, "Sometimes I would reproach Biberti. 'Why do you keep getting at him?' 'He's stupid,' was the answer."[214]

---

213   Biberti in Fechner film
214   Fechner book, p. 204

Mary Panzram – likely a passport photo.

Hilde Longino

It is interesting to hear Marion Kiss (Erna Frommermann), twenty-some years after their divorce, still defending her Harry: "He [Biberti] wanted to snub Harry because he [Harry] was the most gifted of them." As for Frommermann's comedic abilities, Kiss said, "He would have become a great comedian if he did not have this enormous musical talent."[215]

Bootz thought that Harry was not as good a singer as the others: "Generally I have to say that I was very much under Biberti's influence at the time, and that is why I made many misjudgments. Harry was a soft, good-hearted man, who had to suffer quite a bit in the ensemble. Today I see it differently than at that time. Harry, for example, could sing some, if not much, but he imitated instruments very well and learned, at first under my guidance, to arrange very well. When we met again decades later he said, 'You know, you really agonized me by your sharp criticism at the time."[216] Here Bootz may be rewriting history a bit. After all, Frommermann wrote the initial arrangements for the group, before Bootz even became a member. In the story Harry wrote about the Comedian Harmonists, he said that Bootz "had grown into the style and artistical (sic) spirit of the ensemble."[217]

In March 1931, during Bootz' hiatus from the group, there was a move to oust Frommermann but it is not clear who initiated this move or how serious it was. Biberti claimed that the others were not happy with Harry's exaggerated gestures on stage – they thought he was trying too hard.[218] Biberti said in the Fechner film that although he "did not exactly embrace Harry,

---

215 Kiss in Fechner film
216 Fechner book, p. 204
217 Frohman story
218 You can get some sense of this by watching the video of the Comedy Harmonists singing "Creole Love Call." It can be seen in the Fechner documentary.

there are things that just simply cannot be done. And that is why I said, 'Forget about that, that is impossible, Harry stays in the ensemble.'" Marion Kiss confirmed the attempt. She overheard a conversation in a coffee shop among members of the Kardosch Singers, a rival group, who were speculating that Frommermann might become available to them as a result of being forced out of the Comedian Harmonists. She told Harry what she had heard. She believed that Biberti put a stop to the ouster attempt because he realized they could not do without Frommermann's arrangements.[219]

This incident, as well as all the conflict and criticism, naturally worried Frommermann, and he set to work arranging even more songs in order to make himself indispensable: "And then Harry wrote day and night," said Erna/Marion. "I made one coffee after another and Harry wrote his scores, without piano, just out of his head – sometimes the whole night long. And then he went to rehearsals in the morning, and finally slept for a few hours in the afternoon. He worked very hard. For example, in the summer we usually had five to six weeks' vacation. The others would go away and enjoy their vacation. We also would go away, but wherever we were, Harry always kept on writing and writing all the scores for the next season. Today I sometimes think that this was the best deed in my life, that I helped Harry at that time to stay with the Comedian Harmonists."[220]

Biberti had a strong personality and tended to assert himself as the self-appointed leader. Marion Kiss portrayed Biberti as something of a dictator and Biberti did not disagree, "One member is bound to emerge as the leader and to be accepted as such by the others; a man on whom the others can rely for everything…. Occasionally one of the group may have felt he was not getting his share of recognition, but I always took care that no one should ever play a star role." As Bootz put it, "[Biberti] set a limit on all craving for admiration except his own. Of course, it's possible that without him the ensemble would have split up."[221]

Despite their disagreements, the money that the group was earning ensured that they stayed together. None of them could have made that much as a solo. Biberti later said that he understood this.

One of the group's more unusual performances came at the Amstel Hotel in Amsterdam in March 1931, where they helped celebrate the 60th birthday of Dutch conductor Willem Mengelberg, a great fan of the Comedian Harmonists, at a private performance paid for by friends of the conductor. Czada describes the scene: "Suddenly singing could be heard and over the grand staircase in the hall came the Comedian Harmonists, each with a flowerpot in their hands towards the totally surprised Mengelberg and sang the matching song for him as a birthday serenade."[222]

---

219   Fechner book, pp. 216-217
220   Fechner book, p. 217
221   Bootz in Fechner film
222   Czada, p.50

MY FAVORITE COMEDIAN HARMONISTS SONG

If someone were to ask me for my favorite song of the Comedian Harmonists, I would have a difficult time to name just one, but I think one title expresses the message that the music of the Comedian Harmonists wants to tell us all – the song "Die Liebe kommt, die Liebe geht, solang' ein Stern am Himmel steht"* (Love comes, loves goes, as long as there are stars in the sky). Because love is what eventually makes us human.

~Uwe Berger is a Comedian Harmonists enthusiast who lives in the northwest of Germany.

*Recorded by the Comedian Harmonists in 1933.

A review in the *Neuer Görlitzer Anzeiger* of April 8, 1931, gives a pretty good idea of how well the group was being received by its audiences: "Well, this really is something phenomenal, something unique in its form. One has to imagine: There are people, five singers and one concert pianist to be exact, which the group always brings with them, and they get together about 800 to 900 people, on a holiday on top of all, and get them in near ecstasy though their capricious cheekiness or with misty sentimentalities from dance, movies and operettas." The review went on to describe their "perfect harmony of language and singing, mimic and performance," followed by, "How hard must they have worked in order to give the impression of improvisation!"[223]

In trying to explain the appeal of the group, Biberti later said: "The attraction of our concerts consisted for a large part in the factor of surprise. The audience always asked themselves: 'What are they going to do now?' And we knowingly avoided any exaggerated perfection – the kind of artistic singing that dominates so many vocal ensembles today. Our singing did not work like a well oiled machine, it always remained human, personal – and if I may say so – never crossed the borders of taste. That made us lovable and very popular – no other vocal ensemble reached that after us."[224]

The Comedian Harmonists' songs break down into three basic categories. First there are the *schlager*, which means "hits." These are light, popular songs and there were many *schlager* in the Comedian Harmonists' repertoire, such as "Veronika, der Lenz ist da," "Mein kleiner grüner Kaktus," "Ich hab' für Dich 'nen Blumentopf bestellt," "Auf Wiedersehen, my Dear" and "Liebling, mein Herz lässt Dich grüssen." The second category consists of the classical pieces, for example, "Eine kleine Frühlingsweise" (A Little Maytime Song), which is "Humoresque" by Dvorak, "Schlafe, mein Prinzchen, schlaf ein" (Sleep My Little Prince, Sleep) to a melody by Mozart, and several by Johann Strauss, "Perpetuum Mobile" (Perpetual Motion), and "An der schönen blauen Donau" (At The Beautiful Blue Danube). The third grouping is the traditional

223   Biberti Estate
224   Biberti Estate, Biberti notes for 1963 radio broadcast

or folk songs such as "In einem kühlen Grunde" or "Morgen muss ich fort von hier" (Tomorrow I Must Leave Here).[225]

The group recorded 17 different sides for Electrola in 1932, among them "In einem kühlen Grunde," "Schöne Isabella aus Kastilien," "Der Onkel Bumba aus Kalumba tanzt nur Rumba" (Uncle Bumba From Kalumba Dances Only The Rumba), "Auf Wiedersehen, my Dear," "Einmal schafft's jeder" (Everyone Can Finally Make It) from the film, *Der blonde Traum* (*The Blond Dream*), "Irgendwo auf der Welt," also from *Der blonde Traum*, "Maskenball im Gänsestall" (Masked Ball In A Goose Stable) and "Eins, zwei, drei, vier" (One, Two, Three, Four) from the film *Zigeuner der Nacht* (*Gypsies Of The Night*).

Another concert, suggested by their record company, Electrola, was booked at the Berlin Philharmonic for January 21, 1932. Frommermann said, "In those days it was unheard of for artists in the field of light music and entertainment to be offered a chance to appear in a concert hall, which until then had been reserved for serious music."[226] It was a good idea – the hall was sold out – all 2700 seats. Frommermann recalled, "Prior to our appearance Electrola played one of our records. The gramophone was in a corner of the stage, amplified by loudspeakers. And then we entered the stage in single file, as was our habit, and were greeted by huge applause. We were very jittery, but the hall was full. And despite our worries we had developed enough security through prior concerts to cover up our nervousness. It was an indescribable feeling to sing in front of such an audience and such critics."[227]

The success of this concert had a profound effect on the group. First, it gave them more confidence. Second, it enabled them to get a *Kunstschein* or art certificate from the Ministry

---

MY FAVORITE COMEDIAN HARMONISTS SONG

One favorite is "Leichte Kavallerie"*(Light Cavalry). I appreciate the arrangement, the musicality, and the presentation of discernible voices alongside Bootz's piano. It's quintessential Comedian Harmonists! It's a fun piece.

~*Carolyn Speerstra Harcourt is a Comedian Harmonists enthusiast from Oregon who is the Archivist for a portion of the Cycowski papers.*

* Recorded by the Comedian Harmonists in 1931.

---

225   Thank you to Sebastian Claudius Semler for his help with these terms.

226   Frohman story

227   Fechner book, p. 218. Fechner designated a section of his book as what he calls "fictional dialogue" (pages 162 to 275). The information that Fechner communicates in that section is not "fictional" in the strict sense of the word; in fact, in some cases the words are direct quotes heard in Fechner's documentary. So we know that these quotes are not "fictional." In those cases, I have cited directly to the documentary. In other instances, Fechner simply rearranged some words or combined different quotes in order to improve the flow. Clearly, the words Fechner attributes to Frommermann were actually conveyed to Fechner by others who were quoting Frommermann (as opposed to being told to Fechner by Frommermann himself). Any portions of the Fechner book used here that might be "fictional dialogue" are noted as such in the footnotes.

At the Berlin Philharmonic

of Culture, which allowed them to keep a larger portion of the profits by reducing the amusement tax on those profits. Third, concert halls were now competing for their services.[228] They were getting more and more bookings outside of Germany and had to develop their repertoire further, adding more songs in languages other than German. Their music was even heard on the radio in the U. S. The Staatsbibliothek Archive contains some very complimentary fan letters from the U.S. – one referred to their "splendid singing."[229]

An appearance in Würzburg on April 4, 1932, brought this review: "The applause of the audience increased from song to song. They had to give encores over encores, which would have filled an acceptable program by themselves. There was no holding back the enthusiasm at the end and only when the artists finished their encores saying 'Auf Wiedersehen' did the audience calm down. And we would like to shout back 'Auf Wiedersehen' from this place."[230]

In June, 1933, the group hired a new business manager to handle their affairs. They chose Rudolph Fischer-Maretzki, an executive with Electrola, their record company.[231] They toured Switzerland, France, Belgium, the Netherlands, Norway and Denmark in 1933. On November 24, 1933, they made their second appearance at the Berlin Philharmonic, and the hall was sold out. By this time, however, they were so popular that they were the only attraction on the bill.

Although one critic called the Comedian Harmonists "a refined version of the Revelers,"[232] they had now departed from the style of the Revelers with much more intricate arrangements and more emphasis on rhythm and harmony. A review of a performance of December 1933, in the *Bautzener Tageblatt* read in part: "The most beautiful and charming, the most heartfelt really going to the heart, of course, are the folk songs, presented without any affectation, but with a lot of tenderness and with such

228   Fechner book, p. 219
229   Biberti Estate, letter of May 20, 1932
230   Biberti Estate
231   Fischer-Maretzki, born in 1866, managed other artists as well as the Comedian Harmonists.
232   Czada p. 24

beautiful blessedness of the voice, that one would love to remain with this melodiousness for hours. How nice was Mozart's 'Wiegenlied,' how touchingly simple the song 'Vom guten Mond,' how emotional 'In einem kühlen Grunde.' All this was the highest culture of singing with a nearly enchanting impression. In short: It was once again an exquisite enjoyment in the area of perfect art of singing and if the Comedian Harmonists return they will be greeted by the same enthusiasm as given to them this Saturday evening."[233]

Rudolf Lorenzen said that they reached "never imagined popularity."[234] As Roman Cycowski said in 1998, in what was probably his last interview, "[H]ad they not dissolved us by force at that time [1935] and scattered us all into the winds, we could have become maybe more popular than the Beatles."[235]

MY FAVORITE COMEDIAN HARMONISTS SONG

My favorite would have to be "Ohne Dich" (Stormy Weather). This 1933 recording embodies everything I like about an R&B group from 15–20 years later. It has a soft tenor lead, nice background harmony (non-obtrusive), a floating tenor, bass bridge, chiming, and a really nice ending. If you had them sing the same arrangement in English, it would be comparable to what the Delta Rhythm Boys (for example) would have done 15 years later. I know of no other group of the time who sang like that, so as far as I'm concerned, the Comedian Harmonists might be the inventors of Rhythm & Blues.

~Marv Goldberg, noted vocal group historian and author. See: http://www.uncamarvy.com/

Music Context

What was going on with vocal groups elsewhere in the world? Most of the action was in the U. S., where music was in a period of great transition. Besides the Revelers, some other influential American groups from the late 1920s and early 1930s were the Boswell Sisters, the Rhythm Boys (featuring Bing Crosby) and the Mills Brothers, as well as numerous Gospel groups.

The Boswell Sisters, from New Orleans, were Connie (later Connee), Martha and Helvetia (or Vet). The Boswells preceded the Andrews Sisters by about ten years, and helped pave the way for the numerous female groups to come. They were also very innovative and more rhythmic than previous groups. They showed their versatility by each playing an instrument (Connie, the cello; Martha, the piano, and Vet, the violin) and by being members of the New Orleans Philharmonic Orchestra. In April 1931, they had their first chart hit with "When I Take My Sugar To Tea;" later hits included

---

233   Biberti Estate
234   Lorenzen Stories
235   Interview, *Musicwoche* magazine, March 23, 1998

"You Oughta Be In Pictures" (1934) and "The Object of My Affection" (1935), all on the Brunswick label.

The Rhythm Boys were a vocal trio consisting of Harry "Bing" Crosby, Harry Barris and Al Rinker. Crosby and Rinker started as a duet act in Spokane, Washington. They went to California in 1925 and Rinker's sister, singer Mildred Bailey, helped them get started. In 1926, they were asked to join the Paul Whiteman Orchestra. There Crosby and Rinker hooked up with Harry Barris and became Paul Whiteman's Rhythm Boys – the first vocal trio to be regularly associated with a band. Eventually, Crosby began to get solo work and the group disbanded in 1931.

The Mills Brothers – John, Jr., Herbert, Harry and Donald Mills from Piqua, Ohio – were the first black group to have wide appeal to white audiences. When John Jr. died suddenly in 1935, he was replaced by their father, John. They had a huge number of hits (eleven on the R&B charts and 70 on the pop charts). Their biggest songs included "Tiger Rag" (1931-Brunswick), "Dinah" (1932-Brunswick), "Paper Doll" (1943-Decca), "Till Then" (1944-Decca) and "Glow Worm" (1952-Decca).

Music was moving in an entirely new direction. This was the big band era. Where the music of the Comedian Harmonists might have gone is a matter of speculation due to what followed.

*"Ach wie ist's möglich dann"** (Oh How It's Possible)*

Why?

by Jan Grübler

Why did the Comedian Harmonists become so famous and why have they fascinated so many people to such an extent? Why did they rise so fast and why did they have to disband? Why are they still so popular today? These questions are very interesting to me because of my extensive study of the Comedian Harmonists.

In their time they presented a new form of so-called "light entertainment," a never before heard kind of harmony and precision, with an easy, cheerful sound, which nevertheless made evident to the listener the difficulty in accomplishing what they were doing. Their variety was unique, away from traditional choir singing, toward hit songs and known operetta ballads. In this regard, they were not at all unique – other artists performed and recorded the same songs at the same time! Later, they began to include not only film melodies, but also classics and folk songs. They had a sure flair for choosing and compiling the repertoire, knowing the different effects of their songs. And all this in several languages! They sang with wit, ambiguity and humour, with a lacing of frivolity, but always appearing respectable and elegant.

All this could only arise at a time and in a place like the Berlin of the late 1920s. A time shaped by unsteady political and economic circumstances in Germany. A time of desire for entertainment and pleasure, against the background of world economic crisis and mass un-employment. Let's put ourselves into this time: The only existing sound storage medium was the shellac record (78 rpm), and radio was still stuck in its infancy. One had to sing live or on records if he wanted to be successful. Never before or after did Berlin have such a large number of theatres, cabarets and small stages. However, the "Golden Twenties" or "Roaring Twenties" were really golden only for a few. It was in this time that the comet-like but short rise of the Comedian Harmonists began.

Since the mid-1920s, the Nazis had begun polluting the German people with their brown poison. After their takeover of power in 1933, a dictatorship of "German taste" soon followed in the arts, and a denouncing of all modernity, especially American music – jazz and swing. Simultaneously, the Nazis initiated the removal of Jewish people from public life, such as from culture: musicians, composers, lyricists, arrangers, band leaders, painters, sculptors, actors and directors – they all lost the ability to practice their professions. Their works became scorned or forbidden and many of them emigrated. The Comedian Harmonists watched this development, lost many of their colleagues and a large part of their repertoire – but tried to ignore it, because they were blinded by success. Nobody knew what would come later.

Three of them were Jews. The group was more and more rejected by Nazi authorities and concert and radio managers. Notwithstanding this, the ensemble braved the threat until the final ban in February 1935. So they became part of German history.

Today, because of the above reasons, their popularity includes a historical dimension. We know the complete history of the Comedian Harmonists, its members and following groups. We know the historical context of their origin, what was happening in Germany at the time and the development of music from 1945. And there has been scorching technological development, which today enables everyone to hear every Comedian Harmonists song always and everywhere. TV, books, movies and the Internet have brought the Comedian Harmonists closer to many people in the last decades, and they have new fans of every age.

Every enthusiast I know has a different point of view on the "Comedian Harmonists phenomenon." One collects shellac records, another tries to identify the individual voices of the members. One is detecting the original lyrics, another one wants to sing the songs himself. Others – like me – are above all interested in the history of the group and search all over the world for original documentation. Schoolchildren and students look for information for essays and dissertations, some older people met the stars of their childhood and youth. What they all have in common is that unexplainable magic, the rapture and worship for a unique and world famous German singing ensemble.

~Jan Grübler is a Comedian Harmonists enthusiast from Oranienburg, Germany who has studied the group extensively.

*Recorded by the Comedian Harmonists in 1933.

"Wer hat Angst vor dem bösen Wolf"* (Who's Afraid of the Big Bad Wolf)

The Rivals of the Comedian Harmonists
by Josef Westner

Contrary to what one might believe today, the Comedian Harmonists were not the only ones who were enthusiastic about the new style of singing imported from America. In the summer of 1928, a group of four Hungarian singers and a pianist had made German recordings, in Berlin, in the style of the Revelers. With that, the "Abels," the name the ensemble had chosen after its founder and pianist, Professor Pal Abel, were the first to have a recording actually released in this new kind of singing. There was a true flood of vocal groups in the aftermath – if we would name them all, they would exceed the volume of a book. But there were only a few groups that were true competition to the Comedian Harmonists.

For example, the Kardosch-Singers, founded in 1932 by the Hungarian pianist Istvan Kardos, had excellent members in all four voices – Paul von Nyiri (bass), Fritz Angermann (baritone), Rudi Schuricke (2nd tenor) and Zeno Coste (1st tenor); the latter would become a temporary member of the Meistersextett.

The recordings of the "Humoresk Melodios" do not take second place to the quality of the Comedian Harmonists. Herbert Imlau (baritone and later with the Meistersextett) and Fried Walter (piano, who had an audition with the Comedian Harmonists in 1930), among others, were members of the group, founded in 1934 as successor of the "Fidelios." The Humoresk Melodios by the way were the "Godfather" of the song, "Ein bißchen Leichtsinn kann nicht schaden," recording it prior to the Comedian Harmonists' version. Imlau founded the "Spree-Revellers" together with Rudi Schuricke in 1935 upon his leaving the Humoresk Melodios; their records contain new versions of Comedian Harmonists' classics such as "Ich hab' fuer dich 'nen Blumentopf bestellt."

The fact that the National Socialist powers were anything but happy with the new style of singing had immense consequences for the rivals of the Comedian Harmonists as well. Not only were groups with foreign members simply prohibited – as in the case of the Kardosch-Singers – but even the Aryan groups in the sense of the ideology of the race, had to fight big problems and resistance. Whoever did not conform to a certain style of folksongs – such as the Heyn Quartett and the Metropol-Vokalisten – and whoever did not agree to add propaganda songs like "Tod des Verräters" or "Mein Herz geht mit der Infanterie," was under constant suspicion. The "Humoresk Melodios" and the later formation of the "Spree-Revellers" existed until the beginning of 1940, but were able to release only a few recordings. Their modern style was no longer wanted in Germany! It may be a curiosity of history that a homosexual, a so-called "Half-Jew," and a member of the Waffen-SS were still performing on stage with the "Humoresk Melodios" in 1939.

The Comedian Harmonists were certainly the best of the German vocal groups of the 1930s. Despite that, one has say that today they have perhaps been highlighted to the exclusion of the "rival" groups. The Comedian Harmonists were not the only ones singing the new style of music on a high level and they did not develop their style independent of other influences. While the level of popularity of the Comedian Harmonists was not reached by these other groups, the rival groups are still an important part of the history of music.

~Josef Westner is a vocal group historian who has studied the vocal groups of the 1920s and 1930s extensively.

*Recorded by the Kardosch-Singers in 1934.

CHAPTER SIX

"Morgen muss ich fort von hier"[236]

(Tomorrow I Must Leave Here)

**The Weimar Republic and the Rise of the
National Socialist German Workers' Party**

T he Comedian Harmonists were formed during the Weimar Republic, the name given to the period in Germany from 1919 (the end of the First World War) through 1933, when the National Socialists came to power. The Armistice ending World War I was signed on November 11, 1918, two days after the Kaiser had abdicated. In February 1919, the German National Assembly met in Weimar, a small city in central Germany, because Berlin was considered unsafe due to rioting.

The rise of the National Socialist German Workers' Party – or Nazis – in Germany and its impact have been well-chronicled and need not be recounted in any detail. However, a brief review may be helpful to place what happened to the Comedian Harmonists in its proper historical context.

The Nazi Party was formed after World War I, and Adolf Hitler became the party's leader in 1921. The party had about 3000 members at the time and Hitler was already using anti-Semitic themes in his speeches. In November, 1923, Hitler tried to take over the government in Munich by force in what came to be known as the Beer Hall Putsch. The attempt was not successful, and after a more than three-week trial during which Hitler spoke out vigorously against the national government, he was given a light sentence (five years) and had gained a lot of public support. Hitler was paroled after serving only one year of his sentence.

While in prison, Hitler began writing *Mein Kampf* (My Struggle), in which he set out his philosophy of strong German nationalism and anti-Semitism. The book would become the Nazis' bible.

The Nazi Party grew from 27,000 members in 1925 to 108,000 members by 1929. However, in the 1928 elections the Nazis received less than three percent of the vote. With the onset of the Great Depression in 1929, the Weimar government saw a large increase in unemployment and the Reichstag[237] passed a law giving the President extraordinary emergency powers to restore law and order during a crisis. In the 1930 elections, the Nazis received 18.3 percent of the vote and became the second largest party in the Reichstag. [238]

---

236 Recorded by the Comedian Harmonists in 1935.

237 The German legislative body equivalent to the U.S. Congress or the British or Australian Parliaments.

238 All from: http://fcit.usf.edu/Holocaust/timeline/nazirise.htm (accessed January 12, 2008)

In the 1932 presidential elections, Hitler lost to the 84-year-old Paul von Hindenburg, but Hitler received 37 percent of the vote and the same percentage of seats in the Reichstag. The SA or Sturmabteilung, the paramilitary branch of the Nazis known as the "brown shirts," was now 400,000 strong and responsible for daily street violence. On January 30, 1933, Hitler was appointed Chancellor by von Hindenburg.

The Reichstag Building was destroyed by fire on February 27, 1933. The Nazis claimed that the fire was started by a Dutch Communist, and it still is not clear what really happened. In any event, the incident was either created by or seized upon by the Nazis to justify a new set of policies that increased their power under new emergency measures. On February 28, 1933, von Hindenburg, at Hitler's urging, issued a decree instituting "temporary" measures that were never removed during the reign of the Nazis.

The Nazis opened ten concentration camps, the first at Dachau, that initially held mainly political prisoners. An enabling act gave the government the power to enact new laws without passage by the Reichstag. Under these powers, new laws were put in place that excluded Jews from positions in the civil service and from professions such as law, medicine and teaching. April 1, 1933, brought book burnings and a boycott of shops owned by Jews. The boycott was organized by Julius Streicher, editor of the anti-Semitic newspaper *Der Stürmer*, which published lists of stores to be avoided. Guards were placed in front of stores and offices to prevent customers from violating the boycott.[239]

Further actions taken against Jews that month included the firing of civil service workers who were not Aryan and the exclusion of Jewish performers from revues and concert halls. One notable exception to this ban was the Comedian Harmonists. As Cycowski said, "I noticed very little and personally hardly suffered at all. I traveled around just as freely, went abroad, came back, brought in money; but we weren't allowed to take any out."[240]

On April 11, 1933, the government issued a decree defining a non-Aryan as "anyone descended from non-Aryan, especially Jewish, parents or grandparents. One parent or grandparent classified the descendant as non-Aryan ... especially if one parent or grandparent was of the Jewish faith."[241] Because of the way the new laws defined who was Jewish, many people who did not regard themselves as Jewish were now classified as Jews due to their ancestry. One such person was Erich Abraham Collin – all of his ancestors were Jewish. Up to this point, Collin had said that if the Jewish members of the group had to leave Germany, he would stay because he was not Jewish. However, after the decree, the next time Collin saw Frommermann and Cycowski, he greeted them with, "*Shalom aleichem*, now I'm one of you."[242] Cycowski recalled, "And from that

---

239 The store owners were even forced to pay the cost of the placards advising people not to patronize their businesses! They were also required to repair any damages that occurred that day and to do so within a specified time.

240 Cycowski in Fechner film

241 http://www.historyplace.com/worldwar2/holocaust/timeline.html (accessed December 6, 2007)

242 Traditional Jewish greeting meaning, "Peace be with you."

day on he considered himself Jewish, maybe more than the rest of us. Even though he had nothing to do with that. But now he had accepted it knowingly."[243] Many Germans agreed with the non-Aryan decree. Bootz said that his landlord put it this way: "A Jew is a Jew, no water (referring to Baptism) can change that."[244]

April 1, 1933 Boycott (Germans Beware! Do not buy from Jews!)

The year 1933 also saw the beginning of the restrictions on the Comedian Harmonists' activities. The first to act was the film company, Ufa, which would no longer accept the group in its movies. On August 2, 1934, von Hindenburg died and Hitler became Reichsführer (combining the offices of President and Chancellor). At that time, there were about 550,000 Jews in Germany. (In 2006, there were only 120,000 Jews in the country, many of them immigrants from the former Soviet Union.)[245]

Reichsmusikkammer

The Reichskulturkammer (Federal Culture Chamber or RKK) was established in September, 1933.[246] Joseph Goebbels, Nazi Propaganda Minister, was instrumental in the RKK's formation and became the organization's President.

The RKK had seven sub-chambers, each for a different aspect of the arts: theater, literature, film, radio, visual arts, the press, and – the one that concerns us directly – music. The stated purpose of the Chambers was to promote German culture

---

243 Cycowski in Fechner book, p. 48

244 Bootz in Fechner book, p. 48

245 http://www.dw-world.de/dw/article/0,2144,1557320,00.html (accessed December 6, 2007)

246 http://www.axishistory.com/index.php?id=3509 (accessed December 6, 2007)

and to "regulate the economic and social affairs of the culture professions."[247] The music arm of the RKK was called the Reichsmusikkammer or Reich Music Chamber (RMK). The President of the RMK was the renowned composer, Richard Strauss, who lasted in that position until July 1935 when he "resigned" and was replaced by Peter Raabe, a musicologist and conductor. Strauss had run afoul of Goebbels and the Nazi Party by declining to cooperate in anti-Jewish measures, by selecting a Jewish librettist for his opera *Die schweigsame Frau* (*The Silent Woman*), and by refusing to discontinue that collaboration.

The First Decree for the implementation of the Reich Chamber of Culture Law was issued on November 1, 1933, to establish guidelines for the operation of the RKK, including membership policies. Paragraph 10 stated in part that, "admission into a chamber may be refused, or a member may be expelled, when there exist facts from which it is evident that the person in question does not possess the necessary reliability and aptitude for the practice of his activity."[248]

The idea for a central body to deal with the arts had been around for years. There were concerns (among others) about unrestricted access to the profession, lack of standards and incursions by amateurs. But under the Nazis, while these issues were addressed, the creation of the chambers also paved the way for the formal exclusion of Jews from the arts. As early as 1920, the Nazi party had called for the "legal prosecution of all those tendencies in art and literature which corrupt our normal life, and the suppression of cultural events which violate this demand." So-called alien tendencies – code words for non-Aryans, particularly Jews – had to be erased from German culture. [249]

Author Alan E. Steinweis put it this way: "The liberal notion of 'art for art's sake' was, therefore, inconsistent with the tenets of National Socialism. As Goebbels explained, 'we have replaced individuality with *Volk* and individual people with *Volksgemeinschaft*.'"[250] *Volk* means "people" and *Volksgemeinschaft* refers to "the community of the people." In the case of the Nazis, this meant the exclusion of certain elements (non-Aryans) in order to ensure the "purity" of the art and therefore the community.

Aryans were also affected, but only on the basis of their knowledge, not their religion. For example, "To obviate the dangers of dilettantism the Reich Chamber of Music instituted stiff examinations for works bands; failure disqualified them from competing with professional bands for hire at such functions as dances and socials."[251] If you were not a member of the Chamber, you could not work legally in any of the affected areas.

---

247   Steinweis, Alan E. *Art, Ideology, & Economics in Nazi Germany, The Reich Chambers of Music, Theater, and the Visual Arts*. Chapel Hill and London: The University of North Carolina Press, 1993, p. 1.

248   Steinweis, p. 45

249   Steinweis, p. 18-21

250   Steinweis, p. 22

251   Grunberger, Richard. *The 12-Year Reich: A Social History of Nazi Germany 1933-1945*. Cambridge, New York: Da Capo Press, 1995, p. 418

The individual members of the Comedian Harmonists applied for membership in the RMK, but their applications were not acted on immediately. In fact, it would take about 17 months before any action was taken. Concert agencies sought permission from the RMK to allow the Comedian Harmonists to honor their tour of Germany for which contracts had already been signed. Strangely, the RMK allowed the tour to take place, although this was subject to change "without prior notice." The RMK also stated that the permission expired on May 1, 1934.[252] The group had been booked into the Scala in Berlin. In a letter to the concert agent, Levy, the Comedian Harmonists' Secretary, Fischer-Maretzki, said: "This engagement has to be treated with the utmost caution, and I myself am of the opinion, that in these times nothing can be forced, as this would only cause complications, which would be of no advantage to any of the involved persons."[253] Despite the RMK decision, the Scala cancelled the booking, claiming that the Comedian Harmonists were "not able to fulfill the legal requirements" in effect at the time, and that any permission to perform that the group had was revocable at any time.[254]

RMK agents would actually "make the rounds of bars at night searching for 'distorted,' 'dissonant' or overly 'hot' sounds. They could rescind musicians' work permits or alert the Gestapo."[255] By November 1935, Goebbels stated that, "There is no Jew active in the cultural life of our people."[256] While this may not have been true in a literal sense, it was effectively true. For example, some Jews were allowed membership in the RKK or one of its branches for the purpose of ensuring that foreign royalties from their works continued to flow into Germany, although those same works could not be played in Germany.[257]

To ensure that no one hired a Jewish musician by mistake, a book called *Judentum und Musik: Mit dem ABC jüdischer und nichtarischer Musikbeflissener* (Judaism and Music: With the ABC of Jewish and Non-Aryan Musicians) was published in 1935-36. The infamous *Lexikon der Juden in der Musik: Mit einem Titelverzeichnis jüdischer Werke (*Lexicon of Jews in Music: With A Title Index Of Jewish Works) was published in 1940.[258]

252   Biberti Estate

253   Biberti Estate, letter of March 16, 1934

254   Biberti Estate, letter of March 26, 1934

255   Poiger, Uta G. *Jazz, Rock, and Rebels: Cold War Politics and American Culture in a Divided Germany.* Berkeley: University of California Press, 2000, p. 26. (The 1993 movie, *Swing Kids*, Hollywood Pictures, also deals with this subject.)

256   Steinweis p. 111

257   Steinweis p. 112

258   Heskes, Irene. *Passport to Jewish Music: Its History, Traditions, and Culture.* Oxford, Great Britain: Praeger/Greenwood, 1994, p. 156

Secret Police

The Nazis were not content to have only one branch of their government that terrorized and spied on people: they had three. First was the SS (Schutzstaffel or Protective Squadron), which was the military and security arm of the Nazis. The SS was run by Heinrich Himmler and became an extremely powerful force. Second was the Gestapo (Geheime Staatspolizei) or secret state police, founded by Hermann Göring, Hitler's second in command, which came under the overall administration of the SS. Third was the Sicherheitsdienst, the Security Service or S.D., the intelligence service of the SS. The S.D. and Gestapo had similar duties and were often at odds with each other.

By early 1934, the SA (the paramilitary arm of the Nazi Party) was 2.5 million strong and Himmler and Göring convinced Hitler that Ernst Röhm, the head of the SA, should be removed. Röhm favored certain so-called reforms that were opposed by important industrialist backers of the Nazis. On June 30, 1934 – the Night of the Long Knives – the SS arrested and shot several hundred SA leaders, including Röhm. The cabinet gave its approval of these actions, saying that they were required for Germany's defense. After that, the SA steadily lost its influence and was eventually merged into the Wehrmacht or German armed forces.

The Media

One of the major forces for anti-Semitism during this time was the German media – chief among them the newspaper, *Der Stürmer*. Streicher, the publisher, was executed in 1946 after being convicted of crimes against humanity at the Nuremberg trials.[259]

Nuremberg Laws

In September 1935, the Nuremberg Laws were enacted, under which Jews lost whatever civil rights they still had in Germany. Jews became subjects of the state rather than citizens. The Jewish members of the Comedian Harmonists had left Germany by that time so they were not directly affected, although their families and friends certainly were. These laws replaced the April 11, 1933 decree. Jews became a separate race under the Law For The Protection of German Blood and Honor; people were categorized as Jews based on their ancestry rather than their religious preference; and marriages and sexual relations between Aryans and Jews were now forbidden.

---

259   Streicher was also the district chief or Gauleiter of Franconia, a portion of Bavaria. The capital of Franconia
      was Nuremberg and was the site of Nazi Party Congresses. That is why Nuremberg was chosen as the location for the war crimes trials.

Degenerate Art (Entartete Kunst)

The Nazi Party also instituted a policy aimed at the "purification" of art and the elimination of what they called *entartete Kunst*, or "degenerate art." Ironically, the theory of degeneracy in art appears to have originated with a Jewish intellectual named Max Nordau in his 1892 book, *Degeneration*.[260]

Nazi caricature

Nordau, whose real name was Simon Maximilian Südfeld, was born in Budapest in 1849, into an orthodox Jewish family. He earned a medical degree but worked as a journalist, first in Budapest, and later on in Berlin and Paris.

Nordau's theory was that modern artists had "defectively operating senses" which allowed their "brain-centres to produce semi-lucid, nebulously blurred ideas" and subjected them "to the perpetual obfuscation of a boundless, aimless, and shoreless stream of fugitive ideas...." He claimed that the Impressionist painters had "gaps in [their] field of vision, producing strange effects"[261] and predicted that "the degenerate will perish; the strong will adapt themselves to the acquisitions of civilization or will subordinate them to their own organic capacity." Nordau asserted that these aberrations of art had no future and would disappear "when civilized humanity shall have triumphed over its exhausted condition."[262] He suggested various methods for accelerating the "recovery of the cultivated classes from the present derangement," including the boycott of those works.[263]

---

260   Nordau, Max. *Degeneration*. New York: D. Appleton and Company, Second Edition, 1895 (English translation).
261   Nordau, pp. 21 and 28
262   Nordau. p. 550
263   Nordau, pp. 550-558

Although Nordau had been assimilated, the Dreyfuss Affair[264] and other anti-Semitic incidents convinced him to take up the Zionist cause. He, along with Theodore Herzl, helped to found the World Zionist Organization. The Nazis seized on Nordau's theory of degeneracy and perverted it, saying that only racially pure artists could produce racially pure art. They used Nordau's theory to explain what they claimed to be the decline of German culture due to impure (non-Aryan) artists and the influences of modern life.

In this atmosphere we find the Comedian Harmonists, three of whose members were either Jewish (Frommermann and Cycowski) or considered by the German regime to be Jewish (Collin). Bootz's wife was also Jewish. About three-quarters of the group's songs were by Jewish composers or issued by Jewish-owned publishing houses.

Goebbels called their type of music "Judeo-Marxist caterwauling."[265] German conservative newspapers complained about "alien Niggerjazz and jungle dances," which they said would lead inevitably to racial disgrace. A Nazi brochure from a 1938 exhibit on degenerate music shows a caricature of a black saxophone player with a Jewish star on his lapel.

MY FAVORITE COMEDIAN HARMONISTS SONG

Which is my favorite Comedian Harmonists song? That's not easy. I would say: I have none! I love most of their songs, though some of them have quite nonsensical lyrics and some of the early songs are musically deficient. Of course I love the zippy evergreens like "Veronika, der Lenz ist da," "Wochenend und Sonnenschein," "Das ist die Liebe der Matrosen" or "Mein kleiner grüner Kaktus." But I love the quiet and more emotional songs too, such as "Wenn ich Sonntags in mein Kino geh," "Schlaf mein Liebling," "Whispering," or "Creole Love Call." But, if I had to name one favorite, it would be "Irgendwo auf der Welt."* Aside from the wonderful voice of Ari Leschnikoff, I like this song because of its sad and wishful lyrics. When I saw the premiere of the Vilsmaier film in Rostock, together with my wife, at the end, when the final credits ran down the screen and "Irgendwo auf der Welt" was playing, nobody stood up to leave! That is quite uncommon. And then something happened that I have never experienced in a German cinema before or after that day – standing ovations! When they put the lights on, I saw tears twinkling in some people's eyes! But finally, every time I hear one of their songs I remember the characters and their unbelievable, affecting and memorable story!

~Jan Grübler is a Comedian Harmonists enthusiast from Oranienburg, Germany who has studied the group extensively.

* Recorded by the Comedian Harmonists in 1932.

---

264   Alfred Dreyfuss was a Jewish French military officer who was wrongfully convicted of treason in 1895 and sentenced to life in prison on Devil's Island. He was pardoned in 1899 and exonerated in 1906. His case was a cause célèbre and was most famously chronicled by Emile Zola in his work *J'accuse!,* which charged the government with anti-Semitism and with wrongfully convicting Dreyfuss.

265   http://www.metroactive.com/papers/metro/09.02.99/audiofile-9935.html (accessed December 6, 2007)

CHAPTER SEVEN

"Lebe wohl, gute Reise" [266]

(Goodbye, Good Trip)

The Beginnings of the Holocaust Affect the Group

T he Comedian Harmonists first began to feel the effects of the hostile climate in Germany in 1932. There was discussion of a possible concert on the island of Borkum in the North Sea. Borkum has been referred to as "a kind of racist preserve where no Jew dared set foot."[267] A concert agent informed the group that he had written to the organizers asking whether the group would be "exposed to any difficulties." The response came back saying, "If there are Israelite members, then I ask you to send me a picture of the group for detecting if the audience would assume Israelite members among them." Biberti responded bitterly and ironically with an expletive and saying that the group was a "purely Aryan corporation" that had "engaged the two Jewish members for the sole reason of making every endeavor to prey" on the people of Borkum.[268] Biberti claimed that radio stations gave false reasons for declining to book them.[269] In 1933, concerts were cancelled in several places, including Hanover and Lübeck, and in 1934 in Bavaria. Some were cancelled by the group themselves because of the political situation.

According to Frommermann's ex-wife, each member's income before the Nazi takeover was about 50,000-60,000 marks per year – then equivalent to about $19,000 U.S. dollars – an enormous sum compared to what the average German was earning.[270] Taking inflation into account, that $19,000 would be equal to $277,000 in 2005 dollars.[271] They achieved this level of success at a time when Europe and the U.S. were in the midst of the Great Depression. In a form filed by Biberti with the authorities after the war, he listed his income as follows:

---

266 Recorded by the Comedian Harmonists in 1934

267 Niewyk, Donald L. *The Jews in Weimar Germany*. Edison: Transaction Publishers, 2001, p. 76

268 Email from Jan Grübler August 30, 2007. Also, note Biberti's reference to only two Jewish members, referring to Frommermann and Cycowski. At that time, Collin had not yet been classified as Jewish by the government and did not consider himself Jewish.

269 Fechner book, p. 235

270 Kiss in Fechner book, p. 31

271 http://www.measuringworth.com/calculators/uscompare/. The U.S. Consumer Price Index was used as the measure of inflation (accessed December 5, 2007)

Year	Earnings	Occupation
1931	M40,000	Comedian Harmonists
1932	M55,000	Comedian Harmonists
1933	M35,000	Comedian Harmonists
1934	M18,000	Comedian Harmonists
1935	M2,000	Meistersextett
1936	M5,000	Meistersextett
1937	M4,000	Meistersextett
1938	M8,000	Meistersextett
1939	M4,000	Meistersextett
1940	M200	
1941	M1,200	
1942	0	
1943	M500	
1944	M3,000	
1945	M1,500	

Here one can clearly see the dramatic financial effect that the Nazi programs had on the group. [272]

Into 1933 and 1934, more and more, concert agencies and broadcasters engaged in a tacit boycott of the group because of its Jewish members. An appearance in the movie "*Kleiner Mann, was nun?*" (*Little Man, What Now?*) was cut from the film. Local officials began to demand that the 40 percent amusement tax – from which they had been exempted – now be collected. This further reduced the number of places where they could give concerts profitably. According to Biberti, the message was clear: "Do not engage the Comedian Harmonists, this pack of Jews."[273] Frommermann said that he "saw the dark clouds on the horizon" when Hitler took over in Germany.[274]

Frommermann described the scene: "Wherever we went, one of the uniformed people gave the same introduction; everywhere we were greeted with the same enthusiasm. But once in a while there were mischief-makers, first very gently – a whistle or somebody shouting from the gallery, 'Stop it' or 'Jews out of here'! But of course they were always quieted by our enthusiastic audience. And of course these interruptions were mostly initiated by the local authorities…."[275]

---

272   Biberti Estate. It is possible that Biberti's numbers are somewhat overstated as to the pre-1935 time and understated as to the post-1935 time, given the purpose of the form – to claim the highest possible reparations.

273   Biberti in Fechner film

274   Frohman story

275   Fechner book, p. 250 – Likely a "fictional dialogue."

Some of the concert agents tried to help, particularly those with whom Biberti had a personal relationship. Karl Gensberger from Munich, for example, wrote to a radio station in the city that had stopped broadcasting songs by the group. They tried to smooth things out so there would not be disturbances at performances.[276] However, when they were able to give concerts in Germany, there were disruptions and other incidents. The radio stopped broadcasting their songs completely in the spring of 1934, and meanwhile the press continued its attacks.

Cycowski gave a chilling account of a chance encounter on a railway train. Harry, Ari and he were in the dining car: "And suddenly Hitler enters the car! That is to say, first came the whole elite, first Göring, then Hess[277] and Goebbels, but the latter was behind Hitler. They all were on their way to Hamburg where Hitler was to give a speech. So, Hitler enters the dining car, and goes by us real close. He did not look at us, he did not look at anybody at all, he just looked over everybody. Unfortunately I have to admit that the man was very interesting. He had 'Basedowsche' eyes,[278] real piercing eyes and very serious – very, very serious. And, as he passed me, my heart beat very loudly, and Frommermann's too, of course. But at that time it was still not so bad. We had already accepted that there was no place in Germany for Jews. But that had happened before. One hundred years ago and two hundred years ago and three hundred years ago, again and again. And the same thing had happened in other countries as well, in Russia, for example, and in Poland. And now it had happened again and one would have to leave Germany. We thought, maybe they will let us be for a little while, maybe we can stay. But nobody knew what was to come, nobody had imagined that."[279]

A review in the *Rostocker Anzeiger* on February 3, 1934, is interesting given all the problems that Jews were having in Germany by then. A negative review would not have been surprising but this one said: "The whole hall was sold out, including the gallery.

MY FAVORITE COMEDIAN HARMONISTS SONG

My favorite "Comedian Harmonists" recording? Why the one I'm listening to at the moment of course! But "Kleiner Mann, was nun?"* has long been a favorite of mine, with its clever fanfare opening, a catchy melody gliding high to low between the voices, and a bittersweet lyric saying far more than meets the ear … for me it best sums up the "What Was And What Might Have Been" of this wonderful ensemble.

~Peter Becker is the baritone for Hudson Shad, an American vocal group that has an amazingly large repertoire, including songs of the Comedian Harmonists.

* Recorded by the Comedian Harmonists in 1933.

---

276   Biberti Estate, letters from Gensberger, December 1933 and February 1934
277   Rudolf Hess, Deputy Führer and number three in command.
278   Protruding eyes, a characteristic of Graves' disease
279   Cycowski in Fechner film

Rarely does one see so many people flock to a musical event – so much has the fame of this group spread by now. One has to say: rightfully so. One has already listened to them with delight when they started producing records. But their art has significantly developed since then, enabling them to stand up to their idols and their competition. There are five singers and a pianist. The foundation of this ensemble is a nearly fabulous musicality. First they sing with a nearly immovable clarity, and that often in quite difficult harmonic sequences and even in stretches of acappella singing, after which they reunite precisely with the piano, making any doubts (of their art) completely disappear." The review concludes with the words, "One has to say: We would love to hear them again."[280]

The reviews were not all positive. The *Altonaer Nachrichten* of February 5, 1934, contains a strange mixture of praise and mockery: "Goodbye to the Misters Comedian! Your harmonies have been a true pleasure to us and your voices a benefit to our ears. But now, let's be honest: there are more interesting harmonies and much better voices. And anyway there are a lot more singers able to sing much better than you. You are smiling? Yes – and you know it only too well. On the other hand, there are only a few singers who can do what you want to do. And you belong to these few.... You brought much happiness to us, Mister Comedians, and business was good for you. Money is still lying around in the streets, right? One just needs to know how to pick it up. You know how – congratulations to you!"[281]

By this time, they were the last prominent Jewish artists performing in Germany. Many of their colleagues had already left the country, including Werner Richard Heymann (their favorite composer), lyricist Fritz Rotter, Kurt Robitschek (owner of the Kabarett der Komiker), and composer Mischa Spoliansky. But the reality was still difficult to accept:

"We kept thinking – it won't happen to us."
(Erna Frommermann/Marion Kiss)

"We thought that since we were a well known group we would be left alone."
(Biberti)

"We brought in foreign currency, and they didn't mind that."
(Cycowski)[282]

As Biberti said, "We were concerned, but it was not that we talked about it day and night. We did not take the Nazis seriously, just like so many."[283] Their secretary, Fischer-Maretzki, wrote in a February 26, 1934 letter to the concert agent, Gensberger, "It can't be possible that only because of a name and because the ensemble isn't a hundred per-

---

280   Biberti Estate
281   Biberti Estate
282   Fechner film
283   Fechner book, p. 238

cent pure Aryan, that the accomplishments of the gents get subjectively degraded…."[284] Clearly, like so many others, he failed to read the signs correctly.

The Comedian Harmonists knew that they had a highly placed admirer; otherwise they would have already been forced to disband. At a concert in Stuttgart, probably on March 20, 1934, before an audience of 2500, they were singing the nonsensical "Der Onkel Bumba aus Kalumba tanzt nur Rumba" when they were interrupted by a heckler with a whistle. He was removed after almost being thrown from the balcony and then some SS and SA members in the front applauded the group and the singing was resumed. [285] The SS and SA members invited the group, including the Jewish members, for a glass of champagne.

In Nuremberg, they were taken to meet Julius Streicher, the publisher of *Der Stürmer*. Bootz said, "He stood there with an open leather coat and inside on his belt hand a riding crop. He ordered us to sing 'Grün ist die Heide' ("Green Is the Heath")."[286] The group had to decline – the song was not in their repertoire.

MY FAVORITE COMEDIAN HARMONISTS SONG

Being asked for my favorite song of the Comedian Harmonists I can only think of one title. "Der Onkel Bumba aus Kalumba"* has accompanied me since my first encounter with the ensemble. The virtuosity of this composition excited me at an age at which I did not know anything of music of the group, not to mention the singers! Still today, I am impressed by the homogeneous sound the Comedian Harmonists are able to produce despite the nearly inconceivable speed of the piece.

But aside from all the refinements of the arrangements, "Onkel Bumba" impresses me, because it is closely connected with the fate that the Comedian Harmonists had to suffer under the Nazi-regime. At an appearance of the group in Stuttgart in 1934, this song was interrupted by the sound of a shrill whistle, as Roman Cycowski tells us in an interview with Eberhard Fechner. The troublemaker was nearly thrown from the balcony into the orchestra by the outraged audience. After security guards had taken the young man with the whistle out of the hall, the SA and SS members watching the concert from the front row demonstrably applauded the Comedian Harmonists and the concert was continued. It seems rather an embellishment of the anecdote that the Comedian Harmonists continued the song with just the lyric of "the politic is totally forgotten in Kalumba." However the singers were invited by the mentioned SA and SS leaders to have a glass of champagne after the concert – it was one of the last opportunities for the Comedian Harmonists to put a good face on the matter. After that the group was heard in Germany only a few more times, and never again in Stuttgart.

~Josef Westner is a vocal group historian from Germany who has studied the ensembles of the 1920s and 1930s extensively.

* Recorded by the Comedian Harmonists in 1932.

---

284   Biberti Estate

285   Kater, Michael H. *Different Drummers: Jazz In The Culture Of Nazi Germany*. New York: Oxford University Press USA, 1992, p. 101

286   Fechner book, p. 237

Biberti asked the RMK to allow the Comedian Harmonists to continue to perform and this appeal was supported by various concert agencies. One of the agents, Erich Knoblauch from Dresden, received a response on March 16, 1934, from a low-level RMK person who said that, although the applications for membership had been denied, it was up to the RMK's president to determine whether the group could fulfill its commitments. This offhand reference was the first indication that the RMK was going to deny their applications for membership. Despite this, it was another eleven months before they received official written notification of the denial. At the same time, Biberti was informed by letter from the RMK of March 13, 1934, that their concert tour could continue, but that the permission would expire on May 1, 1934.[287] The group completed the tour, but they "constantly lived in fear."[288]

The restrictions placed on the Comedian Harmonists were oppressive to both the Aryans and the Jewish members, although perhaps for different reasons. Marion Kiss recalled an incident involving Biberti: "At one time we had a concert in Switzerland, and we all went to Bern in Biberti's big car. And just after passing the Swiss border, Bob stopped the car, got out and shouted like a madman: 'These pigs! This Hitler-pig! – Finally I can talk, finally.' And so on. And then he got back in, feeling relieved, and we went on our way."[289]

In 1934, only one scheduled concert actually failed to take place – that was in Hof on March 10, where the local authorities would not allow the performance to proceed despite pleas from Gensberger. Another concert – this one scheduled for March 16 in Nuremberg – was also canceled, but that was due to the hall's being co-opted by the SA and not because of the makeup of the Comedian Harmonists.

There was almost a second cancellation – a March 13, 1934, concert in Munich. The Ministry of Culture in Berlin sent a telegram to the concert manager informing him that the performance was to be stopped at once because what the Comedian Harmonists were doing was "degenerate art."[290] But the concert agency, Gensberger, hired an influential lawyer to press the matter, and some other concert managers sent a telegram detailing the financial loss that they would incur. The concert was allowed – with certain conditions. This would be the group's last Munich concert and part of the proceeds had to be donated to the winter relief organization. Also, they had to inform the audience that this would be the last concert because the group had Jewish members and the production therefore constituted degenerate art. [291]

---

287 Biberti Estate
288 Fechner book, p. 250
289 Fechner book, p. 257
290 Frohman story
291 Biberti Estate and Frohman story

Biberti recalled waiting to go on stage: "We all stood in our room, still numb, waiting for our call. Suddenly something unexpected happened. A man came hastily inside, introduced himself as a representative of the local district leader, walked past us and addressed the perplexed audience. The old tiring speeches repeated themselves: The Comedian Harmonists were no longer acceptable due to their Jewish members, their destructive alien music, and their pseudo-art that has to be unacceptable to any true German. The audience would understand this and so this would irrevocably be the last performance in Munich of this group. Nobody stirred, the man returned from the stage, and we walked onto the stage with a fake smile. It remained as still as death, when we bowed, but then – and I still get goose bumps thinking about it – two thousand people got up from their seats as one and an unimaginable storm of applause started. We were totally stunned. Many came to the stage and showed their sympathy by chanting – even hard words and curses against the Nazi regime could be heard. I was thinking uncomfortably about the speaker, who could certainly hear these voices behind the stage. When we sang, as usual, Mischa Spoliansky's 'Auf Wiederseh'n' at the end, the people did not want to let us go.[292] And we felt that there would not be a *Wiedersehen* (see you again). 'Lebe wohl, gute Reise' (Goodbye, Good Journey) was our goodbye song."[293]

The March 13, 1934 Munich Concert.

292   Note that this is not the more famous "Auf Wiedersehen, my Dear" song that is played near the end of the 1997 Joseph Vilsmaier film about the Comedian Harmonists, called in the U.S., *The Harmonists*.

293   Biberti Estate, Biberti notes for 1963 radio broadcast

Frommermann said that when the announcement was made, "The audience sat in their seats silently, expecting tensely what would happen next. In the first row quite a number of Nazi officials, trimmed with decorations and in uniform were seated. They watched how many would leave after that speech. Turned their heads back – frozen-faced. The Harmonists, green-faced (in their turn) and with trembling knees started out onto the podium in their usual manner – in a cadence with verve – but their smile was frozen, unnatural and artificial. A sudden storm of warm applause greeted them. It was a standing ovation – like a protesting answer to the preceding announcement. In this way the singers and their pianist were honoured in the most touching manner. The faces of the uniformed men in the first row were still frozen but even more so. (Apparently they had expected an entirely different effect!)"[294]

It has long been reported that this was the last concert in Germany given by the group. However, documents discovered in the Staatsbibliothek now contradict this. In Biberti's calendars, a concert is listed in Hanover at the Konzerthaus an der Goethe-brücke on March 25, 1934, as well as some ten concerts in between.[295] Frommermann, in his story about the Comedian Harmonists, discusses the Munich concert and then says, "That concert, and for that [matter], all the others that still followed in other cities were all alike in frenetic applause, with encored [he means "encores"] without end but this tour also came to an end – like all things in life."[296]

The resultant decline in the number of concerts in Germany led to dissension within the group, with the Aryan members demanding compensation from the Jewish members for lost revenues. As Biberti said, "Our takings naturally fell appreciably because the whole concert system wasn't as well developed abroad." The Aryans contended that the Jewish members should reduce their take in favor of the Aryans so that the Aryans would not suffer as much financially as a result of the decrease in bookings. However, the contract among the group's members provided that they were all equal partners with each member sharing equally in the profits. Their secretary, Fischer-Maretzki, hired a lawyer, Dr. Helmut Ellerholz, to mediate the claim. Negotiations were held on April 4, 1934 with Biberti representing the Aryans and Collin representing the Jews. Minutes of the mediation survive. They read:

> The following gentlemen came accompanied by their secretary, Mister Fischer-Maretzki:
>
> 1.) Biberti, also as representative for Misters Bootz and Leschnikoff (citizen of Bulgaria)
>
> 2.) Collin, also as representative for Misters Frommermann and Cycowski (stateless).

---

294   Frohman story
295   Biberti Estate
296   Frohman story

Mister Biberti and Mister Collin as well as the other gentlemen represented by them are members of an ensemble known under the name of Comedian Harmonists.

A dispute arose between the three Aryan members, represented by Mister Biberti and the three non-Aryan members, represented by Mister Collin.

Each one of the persons present stated his point of view as follows:

1.) Mister Biberti: Each member of the ensemble has to smooth out difficulties for the ensemble that are being caused by their person – such as non-Aryan descent – sacrificing their personal and financial strength if necessary. The Aryan members would be able to maintain their possibilities of income under the laws currently governing Germany if they separated from the non-Aryan members. Therefore, one would have to conclude that it was in the business interests of the non-Aryan members to remove the above-mentioned difficulties connected to their person at their own expense. Mister Biberti cites as an example: An Austrian member having difficulties performing in Austria due to the political situation would have to overcome these difficulties, at his own expense, in order to be able to perform there.

2.) Mister Collin however pointed out: The Comedian Harmonists are a private partnership and have been working together for six years through thick and thin. The contributions of the non-Aryan members are as much in the interest of the Aryan as the non-Aryan members. One cannot say that it would be of advantage to only the non-Aryan members if the Aryan members would stand up for the non-Aryan members. The advantage is the same for both sides. According to Mr. Collin, the financial side is not the deciding factor in this question. All members represented by Mister Collin consider this a moral and legal decision.

Mister Biberti and Mister Collin agree that this question should be solved by myself without involving the court, but they gave me the option of consulting the Professors Fischer and Kuhlenkampff. Berlin, April 4, 1934.[297]

The lawyer decided that the reduction in income was the problem of *all* the members, just as it would be with any other costs, and said that the contract should not be changed.[298] Obviously, however, things would never be the same.

"Ein Lied geht um die Welt"[299]
(A Song Goes Around The World)

The Comedian Harmonists knew that they had to stop performing in Germany and would have to appear abroad exclusively. They gave four more concerts in Denmark and Norway in April 1934, and then accepted an invitation to go to the U. S. where they were to make about 30 radio appearances on NBC.

---

297 Biberti Estate
298 Czada, p. 68
299 Recorded by the Comedian Harmonists in 1933.

*On the SS Europa. Clockwise from lower left – Biberti, Frommermann,
Leschnikoff, Cycowski, Collin and Bootz.*

The group sailed to the U.S. on May 8, 1934, aboard the *SS Europa*, a large ship
that held almost 2200 passengers, and arrived in New York on May 14. The radio
shows, which were well received by listeners, were mostly performed in Radio City
Music Hall in New York and sent out to the country over the NBC network. Their only
semi-public appearance was on June 12, 1934, on the aircraft carrier *U.S.S. Saratoga*
in New York harbor, where they performed together with the Boswell Sisters and the
Paul Whiteman Orchestra. The occasion was a rare meeting of the Atlantic and Pacific
fleets, which were strung out along the Hudson River for about 25 miles. There were
85,000 listeners, most of whom heard the concert over their ships' radios. Cycowski
said of their trip from the hotel to the *Saratoga*, "Police motorcyclists rode in front of
us as if God himself was expected."[300] They got a tremendous reception after singing
their famous song, "The Way With Every Sailor." Biberti said, "When we had finished
our concert, there was an earsplitting din of sirens and applause. The sailors who had
been listening in pulled the sirens."[301]

June 30, 1934 – Night of the Long Knives

The group members held a serious discussion about whether to stay in the U.S.
and not return to Germany. Naturally, the two Jews, Frommermann and Cycowski were
most in favor of staying; while Biberti was strongly opposed. Biberti later gave as one of

---

300   Cycowski in Fechner film
301   Biberti in Fechner film

his reasons that they had been rejected by the American press. Cycowski disputed that saying that he would have known if such a rejection had taken place.[302] Frommermann later said that it was his "most urgent desire ... to save the ensemble he had organized so devotedly, to save it as an instrument still intact...."[303]

Bootz and Leschnikoff also wanted to stay – at least for a while – to see if the Comedian Harmonists would be accepted by the American audience. However, Biberti was worried about his elderly mother, his property and his apartment. Cycowski said that he believed that Biberti did not want to leave his mother, and that although Biberti and Bootz were not fond of Jews, they were not Nazis either: "They were diplomats who were only concerned about money. That may not sound very nice, but it's the truth." Bootz later

NBC telegram to group on board the "SS Europa"

accepted some responsibility for the decision, acknowledging that he had been influenced by Biberti. Leschnikoff said he would go along with whatever "little Erwin" decided. Bootz was also worried about the competition the group would face in the U.S., which was the entertainment capital of the world. Included in this competition were many who were emigrating from Germany because of the conditions there.[304]

Biberti also had other concerns: "Leaving Germany would have had huge consequences. The three of us were so-called Aryans, which means we would have given concerts and made music abroad together with Jews. That was soon forbidden. And then what would have happened? They [the Nazis] would have taken our passports away. We could not have performed in Germany anymore ... and there you are naked and alone in a foreign place. What is one to live on? Is the ensemble going to work out or not? And we did not know what to expect in one of those countries or in America. Nobody had any idea. Maybe we would have split up in the end anyway. Then we would have been outside, not able to set foot on German soil ever again. The consequences were incalculable." [305]

So, in August 1934, the Comedian Harmonists returned to Europe, even though they knew they could no longer perform in Germany. They stopped in London where Mary Panzram had been staying and she and Cycowski became officially engaged. This was an

302   Cycowski in Fechner film
303   Frohman story
304   Fechner book, pp. 260-265
305   Fechner book, p. 261

"Tea For Two" arrangement

amazing step for her to take considering what was happening in Germany at the time. She returned with the group to Berlin in late 1934.

Fortunately, the group was still allowed to record, and on their return to Germany they cut the classics "Wenn die Sonja russisch tanzt," (When Sonya Does The Russian Dance), "Ein bisschen Leichtsinn kann nicht schaden" (A Little Foolishness Can't Hurt), "In der Bar zum Krokodil" (In the Crocodile Bar), "Schade kleine Frau" (It's A Shame Little Mrs.), "Mein kleiner grüner Kaktus," "Lebe wohl, gute Reise," "Gitarren spielt auf" (Guitars Play On), "Schöne Lisa" (Pretty Lisa), "Tea for Two," and "Whispering" – the last two songs in English. The arrangement for "Tea for Two" is interesting to examine because it shows the pronunciation aids Collin used to help him with his English. For example, above the word "knee" ("Picture you upon my knee..."), he has written in pencil "Ni."[306]

In the early fall they traveled to Paris and in November, they toured Italy, performing in Perugia, Rome, Genoa, Turin, Padua, Trieste, Fiume and Milan. They had some apprehension about how they would be received in Italy, the land of opera and *bel canto* singing. Bootz was worried about whether they should include their vocal interpretation of the "Overture to the Barber of Seville," thinking that the Italians might believe they were poking fun at Rossini. He need not have worried – the crowd was wildly enthusiastic.[307] Another Italian tour was scheduled for the spring of 1935, but circumstances intervened, and what turned out to be the Comedian Harmonists' final concert took place in Fredrikstad, Norway, on January 23, 1935.

---

306   Biberti Estate
307   Czada, p. 71

Forever, Forever

Back in Germany, the Comedian Harmonists met at Biberti's apartment to discuss, for what would be the last time, whether to stay together – which would have meant leaving Germany – or whether to split up. Collin suggested that the group go to Vienna, but Biberti was adamant – he was staying in Germany.

The Reichsmusikkammer issued its final decision on the membership applications on February 22, 1935, in separate letters to Biberti, Bootz and Leschnikoff. Just nine days earlier the group had gone into the studio and recorded two songs, including the prescient "Morgen muss ich fort von hier" (Tomorrow I Must Leave Here).

The letters from the RMK read: "Reference your application, you are herewith accepted as a member of the Reich's Chamber of Music. I have rejected the applications of the three non-Aryan members of the Comedian Harmonists. They have therefore lost the right to exercise their profession. You are therefore no longer able to make music with these non-Aryans. However, you are free to continue your musical activities with other Aryan musicians after adopting a German name instead of the Comedian Harmonists." Not only were performances prohibited but they were barred from rehearsing as well.

There is a poignant moment in the Fechner film, just as they are about to show this letter, and Biberti says, sadly, "In our hearts we knew it was a breakup forever, forever."[308]

So, a one-paragraph letter ended what was one of the greatest vocal groups of all time. That piece of paper probably also saved the lives of the three Jewish members. In order to keep singing, they had to leave Germany – which they did. If they had stayed, they might well have ended up in a concentration camp.

MY FAVORITE COMEDIAN HARMONISTS SONG

The "Overture to the Barber of Seville"* shows the versatility of the Comedian Harmonists, not only to imitate the sounds of various instruments, but to present an arrangement that reflects the breadth of the orchestration as well. That is, rather than just hearing a familiar tune imitated, we're hearing an orchestral presentation with balance and thoughtfulness reflecting the sound of an instrumental rendition. As in all their music, we hear singers willing to blend with one another as the highest vocal priority.

Each plays his own instrument as part of the orchestra, without apparent need to be heard individually.

~Robert Scherr is a retired cantor who is the Jewish Chaplain at Williams College and was a friend of the Cycowskis for many years.

* Recorded by the Comedy Harmonists in 1936 and the Meistersextett in 1938.

---

308   Biberti in Fechner film

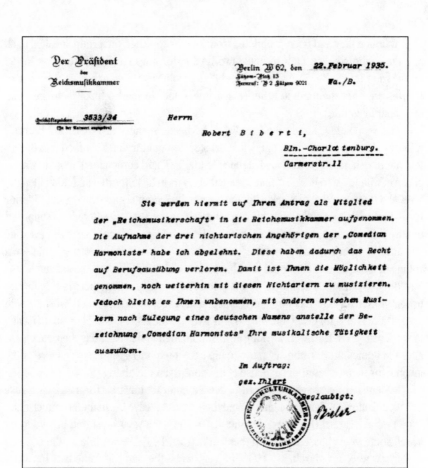

Der Präsident
der
Reichsmusikkammer

Berlin W 62, den   **22. Februar 1935.**
Sützen-Platz 13
Fernruf: B 2 Sützen 9021   **Wa./B.**

Geschäftszeichen   **3533/34**   Herrn

Robert B i b e r t i,

Bln.-Charlottenburg.

Carmerstr. 11

Sie werden hiermit auf Ihren Antrag als Mitglied
der „Reichsmusikerschaft" in die Reichsmusikkammer aufgenommen.
Die Aufnahme der drei nichtarischen Angehörigen der „Comedian
Harmonists" habe ich abgelehnt. Diese haben dadurch das Recht
auf Berufsausübung verloren. Damit ist Ihnen die Möglichkeit
genommen, noch weiterhin mit diesen Nichtariern zu musizieren.
Jedoch bleibt es Ihnen unbenommen, mit anderen arischen Musi-
kern nach Zulegung eines deutschen Namens anstelle der Be-
zeichnung „Comedian Harmonists" Ihre musikalische Tätigkeit
auszuüben.

Im Auftrag:

gez. Ihlert

Beglaubigt:

RMK letter of February 22, 1935

The three non-Aryans never actually received letters from the RMK denying them admission. Copies of denial letters to Frommermann and Cycowski exist in the Bundesarchiv (Federal Archive) in Berlin but, apparently, were never able to be delivered because they had fled to Vienna. The letters state that the applications were rejected because Frommermann and Cycowski did not have "the necessary suitability as required by the Reichskulturkammer Act in the sense of the National Socialist governance." The denials were based on the infamous Paragraph 10 of the First Implementing Provision For The Reichskulturkammer Law of November 1, 1933 ("Erste Verordnung zur Durchführung des Reichskulturkammergesetzes").[309] Of course, the unspoken reason was that they were Jews.

---

309   Bundesarchiv (former Berlin Document Center), Reichskulturkammer.
      Roll 5: Cycowski, Josef, 24.01.1902. Roll 8: Frommermann, Harry, 12.10.1906.
      No letter to Collin was found.

Although they had been prohibited from singing together, the group sneaked back into the studio six days later to make two final recordings: "Ungarischer Tanz Nr. 5" (Hungarian Dance No. 5) by Brahms and "Barcarole" by Offenbach from the *Tales of Hoffmann*. They then met at Biberti's apartment and decided – finally – to split into two separate entities.

At this meeting, Leschnikoff said that he became angry at Biberti for Biberti's refusal to leave Germany – so angry that Ari stormed out. Ari later claimed that Biberti told the Jewish members that Ari had been to the RMK and complained about having to perform with Jews. In turn, Ari maintained that it was in fact Biberti who had written the RMK about not wanting to work with non-Aryans.[310] Frommermann later said, "Rumor has it, that it was one of the boys who secretly went to the Ministry where he is supposed to have said, 'To stand in one line with these Jews and sing, I should say, is an exacting demand.' If true, nobody ever found out, but apart from that the Nazi machine was rolling in those days and it would have happened sooner or later that the ensemble was forbidden to pursue its activities."[311] Other than Biberti's assertion, there is certainly no proof, or even anyone else who has claimed, that Leschnikoff objected to working with Jews. There is also no proof that Biberti ever wrote to the RMK to complain about having to work with Jews. However, working against both men in this regard is their attempt to alter the Comedian Harmonists' partnership agreement in 1934 to secure more of the income for themselves at the expense of the non-Aryan members.

A Vienna concert agency agreed to send a contract for a performance as a ruse that would allow the Jewish members and their wives to leave Germany. Frommermann (and Fischer-Maretzki) left first, on March 10, 1935.[312] Cycowski stayed behind to try to sell some of his possessions and then left in April 1935. Meanwhile, Collin traveled to Paris where, on March 27, 1935, he registered the name, "Comedian Harmonists," with Frommermann, Cycowski and himself as co-owners. Each of the three held a slightly less than one-third interest with French concert agent Wolf holding a four percent share.[313]

Biberti quickly learned that Collin had registered the Comedian Harmonists name in Paris and confronted Cycowski, the only one of the Jewish members who was still in Berlin. Biberti wanted to know where they had obtained the money to register the group since they were not allowed to take any funds out of Germany. Cycowski said that Collin had probably received financial help from relatives and friends in Paris. The conversation got pretty nasty. Biberti said that he would not go to the Gestapo, but, to Cycowski, the mere mention of the Gestapo had a chilling effect: "And then I understood, for the

---

310   Fechner book, p. 266

311   Frohman story

312   Fischer-Maretzki had one Jewish parent, but he had been raised as a Christian. He qualified as a non-Aryan under the April 11, 1933 decree.

313   Biberti Estate, March 15, 1935 Agreement

first time since we knew each other, how the wind blew. We always had gotten along well; we were friends. I said, 'Do, what you want to do. I don't have anything to do with it. I was in Berlin the whole time, not in Paris.'" Biberti proposed that each of them would have the right to use the name without interference from the other and they exchanged letters to that effect. Cycowski wanted to consult with Frommermann and Collin, but Biberti's mother convinced Cycowski to sign.[314] The letter to Biberti read:

> To Mister Robert Biberti, Charlottenburg April 20, 1935.
> I solemnly assure Mister Robert Biberti that the patenting of the name "Comedian Harmonists" on March 27,1935 in Paris does not at all represent a restriction of the public appearances of my three colleagues Bootz, Biberti and Leschnikoff under the name of the "Comedian Harmonists."[315]

Biberti's letter to Cycowski read:

> I herewith solemnly promise Mister Joseph Cycowski that I will not hinder in any way his artistic performances under the name "Comedian Harmonists."[316]

Despite these letters, Biberti was so upset over the use of the Comedian Harmonists name by the Jewish members that he sought legal advice. His lawyers advised against bringing suit and recommended that he try for an amicable resolution of the dispute. The attorneys cited several reasons for their position in a letter to Bootz in May of 1935, saying that all agreements as to continued use of the name had been oral, that both groups had an equal right to the name and that an international court might favor the non-Aryans because of the political situation in Germany. They also cautioned that if the Aryan members lost the case, they might lose the right to use the name themselves.[317]

MY FAVORITE COMEDIAN HARMONISTS SONG

My favorite Comedian Harmonists recording is Offenbach's "Barcarole."* It was recorded illegally, in secret at the Berlin Philharmonie at 5 o'clock in the morning before they split up for the last time. The song is supposed to be light and airy but they infuse a possibly unintentional sadness to it that reflects the time and what was happening to them, and I think you can hear the stress in their voices even though they sing it with an uncommon beauty.

~Pamela Rosen, from California, has studied the Comedian Harmonists extensively.

*Recorded by the Comedian Harmonists in 1935.

---

314 Fechner book, pp. 273-274
315 Biberti Estate
316 Biberti Estate
317 Biberti Estate, letter of May 24, 1935.

The lawyers sent a letter to Paris asking the Jewish members to refrain from using the Comedian Harmonists name. The only response appears to have been a letter from Collin saying that he needed time to consult with his lawyers and noting that their letter contained factual errors.[318] Biberti claimed that he was then "forced" to sue and did so in Berlin in April 1936, alleging unfair competition. The papers were never served – the Jewish members had moved and their new address was unknown. Service was attempted in the Netherlands, but the group was on tour and the papers never caught up with them. Finally, the papers were posted at the courthouse in Germany and service was deemed to have been made. The court decided that it had no jurisdiction over violations that had occurred outside of the country. Biberti then asked the international court in The Hague to void the granting of rights to the name that had been issued to the Jewish members in Paris, but nothing came of it.[319]

MY FAVORITE COMEDIAN HARMONISTS SONG

One song that is maybe the most special to me is "Morgen muss ich fort von hier."* The song itself dates back to the 19th century and is a song about the parting of lovers – very beautiful in its simplicity. This is one of the last recordings the original line-up made, and I think you can hear the special meaning this must have had for each of the Harmonists when they recorded it. After all, at this point they knew the group would be history soon. Many of their recordings are brilliant and funny, but none more moving than this one.

~Karsten Lebl, a member of Ensemble Six, a contemporary German vocal group that is devoted to the old treasures of vocal cabaret and revue of the 1920s and 1930s, including those of the Comedian Harmonists. See www.ensemblesix.de.

* Recorded by the Comedian Harmonists in 1935.

---

318   Biberti Estate, letter of August 19, 1935.
319   Fechner book, pp. 292-293

CHAPTER EIGHT

"Ohne Dich"[320]

(Without You)

The Later Groups

"Love Me A Little Today" [321]

The Comedy Harmonists (The Vienna Group)

For the three non-Aryans, leaving Germany was not easy. Both Frommermann and Collin had lived in Berlin for their entire lives. Even Cycowski, who had been born in Poland, had great difficulty: "I loved Germany very much. I loved everything German. And then suddenly I had to leave all that. I had been glad when I left Poland, but not when I had to leave Germany."[322]

The Oppermanns – Lion Feuchtwanger's novel about this period – includes a passage that illustrates how the three non-Aryans likely felt. In the book, a teenage Jewish boy, who has been accused of certain acts against Germany, has been ostracized:

> He himself felt that he was German in a profounder sense than most of his companions. His head was full of German music, German words, German thought, German scenery. He had never seen, heard, or observed anything else in the seventeen years of his life. And now, suddenly, he was to have no further kinship to these things, he was supposed to be alien to them by nature. How could that be? And why? Who was a German, then, if he was not?[323]

Biberti said of the breakup: "It was a bitter feeling, very bitter. When you have been together day and night, traveling, in trains and on ships, in cars, to a great many places, sharing changing rooms and hotels – and especially on many, many stages and in concert halls – always together, working, earning money together – and all that stops suddenly and abruptly – that is something very dramatic. And the moment came, when we shook hands for the last time. We exchanged words of hope. Everybody told the others: 'Don't forget – we'll come back together.' But that was just eyewash. Nobody showed the others what he really thought. And nobody could have known what tiring years lay ahead of us."[324]

Frommermann's wife recalled: "Biberti's mother once asked me whether I had carefully considered everything. I would be leaving my parents here and going off into an uncertain future without knowing what would happen. I said, 'I'm married to Harry.

---

320 Known in the U.S. and elsewhere as "Stormy Weather" and recorded by the Comedian Harmonists in 1933
321 Recorded by the Comedy Harmonists in 1937
322 Cycowski in Fechner film
323 Feuchtwanger, Lion. *The Oppermanns*. New York: Carroll & Graf Publishers, Inc., 1934, p. 207
324 Fechner book, p. 270

I've shared good times with him and I can't do otherwise.'"[325] Cycowski said about Mary, "My wife left with me to face an uncertain future and I'm very grateful to her."[326]

People leaving Germany were not allowed to take any currency with them. When the Frommermann party reached the Austrian border, they were searched – the women first and then the men. When Fischer-Maretzki's turn came, he somehow managed to slip some money into the women's purses – the women had already been searched.[327] So deftly did he do this that even the women were not aware of it. They lived on this money during their first few months in Vienna, and used it to pay salaries to the new members, while they rehearsed and until they started to get bookings.

Arthur Fleischer, the well-known operatic baritone, helped them get settled in Vienna. Harry and Erna moved into the apartment of Fleischer's ex-wife, also named Erna, and the two Ernas became fast friends.[328]

Once in Vienna, Frommermann, true to form, placed an advertisement for new singers in a local newspaper. There was no lack of response, but Harry was not satisfied with the applicants. Instead, he wrote to Ernst Engel, a pianist that he remembered from the Jockey-Bar in Berlin. Since Engel was Jewish, it could not have been too difficult to convince him to leave Berlin for Vienna and the Comedian Harmonists. But the group still needed a first tenor and a bass. Cycowski had studied with Hans Rexeis, a tenor who was playing violin in a coffee house in Berlin. Rexeis, who was not Jewish and who was originally from Austria, had trained as a violinist but had also studied singing. The bass – Rudolf Mayreder, a very tall, non-Jewish Austrian – was discovered while finishing his studies at the Vienna Academy of Music. With Mayreder, the new ensemble was complete.

Rehearsals were held through the summer of 1935 with the old Comedian Harmonists members supporting the new ones. Frommermann said that he had written about 80 percent of the Comedian Harmonists' arrangements and could use many of them "as long as the scores were still considered modern or evergreens."[329] In contrast to the Meistersextett,[330] Engel, Rexeis and Mayreder were made full partners in the group from the outset and were not just employees. This undoubtedly made for a more stable and pleasant relationship, but the group still had its issues.

Mayreder maintained a diary during his years with the Comedy Harmonists.[331] When he wrote about the other new members, he referred to them as "Engel," "Rexeis"

---

325   Kiss in Fechner film

326   Cycowski in Fechner film

327   In 1938, Fischer-Maretzki is found living in London. In 1964, he returned to Berlin and was a subtenant of Biberti's for a while. He died in 1966 in Berlin.

328   Seeber, Ursula. "Asyl wider Willen. Exil in Österreich 1933-1938." Wien: Picus Verlag, 2003. See, http://www.picus.at (accessed December 6, 2007).

329   Frohman story.

330   The later group formed by the Aryan members of the Comedian Harmonists.

331   Thank you to Michael Hortig and Jan Grübler for providing me with this diary.

and "Kramer;"[332] when he mentioned Frommermann, Collin and Cycowski, it was "Harry," "Erich" and "Roman." There were also some references to trouble they had with each other, but that was to be expected when travelling and living together in close quarters.

From the left: Engel, Rexeis, Collin, Frommermann, Cycowski and Mayreder

The new members were paid salaries until the group began to earn income from performances and recordings. They had to live at a significantly lower level than that to which they had become accustomed. Frommermann said that the original Comedian Harmonists were each earning about 40,000 marks per year just before the breakup. In 1935, they each earned only 150 marks,[333] which would be worth about $900 in 2005 dollars.[334] When the group first began to perform, they had to appear in smaller venues because they had not yet mastered a large repertoire and were not singing at full concert level.

About the new members, Cycowski said: "[Mayreder] had a wonderful voice, but he was no Biberti, because Biberti had a natural humor, which had been good for the group. And Rexeis was no replacement for Leschnikoff, even though he had a great tenor and an easygoing voice. We tried in vain to save the whole ensemble as an instrument, but the luster of the old group could not be restored. That only existed once – that's how it was. The old group, as it existed, would have conquered the whole world, the whole world...."[335]

Liberated from what he felt was the tyranny of Biberti and Bootz, Frommermann flourished artistically. He feverishly wrote new arrangements and was largely responsible for the success of the new group. In the summer of 1935, they sang for the legendary record producer Fred Gaisberg in Paris. Born in the U.S., Gaisberg was a pianist who had entered the recording world during its infancy. He began working for the Gramophone Company in the U.S. in the 1890s and then went to London as a recording engineer for the company's English affiliate. Gaisberg became a producer and was the first person to sign Enrico Caruso to a recording contract.[336] The audition

---

332   Fritz Kramer would replace Engel in 1937.

333   Fechner book, p. 317

334   http://www.measuringworth.com/calculators/uscompare/. The U.S. Consumer Price Index was used as the measure of inflation (accessed December 5, 2007)

335   Cycowski in Fechner book, pp. 316-317

336   http://www.bbc.co.uk/music/features/vinyl/1900/ (accessed December 6, 2007)

was a success and Gaisberg convinced the group to change their name to the "Comedy Harmonists," which sounded better to the English ear.[337] The first song they recorded was the American number "The Continental" on July 19, 1935. That same day they also recorded "Guitare d'Amour," a French version of their great song, "Gitarren, spielt auf," which was performed by the original group and is featured poignantly in the Fechner film.

The group used the new name on their recordings but still used the Comedian Harmonists name for most concerts and in films such as *Katharina die Letzte* (*Katherine The Last*) (1935) in Austria, which is probably the best appearance for any of the groups on film. In the film, they appeared as themselves in a nightclub and performed a number – "Du passt so gut zu mir wie Zucker zum Kaffee" (You Suit Me As Well As Sugar With Coffee) – on screen. They also sing "Auf Wiedersehen mein Fräulein, auf Wiedersehen mein Herr" (Goodbye Lady, Goodbye Sir) in the film.

The Comedy Harmonists' first live performances took place in Geneva in August 1935 and then in Nice in September. In November, they sang at Ronacher's music hall in Vienna and were well received. However, they were back to performing in revues (along with other acts) and continued to sing in lesser venues until the new group gained a reputation.

In Paris they teamed up with Josephine Baker for recordings in French of "Sous Le Ciel d' Afrique" (Under The African Sky) and "Espabilate" on September 29, 1935. Baker was a friend of Collin's, which was how they made the connection. Frommermann wrote the arrangements, but Baker had great difficulty in learning them, and Harry had to spend a lot of time helping her. In November, they recorded two more numbers for His Masters Voice (HMV) in Paris: "D'Ajaccio a Bonifacio" and "Il Pleut Sur La Route" (It's Raining On The Road). These recordings in Paris were all in French.

Frommermann and Collin lost their German citizenship when they were ordered to report to the German embassy in Vienna and failed to do so. There were rumors that if they went to the embassy, they would be forcibly returned to Germany. The women, who were all Aryan, were informed that they would be allowed to return to Germany if they divorced their Jewish husbands (Mary, who was not yet married, would simply have to leave Cycowski). The women all declined. Special passports were provided by the Austrian passport office in Vienna that allowed them to travel, but these passports became invalid in the spring of 1938 after the Anschluss.[338]

December 26, 1935, in Vienna, marked a milestone for the Comedy Harmonists – their first solo concert since the breakup. The performance went very well and led to new bookings in Paris, Scandinavia and Italy for early 1936.

---

337   Frohman story

338   "Anschluss" means "connection." Here it refers to the 1938 annexation of Austria by Germany

Germany Invades the Rhineland on March 7, 1936

In May 1936, the Comedy Harmonists traveled to Tiflis via Kiev to begin a tour of the Soviet Union, which they viewed as an ideal place to try out their new program and for further rehearsal. However, there was also some uncertainty, as this was a new audience for them. The men traveled first, followed by the women a week later. When the women reached the border they picked up a package from Frommermann that contained rubles. Since any rubles that the group earned had to remain in Russia, why not spend them? The tour was a success. Marion Kiss, Frommermann's ex-wife, said, "We earned a lot of money and traveled around with suitcases stuffed with rubles."[339] They gave four weeks of concerts, including in the Hermitage Garden – their first concerts outdoors – alternating evenings with the Dutch-German classical pianist, Egon Petri.

During the tour, Rexeis, Frommermann and Collin all became ill. In some cases, they sang at less than full-strength; some concerts had to be cut short or cancelled but fortunately the group had insurance. On a more pleasant note, they met Sol M. Hurok in Moscow in June. Hurok, who was probably the foremost impresario in the world at the time, had been born in Russia, but emigrated to the U. S. in 1906. After listening to the Comedy Harmonists, Hurok signed them to a contract for a North American tour in 1939. The contract was signed on the back of a "dining card."[340]

The First Gypsies are Sent to the Dachau Concentration Camp on July 12, 1936

The tour concluded at Volodarsky Park in what was then Leningrad, but the group delayed their departure so that they could spend the rubles they had earned and were prohibited from taking out of the country. After Russia, they went by ship to London in August 1936.

The Summer Olympics are Held in Berlin in August 1936

Hitler and Mussolini Sign Their Axis Agreement on October 25, 1936

From London, the group traveled to Belgium and Paris, and then on to Scandinavia. The quality of their singing improved due to Frommermann's prodding and extensive rehearsal time. The repertoire had to be updated constantly, and the group also had to sing in foreign languages in order to win over their new audiences. This required intensive phonetic rehearsing, as only Collin had a good knowledge of foreign languages. According to Marion Kiss, "Collin was very talented with languages. He would go to another country, buy a newspaper and then was somehow able to read it."[341] But the group's profits did not approach what they had earned with the Comedian Harmonists.

---

339 Kiss in Fechner film
340 Frohman story
341 Kiss in Fechner book, p. 45

From the left: Collin, Kramer (at the piano), Mayreder, Rexeis,
Cycowski and Frommermann.

Czada attributed this to fewer concerts, longer travel times (due to the need to avoid Germany) and the inability to perform in the lucrative German market. [342]

While in Paris, Ernst Engel was dismissed from the group for being difficult to work with and unreliable, likely due to a drinking problem,[343] although Frommermann said Engel left to stay in Paris with his family.[344] Engel was replaced by Fritz Kramer, a gifted pianist, but that meant more downtime while the group rehearsed in Vienna. Kramer's widow, Eleonore, tells the story that her husband was playing piano and conducting the Vienna Volksoper when he was heard by members of the group. They approached Kramer about joining the group and then "locked him in a room" and tested him extensively on his ability to memorize and arrange before offering him the position.[345]

When the group felt ready to perform, they returned to France, where they received an offer from the Australian Broadcasting Commission for an extended concert tour. They stopped in London first, and Roman and Mary were married before they sailed. The couple had tried to get married in Austria, but the rabbi had refused because Mary was German and the rabbi was afraid that he would anger the authorities by marrying an Aryan and a Jew. This, even though Mary had earlier converted to Judaism.[346]

---

342 Czada, p. 95

343 Interview with Eleonore Kramer, September 11, 2007

344 During the War, Engel was interned at a camp in Gurs in southwest France. He survived and earned his living playing piano at bars in Paris. He died in 1958.

345 Interview with Eleonore Kramer, September 11, 2007

346 Cycowski in Fechner book, p. 325

The group also made eight more recordings from April 22 to 28, 1937, including "The Way You Look Tonight" (in English), the "Overture To The Barber of Seville" and "In A Persian Market" for Gramophon in Hayes, where the company had its headquarters. In June, they made more recordings for HMV, including the poignant "Love Me A Little Today" and "Du bist mein Baby" with lyrics by Gerd Karlick. In all, they recorded 25 sides in 1937, including 16 in Paris. They sang in English, German, Spanish, Italian and French, as well as two sides – the Overture to the Barber of Seville, Parts I and II – without lyrics. Incredibly, all their recordings were done in one take with a single exception – "The Way You Look Tonight."[347] Given the complexity of Frommermann's arrangements and the exquisite timing needed to perform their songs, the fact that they were able to do so many in one take is astonishing.

The lyrics of "Love Me A Little Today" are particularly moving:

Love me a little today,
Show the way to the world, show the way.
For they say, "Every day it's the duty
of youth and beauty to lead the way . . . .
There's always some upset or other
Man is most unkind to man, and since
the world is one big brother we should all
do what we can. But can a nation love a nation,
if even I can't agree with you? Let's demonstrate
cooperation and show Geneva what love can do.[348]

Roman and Mary

---

347 Czada, p. 95 and Andreas Schmauder discography.

348 By Alan Herbert and Nicholas Brodszky. The group also did a beautiful version of this song in French, "Si Vous m'Aimez En Secret"

At the end of June 1937, the Comedy Harmonists sailed for Australia. Journeys such as these were not very profitable because of the long travel times, the fact that they made no money during the voyages and the added expense of bringing their wives along. On the plus side, the travel provided them with a lot of rehearsal time and the ability to learn new songs. The group disembarked in Perth in Western Australia on July 20, 1937, while the women went on to Sydney.

Mayreder maintained a diary for the first four years of his time with the group. His entry for the arrival day reads: "A day full of surprises. At 7 o'clock a. m. there was a medical check; only then did we go on into the port. Just as we landed, we were welcomed by the local manager Charlton and his wife, who brought us the surprising news that we had to disembark because our concert tour was to begin in Perth, so we quickly packed and got off. We made a tour through Fremantle, then went by car to the hotel where we reserved our rooms. After that, we went back to Fremantle because the wives of my colleagues went onboard again to proceed with their travel to Sydney. We went to the studio to start our rehearsals right away. In the evening we visited the city. We were very surprised to find such a bustle in a town like Perth with 250,000 inhabitants. The first impression that we have is more than surprising which might get even stronger later on, when we have gotten to know everything a bit more. Already the fact that we had a delicious meal in our hotel 'King Edward' – in contrast to the ones we had during the last days – is a great joy for us. We will have two concerts in Perth and there is already great interest here. Reporters and photographers have 'confiscated' us. The people are unexpectedly friendly. We are simply perplexed by everything we are able to see and experience. Now it is up to us not to disappoint these expectations and we are working without rest for the first concert."[349] A portion of the actual entry appears on the opposite page.

Their first Australian concert took place in Perth on July 22, 1937, at His Majesty's Theatre. This appearance marked Fritz Kramer's concert debut with the group.[350] They were so well received that they were asked to give fourteen concerts in Western Australia instead of the six originally planned. They eventually gave 55 concerts (they had originally contracted for 37) as they made their way across Australia – all sold out and all broadcast on radio. Newcastle, Brisbane, Canberra, Adelaide, Melbourne and Sydney were the stops they made, although some of the dates had to be rearranged due to the increased number of concerts. The Comedian Harmonists were fairly well known in Australia, mainly from their previous recordings; but the press agents were, apparently, unaware of what had happened in Germany: They mentioned Biberti and Leschnikoff as members of the group, and it was not until an interview with Collin in early August that the public learned of the split between the Jewish and the Aryan members.[351]

---

349   Mayreder Diary
350   Email from Jan Grübler, November 5, 2007
351   Czada, p.99

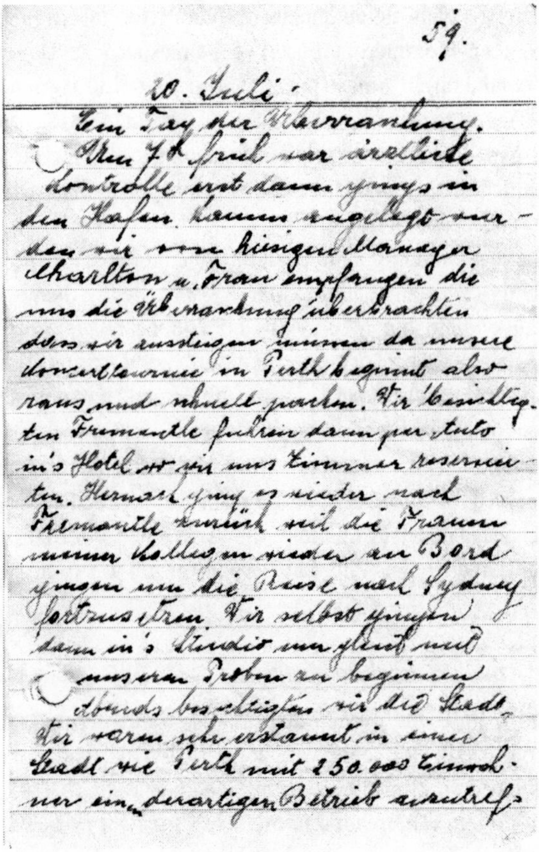

59.

20. Juli.

Ein Tag der Überraschung.
Um 7h früh war ärztliche Kontrolle erst dann gings in den Hafen. Kaum angelegt wurden wir vom hiesigen Manager Charlton u. Frau empfangen die uns die Überraschung überbrachten dass wir aussteigen müssen da unsere Konzerttournée in Perth beginnt also raus und schnell packen. Wir besichtigten Fremantle fuhren dann per Auto in's Hotel wo wir uns Zimmer reservierten. Hernach ging es wieder nach Fremantle zurück wo die Frauen meiner Kollegen wieder an Bord gingen um die Reise nach Sydney fortzusetzen. Wir selbst gingen dann in's Studio um gleich mit unseren Proben zu beginnen. Abends besichtigten wir die Stadt. Wir waren sehr erstaunt in einer Stadt wie Perth mit 250.000 Einwohner einen derartigen Betrieb anzutref-

Mayreder Diary, July 20, 1937

While on tour, the group did the things that celebrities do. A photograph from an unidentified Australian magazine from July 1937 shows them visiting sick children in a hospital in Hobart. The article says that they will be giving a concert at City Hall in aid of "Patriotic funds." The Fremantle newspaper (no date is on the clipping) included a picture of "Wives of Four Members of the Comedy Harmonists Sextette, who arrived in the Orford yesterday" and showed "Mrs. J. Cycowski, Mrs. F. Kramer, Mrs. Abraham Collin and Mrs. H. Frommermann." A headline on a short newspaper article from an unidentified newspaper reads, "Vocalists' Wives Decorative" and goes on to describe the outfits of Mary, Erna and Gerty Kramer.[352]

Another article from the same newspaper referred to them as "Austrian Entertainers" and said that they "had to adapt their programmes to the different national temperaments" of the many countries in which they appeared: "Reverting to the ideas which moved Herr Frommermann and his colleagues in forming the group, Herr Collin made an analogy with the string quartet. 'Why should there not be something like that for voices?' The great difficulty was the comparatively small range in the compass of men's voices, from bass to tenor. So they had to search for an extremely high tenor on the one hand and an extremely deep bass on the other." A report in an unidentified newspaper from Sydney referred to a "tumultuous reception" and said, "There was sustained applause which brought the performers back on to the platform time after time, until they were finally obliged to sing encores."[353]

352 Cycowski Archive (all Cycowski Archive materials are courtesy of Carolyn Speerstra Harcourt)

353 Cycowski Archive

As a result of their great success with the audiences, they added a stop in New Zealand in November and December. Frommermann said of their experience Down Under: "We had conquered a continent!"[354] A newspaper there referred to them as "Brilliant Vocal Acrobats" and went on to say, "The National Broadcasting Service has been responsible for bringing to New Zealand a number of outstanding artists in recent times, but no individual or combination has caught the public imagination to the extent that the Comedy Harmonists has succeeded in doing."[355]

By contrast, the group did not get much of an opportunity to conquer Italy when they visited that country at the end of February and into March, 1938. Before the war, Italy had not been particularly anti-Semitic, but in 1938 Mussolini published his *Manifesto of the Race* that declared Italians to be Aryans and Jews to be non-Aryans. The *leggi antiebraiche* (anti-Jewish laws) came into effect while the Comedy Harmonists were in Italy and the group was not allowed to continue its tour.

Unable to perform and prohibited from taking out of the country the money they had already earned, the group stayed for four weeks in the resort town of Santa Margherita, near Portofino on the Ligurian coast. From there, the wives decided to return to Vienna and then meet their husbands in Scandinavia where the group was to begin a major tour on March 14.

March 12, 1938 – The German Army Crosses Into Austria

On the night of March 12-13, 1938, the women detrained in Vienna. Frommermann picks up the story: "And our friend Fleischer[356] was at the station and said: 'You must be out of your mind!... Hitler invaded, don't you hear the enthusiasm?' That was the famous Anschluss. 'You will go into a little hotel in the side alley right away, but before that, you will buy a ticket for the first train to Zurich and leave this place as soon as possible. Don't touch your bank accounts, don't go to the apartments – you never know.'" [357]

When the women reached the border, the Austrian customs officer asked for their passports. In the passports was a space to list one's profession. The women's passports simply said "artist's wife" in this space. The Austrian customs officer was already accompanied by a German officer. The Austrian turned to the German and said – according to Frommermann – who repeated the words in an Austrian accent: "Well, ladies, you are artists' wives? I guess you are going to an engagement of your husbands? Well, that's nice, that is okay." And the customs official turned to the German officer, who nodded and they were allowed to pass. What Frommermann was likely saying was that the Austrian customs officer knew that the women were trying to escape and decided to help them knowing the German officer would not be able to figure out the language about their "profession." "And what our wives saw at the border – all

---

354   Czada, p. 100

355   Cycowski Archive

356   Opera singer, Arthur Fleischer

357   Radio Bremen Frommermann Interview

Jews had to leave the train, go down to the platform and they were searched – body checks of ladies, gentlemen, children who traveled with their parents. It was very tragic. What they saw there made them feel sick to their stomach."[358]

April 10, 1938 – Anschluss Confirmed by Austrian Plebiscite

Suzanne Collin, Neuilly, 1944/1945

Hitler had followed them to Austria. On March 12, 1938, the German army crossed the Austrian border. The Austrian army offered no resistance and in fact welcomed the Germans. Hitler announced the Anschluss with Austria and proclaimed the German army as "liberators." The takeover was given legal effect by an act of the legislature on March 13 and was confirmed in an April 10 plebiscite where it was approved by 99.73 percent of the voters.[359] Although there were significant irregularities in the election process, there is no question that most Austrians were in favor.

The women finally reached Zurich, but they had now been forced to leave their second home. Because Switzerland would not accept Austrian refugees, they continued on to London. The Comedy Harmonists were now truly stateless: Germany had required all Austrian citizens to exchange their passports for German ones, but, obviously, this was not something that four of the six (Mayreder and Rexeis were not Jewish) could do. Instead, because their Austrian passports were no longer valid, they used their recording company's contacts in London to obtain Nansen passports. Nansen passports were internationally recognized identity cards that had been issued by the League of Nations to stateless refugees.[360]

The Comedy Harmonists traveled with their wives – partly because they had no home. Only Fernande did not tour with them: Collin's daughter, Suzanne, was six years old and Collin did not think that she should travel with the group. Fernande and Suzanne stayed with relatives in the Paris suburb of Neuilly and Suzanne attended a convent school. The Collin family could not have imagined that it would be eight years before they would be together again.

The phenomenon of musicians who "fool around" while on the road did not originate in the rock-and-roll era. As Bootz said, all of the group members "dined a la carte" when it

---

358   Radio Bremen Frommermann Interview

359   http://www.ibiblio.org/pha/events/1938.html (accessed December 6, 2007)

360   Nansen passports, initiated in 1922 by Fridtjof Nansen, would eventually be honored by governments in 52 countries and were the first refugee travel documents. Approximately 450,000 were issued, making them one of the League of Nations' few successes.

came to women. Collin had a serious affair with a young Swedish woman and, according to Marion Kiss, even considered divorce. Cycowski said, "Erich was a little careless and loved the change.... I couldn't quite understand it, as his wife Fernande was very pretty and likeable."[361] Fernande later said, "I don't want to get into details. Nobody is perfect."[362]

The group embarked on an extensive international tour and reached South America in May, 1938. They performed in Brazil, Uruguay, Argentina and Chile, and earned good reviews – although the South Americans took a while to warm up to the group. However, after their records were played on the radio and they added some Latin numbers to their repertoire, they began to win over the audiences. After a performance in Santiago de Chile, a review in the newspaper *La Nacion* said, "These friendly international artists, performing at the Teatro Municipal, have brought a light spark of humor and good mood into our melancholic Chilean atmosphere. They sing in a fresh and easygoing way, like six good friends, with the common target of bringing a good mood to their audience for a few hours."[363] The group became so popular that their tour was extended.

While in Buenos Aires in the summer of 1938, Cycowski heard from his sister in Poland. She said that the family wanted to emigrate so that they would not suffer the same fate as the Jews in Germany. Cycowski used his influence to obtain an entry permit, but his family then wrote to say that they were going to stay on for one more year. As Cycowski said, "It was one year too late. That's fate."[364] Three of his four siblings died in concentration camps – his sister was the only one that survived.

The Comedy Harmonists' final South American concert took place in Rio de Janeiro on October 24, 1938. They then sailed for England where they made some appearances. In December 1938, they did six recordings in London (in English and French) and then two more in London in January 1939 to conclude the group's recording career. Among the December 1938 recordings were "Donkey Serenade," "Whistle While You Work" and "Ti-Pi-Tin" – all in English.

A November 1938 program from the London Coliseum bills them as "The Six Comedian Harmonists – First Appearance in England of the World-Famous Vocal Ensemble. With all the ease in the world they imitate various musical instruments and unite their voices into one grand chorus of sound, resembling a symphony orchestra in full swing."[365]

---

361   Cycowski in Fechner book, pp. 47-48

362   Fechner book, p. 48

363   Czada, p. 103

364   Cycowski in Fechner film

365   Program from the author's collection

Program from London Coliseum

Kristallnacht Takes Place on November 9, 1938 [366]

In February 1939, the Comedy Harmonists began the tour of Canada and the U.S. that they had arranged with Sol Hurok in Russia in 1936. The tour was a success, so much so that they were booked for a return tour in 1940. But first, they had scheduled another trip to Australia with a stop in South Africa for several concerts. They reached Australia in June 1939. While Cycowski's family had decided to delay their departure from Europe, Collin's sister, Anne-Marie, emigrated to Australia in August 1939.

The tour began in Perth again. The program covered the entire tour and contained information on 80 songs – and each night the audience was told which songs would be performed. Once again, the Down Under audiences loved them. A report from *The Truth*, a Melbourne tabloid, said: "I have never seen the Town Hall this crowded as on Thursday night's concert of the Comedy Harmonists. The people sat on the steps, the organ bench and nearly on the chandeliers. The smartest people were those four, which were seated at the organ bench. As soon as the floodlights came on, they took

---

366   Called the "Night of the Broken Glass," Kristallnacht was a series of riots against synagogues and Jewish homes and businesses. Approximately 30,000 Jews were taken away and sent to concentration camps at Dachau and elsewhere. Hundreds of synagogues and homes were damaged or destroyed. See, http://www1. yadvashem.org.il/ (accessed November 6, 2007)

sun glasses out of their pockets and kept them on during the entire concert."[367]

The group decided to settle in Australia. They bought a large house in Sydney that could hold them all, and they began the process to become Australian citizens.

On September 1, 1939, German Troops Invade Poland,
Marking the Beginning of the Second World War

Britain and France Declare War on Germany on September 3, 1939

The Comedy Harmonists were driving to a concert in Sydney when they heard the newspaper boys shouting, "Germans Bomb Polish Cities."[368] Naturally, they were worried about the reception they would get from the audience that evening. They needn't have been concerned. The concert was sold out: 3000 people attended and cheered them enthusiastically.

They listened to British Prime Minister Neville Chamberlain's speech on the radio.[369] With the beginning of the war in Europe, all Germans and Austrians in the country were interned, even if they were married to Australians. The members of the group were all from Germany – including the Austrians after the Anschluss – and were worried that they might be interned. But they were not. The *Daily Telegraph* newspaper in Sydney reported on the internments but said that the Comedy Harmonists would not be affected because they had British documents.[370] That statement was inaccurate – the group members actually carried Nansen passports, as did others who had been interned. It appears that the Australian Broadcasting Commission had used its influence with the Ministry of Defence to allow the Comedy Harmonists to continue with their tour.

Internment was, however, a real concern. For example, the Weintraubs Syncopators were an extremely popular – and mostly Jewish – jazz band in Germany at about the same time as the Comedian Harmonists. The Weintraubs appeared in all the Berlin clubs and in the 1930 movie *Blue Angel* with Marlene Dietrich. When the Nazis came to full power in Germany in 1933, they were on a foreign tour. The band members decided not to go home. They had continued success touring in Italy, Scandinavia and Asia and then Australia, where they finally settled. However, when the Japanese attacked Pearl Harbor, some of the Weintraubs were interned, along with most German citizens living in Australia. That spelled the end of their extraordinary ensemble.[371]

---

367 Czada, p. 110

368 Cycowski in Fechner film

369 Chamberlain was Prime Minister from 1937 to 1940 and is best known for his policy of appeasement towards the Nazis. He resigned his position after Germany invaded France, the Netherlands and Belgium, and died of cancer shortly after leaving office.

370 Czada, p. 110

371 http://www.nfo.net/euro/ew.html#Weintraub (accessed December 16, 2007). A documentary on them – *Weintraubs Syncopators (To The Other End Of The World)* – was released in 2000.

Frommermann in Australia in 1939

A short article in an unidentified Sydney newspaper used the headline "Polish Comedy Singer's Fears" and went on to say that "Roman Cycowski, baritone of the Comedy Harmonists, is one of the most worried men in Sydney today. Three younger brothers are in the Polish army ... 'I had a letter from my father while we were in Adelaide, four weeks ago, and it was frightening,' said Mr. Cycowski."[372]

In all, the Comedy Harmonists gave 76 concerts during their Australian tour and all of the concerts were sold out. The final concert in Brisbane on December 13, 1939, drew an audience of 2500. The group was so popular that a racehorse was named after them, which led to a photograph of Frommermann sitting uncomfortably on the horse.

The members were unhappy with HMV because "they [had] heard a good many of their records being broadcast over the Broadcasting Networks" and did not believe that their talent was being properly "exploited" as it had been in Germany. Apparently the members believed that if their records were played on the radio, the public would be less likely to attend concerts and buy recordings. A letter from a Gramophone executive in Sydney to his home office in Hayes, England, says that he pointed out to the group that they had played to full houses every night and that the broadcasting "[had] not done [them] any harm but [had] done [them] good." The executive also said, "After the outbreak of the war they were not so popular and they have been living quietly and not giving any concerts or broadcasts for some time.... I believe Collin and Frommermann are both Germans and, while they have stated that they are not in sympathy with 'Nazi' principles that is an easy way out of it. What amazes me with Germans and some of the

372 Cycowski Archive

other Refugees is the way they can so easily change their 'nationality' when it suits them, and even when they are in a hospitable country they have the audacity to criticize."[373]

After the tour, the group had to decide what to do now that the war would limit their ability to travel. Harry's wife did not want to stay in Australia, fearing they would be interned, even though the Australian Broadcasting Commission had asked them to stay and said that they could become Australian citizens. At the end of January 1940, the group sold their house, left Australia and sailed for Hawaii. Collin's sister, Anne-Marie, was not allowed on the ship and had to remain in Australia. She said, "I felt things couldn't get worse. I wasn't allowed on the ship because it was wartime. They all left and I was alone in the vastness of Australia. It was a difficult time."[374]

They gave four concerts in Honolulu and then went on to San Francisco. The women stayed in the Bay area while the group went on tour. Czada lists their itinerary for April 1940 – certainly a diverse set of venues.[375]

April 1 – Chapel Hill, North Carolina/Memorial Hall[376]

April 3 – Greenville, North Carolina/Wright Auditorium

April 5 – Columbus, Missouri/Whitfield Auditorium

April 8 – Winfield, Kansas/Richardson Hall

April 9 – Oklahoma City/Shrine Temple

April 10 – Wichita, Kansas/High School East

April 12 – Tyler, Texas/Gary Auditorium

April 13 – Longview, Texas/Junior High School

April 15 – Laredo, Texas/Martin High School

April 20 – Seattle, Washington/Moore Theater

April 22 – Bellingham, Washington/ High School Auditorium

April 23 – Everett, Washington/Elks Auditorium

April 27 – Aberdeen, South Dakota

April 29 – Oshkosh, Wisconsin/Grand Opera House

May 1 – Richmond, Indiana/Tivoli Theater

The program for the Chapel Hill appearance shows that their repertoire reflected their travels. The songs they sang included "D'Ajaccio a Bonifacio" (a Corsican Barca-rolle), Disney's "Whistle While You Work," Spoliansky's "Congo Lullaby," the American "Let's Call The Whole Thing Off," and "Allegre Conga En El Rancho Grande" (reflecting

---

373   Letter from The Gramophone Company Limited, Sydney, Australia, to the Gramophone Company Ltd., Hayes, England, dated February 5, 1940.

374   Anne-Marie Collin in Fechner film

375   Czada, p. 114

376   Memorial Hall is on the campus of the University of North Carolina, my alma mater.
       It was also from here that Mayreder wrote a letter resigning from the group, which is covered below.

Tivoli Theater, Richmond, Indiana

the time they spent in South America). They also sang "Ti-Pi-Tin," partly in English and partly in Spanish.[377]

A concert at the unassuming Tivoli Theater in Richmond, Indiana, turned out to be the final performance of the group.

Their U.S. reception did not match the adulation of the Australians. Frommermann thought that the Americans were put off by the German accents. Their earnings were about one-sixth of what they had been making in Australia.[378] Although they tried to sing in English, their thick accents were not pleasing to Americans, especially during wartime. The group received an offer from the Australian Broadcasting Commission for a third tour. The offer was accepted but passenger ships were ordered to remain in port due to concerns about German submarines and the group stayed in the U.S.

April 30, 1940 – A Jewish Ghetto is Established in Lodz, Poland – Near Cycowski's Hometown

May, 1940 - The Auschwitz Concentration Camp is Established Near Oswiecim, Poland

July 9, 1940 – The London Blitz Begins

November 15, 1940 – The Warsaw Ghetto is Sealed Off

The Comedy Harmonists came to an end for a variety of reasons, but two events – one seemingly trivial, the other not – certainly affected the group and likely hastened the breakup. First, Collin and Mayreder had an argument. Mayreder thought that Collin was mugging it up on stage with exaggerated facial expressions, and Collin countered by making a reference to Mayreder's physiognomy. Mayreder was sensitive about his looks – he was tall and thin and caricaturists always seemed to accentuate his nose. He was apparently extremely offended by Collin's comments and on April 1, 1940, gave three months' notice of his intention to leave the group. A replacement was found and they held some rehearsals, but other events intervened.

At about the same time, Cycowski received some horrible news. A letter from the Red Cross informed him that his father was dead, while a letter from his sister said that their father had been attacked in the street and killed, not by the Germans, but by Poles. Cycowski's father had been beaten severely; his beard had been torn off and he had been left for dead. A Christian woman found him and took him to her house, where he survived for three hours before dying. Cycowski said, "The Poles killed him; they wanted to do it even better than the Nazis. They were collaborators." After receiving

---

377   Cycowski Archive
378   Czada, p. 114

the news, Cycowski made a life-changing decision: "When I got the letter I said to my colleagues, 'I promised my father that I would be a cantor.' I said to Frommermann, 'I'll give you three months to find a replacement for me.' I immediately took up a post as cantor in Los Angeles. I hadn't set foot in a synagogue for 20 years, but I immediately felt at home again."[379]

Cycowski left for Los Angeles in the summer of 1941 and, effectively, that was the end of the Comedy Harmonists. Frommermann and Collin wanted to return to Australia, but the war made that impossible. Mayreder joined the Radio City Choir in New York, then sang with Metropolitan Opera Company and also tried to form a group he called the Master Singers. He returned to Austria in 1955, married, worked in a photo shop and died in 1978. Kramer and Rexeis went to Cuba where they were musicians and music teachers. They hoped to be able to emigrate to the U.S. from there. Kramer later became a bar pianist and then taught at New York University and the Manhattan School of Music. He died in 1988. Rexeis later went to Italy where he ran a music school. Vision problems plagued Rexeis and he lost all of his money due to heavy medical expenses. He was deported to Austria where he died, penniless, in 1980. Frommermann tried to find some new singers but did not have the money to pursue it properly and his efforts went nowhere.

June 22, 1941 – Germany Invades the Soviet Union

December 7, 1941 – Pearl Harbor

December 11, 1941 – Germany and Italy Declare War on the U.S.

MY FAVORITE COMEDIAN HARMONISTS SONG

I have a favorite song of my father's and I think that the Comedian Harmonists were one of the best interpreters the song ever had. It is: "Irgendwo auf der Welt." It is THE song for love and peace, because everybody is longing for the little piece of luck and in everybody's heart is the knowledge that we can find it. "Somewhere in this world the way to heaven starts..." begins this song and it is like steps leading us up. In 2005 my beloved mother died and I let this song play at her funeral. This was so touching, because it was not sad, it was the hope for a reunion ... "Who knows when, who knows where, who knows how." It was also the "Lieblingslied" [favorite song] of my father. He wrote not only the music, but also the refrain lyrics. Somehow his own music was the best therapy for all the bad things that happened in his life. And I am sure that this is the same for many, many people with open hearts and a longing for a better world.

~ Elisabeth Trautwein-Heymann is the daughter of the great composer, Werner Richard Heymann, and in her own right has studied music (piano, flute and percussion), dance and the teaching of dance. She is a graduate of the Mozarteum Conservatory in Salzburg. She appeared as a dancer in Paris, Salzburg and Stuttgart, and has worked as a dance instructor, dance therapist and health consultant. Since 1998 she has been in Berlin, where she has devoted herself solely to the music, interpretation and performance of her father's work.

---

379 Cycowski in Fechner film. Also, in a February 1957, letter, Cycowski wrote to Biberti: "I left the group in 1941, because it wasn't possible for me to work with Harry any longer."

"Wenn ich vergnügt bin, muss ich singen" [380]
(When I Am Happy, I Have To Sing) – The Meistersextett

The other half of the Comedian Harmonists did not remain idle either. Biberti, in turn, quickly formed a group with all Aryan members. Their name – the Meistersextett – was perhaps an homage to Biberti's father's group, the Meistersänger-Quartett. Leschnikoff and Bootz belonged to this new group along with three other members that Biberti found by – you guessed it – placing an ad in the *Berliner Lokal-Anzeiger* on March 3, 1935, that read: "World-famous German vocal ensemble is looking for two tenors and one baritone, no more than 30-years-old. Detailed resume required with activities so far…" followed by an address for a response.[381]

Although the ad did not specifically mention the Comedian Harmonists, it must have been clear which group was seeking new members. Why Biberti chose this approach to finding new members is somewhat of a mystery. When Harry advertised in 1927, he was a beginner. In 1935, Biberti was an established international star. Josef Westner, a vocal group historian, suggests that Biberti was looking for unknown singers.[382] Nevertheless, he placed the ad and, as one might expect, the response was overwhelming. Biberti was unhappy with the talent level of the auditioners, but he had to do something, so he picked the best of the lot. As we will see, the title of one of the best efforts of the Meistersextett – "Wenn ich vergnügt bin, muss ich singen" (When I Am Happy, I Have To Sing) – stands in cruel irony to the unhappiness of their story.

Richard Sengeleitner replaced Collin as second tenor and Walter Blanke took Cycowski's place as the baritone. Hungarian Janos Kerekes is listed in some references as the buffo tenor, but his contract with the group lists him as pianist (unusual because they had Bootz), arranger and Korrepetitor – or vocal coach.[383] Walter Gorges apparently sang with them for a short time in 1935, but he left for medical reasons and it is not known which position he held in the group. The newcomers joined the new group as employees, not as partners, allegedly with the assurance that they would become partners if they remained for three years.

Contracts with the new members were initially for one year. Tenor Sengeleitner's contract contained this clause: "We engage you herewith to perform as part of our ensemble until June 30, 1936. You are obligated to fulfill all required services for the duration of our contract. In exchange you will receive a monthly salary of 500 Reichsmark and you will be reimbursed for travel and hotel charges in connection with the work. If not cancelled, the contract will be considered extended for another year."[384]

---

380   Recorded by the Meistersextett in 1936.

381   Biberti Estate

382   Email of June 18, 2007

383   Email from Jan Grübler, September 18, 2007. Kerekes, who was from Hungary, later became conductor of the Budapest Opera and also conducted the famous soldiers' orchestra, Honvéd.

384   Czada, p. 75

The Meistersextett featured two of the better voices from the Comedian Harmonists, with Leschnikoff at the top and Biberti at the bottom. As Biberti said, dismissively, "Only the middle voices went away." On the other hand, Biberti later said that neither the Meistersextett nor the Comedy Harmonists could maintain the standard set by the original group because the relationship wasn't there.[385] But the "middle voices," as Biberti referred to them, are crucial for a vocal group. They provide the heart of the harmony and are the real fabric of an ensemble. Also, Cycowski was a world-class singer in his own right. Even more important, however, was the absence of Frommermann. You only have to listen to the Meistersextett version of "Blumentopf" to hear the difference between the Comedian Harmonists and the Meistersextett. The Meistersextett's version is hurried and lacks the great musicality of the original.

Biberti very much wanted to keep using the Comedian Harmonists name in order to capitalize on their prior success, so he went to a meeting with the RMK's president, Peter Raabe. The conversation was brief. Biberti, "Why can't we use our name? It's a well-known brand name, you can't just…" Raabe, "No, that's not possible." Biberti, "Could you tell me why?" Raabe, "No."[386]

Not to be dissuaded so easily, Biberti sent a letter to the RMK on April 28, 1935, in which he once more pleaded his case for retaining the Comedian Harmonists name. The reasons he advanced were that the name was known throughout Germany and "the whole civilized world," had been established "only by long years of hard work and great deprivations," and had "advertised German music and a sense of German appreciation for music in a very positive way." Biberti said, "If the loss of our name would come in addition to the very difficult change in our group, we would not only lose the trust of our business partners, but we would have to give up, looking at the hopelessness of our huge amount of work."[387]

The RMK relented somewhat by saying that the group could bill themselves as the "Meistersextett – Formerly Comedian Harmonists." In a telephone conversation on June 27, 1935, the RMK's Mr. Vedder said, "Okay, the use of just that name [Comedian Harmonists] is impossible! And that is, according to [Heinz] Ihlert,[388] for the following reason: this is not even a favor to the people (the members of the ensemble) because there will be many assaults in the provinces – this will not be very peaceful. We have to do it in a way that the people – very few – find a new name, which could be anything, and you can print 'Comedian Harmonists' next to it in big letters. And slowly over the years we will change the relation. The other name will become larger and the old one smaller and finally the old name will disappear. Mr. Ihlert says, you can count on it, if they go to Nuremberg now with the old name, then we will have big disturbances and what would

---

385   Biberti in Fechner film.

386   Biberti in Fechner film

387   Biberti Estate

388   Heinz Ihlert was the General Manager of the Reichsmusikkammer

we gain from that? Only trouble!" On November 21, 1935, the RMK sent Biberti a letter confirming that the new name would be "Meistersextett – Formerly Comedian Harmonists" to "avoid financial and artistic disadvantages for the ensemble."[389]

But a letter in December of 1935 reminded Biberti that the size of the print for the name "Meistersextett" had to be at least double the size of the words "formerly Comedian Harmonists" or the permission would be revoked.[390] The extent of the reach of the RMK is demonstrated by a letter on October 29, 1936 noting that a radio program had announced that "the Comedian Harmonists are singing in Copenhagen." They were asked for their "comments." It turned out it was the Vienna group, but the message was clear – "we are watching you, so behave."[391]

In the meantime, in May 1935, Biberti received an ironic letter from the great composer, Werner Richard Heymann, who had left Germany in 1933 and was trying to entice the Comedian Harmonists to come to Paris.[392] Apparently, Heymann was unaware that the Comedian Harmonists had disbanded.

Fairly soon after their formation, the Meistersextett experienced their first change in personnel. In July 1935, Friedrich (Fred) Kassen was brought in as buffo tenor – a change that Biberti would later regret. Kassen was multi-talented. He was both a singer and a pianist and had been a bar pianist at the Texas-Bar at the Femina Palace, a large dance hall in Berlin.

The Meistersextett – with Leschnikoff in fine voice – made their first test recording for Electrola/HMV on August 20, 1935.[393] The song was "Tausendmal war ich im Traum bei Dir" (In My Dream I Was With You A Thousand Times), a slow number from the film *Amphitryon*. A version recorded on September 16, 1935 was the one that was finally released. The flip side was "Drüben in der Heimat" (In My Homeland) another slow song, this one from the operetta *Glückliche Reise* (*Lucky Trip*).[394] Their next recording was "Was mit Dir heute bloss los ist" (What Is Wrong With You Today), where they tried some instrument imitation, but the effort was clearly not up to the standard set by the Comedian Harmonists. In all, the Meistersextett completed six sides that year. All of the Meistersextett's recordings were done in Berlin, not only in 1935 but for as long as they continued recording. They recorded 26 sides in 1936; 18 in 1937; 31 sides in 1938. They finished with eight in 1939, the last ones being "Penny Serenade" and "Bel Ami" in May, neither of which was released. Their last actual releases were

389   Biberti Estate

390   Biberti Estate

391   Biberti Estate

392   Email from Elisabeth Trautwein-Heymann, December 16, 2006.

393   HMV was the label of the British Gramophone Company and Electrola was the German subsidiary company of Gramophone. In 1931, Electrola (and Gramophone) merged with Lindström (and its parent, Columbia Gramophone) and formed Electric & Musical Industries Ltd. (EMI). At first, in Germany it was called Lindström-Electrola.

394   Schmauder

"Jetzt oder nie" (Now or Never) and "Holla Lady," from recording sessions held in February, March and April, 1939. A few of the old German booking agencies stayed loyal to Biberti. They were able to get some concert engagements; however, at first their repertoire was severely restricted. Biberti said: "We were only allowed to sing songs that were irreproachable in the Nazi sense, i.e., no Jewish composers, no Jewish librettists, no Jewish publishers. Those were three conditions that could hardly be fulfilled in the world of top-class international hits. And in this respect the Nazis were particularly strict...."[395] Consider the songs that they could no longer perform: "Veronika, der Lenz ist da," "Auf Wiedersehen, my Dear," "Liebling, mein Herz lässt Dich grüssen," "Das ist die Liebe der Matrosen," "Ein Freund, ein guter Freund," "Wochenend und Sonnenschein" – and many others. Czada said that they were able to keep two songs by Jewish composers in their repertoire for a while – "Mein kleiner grüner Kaktus" and "Lebe wohl, gute Reise," both by Bert Reisfeld and Rolf Marbot because they had been written under pseudonyms.[396]

On September 10, 1935, the Meistersextett had its debut concert in Dresden, with only about 15 songs in its repertoire. Both of the new groups were now working in Europe and the Comedy Harmonists – naturally – were using the "Comedian Harmonists" name. According to Czada, "This competition in the succession had worried Biberti ever since the separation ... and he did everything he could to convince the concert agencies of the artistic advantages of 'his' ensemble, leading him occasionally to untrue or even defamatory statements."[397]

In late 1935, the Meistersextett was successful enough to be able to hire a Secretary and they chose Hans-Adolf Grafe. But the issue of their repertoire plagued them. One agent, Richard Hoppe of Breslau, sent a letter to Biberti on May 11, 1936: "You promised me ... a partly new program.... You did not keep this promise, as the program contained 15 songs – all already performed here – and only one new song. You cannot call that a partly new program. The consequence of this was a low attendance on both evenings."[398]

A review of a performance in Aschaffenburg must have been encouraging, especially to Bootz: "The parody and the mood, as in the Vienna Waltz and the song from 'Amphitryon' are really the important factors of this kind of singing, which does not as much come from the art of singing as one would assume, but rather from the instrumental arts. The root is the form of dance music cultivated today whose character of improvisation is put into a definite form. And that explains the noticeable preference of the musical colorfulness expressed by the special treatment of the human voice as well as the piano and the composition. The singers know the art of giving color as does

---

395   Biberti in Fechner film
396   Czada, p. 80. They were written under the names "Dorian/Herda."
397   Czada, p. 80
398   Czada, p. 80. Breslau in former Lower Silesia, is today Wroclaw, Poland.

the pianist, who at the same time is the mentor of this Meistersextett and a masterly representative of his art."[399] The group also met with resistance from some of the press because of their previous association with the Jewish members and what was perceived as the frivolous nature of some of their music.

What would have been an interesting meeting almost occurred in late 1936, when two advertisements appeared on the same page in the *Haagsche Courant* in The Hague, Netherlands on December 24, 1936. One ad was for a concert at the Dierentuin by the "Meistersextett – Comedian Harmonists," which was, of course, the Aryan group, while the other ad was for the "Comedian-Harmonists" at the Scala, a concert by the Frommermann/Cycowski/Collin group. However, although the two groups were in The Hague at about the same time, they did not meet.

A contract draft sent by the Legal Department of the RMK to Biberti in May 1936 shows the extent of government involvement in the Meistersextett's affairs. The draft is an employment agreement with the new members and states that the contract was drafted "so that the social aspect cannot be questioned and to provide a healthy basis for the joint employment relationship." [400] If that is what the agreement was supposed to accomplish, it failed miserably, as we will see.

Ari Leschnikoff, Robert Biberti, Walter Blanke, Fred Kassen,
Richard Sengeleitner and Erwin Bootz at the piano.

399   Biberti Estate
400   Biberti Estate

Further personnel changes in the Meistersextett were inevitable. Biberti and Bootz were both perfectionists, and then there was the impossible task of trying to recreate something that was unique – the original Comedian Harmonists. Sengeleitner was unsatisfactory and Biberti and Bootz selected Rudi Schuricke of the Kardosch Singers to replace him as second tenor. However, Leschnikoff vetoed the choice, allegedly because Schuricke was tall and would be standing next to Leschnikoff, who was short. Biberti told Schuricke that there were also concerns about conflicts between Schuricke's recording obligations and the needs of the Meistersextett. They needed a singer immediately because of scheduled recording dates, so they brought in Zeno Costa, also of the Kardosch Singers. He sang with the group for only about one month in 1936.[401]

They found a more permanent solution to the second tenor problem when Alfred Grunert joined the group in September 1936.[402] That same month, Herbert Imlau, formerly of the Spree-Revellers and the Humoresk Melodios, replaced Walter Blanke as the baritone. This membership – Biberti, Leschnikoff, Bootz, Grunert, Kassen and Imlau – remained constant for the next two years – but the group still had its problems.

Herbert Imlau, Rudolf Zeller, Robert Biberti, Fred Kassen,
Alfred Grunert, Ari Leschnikoff

---

401   Several references were found to a Meistersextett member with the last name of Walther. This may have been a fictitious name used for various people so that it would not look as if they were frequently changing members.

402   Grunert had been banned for a time by the RMK for having an affair with a non-Aryan singing teacher, but was re-admitted.

A letter from the RMK on April 26, 1937 asked them to ensure that the former name, Comedian Harmonists, would no longer appear in concert announcements or other events: "The whole sense of your name change was that foreign-sounding names should disappear. The use of the subtitle can be seen as a way to get around this." The letter went on: "In addition I would like to suggest that you reconsider your current name 'Meister-Sextett.' Without considering this a degradation of your abilities, you will realize that the word 'Meister' in the artistic field is connected with certain expectations, causing me to consider this name as very inappropriate."[403] Biberti fought hard to keep the reference to the old group in their name. In a letter to the RMK in May 1937, he set out the "compelling reasons" for his position: "We have become world famous with our former name 'Comedian Harmonists.' No German group of artists has experienced a similar career during the last years. If such a group has to suddenly rename itself, it would mean having to do a complete new start." Biberti also claimed that it would cause confusion for the audiences.[404] But all of his protests were to no avail.

The RMK was kept informed of the Meistersextett's activities, for example, in a letter dated May 25, 1937, concerning a proposed concert in June in Salzburg, Austria: "The 'Vienna' Comedian Harmonists have been in Salzburg recently and they were not convincing artistically. In addition the concert had poor attendance. One knows that Jews are with the group and the nationalist-minded circle did not attend it." The letter went on, "The concert in Salzburg has been suggested by and will be supported by the Gauleiter of the Bund der Reichsdeutschen (who has National Socialistic tendencies), which was not the case with the last concert of the Comedian Harmonists." The letter concludes with a statement that the group would receive 500 Schillings for the concert at a profit of 80 percent. The letter's author is not identified on the copy in the Archive.[405]

A November 8, 1937, letter from the RMK brought more aggravation for Biberti. The RMK claimed that the Meistersextett name was too "Weimar." Biberti argued against the elimination of the Meistersextett name claiming that it reflected the quality of the group and that they were helping the German people to withdraw from "purely commercial hits. . . . "[406] Nevertheless, Biberti was given until April 30, 1938, to change the name – and the new name could not include the word Meister.[407] For some reason, however, that directive was rescinded on May 9, 1938, and they were allowed to continue to use the name.[408]

In August 1940, Biberti made one last attempt to regain the right to use the old Comedian Harmonists name, but the request was denied, saying that, at least during wartime, the use of the old name would be "considered an offense against the current national

---

403   Biberti Estate
404   Biberti Estate, letter to RMK of May 10, 1937
405   Biberti Estate. Normally, a Gauleiter was the leader of a regional branch of the Nazi Party, but in this case it was the district head of the Union of Reich's Germans in Austria.
406   Biberti Estate, letter to RMK of May 10, 1937
407   Biberti Estate, letter of November 8, 1937
408   Biberti Estate

feelings."[409] And the government was always watching. A letter from the RMK in March 1939 pointed out that there had been a concert advertisement for Berlin in which the words "Formerly Comedian Harmonists" had been noticed. They were warned that if it reoccurred, legal action would be taken.[410]

And there were still more troubles. On December 17, 1937, a new regulation required record companies to purge all recordings by Jewish artists from their catalogs. The Aryan members of the group had been receiving substantial royalties from the sale of Comedian Harmonists records, but this income would now be lost.

Bootz left the Meistersextett in June 1938; he said later that it was to further his musical development. He became the musical director of the Kabarett der Komiker where the Comedian Harmonists had starred some ten years earlier. The engagement involved "a very good contract and an 11-man orchestra. It was a very good cabaret with a revolving stage – very high class. The audience sat at little tables…. After all, I wasn't just a musician; I also wrote texts and entire revues – for instance, the revue, *Ich träum von Dir* (I Dream of You)."[411]

Bootz's departure complicated matters since, in addition to being the pianist, he was also the Meistersextett's arranger. In many ways, the arranging was much harder to replace than the piano-playing. Biberti found a new pianist, Rudolf Zeller, but Zeller was not an arranger, so Siegfried Muchow[412] and Bruno Seidler-Winkler[413] were brought in to contribute arrangements.[414]

The first sign of serious issues within the group arose in connection with a trip to the U.S. that Biberti was planning for July and August, 1938. Biberti's absence meant that the salaried employees – Kassen, Grunert and Imlau – would get no pay during that summer. As a result, they wanted twelve-month contracts rather than seasonal ones, and said that they would not sing with the group in the fall if they did not get some pay for the summer. The dispute was resolved by the signing of new contracts at a higher salary. In a letter to Hilde of July 11, 1938, Biberti said that the employees' "bluff resulted in nothing" and that Grunert had been keeping him informed on what was happening.[415] Biberti's intransigence on this issue is interesting when you remember that the original employee-members were given annual contracts.

In an August 20, 1938 letter, written by Biberti from the ship bringing him back from the U.S., to the still-friendly Leschnikoff, he confirmed that the three employees

---

409   Letter from the Reichsministerium für Volksaufklärung und Propaganda (RMVP or Ministry for Peoples Education and Propaganda), September 20, 1940.

410   Biberti Estate, letter of March 28, 1939

411   Bootz in Fechner film

412   He shows up as late as 1986 on the web site, http://www.dres-schulze.de/widmungen/widmunge.htm, as composer of the work, "Edda Symphonische Dichtung für Orchester." (accessed December 6, 2007)

413   Known primarily as a conductor of classical music.

414   Czada, p. 82

415   Biberti Estate

had signed on again at a rate of 700 Marks per month for Imlau and Grunert and 800 marks per month for Kassen, who had additional duties such as arrangements and direction of rehearsals. Biberti boasted, "Well, little Robert still has the stronger nerves!"[416]

In March 1939, the Meistersextett traveled to Italy for what turned out to be their final tour. Things were not going well, either with the music or the relationships among the members. Biberti said: "Bootz's absence upset the balance of the ensemble. Now Leschnikoff, Kassen and another new man were there and it led to animosities towards me, reappearing in a more or less unfriendly, even hostile, way."[417] As you might expect, the others saw things differently. Bootz said; "Bob unfortunately had a way of showing [Leschnikoff] up without reasons. His poor German speech also led to him being made fun of by Biberti.... Ari's German was very insufficient. He did not always understand what was said. Sometimes we would make jokes that required a certain previous knowledge. And Ari always laughed with us, so as not to show that he did not understand. And Biberti would ask, 'Why are you laughing, Ari?' And Ari did not know what to say. For Leschnikoff it must have been sheer horror, because he could not answer back.... It was pure baseness, nothing else. And if something like that goes on for years, then it can poison the atmosphere between two people."[418]

Relations between Biberti and Leschnikoff became very strained. Leschnikoff failed to show up for rehearsals and telephoned the other members to cancel rehearsals without informing Biberti, the self-proclaimed leader of the group. Once when Biberti called to tell him about a rehearsal, Leschnikoff screamed, "I will heat the ground under your feet so you can't stand here anymore!"[419]

Biberti had even more difficulty working with Kassen. A full partnership in the group had been promised by Biberti to those new members that stayed for three years, but he reneged on the agreement. Kassen protested – with Leschnikoff's support – but Biberti was adamant. Ari recalled Biberti saying, "Don't be a fool! I'm not letting any strangers into the ensemble. That's out of the question." Ari replied, "You promised him. A promise is a promise; I learned that in Germany."[420] Kassen no longer showed up for rehearsals and Biberti felt the situation to be unbearable.

In April 1939, Biberti decided to submit the dispute to the RMK president, Raabe, for resolution. Perhaps Biberti made this decision because he thought that if one of the other members planned to go to the RMK, it would look better if Biberti was the first to report the problems. Jan Grübler found documents written by Biberti in which the bass said that he went to the RMK because of the lack of discipline in the group and because

416   Email from Jan Grübler, August 20, 2007
417   Biberti in Fechner film
418   Bootz in Fechner book, pp. 93 and 302
419   Email from Jan Grübler, August 11, 2007
420   Leschnikoff in Fechner film

he was afraid that the artistic level of the group would decline. Biberti never mentioned the issues raised by the others. A June 5, 1939, letter to the RMK from Biberti claimed that Leschnikoff was "endangering the peace and order in the group" and demanded that Leschnikoff respect Biberti as the founder and leader.[421]

The RMK summoned the two men to its offices where they were questioned separately. Biberti said, "I felt I had to use its [RMK's] influence to make people see reason.... We spent the whole day there being separately interrogated."[422] Wachenfeld, a high-level civil servant in the RMK, agreed to arbitrate, but Leschnikoff rejected this alternative.

Biberti claimed that Grunert said that Leschnikoff and Kassen had told the RMK that Biberti was against the Nazis, had refused to give the Hitler salute at concerts in Italy, and had disparaged the Kraft durch Freude (Strength Through Joy or KdF). The KdF was affiliated with the State labor organization and was responsible for leisure activities in Germany, including concerts at which the Meistersextett performed. Leschnikoff vehemently denied the accusation, saying, "Lies! Lies!... They stuck a knife in my back." Imlau and Zeller stayed out of the dispute. When Biberti asked Imlau what was going on, Imlau declined to speak and said that he had given his word not to.[423]

Biberti later claimed to have been subjected to harsh interrogation for months by the Nazis at Gestapo headquarters at Prinz-Albrecht-Strasse.[424] In the Fechner film Bootz called the reporting of Biberti to the Gestapo a dirty trick and said that he had been called in for questioning and "settled the matter in Biberti's favor."[425] Biberti, however, said it was not Bootz who resolved the matter but Göring's wife, Emmy, who was a friend of Biberti's brother, Leopold. Biberti received a letter from the Reichsministerium für Volksaufklärung und Propaganda dated September 17, 1940, telling him that the resolution of the matter would be postponed until after the "victory."[426]

Given Biberti's history of prevarication, there is doubt as to whether he had actually been forced to undergo questioning and physical abuse as serious as he had maintained. To this point, no documentary evidence has been found that supports Biberti's claim.

Meanwhile, in April 1939, Biberti started litigation against Leschnikoff on the grounds of intimidation and threat, which were criminal violations under German law, but the Prosecutor refused to pursue the matter and referred Biberti to the civil courts.[427]

---

421   Biberti Estate, letter of June 5, 1939
422   Biberti in Fechner film
423   Fechner book, p. 304-306
424   Biberti in Fechner film
425   Bootz in Fechner film
426   Fechner book, pp. 307-308
427   Jan Grübler email August 11, 2007

The Meistersextett cut what turned out to be their final recordings on May 3, 1939. The artistic problems they were experiencing are best exemplified by a letter from Electrola that referred to those recordings:

Dear Mister Biberti,

Our committee has reviewed the recordings of "Bel Ami" and "Penny Serenade," chosen by you, and we unanimously decided that we cannot publish these recordings, especially not "Bel Ami." The recordings are lacking the life and unmistakable difference and harmony that you usually praise as the outstanding advantages of your ensemble.[428]

The rejection must have been bitterly disappointing for Biberti, but "Bel Ami" was a mediocre effort that lacked energy and originality, and "Penny Serenade" was only marginally better. The Meistersextett made no further recordings. Another source of revenue had been cut off.

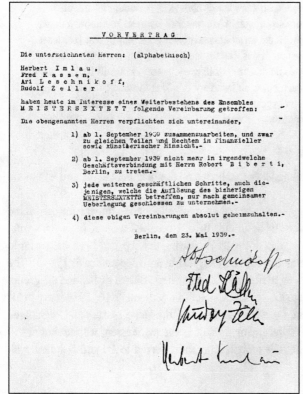

May 23, 1939, Letter of Intent

An interesting document, only recently come to light, reveals quite a bit about the relationships among the members of the Meistersextett and, perhaps, why their later recording efforts were so lackluster. In a "Letter of Intent" dated May 23, 1939, signed by Imlau, Kassen, Leschnikoff and Zeller (only Grunert was missing), the four agreed to work together as equal partners both artistically and financially from September 1, 1939, forward; to have no further business relationship with Biberti after that date; to work together on future steps – including the dissolution of the Meistersextett – and to

428   Czada p. 84

keep the agreement confidential.[429] This letter was never mentioned in Leschnikoff's interviews with Fechner or in any other forum. It is likely that Leschnikoff's return to Bulgaria prevented the others from implementing the plan because without Ari, their power was lessened considerably – he was, after all, a 50 percent partner in the group – as was their appeal to concert agents.

In another recently discovered document – this one a letter from Zeller to Biberti dated August 25, 1939 – we catch a glimpse of what life within the Meistersextett was really like:[430]

> Leaving aside the financial side and only considering the ideal aspects of my membership in the Meistersextett, I came to the conclusion that there are human perspectives in this situation that if you take a closer look at them are very unpleasant. Of course I had been at the mercy of employers before when I worked at the bar; however in the artistic aspect I had been a free man to a certain extent. I could be a pianist there and not only an accompanying copycat as is the case elsewhere…. Last, but not least, a few words about the 'camaraderie' among the ensemble members so praised by you in November of last year. You know yourself that the atmosphere between the members had gotten worse day by day. Let's leave aside the question whose fault it was. But for me it is not fun to travel all over Germany together with people that are insulting each other on a daily basis or avoid each other or threaten each other, and who are breaking the little collective group into smaller parties or loners again and again for reasons of jealousy, distrust and improper craving for recognition. Then I'd rather earn my living among the drunken, because they can either be brought to their senses with good words or, if not, they can be kept away by force.

An astonishingly revealing letter that leaves no doubt about the discord within the group.

In August 1939, the usually punctual Leschnikoff failed to appear for scheduled rehearsals and was nowhere to be found. Biberti received a letter from Ari's wife, Delphine, who was in Sofia, dated August 26, saying that Ari had been called up to the army for several weeks and would be unavailable until September 5, 1939.[431] The future of the group was put on hold and, after a few days, Biberti disbanded the group. Given all that had happened, this was inevitable. In a September 16, 1939 letter to his brother Leopold, Biberti said that he had dissolved the Meistersextett and "dismissed the two gentlemen, Grunert and Imlau, as well as the pig, Kassen, without notice."[432] He also mentioned Leschnikoff's mobilization and referred to Ari and Delphine with an expletive.

---

429   The letter was discovered in the papers of Herbert Imlau by Josef Westner.
430   Again, thank you to Josef Westner.
431   Biberti Estate
432   Biberti Estate

Another document written by Biberti leaves no doubt about his view of Kassen:

I gave him the job of the so-called 'middleman' of the group – to do mostly the easier parts of the performance – as his voice was not sufficient for more serious tasks.... Kassen had never before in his life received such an advantageous contract. When I hired him, he lived in a modest condition, and he built himself a new ambience with the income he now received regularly. A few days after he was hired, Kassen created a certain restlessness during the rehearsals. He tried to assert himself by boasting at any possible opportunity of his excellent connections to the party ... his longtime strict National Socialistic mindset. He declared that he was a member of the party and the SS for a long time.... His bumbling and his craving for recognition could have been tolerated, had he not campaigned against and threatened various members of the group, without reason and in a nasty and challenging tone, just because they did not show him the expected respect.... If I had known more about Kassen's past at that time, he would not have been hired.... To my greatest surprise even his information about belonging to the party and the SS was years later proven to be incorrect.... Kassen borrowed large amounts of money from me several times, pretending urgent personal needs. Today, more than at that time, I am convinced that Kassen used these amounts for criminal purposes.... A person whose only thought is to cause fights, to make his employer look impossible through malicious libel, to try to push himself into the position of the employer, and to destroy a performance that had been reached after hard work – such a person does not have the right to be a member of the group whose vocation is to be an example for German ensemble art inside the country as well as abroad.[433]

Biberti apparently realized that without Leschnikoff's magnificent voice any new version of the Meistersextett would be less marketable, so in October, 1939, he wrote to Delphine to inquire about Ari's return to Berlin.[434] She responded with a handwritten letter saying that Ari had been detained but was expected back around the 20th.[435]

Again, on November 9, 1939, in a letter to his brother, Biberti claimed that he did not know if Leschnikoff planned to come back and wondered if Ari had really been mobilized: "Perhaps he doesn't dare to return because of his defeat at the RMK." It is not clear to what defeat Biberti was referring or if there even was a defeat. Biberti went on to say that he was looking for a new tenor (as if voices like Leschnikoff's were easy to find). Biberti followed this with a November 14 letter to Delphine stating that because of Ari's failure to report, he regarded the contract as dissolved.[436]

In fact, Leschnikoff had returned to Sofia, with Delphine and Simeon, because he had been mobilized by the Bulgarian army.

---

433   Biberti Estate, handwritten notation – "im Februar 1940" at the end.
434   Biberti Estate, letter of October 9, 1939.
435   Biberti Estate, letter from Delphine David, dated October 16, 1939.
436   Biberti Estate

However, Leschnikoff did return in December, and on the 28th Biberti received a telephone call from Ari's lawyer saying that Ari was going to enter into a contract the next day with the other group members and that Biberti could attend if he had any interest in joining them! One can only imagine Biberti's outrage. Biberti's lawyer contacted Leschnikoff's lawyer and a legal battle was on. In mid-January Biberti and Leschnikoff finally met and were willing to work together; however, Biberti insisted that Kassen could not be part of the group. Biberti wrote to his brother that Leschnikoff was insisting on having Kassen in the group, not for the stated reason of being worried about the time required to break in a new buffo, but because he did not want to be without his "friend and counsellor" in having to deal with Biberti. [437]

Leschnikoff returned to Bulgaria on February 17, 1940. In a March 5 letter to Leopold, Biberti referred to what had transpired and spoke of Leschnikoff in extremely derogatory terms.[438] Biberti again turned to the RMK to support his position that Leschnikoff had neglected his obligations to the group. The RMK responded by suggesting that Biberti address his questions about Leschnikoff's activities to the German authorities in Bulgaria.[439] Eventually, they would confirm Ari's side of the story. Despite this, Biberti wrote to Leschnikoff on April 11, saying, "Dear Ari! What's the matter with you? Where are you staying? I have to talk to you unconditionally! I'm not well! I hope this letter will catch you! Write me instantly, please!"[440]

Biberti and Leschnikoff had been the owners of the group – Bootz had allegedly waived his ownership share in exchange for the assumption of some debts when he left. Now, Biberti became the sole owner – not that there was much left to own – and his dictatorial manner went unchecked. Ari had not formally relinquished his ownership, but was gone and did not return to Germany until late 1941.

Biberti re-formed the group in July 1940, with Grunert and several new members. Biberti said that he had to lower his standards because he wanted members who would not be called up for service. He ended up with two singers from the Netherlands – Willy Vosmendes (Willem Hendrik Gerard Vos), a tenor, and baritone Bernard Taverne (Bernard Diamant) – along with tenor Erwin Sachse-Steuernagel and pianist Willy Hermann (Zeller had died in March 1940 of heart failure). This array performed a few times in late 1940 and January 1941, before Sachse-Steuernagel and Hermann were drafted. Günter Schroeder replaced Sachse-Steuernagel for a short time, but effectively, this marked the end of the Meistersextett.

When Leschnikoff returned to Germany in 1941, he tried to get work as a solo artist. He wrote to Erich Knoblauch, an agent who was a friend of Biberti's: "I would like to restart my activities – in front of the microphone, radio-transmissions, concerts,

---

437   Email from Jan Grübler, August 11, 2007
438   Biberti Estate
439   Biberti Estate, letter of March 20, 1940.
440   Biberti Estate

etc. – and this is why I am writing to you. But I would like to remark that I am no longer with my colleagues, but on my own…. Concerning Biberti and myself, you will later hear about it in detail. I am in possession of a declaration by the Bulgarian Minister of War that I was recalled to duty."[441]

Not only did Knoblauch fail to find any work for Leschnikoff but, in spite of Ari's request to keep his inquiry confidential, the agent passed the letters on to Biberti.[442] Biberti also wrote to the agent Gensberger, saying that Leschnikoff would probably be contacting him looking for work. Biberti said he would be grateful if Gensberger would "ignore that bastard, who wanted to finish me off in a convenient way."[443]

Ironically, even though all its members were Aryan (and in any case were no longer performing), on November 24, 1941, according to Biberti, the Meistersextett too was formally banned by the RMK. Biberti said of the letter, "I shall never forget that sentence. 'The type of entertainment offered by your ensemble is unsuitable for boosting the combat morale of the German people.'" Biberti said that he concurred: "And there the Nazis were right. 'I've Ordered A Flowerpot For You' or 'The Crocodile Bar' or 'You've Got a Cactus On Your Balcony' – some of these songs weren't suited to encourage a fighting spirit."[444] However, no copy of any letter of this type has ever been found in Biberti's papers. Given that he kept everything else he ever received, it is entirely possible that Biberti invented this RMK banning to explain away the Meistersextett's demise.

Biberti's issues with Kassen did not end there. After the war, Biberti and a publisher who also had a problem with Kassen issued an 80-page document that attacked Kassen. Biberti also wrote some anti-Kassen letters, including one to Ursula Hammil (Bootz' first wife) in 1948, in which he claimed that, "Immediately after the breakdown [of the Nazi regime] I took up the fight against Kassen and brought this bastard into prison with help from other persons injured by him."[445] In a 1947 affidavit, Biberti asserted that Kassen demanded a showing of an anti-Semitic attitude by the group (no connections with anyone or anything Jewish) and claimed Kassen tried to dominate the Meistersextett "in a Nazi sense and threatened them with the concentration camp."[446]

Kassen wrote to Bootz in May 1948, claiming that Biberti had denounced him to a court in Würzburg, which Biberti admitted in the Fechner film. In the letter, Kassen referred to Bootz's 1939 appearance at the Gestapo, which occurred at Biberti's request, after he had been questioned by the Gestapo – but about what, we do not know.

Despite all this, in 1951 a Munich court wrote to Biberti saying that, "it is proven after a review of the document center that Kassen was neither a member of the NSDAP

---

441 Biberti Estate, letter of November 17, 1941.
442 Indeed, several "confidential" letters from Leschnikoff to Knoblauch from 1941 reside in the Staatsbibliothek in the Biberti Estate papers.
443 Biberti Estate
444 Biberti in Fechner film
445 Biberti Estate
446 Biberti Estate

[Nazi Party] nor of any of her organizations." The court suggested that Biberti produce evidence or eye-witnesses. That never happened. After the war, Kassen owned an artists' bar called Das Stachelschwein (The Porcupine) in the Schwabing area of Munich, where he performed as bar pianist and singer and founded the cabaret ensemble Münchener Lach-und Schiessgesellschaft, that performed in the bar. In 1959, Kassen opened a cabaret in Cologne called Das Senftöpfchen (The Little Pot Of Mustard). He died in 1972. His second wife, Alexandra, and his children, Klaus and Alexandra Franziska, live in Germany.

Herbert Imlau formed the Comedien Quartett in 1947 and also recorded with Die Sieben Raben (The Seven Ravens). Unable to let go of the past, Biberti, in a letter to Imlau of April 11, 1948, said: "In that debacle then, which almost suffocated me, I would have been very thankful if you had declared to me openly and directly that you did not identify with the evident and lousy attempts of both bastards – Kassen and Leschnikoff – to give me hell. But you were silent as a grave, even after your interrogation by the RMK about the items they asked you, items that were able to extinguish me professionally." Imlau responded on June 17, 1948, reminding Biberti about the dispute in the Meistersextett regarding partnership for the new members, and Biberti's request that Imlau side with him against Leschnikoff and report to Biberti about what the other members were doing. Imlau said it had been Biberti's rejection of their demands that led Leschnikoff to go to the RMK. Imlau claimed that he had never learned the outcome of that.[447] He died in 1983 at the age of 79.

Grunert worked as an entertainer in Hamburg and died there in 1982. Sengeleitner made some solo recordings for Deutsche Grammophon and after the war taught music at a university in Berlin. He died in 1980 in Berlin. Grafe worked for Ufa in the 1960s, owned a small cinema and later worked in the press departments of several film-rental companies. The last known mention of him is a letter to Biberti in 1981.

Taverne's real name was Diamant, but he called himself Taverne (his mother's name) because his father was Jewish. After the war Bernard Diamant became a famous singer and teacher in the Netherlands and later in Canada. He died in the Netherlands in 1999. A recording survives of Willy Vosmendes singing in Austria in 1948.

Biberti and Leschnikoff met one more time, by chance, in late February 1942, in Berlin. Biberti described the meeting in a letter to Knoblauch: "Yesterday I ran into Leschnikoff in a restaurant. The bite stuck in his throat literally when he saw me! I greeted him briefly and asked for his telephone number. He ignored my question and asked when he could contact me. I told him and left on the spot."[448]

---

447   Biberti Estate
448   Biberti Estate

"Du hast mich betrogen"*
(You Have Betrayed Me)

by Jan Grübler

In the spring of 1939, the problems between Leschnikoff and Biberti reached a new height. The reasons were probably the differences between the "old" and the "new" members of the Meistersextett. Biberti wouldn't keep his promise to make the new members equal partners with the same rights as the old ones and one-sixth of the revenues. He wanted to keep them as employees with a fixed salary. Leschnikoff supported the new members (Kassen, Imlau, Grunert and Zeller) in their attempt to advance their interests.

In all the later documents he wrote about the history of the group, about Leschnikoff or Kassen, Biberti represented that he himself turned to the Reichsmusikkammer because of a loss of discipline and the opposition against the existing structure of the group. He assumed that the other members (Imlau, Grunert, and Zeller) could get set against him by Leschnikoff and Kassen and furthermore he was afraid that the artistic level of the group would decline. But he never mentioned the valid demands of the other members.

I think knowledge and understanding of this dispute is important for the evaluation of the following developments. In my opinion, Biberti was driven by his desire for power and his greed for money! The other four members had a weak position for negotiations. Leschnikoff was the only one who had the same rights as Biberti. So Biberti had to oppose Ari to hold his authority and in particular – his earnings! Biberti also claimed a payment for his efforts as the leader of the group. He never told the employees the real level of receipts and told the concert managers to be silent on questions of receipts. So he earned much more than the others. Now Leschnikoff was a danger because of his solidarity with the employees. So Biberti used every means to oppose Leschnikoff, to make him implausible, to accuse him and to bring him to silence. He even used denunciation to the RMK. And it seems probable that Biberti in fact used an indirect denunciation to the Gestapo, too.

Later Biberti denied having denounced Kassen. That's true in fact, because he didn't denounce him at the Gestapo – but he sent a question to the National Socialist German Workers Party and he must have known what trouble that would cause! (Incidentally, there's no proof that Biberti himself was summoned to the Gestapo, or that he was arrested or maltreated, as he later claimed.)

The following is well known: Leschnikoff didn't appear for the rehearsals to prepare the next concert season. The next series of concerts was planned in Bavaria from August 3, 1939; however, Leschnikoff and his wife left Germany on August 1 or 2.

Now one can put any kind of hypothesis in this story. Is it true that Leschnikoff became an officer in the Bulgarian army? Was there a mobilization in Bulgaria? Was he still a Bulgarian citizen? Was it his intention never to go back to Germany, as Biberti suggested? Was he afraid about the dispute with Biberti or the RMK? Did he fear an interrogation by the Gestapo?

I believe that Leschnikoff was really impeded in his return and that he had the intention to go back to Germany. In the meantime, there was that secret letter of intent among Leschnikoff, Imlau, Kassen and Zeller of May 23, 1939. (Biberti suspected something about these happenings, but nobody actually told him anything. Later, Biberti reproached Imlau for that.)

And Leschnikoff, with his excellent voice, had great chances for a career in Germany – with or without Biberti! We have to consider the political situation in Germany at that time! The war stood immediately before them, and any kinds of measures on the Bulgarian side are imaginable.

I think the following will show that my view is correct – although there is some contradiction.

This development shows in my opinion the real intentions of Biberti. Although he insulted Leschnikoff, he used that situation as a chance to get rid of him. But he didn't count on Leschnikoff really coming back! His re-entry to Germany happened on December 21, without any communication with Biberti, and at once Leschnikoff tried to re-organize the group behind Biberti's back. (In April 1940 Biberti got an answer to his inquiry to the Bulgarian Department of Foreign Affairs: "Mr. Asparuch Leschnikoff entered Bulgaria in company with his wife Delphine on August 4, 1939 and left the country on December 18, the same year.")

I can imagine Biberti was foaming with rage! All his plans were forestalled and his arch-enemy Leschnikoff was back again! And Biberti of all people got an offer to take part in a new group being organized by Leschnikoff. Unacceptable! Biberti saw himself as the one and only founder and leader!

It seems that Biberti believed he would be successful in a quick reestablishment of old circumstances. So he wrote on January 17, 1940, to a concert manager in Rome, saying that Leschnikoff had returned from Bulgaria and the group would be ready to appear with a new program in about five weeks. A letter from Biberti to the agent, Hermann Kempf of Frankfurt am Main, from February 6, 1940, says, "I can only tell you that I have to make a struggle to the knife to forestall the attempts of two bastards to wrest the group from me."

But now the story took another unexpected turn: Leschnikoff returned to Bulgaria on February 17, 1940. The real reasons are unknown. Perhaps he saw the desperate dealings with Biberti and felt in a hopeless position. But now Biberti's dreams cracked anew! Again Biberti contacted the RMK! It seems he sought authority from a legitimate public institution to be able to clarify those problems and to discipline the members.

In the meantime there was further correspondence between the lawyers about the dismissal of Leschnikoff. Leschnikoff agreed to his cancellation, but he reserved the right to found a new group with the name "Meistersextett." Furthermore, there was some quarrel about an amount of money Biberti owed him.

Astonishingly Biberti didn't give up his efforts for the group. We have to consider that Germany was at war. Biberti had to worry about his own mobilization! So it was probably in his interest to get the group going again and to make himself irreplaceable.

After 1945, Biberti omitted no opportunity to insult and to persecute Leschnikoff, even to official authorities: He accused Leschnikoff and Kassen of being responsible for the difficulties after 1939 and for the break-up of the group. Meanwhile, we know that the group couldn't exist any longer after 1941, even with Leschnikoff and Kassen, because of the special circumstances in Germany. But Biberti needed a culprit and never confessed his own contribution to the disaster. Here for the first time appear accusations of alleged reports against Biberti by Kassen and Leschnikoff to the RMK and the Gestapo!

In a letter from December 1955, Biberti wrote to Bootz, "Have you heard anything about Leschnikoff? My last – unverified – information was: 'dead!'" That's the reason why Leschnikoff was listed as being dead in a 1957 *Constanze* magazine article. Biberti justified the *Constanze* article in a letter to Imlau who had criticized the article in a letter to Biberti. About Leschnikoff, Biberti said: "Leschnikoff was vocally divine. Otherwise he was worthless, unlettered up to the excess, as a person the least!"

After the joyful correction to the *Constanze* article in March 19, 1958, everyone knew that Leschnikoff wasn't missing or dead.

And then Biberti accused Leschnikoff in connection with the 1935 break-up of the Comedian Harmonists! In a letter to Collin of July 21, 1959, Biberti wrote: "Perhaps you remember that it was Leschnikoff who accelerated the break-up of the ensemble that time by his intervention at the RMK? That was told to me by Rudolf Vedder** and Fischer-Maretzki. Leschnikoff said that 'nobody could make him collaborate with Jews any more.' Except for the fact that the Comedian Harmonists would get dissolved in the foreseeable future, that was a rotten act!" No evidence has been found to support Biberti's claim.

~Jan Grübler, from Oranienburg, Germany, is a Comedian Harmonists enthusiast who has studied the Biberti Estate documents.

* Recorded by the Comedian Harmonists in 1928.

** Vedder was with the RMK until 1935, after which he became a concert agent. He booked some of the Meistersextett's concerts, including those at the Berlin Philharmonic.

CHAPTER NINE

"Irgendwo auf der Welt"[449]

(Somewhere in the World)

"My God, Mary, they have all become old!"[450]

Eric Collin[451]

Eric Collin

While Collin was touring with the Comedy Harmonists, his wife and daughter Suzanne went to Neuilly, near Paris, in 1939 for Suzanne's education. When the war broke out, they were unable to leave. During the war, Fernande and Suzanne lived in a boarding house owned by friends of the family. Fernande's "job" was to stand in line for food-ration tickets. When the Germans approached Paris, people tried to head south in order to avoid them. Fernande and Suzanne started south with two other people, but Fernande got separated from them. The other two took Suzanne with them, figuring that it was better that Suzanne be saved rather than stay behind. By luck, they met up with Fernande farther south, but were stopped by the Germans and made to return to Paris.

Back in Neuilly, everyone had to register at the town hall. Fernande's papers listed her family name as Abraham, which was Erich's official last name. Fernande still, however, had French citizenship. An official told her to go home and burn any papers with "Abraham" on them, and she did. From that time on, Fernande spoke only French and stopped speaking to Suzanne about Erich. Near the end of the war, the Gestapo came to the boarding house looking for Fernande. She was not home and the owner told the Gestapo that she no longer lived there. Luckily, the Gestapo never came back.[452] In 1939, Collin's mother managed to escape from Berlin to Switzerland, where her daughter Charlotte lived.

In 1941, after the breakup of the Comedy Harmonists, Cycowski tried to persuade Collin to join him in California. Cycowski's cousin owned a bar and Collin could work

---

449 Recorded by the Comedian Harmonists in 1932.

450 Comment by Roman Cycowski on viewing his former colleagues on film in 1976, after not seeing some of them for 40 years. Czada, p.131.

451 Collin changed the spelling of his first name from "Erich" to "Eric."

452 Interview with Deborah Tint, September 23 and 26, 2007

there as a bartender. Although this was not Erich's first choice for employment, he did not dismiss the idea entirely.

When Collin finally went to Los Angeles, he worked for a time in a wine shop, but the store closed down and he was unemployed again. In an effort to boost his chances of U.S. citizenship, Collin traveled to Canada to obtain a work permit and then returned to the U.S. He went to New York where, armed with a letter of recommendation from Albert Einstein, his father's old friend, Collin found a job as a German music instructor at New York University. The job did not last. He then sold encyclopedias for a year and later worked in a ladies-clothing store. Finally, after moving to California, he took a course in plastic technology and found work in a fiberglass factory in 1952.

Erich's wife and daughter were still living in Neuilly. He had sent some money to France so that his family could join him in the U.S., but he had not heard from them. He considered divorce, but it was a complicated matter and would take a lot of money. Eventually, in 1947, Fernande came to Los Angeles with Suzanne. Collin's employer, a man named Bill Sucor, paid the travel expenses.[453]

Anne-Marie (Collin's sister) said, "[Erich] was having a very difficult time. When Fernande and Susie arrived, he had only a tiny apartment. They lived in very poor circumstances."[454] Cycowski added: "But he never showed any sign of it. I would have lost heart, but he wouldn't. He was always trying to make his way again. Every time I came, he was the same old Erich. Perhaps it's a good thing to be like that. He never let on that he was not doing well."[455]

Suzanne, a little girl when Erich had last seen her, was now a young lady. Fernande found a job at the Mays Department Store in Los Angeles. Erich's job with Sucor did

Fernande Collin

not last and in 1948, Collin put together yet another group. Cycowski declined to join as did Frommermann (who was now calling himself "Harry Frohman") at first. Collin was aided in his efforts by Bert Reisfeld,[456] who had written several songs for the Comedian Harmonists, including two of their more successful efforts, "Lebe wohl, gute Reise" and "Mein kleiner grüner Kaktus." Collin secured some European bookings for the new group, whose members were Collin

---

453   Fechner book, p. 368

454   Anne-Marie Collin in Fechner film

455   Cycowski in Fechner film

456   Reisfeld, born in Vienna in 1906, emigrated to the U.S., where he became a successful Hollywood film composer. He died in Germany in 1991. http://www.imdb.com/name/nm0718434/ (accessed December 6, 2007)

(now a baritone), Fred Bixler (1ˢᵗ tenor), Murray Pollack (2ⁿᵈ tenor), Nicolai Shutorev (comic tenor), Arthur Atkins (bass) and Jack Cathcart (piano).[457]

Collin's group began their tour in Scandinavia, where the comic tenor, Shutorev, died suddenly in September 1948. Collin urgently asked Frohman to come to Oslo to replace Shutorev for the remainder of the tour. Harry accepted – he had no steady employment and the real estate office he had tried to establish in Switzerland had not been doing well, so he closed the office down immediately and took the next flight to Oslo.

Harry found the group "lacking the discipline and willingness to rehearse [in the way] that he had expected and was used to from the previous groups." Of his first performance with them, in Slagelse, Denmark, he said: "I hadn't been on a stage for eight years. The unfamiliar sensation, new colleagues, a new repertoire, newly learned, insecurity – all of this came upon me like a burdensome lid that lowered itself upon all of us, suddenly, nearly depressing. I had lost my confidence, and this spark got hold of my colleagues. They stood there like a block of cement. Their singing and movements were wooden and the first song came to the end. Clap! Clap! Clap! A cold atmosphere down there. Nobody dared to look at one another." As they began the second song, Harry felt he had to do something, so he improvised by imitating a clarinet. The ice was broken and the audience was theirs.[458]

The tour continued – on to Brussels and Paris and then The Hague and Rotterdam. By February, they had reached Switzerland, where they cut six sides on the Chant du Monde label, including "You And The Night And The Music" backed by "The Donkey Serenade."

The press reviews were positive. A February 2, 1949, review in the *Baseler Nachrichten* said: "The Comedian Harmonists are six stars, one at the piano and five singing. In their program, they sailed under the American flag this time, unlike before the war. But they sang the 'In einem kühlen Grunde' so authentically that the audience soon started their 'nationality research'…. We think the best of the Comedian Harmonists is their artful imitation of noises. The audience, happy about the comeback, literally tyrannized them with never-ending applause, and the six surely remained on the stage with dead vocal cords after the last curtain."[459]

Erich and Fernande, Santa Monica 1949

---

457 Cathcart's credits include being the music arranger for the 1954 film, *A Star Is Born*.

458 Czada, pp. 121, 123-124

459 Czada, p. 125

The American Group – Frohman at upper left and Collin at upper right.

The group was offered a contract to extend the tour, but they needed new material and so extensive rehearsals would be required. According to Erika von Späth, Frohman's companion during the last years of his life, the younger members did not have a good work ethic and were loath to rehearse. However, von Späth was not with the group during the tour and so could only have been repeating what Frohman told her later. Harry's disappointment was made worse by the fact that this group actually performed quite well when they wanted to. Frohman revoked his consent for the use of the "Comedian Harmonists" name and the group dissolved in March 1949.[460]

In 1955, Collin made a last desperate attempt to re-form a group with Fred Bixler (1st tenor), Bill Parsons (2nd tenor), Murray Pollack (tenor or baritone), Collin (baritone) and Bob Hunter (piano and arranging). Harry Frohman was to be the buffo.

There is some interesting correspondence between Collin and Frohman about the formation of this group. Collin wrote Frohman: "I would never consider restarting the C.H. without you. And that not only because of legal reasons, because I would like to have the founder of the group as member, but especially because of artistic reasons at hand. Therefore the buffo-spot – your old position you had for years with the old ensemble – is self-evidently reserved for you."[461] Harry talked about the type of music they would sing: "I would like to write the arrangements. It remains to be considered,

---

460   Fechner book, p. 353
461   Letter, Collin to Frohman, June 8, 1954. (All of the Frohman-Collin correspondence from the 1950s is courtesy of Marc Alexander and Pamela Rosen.)

besides the already mentioned thoughts, whether we want to sell hits that we made 19 years ago as still 'new.' Can we do this in the 20th century, if you do not make a new version with a more modern direction? But why not something new?" Frohman also wanted to perform a solo act on the same bill as the group: "When I start performing my one-man act and am still a member of the group, I should have 2/7 of the income, because the price will be higher due to this addition, and the performance time in nightclub shows would be longer by 8-12 minutes, not to talk about saving the group some repertoire – which is especially important in the beginning. And it should not be underestimated that this group would be the only one that would have such a unique enrichment connected to its name...."[462]

Money was an issue. Collin wanted Harry to write the arrangements for the group, but there was no money. Collin proposed that Harry would get 5 percent off the top of the group's fees until the arrangements were paid for. They expected to get $1500 per night and, at that rate, the arrangements would be paid off quickly.[463] Harry was all right with the delayed payment but did not want to start work on the arrangements unless he was sure that they would be used. This meant that Harry and Eric had to agree on the style of the new group. Harry wrote to Collin: "Eric – old boy, you still did not answer me to my question on the subject. Again you ask for scores of the old group's repertoire. If you want to make recordings why, for God's sake, not new material, because who would care for 'Gars de la marine'? – on records as on TV these days – unless I give the score a new twist and you sing it in English."[464]

Collin wanted to pass the group off as foreign – not American, perhaps French. Frohman urged caution, saying that the audience would quickly detect the American accents of the members other than Collin.[465] Collin wanted to call the group the American Harmonists while Harry preferred simply to call them the Harmonists.

At one point, Harry wrote suggesting that when he joined the group as comedian, Collin should step aside and just handle the management for the group. Harry believed that the new second tenor and baritone were both better options than Collin.[466] Both wanted Fritz Kramer to be the pianist, but Kramer was not available right away. Harry wanted to start with another pianist and then have Kramer step in later; Collin was not willing to consider this. There were problems with rehearsals, Collin worked a swing shift and the others had regular day jobs. Frohman wanted to travel to Los Angeles for rehearsals, but he had no money for lodging. Collin tried to find someone who would let Frohman stay at their home. Frohman also considered forming his own group in New York with Kramer and Mayreder.

---

462 Letter, Frohman to Collin, July 7, 1954.

463 Letter, Frohman to Collin, August 16, 1954. Collin was making $85 per week at the factory.

464 Letter, Collin to Frohman, August 19, 1954.

465 Letter, Frohman to Collin, August 25, 1954

466 Letter, Frohman to Collin, October 6, 1954

There were some rehearsals on the West Coast, without Harry. In the end, it did not matter. Harry wrote in March 1955, telling Collin to start without him.[467] With all the delays – Collin was trying to get top dollar from European agents and Bob Hunter, the pianist, was considering an offer from Freddie Martin, a leading U.S. band – and after a lot of work, they had to drop the idea; they never could manage to put the whole thing together.

Collin opened a small shop in Los Angeles where he made plastic items such as store-window decorations. He got by on that for a few years, but things began to look up in 1956 when he got a job at Northrop Corporation (now, Northrop Grumman) working on the assembly line. He worked in a shop at night to earn extra money and beginning in 1960 he and Fernande also received some compensation from the German government. Collin changed the spelling of his name to "Eric," dropping the "h" at the end.

Meanwhile, Collin's sister, Anne-Marie, was still in Australia where she worked as a teacher. Mimi, as her family called her, visited Eric in the U.S. over the long summer holiday at the end of 1960, and they celebrated a family reunion after 21 years.

Then, in April 1961, Eric went into the hospital for a routine appendectomy. Fernande said that he was not worried because so many people had appendectomies every day, but his heart stopped during the operation and he did not survive.[468]

Anne-Marie said, "He took life as it came. If something didn't run smoothly, he accepted it. He was devoted to Fernande; when she was there, everything was all right."[469] Cycowski added, "He was the complete opposite of Biberti ... he couldn't tell a lie. That was his nature."[470]

After all Collin had been through, when he settled in the U.S., he considered himself Jewish. His daughter, Suzanne, formally converted (which was necessary because Fernande

---

MY FAVORITE COMEDIAN HARMONISTS SONG

I like "Quand il pleut,"* because it is a song on which I can clearly hear my grandfather's voice, and it is in French, which connects it strongly to my mother and grandmother, and for its connection to jazz which placed them firmly in the international popular music of their time and made them completely unacceptable to the Nazis. And lastly because it speaks of separation which played such an important part in my grandparents' lives.

~Deborah Tint is Erich Collin's granddaughter. She is an artist living in New York.

* Recorded in 1933. This is the French version of "Ohne Dich" and both are translations of the great American song, "Stormy Weather."

---

467   Letter, Frohman to Collin, March 6, 1955
468   Fernande (Collin) Currie in Fechner film
469   Anne-Marie Collin in Fechner film
470   Cycowski in Fechner film

was not Jewish). Collin's grandson, Marc Alexander, is an attorney in Irvine, California, and his granddaughter, Deborah Tint, is an artist living in New York. Collin and Cycowski stayed in touch over the years. Suzanne died in 1994 and Fernande in 1995 in California.

Deborah and Marc, 1967

"Quand il Pleut"*
(When It Rains)

by Deborah Tint

I am writing this essay to provide information which is lacking from the record due to my grandfather Erich's not being alive at the time of Fechner's wonderful documentary and my grandmother Fernande's reticence during the making of it.

When Eberhard Fechner came to Los Angeles to make his documentary, "Six Lives," my grandmother, though delighted that the documentary was being made, was at the time remarried. Her second husband, who was fascinated by the production, attended the interviews whenever he could. My grandmother felt constrained by his presence and didn't want to hurt him by reminiscing about her exciting life with her first husband. So she said very little and Fechner, though very gracious, was frustrated and furious with her. She felt keenly that she had failed Erich in not speaking up and years later wrote Fechner a letter to explain herself, but I am afraid it was never sent.

I imagine because of this information vacuum, Vilsmaier, in his film *The Harmonists*, felt free to create a cartoonish character for Erich, and attach him for dramatic effect to a French whore. Though clearly this is not my grandmother it would have irritated her. My grandmother,

Fernande Holzamer, was born in Paris in 1909, the daughter of a German tailor who had ambitions to become a violinist, but not the money to study, and his French wife. The family, though preferring France, was required to move to Frankfurt after the First World War as Germans were not tolerated in France at that time. As a girl Fernande was interested in being a clothing designer and she was apprenticed in a dressmaker's shop in Frankfurt at the time she met my grandfather. She made many of her own clothes for herself and my mother with flair.

The characterization of Erich in the movie, though it supplies comic relief, bore no resemblance to the stories I heard of my grandfather growing up. My mother and grandmother spoke of him as a relaxed, playful, earthy, and cultured man, and in no way prissy. My mother Suzanne Collin wrote in a note to Fechner upon reading his book of the documentary: "I of course do not remember my father very well when he was young and 'a pretty boy,' as Leschnikoff says, but 'dumb' he never was. My father is the person with whom I had interminable conversations when I was a teenager about music, about religion and philosophy and politics. He gave me pleasure in those realities, and the habit of good conversation."

My grandmother's story of how they met: Fernande was at a nightclub which she characterized as "not crowded, dignified" and Erich asked her to dance. He then invited her to see him in concert the next day. She persuaded a friend to take her to the concert. Her friend was not enthusiastic about the show and wanted to leave early. After he drove her home she taxied back to the concert and met Erich. Some months later he wrote her a letter misaddressed to Fernande Holzauer. She was insulted and thought he had confused her with someone else. She said with her characteristic delicacy, "He was an entertainer, they had a reputation..." and she didn't answer his note. He wrote her one or two letters asking why she didn't respond - by now he had the correct name. A few months passed and he returned to Frankfurt on tour and called her. She explained why she didn't respond and he apologized for his mistake. In a short time they were married.

There is an interesting story my mother Suzanne told about the days leading up to the war. Roman Cycowski went to pick Suzanne up from day school where the children had been celebrating Purim, the festival that commemorates the deliverance of the Jews of ancient Persian from Haman's plot to annihilate them. Mom was riding on Roman's shoulders and on the way they passed a parade of brown shirts. Fresh from the pageant she had just participated in, my mom yelled, "Haman, Haman, rash, rash, rash!" Roman whisked her under his coat and fled.

This was the only reference I ever heard of to Judaism in her upbringing.

We know that Eric's younger sister Annemarie and her friend Landsie (Gertrude Landsberg) worked in a Jewish day school. We don't know if my mother attended and Annemarie taught there by inclination or because the government was driving children and teachers who were Jewish (i.e., "racially" Jewish per Nazi laws) out of the public schools and into Jewish schools.

In 1939, while on tour in Australia, Erich tried to get my mother and grandmother out of France, but their papers were delayed. By the time the papers came they were torpedoing boats of refugees. My grandmother said she would have gone if she had been alone but didn't want to risk it with Suzanne. When the Exode happened my mother and grandmother fled in a car with another couple to rendezvous with friends in the Pyrenees. Along the way they stopped in a small town. Nana went off to get provisions or gas. While she was gone something happened to make the couple panic and leave with my mother. They left a note that read, "Better to sacrifice one life than four." Nana managed to meet up with them at the next town. On their way they were stopped by the German advance and made to return to Paris.

All Parisians were required to register at the city hall. Fernande went in all innocence with her papers stating her married name as Fernande Abraham-Collin. The German officer took one look at her and said, "I have not seen you or your papers. You'd better go and divorce your husband immediately." She returned home, burned all the papers she had recording her marriage and decided to keep a low profile at a friend's boarding house. It was automatic at the time that a married woman took her husband's citizenship, but luckily it required some officiating action that she had been too lazy to do. They had arrived in France with "German" (Austrian) papers. Fernande declared herself stateless because everyone at the "pension de famille" where she was staying had done the same to disassociate themselves from the Germans. She had my mother baptized, put her in a catholic school, ceased speaking German and never spoke of my grandfather. My mother, who was eight years old, instinctually never asked. She did not know until the war was over that her father was Jewish.

During the occupation my grandmother's job was to stand in line for rations with her coupons for the household. They told me they ate mostly rutabagas and a fish called "chien de mer," and got a thorough hatred of both for the rest of their lives. Some time near the end of the war the Gestapo came to the boarding house asking for Fernande. By chance she was out and the owner said she had moved away leaving no address. They never came back.

For eight years my grandparents had no news of each other. In 1947 a family friend came to Paris, traced Fernande and put her in contact with Erich. My mother and grandmother arrived stateless to join Erich in the U.S. in 1947.

~Deborah Tint is Erich Collin's granddaughter. She is an artist living in New York.

* Recorded by the Comedian Harmonists in 1933. This song is known in the English-speaking world as "Stormy Weather."

Collin grave in Los Angeles

"Guter Mond, Du gehst so stille"* (Good Moon, You Go So Quietly)

A New Look At Collin
by Theo Niemeyer

The publishing of this book presents us with an opportunity to re-evaluate the role of Erich A. Collin, the second tenor of the Comedian Harmonists. Prior publications cast a rather pale light on him – a misleading impression – because Collin had a big influence on the development of the ensemble and its successor formations.

For this it is first necessary to correct a fact regarding his joining the group. Previously, he was considered the direct successor of Walter Nussbaum, who had been given notice of his termination from the group on February 28, 1929. But after that, there was a short intermezzo with a previously unknown member: In March 1929, Willi Steiner took over Nussbaum's position during a one-month guest tour at the Hansa-Theater in Hamburg. Steiner, just as with Bootz and Collin, had been a student at the Staatliche Hochschule für Musik in Berlin. But Steiner's engagement with the Comedian Harmonists ended in April, because his voice was not suitable for the group. The time for Collin to join the ensemble had come to take over the demanding position of the second tenor. But he also took over another position that so far has not been highlighted.

After the failure of a planned concert tour under the direction of a Berlin concert agency around the end of the year 1929/1930 and upon separating from the first manager of the group, Helmut Jaro Jaretzki in May of 1930, after only five months, the Comedian Harmonists made an agreement "to re-establish fruitful activities of the ensemble." The heart of the agreement was that they would carry on the business affairs on their own. Under the header "Business," it was determined that Biberti and Collin were entrusted with the business affairs, with Collin being in charge of all the administrative work. He therefore represented the Comedian Harmonists as manager, along with Biberti, a position that Collin certainly was able to fulfill because of his education. Internally the members maintained equal rights in financial and legal aspects.

Collin's role as a manager was primarily in the planning and execution of the many concert tours inside the country and abroad. His work can be seen in many letters to concert agencies, theaters, radio stations and movie companies, but also in answers to fan letters. He was responsible for the important salary negotiations in financially hard times, and also coordination with the record company, Electrola, on publicity in connection with concert appearances.

Relief from some of these tasks came in 1933 and lasted until autumn 1934 with the employment of Rudolf Fischer-Maretzki as secretary of the ensemble – the business affairs during the last months until the separation of the ensemble in March 1935 were again taken care of by Collin. He continued his administrative lead management without interruption with the Vienna group, and also with the American group.

I am happy to be able to share these mostly new research results with the fans of this group and to be able to recognize the considerable merits of Erich Collin for the Comedian Harmonists.

~ Theo Niemeyer lives outside of Hamburg, Germany. He has studied the Comedian Harmonists extensively and is the official Archivist for the Comedian Harmonists.

* Recorded by the Comedian Harmonists in 1933.

Erwin Bootz

Bootz' marriage to Ursula ended in divorce in 1938.[471] Both Cycowski and Marion Kiss said that Bootz did it for his career – because Ursula was Jewish. Bootz himself said that it was because he was too immature and that he was no longer in love with her. Bootz' widow, Mrs. Helli Bootz, disputes that the divorce had anything to do with Ursula's religion. Mrs. Bootz was also particularly distressed at how the Vilsmaier film, *The Harmonists*,

Erwin Bootz

Helli Bootz in 1957

portrayed Bootz' treatment of Ursula, saying, "That was so unlike him – it could not have been worse. For me that was a defamation of his likeable character. He always behaved courteously, especially towards women, and treated them with a lot of charm. Also, the couple had separated amicably at first – the trouble came later."[472]

For two years after Bootz left the Meistersextett, he worked for Willy Schaeffers at the Kabarett der Komiker. Writing shows for cabarets at that time was a tricky business: You still had to be clever and relevant, but take great care not to offend the government. Once the war started, Bootz left KaDeKo and went on tour. In 1940, he married his sweetheart from his teenage years, Ruth Sametzki, who, like Ursula, was the daughter of a sculptor. Bootz said of his second father-in-law, "He was a delightful man. A Nazi, but one of the sort who really believed and had personal integrity."[473] Bootz and Ruth had a son, Michael, in 1944, and a step-daughter of whom he was very fond.

Bootz was drafted into the German army in 1942 and had a difficult time at first. He would perform for his fellow soldiers in the evenings, doing parodies of army life. Someone noticed and assigned him to the Berlin Artists' Tour. He also toured with the Variety Troops. In the end, his stay in the army was a fairly easy one.

---

471 Ursula emigrated to the United States and married television writer Joel Hammil. She died on March 1, 2004 in Beverly Hills, California, at the age of 93.

472 Letter from Mrs. Helli Bootz to the author, September 27, 2007

473 Bootz in Fechner film

When the end of the war was near and they could hear the guns in the distance, Bootz and his colleagues began to burn all the papers. The officers urged them to fight and wanted Bootz to become a section leader. However, Bootz demurred: "I said I had asthma and thought a leader ought to be in front, not behind. The officer responded, "But you're an intelligent man." Bootz countered with, "That's why I advise you not to appoint me."[474] Finally, the soldiers were told that they could leave. Bootz removed his uniform and became a civilian again.

Almost immediately Bootz found work, or to be more accurate, it found him. An acquaintance told him about a cabaret in Zehlendorf[475] where they needed a "star." Bootz had no way to get there so the acquaintance picked him up every evening with his bike and took him to the cabaret performance.[476]

Bootz also worked again at KaDeKo and even assembled a female vocal octet called The Singing Stars.[477] After his divorce from his second wife, he spent ten years working as a dubbing author and director in Berlin and Hamburg for MGM and in Munich doing dubbing work as well.

In 1959, Bootz decided to go to Canada, probably to escape some tax liabilities. His sister was living there and she sponsored him. He ran into an unexpected problem when he learned that he could not get into the musicians' union until he had been in Canada for one year. So he became an insurance agent instead. When the year was up, he became a member of the union: The union man said, "So, you're now a professional musician.' I said, 'Thank you, but I've been one for some 30 years now.'" He became a bar pianist – it was an elegant bar, he was quick to point out, not a joint – and he made some appearances on radio and TV.[478]

On July 23, 1961, Bootz married a woman named Helli Gade, whom he had met before he emigrated.[479] They were introduced by a friend at an "open house" held by a Hamburg painter for others in the arts. She was 26 years younger than Bootz and a student at the Hamburg art school.[480] Bootz had told her that he would send for her when he was settled in, knew he could make a living in Canada and had an apartment – and he did.

MY FAVORITE COMEDIAN HARMONISTS SONG

What is my favorite Comedian Harmonists song is a bit difficult for me to answer – because I really don't have a favorite. But if I have to, then I would pick all those with a classical background – for example, 'Ungarischer Tanz Nr. 5,' 'Perpetuum Mobile,' 'Menuett' and the 'Barcarole' from *Tales of Hoffmann*.

~ *Mrs. Helli Bootz, widow of pianist, Erwin Bootz*

474 Bootz in Fechner film
475 A section of Berlin
476 Bootz in Fechner film
477 Czada, p. 135
478 Fechner book, p. 383-384
479 Mrs. Helli Bootz lives in Hamburg today
480 Interview with Helli Bootz, September 11, 2007.

Helli Bootz described their wedding day: "We had decided to get married when we were in Canada. It was a house wedding, so to speak, on a very small scale. We were sitting in the living room playing cards when suddenly Erwin jumped up and said, 'My God, we're getting married' and left the house. I thought, he's not coming back, he's scared. Five minutes before the ceremony he came running back with a bunch of roses. 'Come quickly, the pastor's waiting.' Then we drove to the church. Ten minutes later it was all over."[481]

The couple returned to Germany in 1971 and Bootz was hired by Peter Zadek[482] as musical director at the Bochumer Schauspielhaus.[483] The first production on which he worked was *Kleiner Mann, was nun?*[484] Ironically, the 1933 movie version of this story had included some scenes with the Comedian Harmonists that were removed because of the Jewish members in the group. Bootz continued working at various musical positions throughout his life, usually as a musical director, and died of a heart attack in Hamburg in 1982. He was the only one of the Comedian Harmonists to continue to work full-time in music. He also received some royalties from the reissues of the Comedian Harmonists recordings.

Helli Bootz said that he viewed his writing of music for the theater as his most significant work.[485] Bootz commented on his career, "If I do something well and the people like it, then I am happy just like a little kid. Then I would like to rejoice, 'Look, how beautiful.' I think the true sense of life is to bring happiness to others and love. People learn best when they laugh and are entertained – both together if possible. And I think I did that."[486]

Bootz grave in Hamburg

481   Helli Bootz in Fechner film
482   Zadek was born in Berlin in 1926. His family emigrated in 1933 to London. There, he worked in theater and eventually returned to Germany.
483   Bochum is a city of approximately 400,000 in North Rhine-Westphalia.
484   From Hans Fallada's 1932 novel.
485   Interview with Helli Bootz, September 11, 2007
486   Bootz in Fechner book, p. 386

Roman Cycowski

In 1941, when Cycowski heard from the Red Cross about his father's death in Poland, he decided to fulfill a promise he had made to his father and become a cantor. Roman and Mary rented a car and drove from New York to Los Angeles, where he had a cousin. Bizarrely, Roman took his savings from the Comedy Harmonists years and opened a night club with his cousin in Indio, near Palm Springs. Mary opposed the decision. Cycowski recalled his reaction when he finally saw his investment: "I felt sick to my stomach. The whole thing was made like a Hawaiian imitation, lots of bamboo and such things. There was a bar with a four-bar mixer and a big orchestra. My cousin thought I would like this because I am an artist. But he did it with my money. I risked my neck and lost."[487] Actually, the club started out reasonably well, but after Pearl Harbor business dropped precipitously, and Cycowski lost $40,000 in the venture. They sold the club and Roman considered himself lucky to escape without any debts. Soon thereafter, the bar became a great success due to the patronage of soldiers who were training in the area.

Then a bit of luck came Cycowski's way: He was offered the position of cantor at the Shaarei Tefila Congregation in Los Angeles. Roman had not been in a synagogue for 20 years, but as he said, "in my heart I always stayed religious."[488] Roman and Mary applied for immigrant status – they had already been in the U.S. for over two years – but were told that they had to leave the country and then return. They traveled to Portland and then Roman crossed into Canada where he had to stay just one day in order to qualify to return. Because Roman was Polish, Canada gave him no trouble, but Mary was German and they needed additional paperwork, which took three weeks. Finally, Mary was able to get into Canada, but on the return trip, while in the bathroom on the train, she was thrown against the wall and suffered a concussion. It took a while but eventually she recovered.

Cycowski lived an almost surreal existence. After experiencing great fame and fortune in Europe, he shifted into a comfortable middle-class American life; however, his thoughts were frequently with his family in Poland and his complete lack of knowledge about what had happened to them. Once the war ended, Roman learned that his entire family, with the exception of one sister, had been murdered in Auschwitz. There had been seven siblings.

Before the war, Cycowski would send his old suits to Poland for family members who wore the same size. Roman's sister learned about the fate of their brothers while sorting through some clothes at the factory to which she had been assigned. She recognized those suits and knew that her brothers were dead. After Auschwitz was liberated, she went to Paris and married, but died in 1966 when she was only 59 years old. Although Roman's work was very satisfying, the fate of his family devastated him: "I became very popular, just like during the time with the Comedian Harmonists. Every

---

487   Cycowski in Fechner book, p. 418
488   Cycowski in Fechner book, p. 75

Cantor Cycowski

child knew me. I was 'somebody.' On the other hand, I lost any ambitions for a long time. I asked myself: 'If what happened over there in Poland can happen, what is all of this good for?' For nothing! Of course, life goes on, one has to go on and serve God. But my family's fate destroyed me."[489]

Cycowski spent six years in Los Angeles, where in addition to his substantial duties as cantor, he opened a singing school in Hollywood for the training of singers and cantors. In 1947 he was offered a position as cantor at Temple Beth Israel in San Francisco (now Congregation Beth Israel-Judea). Both Mary and Roman were ready for a change. Beth Israel was the oldest temple in California and was quite large – seating 1600 congregants. Roman stayed there for the next 25 years and led a 40-voice choir: "I had a wonderful choir, 18 professional singers from the opera in San Francisco. I was not only the cantor but also a singer. I sang opera, jazz and conducted as well. I composed new pieces. I introduced a system of annual concerts in the temple."[490] Cycowski received many awards, and he and the rabbi at Beth Israel became great friends – more like brothers. Arthur S. Becker, a congregant at Beth Israel-Judea who knew Cycowski, said that Cycowski was a bit "stand-offish at first but mellowed over the years. . . He enjoyed being a cantor very much and at times would show off his voice from the bema (pulpit)." Over time, Becker became aware that Cycowski had been a member of a vocal group and was very proud of that, but it was not until the Vilsmaier film that people realized how famous Cycowski had been.[491]

In 1948, Roman declined to join the group organized by Collin, calling it, "a copy of a copy." He advised Collin to concentrate on providing for his family and not to pursue the new venture.[492]

After living in an apartment in San Francisco for three years, Roman and Mary built a house in San Rafael on the other side of the Golden Gate Bridge. In 1971, they retired to Palm Springs. For a while he commuted back to San Francisco to sing on holidays, but eventually he got bored.

489   Cycowski in Fechner book, pp. 423-424
490   Cycowski in Fechner film
491   Telephone interview, July 12, 2007
492   Cycowski in Fechner film

Roman and Mary in 1976

Fortuitously, Cycowski received a telephone call from a young rabbi at Temple Isaiah, a new congregation in Palm Springs. It was an ideal situation. The temple was open for only nine months a year, so Cycowski would have three months off. He said that the desert weather helped his voice, and besides working at Temple Isaiah, he gave voice lessons and taught German.

In 1977, the 50th anniversary of the Comedian Harmonists, Roman and Mary went to Berlin, where he had a reunion with Biberti. Roman and Bob also met with Erika von Späth in Bremen.

Eventually, he became the oldest practicing cantor in the U.S., singing into his 90s. He lived to see the renewed interest in the Comedian Harmonists and saw the Vilsmaier film shortly before his death on November 9, 1998, in Palm Springs – two months shy of his 98th birthday. His obituary appeared in both the *Los Angeles Times* and the *New York Times*. Mary, who had bravely converted to Judaism, contracted Alzheimer's in her 90s, and died in Palm Springs, in January 2006, at the age of 98.

Cycowski summed up his life after the Comedian Harmonists: "I feel that I've achieved something, not just drifted along. I'm proud that I left the group to become a cantor. It was a new life for me. My life started with music and I want it to end with music. I'm preparing myself for the other side. What will that be? If there's anything there, I'm ready to account for myself. And then, as one says, 'I'll take the medicine,' whatever I have coming. One has to be well prepared. I know I have not always been good in my life … I am only human. Everybody says, 'if I could live my life again, with what I know today, I would have lived differently.' I certainly would have done a lot differently – especially if I could have saved my family in time from Poland. Sometimes I did something bad, even unknowingly. Sometimes it is the temperament. One forgets oneself and loses one's head. My wife has worked with herself a lot during the last years and reminds me: 'Don't hate.' I also won't hate. Not even the people who are responsible for the misfortunes in this world. I think, if there is a God, an Almighty, He will take care of it."[493]

Cycowski grave in Palm Springs

493   Cycowski in Fechner film

"Ein Freund, ein guter Freund"*
(A Friend, A Good Friend)
by Robert Scherr

When I first heard Roman Cycowski sing, my head, heart and soul were set into motion. I heard a cantor unlike the voices I had known growing up. He was a powerful baritone voice, emotionally expressive, fully holding his own with a professional choir and large organ in a large sanctuary that held over one thousand people. Yet his interpretation was so sweet, accessible, and joyful. His physical appearance was elegant, standing regally at the pulpit, and finely dressed as he greeted congregants after the service. When I introduced myself to him as the protégé of his colleague, his warmth toward me was immediate and embracing. We soon began to meet regularly after services to share a cup of tea and enjoy a growing friendship, talking about synagogue music, my studies (I was a college student), and the tumultuous state of the world in the mid-1960's. Roman became my mentor and friend for over thirty years.

I was fascinated by his personal sweetness and complete joy in service to his synagogue and the Jewish people. Early in our friendship, Roman made vague references to a successful singing career in Europe, and how, following the murder of his father by the Nazis, and his emigration to the United States, he decided to return to his essential love and pursue life as a cantor. I was fascinated by this man who had every reason to be bitter about losses in his life, but who instead chose to bless God for being alive, and expressed that blessedness in his voice.

Roman was beloved by his congregation. The musical program of the service was always beautiful. The professional singers in choir were the finest voices available, creating an atmosphere of prayer in Congregation Beth Israel on the highest esthetic level. The children in his junior choir adored him. He never spoke down to children, but offered them grandfatherly encouragement, and a sense of pride in themselves. Students whom he prepared to become bar mitzvah and bat mitzvah were likewise devoted to him. He commissioned new music for the synagogue and gave concerts of Jewish music. He was revered by his cantorial and rabbinic colleagues not because he had been a renowned singing star, but rather because he was a pious and learned clergy leader in his community.

Roman was such a superb musician, instinctive as well as educated. He was a high baritone who could demonstrate a piece with high notes, but emphasized that the beauty is not in the high note, but in all that comes before and after. He taught me to look within a composition, again and again, to find new meanings and nuances. One could perform a liturgical—or classical— composition many times over and never repeat oneself. The voice always depends on technique. Trust your technique, he would say, then, whether you feel well or not, your voice always will be well.

Roman understood change, and never seemed to despair of living in a world that sometimes seemed to turn itself upside down. His wife, Mary, was likewise a force of spiritual imagination. They lived lives of simple elegance, comfortable in their home in Tiburon, or later in Palm Springs. Pleasures in life were offered by the bounty of their fruit trees, the warmth of the sun, the love of their cats, or the tasty food that Mary served with graceful elegance and love.

~Robert Scherr is a retired cantor who is now the Jewish Chaplain at Williams College in Massachusetts. He was a friend of the Cycowskis for over 30 years.

* Recorded by the Comedian Harmonists in 1930.

"Marie, Marie"*

by Carolyn Speerstra Harcourt

Mary's eyes glowed when she whispered, "Roman, that's Roman!" Music of the Comedian Harmonists was coming from the little blue CD player on a small table, the late afternoon desert sun streaming through the window behind her and flooding the photographs of an earlier life that lay before us on the dining table. Each time Roman's voice surfaced in the old recordings, Mary tenderly spoke his name.

It was a Sunday – February 18, 2001 to be exact – and I was with Mary Cycowski in her Palm Springs home on a quiet street in the shadow of the San Jacinto Mountains. Mary would celebrate her 94th birthday in a few weeks and although her memory faded quickly from moment to moment, it was clear she treasured the circle of photos and music that awakened her senses.

I brought the CD player as a gift for Mary, along with several Comedian Harmonist albums when we met that first time. She examined the compact discs and asked me what they were; it defied imagination that Roman's music recorded 70 years before this moment could somehow be connected to them! While the music played, we flipped through Mary and Roman's photo albums and scrapbooks together. She enjoyed naming each person in the pictures as her mind came alive; she spoke sometimes in German, sometimes in English. I regret that she was unable to elaborate on specific events, but it was delightful to watch her recall names of people from the past. My own mind was awash with wonder that I was helping Mary remember while sitting in Roman Cycowski's chair at their dining table.

The Cycowski home sat on a corner lot, a one-story 1950s white stucco with tile roof, desert palms and white rocks in the front yard, an immaculately-kept swimming pool and patio in the back. Inside, one could imagine it was 1975 and Roman had just stepped out for lunch; I could feel his presence all around. The walls and cabinets were adorned with many certificates and awards given to Cantor Josef Roman Cycowski, and several framed paintings by Mary were installed in the living room. Their furnishings were well worn and comfortable; one could feel that there had been some sweet and lovely and also sad times in this place together – it was a home with a heart.

I saw Mary several times in the years that followed our first visit. Each time, I brought her music and we looked at the same photographs together. Although I know she did not recall that we had met before, she always greeted me with a warm smile and a welcoming hug.

Mary's life was greatly enhanced and perhaps would not have been so long and healthy had it not been for the remarkable love and devotion of her caregiver, Margo Morgan. It was Margo who wrote to me regularly on Mary's behalf, and it was Margo who made my afternoons with Mary possible. It was Margo who understood how important it was for me to capture a few memories before they were gone forever, and it was Margo who assured that I was notified of Mary's death on January 18th, 2006, a few months short of her 99th birthday. I am deeply grateful for her kindness and generosity.

~ *Carolyn Speerstra Harcourt is a Comedian Harmonists enthusiast from Oregon who is the Archivist for a portion of the Cycowski papers.*

* Recorded by the Comedian Harmonists in 1931

Ari Leschnikoff

Clearly, the saddest of the post-war stories belongs to Ari Leschnikoff. Ari left the Meistersextett in 1939 and returned to Sofia because he had been mobilized into the Bulgarian army. Delphine and son Simeon went on ahead while Ari completed some performances with the Meistersextett. Using the money he had earned while with the Comedian Harmonists, Leschnikoff bought a four-story apartment building. His family lived on the second floor and leased out the other units.

Ari Leschnikoff

By 1942, Leschnikoff's position in the army was as adjutant to the commandant at the central station in Sofia. Ari related what happened on the morning of January 10, 1944: "I had the night shift at the train station. Suddenly there was an air-raid warning that lasted for several hours. In the morning around eight o' clock, some people came, saying that a lot of bombs had fallen in Wenelin Street, close to the Zoo. I tried to get there by car, but that did not work because everything there was broken. The telegraph poles had fallen down and electrical wiring was lying around. I ran like a madman until I reached our street. My God how it looked over there! A bomb had fallen on our house, from the fourth floor all the way to the ground floor, and had destroyed everything. The houses next to ours were on fire and I saw that my wife had wrapped our son and all the other kids in wet blankets, and had brought them to the basement and saved them. But we had lost everything, everything."[494] Ari had no insurance and was left penniless – this although he had some funds in Germany to which he was not able to gain access.

At first, Ari slept at the train station, while Delphine and Simeon lived with an ex-pat Englishwoman who was married to a Bulgarian. In March, Ari asked to be demobilized and the army complied. He worked as a freelance singer, and after the Russians began their occupation in September 1944, as an entertainer in the cultural department. Delphine, meanwhile, gave English lessons.

At this point we are confronted with different versions of what happened. The way Biberti told the story, Delphine's father died in 1947 and she and Simeon went to England for a one-month visit and never returned. Ari, devastated, later remarried. Leschnikoff's English granddaughter, Jessica, wrote that when Delphine and Simeon left Bulgaria, it was not for a funeral but because they were destitute. Bulgaria was then under strict Communist control and when Ari attempted to accompany them, the

---

494   Leschnikoff in Fechner book, p. 407-408

Ari arriving in Sofia in 1940

Leaflet for Mikrofon Records

Russian authorities would not allow him to leave.[495] According to the family, letters between Ari and Delphine talked about how to get Ari out of Bulgaria so that he could join his family in England. However, it was not Ari who got a "Dear John" letter, but Delphine, who was devastated to learn that Ari had had their marriage annulled and was married to someone else.

Given Biberti's difficulties with telling the truth, and the fact that the Leschnikoff family would have no reason to fabricate this story, we have to assume that the family's version is the correct one.

Delphine had a difficult time of it back in England. In most places, lodgings were not available to unwed mothers, and because people thought she was unmarried, Delphine was unable to find a place to live. Her family in England helped but she had to place Simeon in a hostel so that she could get a room. Simeon never saw his father again. Delphine died in 1999 after a difficult life, including the death of Simeon in 1994. Simeon and his wife, Ann, had two daughters – Nancy and Jessica, both involved in the arts.

For a while after the war Ari sang on the radio with a gypsy orchestra; they also gave Sunday concerts in cinemas in small towns. Leschnikoff had made some solo recordings, probably in Berlin in the mid-1930s, that were released in Bulgaria in the 1940s under the Orfej or Orpheus label. In 1939, a new record company was established in Sofia called Mikrofon or Microphone. Ari was listed as head of their musical department as evidenced by the leaflet shown here. It states that Leschnikoff is "the warranty for the high musical and manufacturing quality of Microphone records." It is likely that these recordings were also made in Berlin. There were about 110 releases on the two labels featuring Leschnikoff as a solo performer. A few attempts at singing with vocal groups in the 1950s went nowhere.[496]

Ari met Saschka Siderova, who was studying to be a kindergarten teacher. It was Ari's 48th birthday and a friend asked Saschka if she would like to meet Ari. Saschka went along and brought Leschnikoff a bunch of flowers. Ari was happy to get flowers from the young blond woman, saying "She was poor, just like me."[497] They married in 1952, and had a son, Anri, in 1958. Leschnikoff stopped singing: "The modern music really threw us old ones out and it was rough, very rough. Just like being killed."[498] Anri, whom Leschnikoff referred to as a "difficult boy," now works in the textile industry.

495   September 12, 2007, posting by Jessica Leschnikoff on http://www.comedian-harmonists.com/ (accessed September 15, 2007)

496   Thank you to Bernd Meyer-Rähnitz for this information.

497   Leschnikoff in Fechner film

498   Leschnikoff in Fechner film

In a sad, handwritten letter of August 16, 1957, Ari appealed to Biberti for financial help:

Dear Bobby,

17 years have passed since we saw each other last. Is that possible? It seems as if it was yesterday. You think so, too, Bob? Everything is like a dream – just pictures over pictures. As chorus members in the Grosses Schauspielhaus, then our ensemble, the Comedian Harmonists, the Meistersextett and so on and so on. Concert tours, a lot of money, the good life. It was just like a dream. But enough of sentimentality. I lost everything since I left Germany: my house because of bombs, Delphine divorced me, my mother died. And today, after 17 years, we cannot see or talk to each other; we can only write to each other. By coincidence I found the February edition of the magazine *Constanze*. It told a lot about the Comedian Harmonists. I cried when I read it. How nice everything was!

You probably have become a great photographer, because you used to work with the camera and the records a lot. Talking about records – mine have all been destroyed by bombs, nothing is left. Could you send me one or another? I would be particularly happy about the German folk songs, the 'Serenade' by Schubert and 'Die Liebe kommt, die Liebe geht' and of course 'Ein Lied geht um die Welt.'

I have also written to Electrola in London and would like to know what happened to the money for our royalties and what my part of that is. I am asking you in the name of your dead mother, if you know something, then let me know. Like me, you have always been honest with the money and the accounting. I also wrote many times to Radio Berlin and the Frankfurt recording company, but never got an answer. Otherwise I am doing okay. I am healthy and robust. How does the old saying go: If you feel well, you don't have to remember your age.

My voice is still good, what a pity I cannot be there to sing the high 'c' for you! I work as gardener for the parks of Sofia now, I have to keep the paths clean and so on. But the money is not enough. Please, Bob, can you help me? It is only a friend that one asks for help in time of need. There is still some of my money in Italy – can you send that to me? In dollars and via a bank? Or buy a nice new radio from that for me. My 'Koerting' [a radio brand] that you might remember, was destroyed by the bomb. And I still have a little bit with the Deutsche Bank at Savignyplatz. Please look at it and let me know what's going on. In 1939, shortly before the war, there were 2000 marks in that account.

And I am asking you for another favor: Can you get glasses for my frames? For the left eye +1.50/4 and for the right +0.50/3. I cannot get them here. Tell me all that happened in the past years, who is still alive and where everybody lives today. What about Erwin Bootz and your brother Pelle? Greetings to my Berlin and to all the friends and acquaintances we had. Lots of greetings and kisses from your very unhappy Ari

PS: I am impatiently waiting for your answer.[499]

---

499   Biberti Estate

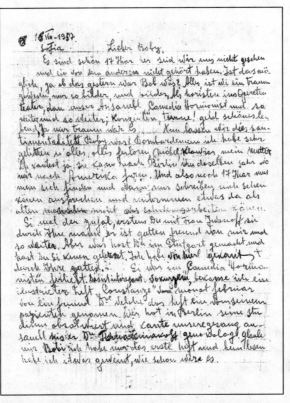

First page of the August 16, 1957, letter from Ari to Bob

Biberti said, "I would not have minded sending him a few hundred marks per month. He could have lived like a king with that in Sofia." Biberti's wife, Hilde, urged him to send money but he did not. Instead, Biberti, who was still holding a grudge from the Meistersextett days, did not respond. "[I]f what Ari did at the time had succeeded, I would not be alive today; I would have probably died in one of the concentration camps or would have ended up in a penal colony." Nor did Biberti send any records or glasses.[500] Two years later, Leschnikoff again wrote to Biberti and requested the transfer of royalties to him from Biberti as trustee of those royalties. Ari also asked for the settlement receipts that were due him from Electrola. He finally received the recordings he had requested, but not from Biberti – Electrola sent him some records.[501]

Several years later, with Leschnikoff still living in poverty, Biberti said (in a letter to Bootz of December 26, 1964): "Apparently he's not very well in Sofia and I could help him easily. But imagine that my wife Hilde would be a widow today living on income support if his dirty plan would have come true. That lets me be and stay firm."

---

500   Fechner book, p. 412
501   Biberti Estate

Saschka, Anri and Ari Leschnikoff

The extent of Biberti's enmity toward Leschnikoff can be seen in a document found in the Staatsbibliothek, undated, but clearly written after the breakup of the Meistersextett. In it, Biberti refers to Leschnikoff as being "completely uneducated" and having "notoriously limited comprehension." As for Leschnikoff's musical talents, Biberti said, "Leschnikoff did not have anything qualifying him for the work in this ensemble, which one day would become world famous, but a very small, but very nice voice. I was able to educate L., together with the former musical tutor and pianist of the group, Erwin Bootz, after long years of intensive work in order for L.'s heavy human and musical deficits not to have too much of an inhibiting effect on the artistic activities of the group."[502] Had Biberti somehow convinced himself of this?

Leschnikoff retired in 1962; because of his years in Germany, his pension was quite small. In 1965 in Sofia, he introduced himself to some German tourists. One of these tourists knew Hellmuth Näther, an educator who was a big fan of the Comedian Harmonists and a collector of their records. Näther contacted Leschnikoff and an invitation was issued in 1965 to visit several cities in what was then East Germany: "They arranged for special record-evenings in schools and theaters and many people came – sometimes 600 to 800 people. They played the old records. I told them stories and I was happy."[503]

In 1968, Leschnikoff again went to East Berlin on an invitation from Näther. There, in the Friedrichstadtpalast, where the Comedian Harmonists had appeared in 1928 when it was the Grosses Schauspielhaus, he was made an honorary member of the theater.

At about the same time, in connection with the dispute about the Electrola royalties, Biberti convinced Bootz and Dr. Grafe (the former Meistersextett Secretary), and Irene Hunold (a former Electrola representative) to testify that Leschnikoff owed Biberti sums for debts of

---

502   Biberti Estate
503   Leschnikoff in Fechner book p. 413

the ensemble, including amounts owed Electrola for advance payments that far exceeded any royalties that might be due. Biberti drafted the affidavits that he wanted them to sign, and they did.[504]

One positive result came out of the trip to East Germany: the publicity apparently helped Leschnikoff to get a better apartment and a slightly higher pension. In 1977, Bulgarian radio commemorated Ari's 80th birthday and he received an Art and Culture medal.

In his retirement, Leschnikoff's income consisted of his pension, a small amount of royalties from the sale of a few of his Bulgarian records and some financial assistance from people in Germany after the Fechner film appeared in 1976. Ari's wife earned a small salary as a kindergarten teacher. She died in 2003.

Leschnikoff said of his music career: "I sang for 40 years. I know I did not live in vain. Every man should love his profession. It is wonderful to sing, and that is why I was happy with my work. It was a big honor for me, wasn't it? Because I was able to give something to the people, no matter whether they were Germans, English, Bulgarians, French, Americans or what have you."[505]

On July 31, 1978, the German press agency received a telegram that read: "Today, on July 31 at 14 o'clock, the golden nightingale stopped singing forever. The knight of the high 'f', the famous former tenor of the Comedian Harmonists, Ari Leschnikoff, died at the age of 81 years. He remained a faithful friend of the hard-working, industrious music-loving German people until his last breath. In deepest pain." It was signed by his close friend, Georgi Dimitrov,[506] Leschnikoff died in extreme poverty. When asked by a German newspaper for his reaction to the death, Biberti, true to form, harkened back to his claim that Leschnikoff had reported him to the Gestapo and said that Leschnikoff had "disappeared secretly."[507]

In 2006, Comedian Harmonists enthusiast Jan Grübler arranged for an engraved photograph of the Comedian Harmonists to be placed on Ari's gravestone in Sofia. It was placed there by another enthusiast, Uwe Berger, together with Ari's son, Anri.

Ari Leschnikoff's gravestone in Sofia with the newly-placed photograph in the upper right-hand corner.

---

504 Biberti Estate, Statement of Irene Hunold, March 27, 1970.

505 Leschnikoff in Fechner film

506 Fechner book, p. 414

507 Biberti Estate, Newspaper clipping of August 23, 1978. The paper is not identified.

Robert Biberti

Biberti's apartment house in Berlin was hit by an air raid on October 20, 1940, and he received a medal for his actions in connection with the fire that resulted and the rescue efforts. After that, Biberti worked for the police and was assigned to the Berlin Air

Raid Warning Center, where his job was to receive reports of flights of enemy aircraft, plot them and then sound the appropriate air raid warning signal: "I felt very important. We pressed a button and the horrible sound started."[508]

In 1943, Biberti was drafted into the army and was fearful of being sent to the front: "This fear encouraged a great determination in me and a will to survive. You must make yourself so indispensable that they won't send you to the front."[509]

Robert Biberti

Because he had some knowledge of weaponry, he managed to get himself transferred to the Alexander Barracks in Spandau where he stayed for about one year. [510] Biberti said: "Although my pay book listed 'concert singer' as my profession, I was able to develop some ideas on the treatment of weapons. I even applied for a few patents. I enjoyed this very much because I was forced to attract attention to myself through my own achievements. The battalion commander suggested me as a member of the research and development team in Zoppot.[511] The laboratory was concerned with the remote control of rockets with the V1, V2 and tracking torpedoes, etc."[512]

Before leaving for Zoppot, Biberti married his longtime companion, Hilde. He said he got married so that Hilde would not have to spend her life as "Fräulein Longino," dependent on Social Security, if he did not return.

By February 1945, the Russians were advancing and Biberti and his colleagues left their lab behind and retreated toward Berlin: "We drove for two days and three nights over snow-covered roads to Berlin."[513] Once he reached Berlin he did something

---

508 Biberti in Fechner film

509 Biberti in Fechner film

510 Spandau is the westernmost borough of Berlin and is located at the confluence of the Havel and Spree rivers. After the war Spandau was part of the British Occupation Zone and Spandau Prison housed Nazi war criminals convicted at the Nuremberg trials. Rudolf Hess was the prison's last occupant; the prison was destroyed after he died in 1987.

511 A town in Eastern Pomerania, in northern Poland, on the southern coast of the Baltic Sea – called Sopot in Polish.

512 Biberti in Fechner film

513 Biberti in Fechner film

Biberti Wedding Announcement ("We Were Married Today")

that he later said he regretted: "The first thing I did was to get hold of a typewriter. I wrote a letter to the De-Nazification Commission (Entnazifizierungkommission) and denounced five people, including Leschnikoff and Fred Kassen, for behavior that was now punishable according to recently issued regulations. I must admit that it was pure revenge on my part."[514] Still, in a 1948 letter to Collin, Biberti claimed that in 1939, Leschnikoff's apartment was opulently decorated with Nazi symbols, a claim that has never been substantiated.[515]

Biberti found his apartment ruined. Most of the contents had been stolen – he believed, by his neighbors. His wife became ill, but he had to scrounge for the nourishment that she needed to recover, which was no easy task in early post-war Berlin. Some valuables that he had hidden in the basement were untouched, and he was able to trade those for the food he needed. He described himself as a kind of prehistoric animal that could survive solely on potato peels.[516]

The period from 1945 to 1948 was a difficult one. Biberti sold a pen with a gold tip to bring in food for a month, and he traded in the black market in order to survive. At night, he secretly collected wood from the flooring in abandoned houses and used it for fuel. Because they were able to heat at least one room, their apartment became a gathering place for friends seeking warmth: "It really was a strange time. The misery, the hunger and the cold created a feeling of togetherness among people, the likes of which I have never seen again. Later, when prosperity returned, everybody kept to themselves

---

514   Biberti in Fechner film
515   Email from Jan Grübler, August 11, 2007
516   Biberti in Fechner book p. 400

again." Berliners were being required to turn over a portion of their apartments to other families, but Biberti avoided this by bribing an official.[517]

Biberti set up his old workshop and began doing carpentry as well as precision machine work. As one who was classified as having suffered financially because of persecution by the Nazis, he received compensation based on his earnings during the successful years of the Comedian Harmonists. Other than that, his income was derived "bisschen dies und bisschen das" – a little bit of this and a little bit of that. He bought antiques, repaired them and sold them at a profit. He sold photographs from the Comedian Harmonists days. When his brother, Leopold, died in Switzerland, he left Biberti some money, which Biberti said was because he had done of lot of free work on Leopold's house. He was no longer a high liver. He re-soled his own shoes and did his own laundry. Later, a larger source of income was royalties from Comedian Harmonists records (LPs).

Biberti thought about trying to form a new group, but was deterred by food shortages and transportation difficulties.[518] In a 1960 letter, Imlau suggested that they try to put the Meistersextett back together again, even if only for an appearance on television; but Biberti was not interested, especially in working with Leschnikoff.[519]

In a 1957 letter to Biberti, Bootz said that he had heard of Biberti's financial difficulties. (Biberti was even trying to sell his grand piano to raise funds.) Bootz then chastised Biberti, saying that Biberti should have put his strength into resolving those difficulties rather than involving himself in various legal proceedings, "the profitability of which is very questionable." Bootz referred to Biberti's intention to leave Germany and points out the difficulties in doing that.[520] Biberti never did leave Germany, but, as we have seen, it was Bootz who emigrated – to Canada – several years later.

Biberti and his wife, Hilde, traveled extensively – all over the world. Hilde died in February 1968 at the age of 59: "I did not recover from that even up to today, and I never will. Now and again I still have these thoughts: 'You really are alone. Your wife is gone. The person with whom you lived for 34 years.' There is no replacement and there can never be one, even though I have friends, who are very nice and on my side. But this person 'Hilde' is irreplaceable to me. Sometimes, when I walk through my big place I think: 'God, if only she was here and would say, 'Bob, coffee's ready!'"[521]

He followed this with, "The best thing in my life was certainly my initiative with the Comedian Harmonists, when I tried to do everything possible to avoid a breakup and to maintain the thought of the collective, the human togetherness. I am convinced that this was my best deed."[522]

---

517   Biberti in Fechner book p. 401

518   Biberti in Fechner film

519   Email from Jan Grübler, August 11, 2007

520   Biberti Estate, letter dated February 9, 1957

521   Biberti in Fechner film

522   Biberti in Fechner film

Biberti spent the last years of his life in a Berlin apartment in an unassuming building on Schlüterstrasse.[523] He had a workshop and was able to occupy himself with his hobby – mechanics – and sometimes was able to earn some extra money that way. But he claimed that he had enough money on which to live and that it was unlikely he would "end up in the workhouse."[524]

He made appearances on radio and TV. Sebastian Claudius Semler, who maintains a Comedian Harmonists web site,[525] met Biberti in 1980, and described him as a very funny conversationalist and "a typical boy of the old Berlin."[526] Biberti's evenings were spent holding court at Diener's, a bar in Charlottenburg near his apartment that served as a meeting place for writers and actors. Decades after the breakup of the Meistersextett, Biberti was still using stationery that was headed: "Comedian Harmonists ('Meistersextett') – Leitung [manager]: Robert Biberti."[527] Amazingly, his listing in the Berlin telephone book used the words "Comedian Harmonists" beside his name right up until his death.[528]

Biberti's personal record collection naturally included many recordings by the Comedian Harmonists as well as songs by the Revellers, Paul Whiteman, Richard Tauber

Grave of Biberti and his wife in Berlin. The other person named on the stone, Ingeborg Bibert, was his cousin by marriage.

---

523 Biberti's apartment was, however, large and well-furnished.

524 Biberti in Fechner film

525 http://userpage.fu-berlin.de/~sese/Barbershop_Boys/ComedHrm/Comedian_Harmonists_Story.htm (accessed December 16, 2007)

526 Email of November 18, 2006

527 Documents in Biberti Estate (B 20, 37, for example)

528 Czada, p. 140

and more modern music such as the score to *My Fair Lady* and classical music as well – Beethoven, Schubert, Liszt, Tchaikovsky, etc.[529]

In 1973, the Senate of West Berlin wanted to reunite the Comedian Harmonists for the forty-fifth anniversary of the group. Biberti wrote to Cycowski suggesting that they agree, and that he would be willing to work with both Ari and Harry again. As Collin had died, Biberti proposed that Grunert take his place. He thought that they should sing only one song and suggested that the song be "Wochenend und Sonnenschein." The reunion never happened.[530]

Biberti died of kidney failure on November 2, 1985 in Berlin. He seems to have saved every scrap of paper on the Comedian Harmonists (and everything else) that he ever received, which was probably made easier because he lived in Berlin for most, if not all, of his life. His considerable collection of Comedian Harmonists memorabilia and information now mainly resides in the Staatsbibliothek (State Library) in East Berlin; the material has been scanned digitally and fills 20 CD-ROMs. The originals are contained in large file boxes and both can be viewed only with special permission.

Harry Frommermann

Harry Frohman

After the last concert of the Comedy Harmonists in 1940, Frommermann went to New York to try to form a new group. But problems kept cropping up and he never got that group off the ground. Erna and Harry were facing very difficult times financially: "My savings from the last Australian and American tours were coming to an end. I had to sustain my wife and myself the best I could by doing odd jobs in factories," said Frommermann.[531] Despite this, Erna continued to spend money as if they were still well-off. Cycowski sent him some money, which embarrassed Frommermann, but Roman said, "I've lost a lot in my life, but you're my friend. The time will come when you'll be able to pay me back." The couple also received some money from a Jewish relief organization.[532]

Frommermann asked Ernö Rapeé, a Hungarian-born conductor and film-score composer, whom he knew from filming at Ufa, for assistance. Rapeé was serving as the director at Radio City Music Hall in New York, and with his help, Harry put together a new

529   List found in the Biberti Estate
530   Email from Jan Grübler, August 11, 2007
531   Czada, p. 117
532   Cycowski in Fechner film

group. The new formation made its debut at a charity function at the Waldorf Astoria Hotel in New York in February 1943. They opened with the "Overture to the Barber of Seville" while the curtain was still down. The audience thought that it was an orchestra, and when the curtain went up and they saw only five singers and a pianist, they broke into applause.

However, despite that initial success, the group was unable to go further. Frommermann worked at various non-entertainment jobs – taxi driver, factory worker, etc. – without success, and then joined the U.S. Army in May 1943. Harry was not really suited for army life, and finally ended up in the entertainment section. He had applied for U.S. citizenship while in Hawaii and being in the Army was a way to expedite the process. On February 13, 1944, Frommermann became an American citizen. He also changed his last name to "Frohman."

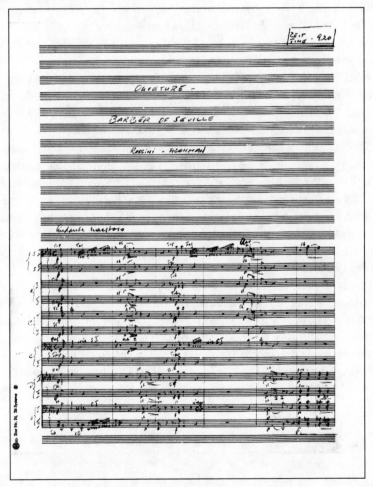

Frohman arrangement for Barber of Seville

Erna was left to fend for herself. She received a $50-per-month payment from the U.S. Army because of Harry's service, but her rent was $25 and that just for a room in a friend's apartment. Using borrowed money, she went to school to learn beauty care. The school was on 42d Street, and although she lived on 110th Street, Erna walked back and forth each day to save the subway fare. She had difficulty finding work and did not speak well of the American vocational education system: "When one leaves school here one isn't fit for any job." But eventually, at the end of 1943, she landed a hairdresser's job. The shop was owned by the man who would become her husband after she and Harry divorced several years later.[533]

When the war was over, Erna – who by then had changed her first name to "Marion" – still did not know whether her parents were alive. One day she received a letter from a British officer stationed in Hanover, Germany. Her parents had asked the officer to write (although she never found out how he got her address): "It was one of the happiest days in my life when I heard that they were both still alive, that the house was still standing – damaged, but standing."[534]

When Harry was discharged from the Army in August 1945, he was at loose ends. There was no money to form a new group. One evening, while visiting with friends, Harry and Marion met a soldier who was scheduled to go to Germany as a translator for the Nuremberg trials. The soldier was getting married and did not want to go. The next day, Harry took a test, qualified as a translator and was able to take the soldier's place. Harry did not work at the actual trials, but he was involved in the preparations.

In 1946, after the trials were over, Harry went to Berlin and was hired as a control officer for American radio in Germany called RIAS (Rundfunk im amerikanischen Sektor Berlin or Radio In The American Sector).[535] RIAS had begun broadcasting in early 1946 and, in September 1946, went on the air with a proper 800-watt transmitter.[536] RIAS employed mostly Germans, but was managed by American control officers, including Frohman.[537]

One day at RIAS, Harry ran into Biberti, who later said, "I was completely flabbergasted. I said, 'You're here, after all these years, in Berlin, and you didn't contact me?'" Harry said that he had meant to contact Biberti but had been too busy. Biberti claimed that the Manager of RIAS, Dr. Franz Wallner-Basté, was interested in hiring him. There was a meeting, which Frohman attended. The station director said that he wanted to hire Biberti; Biberti later said that Frohman started to praise him, but suddenly changed course and spoke out against the hiring, saying that Biberti was a "dictator." Biberti

533 Fechner book, p. 344

534 Kiss in Fechner film

535 After the war, Berlin (and also Germany itself) was divided into four sectors, each under the control of one of the victorious powers – American, British, Russian and French.

536 http://www.riasberlin.de/rias-post/rius-post-trans.html (accessed December 6, 2007)

537 The overall manager was Ruth Norden, who later became a translator and author.

Harry Frohman at RIAS (second from right). The woman is Ruth Norden.

did not get the job. Biberti seemed most upset by the fact that the RIAS job would have enabled him to get a top-priority ration card and perhaps a small car.[538]

While at RIAS, Frohman also met up with Fried Walter who had almost been selected to replace Bootz in the Comedian Harmonists when the pianist briefly left the group at the end of 1930. (Walter was the entertainment music manager at RIAS from 1947 to 1972.)[539]

Things got very political at RIAS. Some people thought that the American control officers, particularly Ruth Norden, were too left-wing and sympathetic to the Soviets. In early 1948, all of the American control officers left – including Frohman. They were not fired officially, but in effect they were fired. Their contracts had expired, but were it not for the political issues, would have been renewed.[540] Although the official reason given to Harry for the non-renewal of his contract was that he had been a citizen of the United States for only three years and in view of that could not properly represent the U. S. interests, he believed otherwise. In a letter to his wife he said, "I got the thing with my job ("Jew") confirmed by a strictly confidential party two weeks ago."[541] By this he meant that he had been told that his contract was not renewed because he was Jewish.

Harry then met a woman named Erika von Späth, who had missed her train connection in Hanover and was trying to get home to Bremen. Undaunted, she went out on

---

538   Biberti in Fechner book, p. 347-348

539   Czada, p. 118

540   Schivelbusch, Wolfgang. *In A Cold Crater: Cultural And Intellectual Life In Berlin*, 1945-1948. Berkeley and Los Angeles: University of California Press, 1998, pp. 118-121

541   Czada, p. 119

the highway to hitch a ride: "And finally comes this little BMW. I waved and I see, 'My God, it's an American license plate.' When he stopped I thought I'd rather not go with him. But he had already gotten out of his car and introduced himself in English. I had known the Comedian Harmonists since my early youth and loved them dearly, but Harry called himself 'Frohman' now and the name did not ring a bell to me."

"But I got into the car, because I had promised my father to be on time. We had to drive very slowly, because the engine had new pistons, and so we crawled over the highway to Bremen at 40 kilometers-per-hour." Von Späth's husband was missing in action on the Russian front and it had been years since she had received any news. Harry and Erika seemed to find each other at the right time and spent a few days together. At first, they spoke only in English, which Harry did without an accent. Von Späth then told Harry that they could speak in German. When Harry asked her how she knew he was German, she said it was because he had introduced himself so formally – something only a German would do.[542] After a few days together, Harry left for Switzerland, where he had a failed attempt at working in real estate. He sent von Späth one letter a few months after their meeting and then nothing else for years.

Then came a message, in the spring of 1948, from Erich Collin, who was touring in Europe with his new group. Harry had heard from Collin when the group was first being formed, but at that point Harry still had a good job with RIAS. Now things were different.

Marion (Erna) was still back in New York working as a hairdresser: "He could have sent for me. I would have liked nothing better than to go to Germany. But Harry always had some excuse. Then I learned he was living with someone else. I've forgotten her name."[543]

After the breakup of the 1948-49 group, Harry obtained a job in Rome with R.A.I. (Radio Audizioni Italiane), which was still privately owned at the time.[544] He headed up R.A.I.'s entertainment department which needed revitalization after the war. When Harry completed that task, the station offered him the opportunity to found a vocal group for the station. A dream come true? He found some singers and formed a sextet with two women (including a soprano from Canada) and four men, plus a pianist, and completed 54 new arrangements. They called themselves "Harry Frohman and his Harmonists – Sei Voci e un Piano."[545] Harry was particularly impressed with the alto (who, he said, "combined all the qualities of a jazz singer with a high musicality") and the tenor (whose "melting voice reminded [him] of Ari Leschnikoff").[546]

The group sang on the radio some 60 times, but they never recorded and no transcriptions of the broadcasts exist. Newspaper accounts referred to the "unusually

---

542 Erika von Späth in Fechner book, p. 349-350
543 Kiss in Fechner film
544 R.A.I. became publicly owned in 1954
545 Translated as "Six Voices And A Piano"
546 Fechner book, p. 354

Harry Frohman and his Harmonists

brilliant arrangements" and called them a "true vocal orchestra, with a colorful sound." The same reviews described Frohman as "a very gifted and talented 'music comedian,' who can transform his voice into the sound of a clarinet, a tuba, a horn or a drum, whatever is needed at the time. In short, he is the 'little crazy musical lad,' the goblin of the Harmonists, who contributes to their musical ballgame with his liveliness and extraordinary good taste."[547]

Harry could not have asked for better reviews. In a letter to Biberti, Harry said: "[We] had success and had offers for international tours, but we could not accept any contracts. One of my singers got engaged and I could not find a replacement soon enough, as the girl was very musical and I had to be ready with the repertoire prior to the start of the tour. Her fiancé did not want her to 'discover the world' prior to their wedding – was that a man with an inferiority complex!" The events gave Harry stomach ulcers, so he cancelled all his plans and disbanded the group.[548]

Frohman went to Lausanne, Switzerland in 1950 and tried to establish a business. When that failed, Marion sent him some money and he returned to New York in 1952 and lived in a rented room. Marion supported him while he looked for work. As a former soldier, Harry applied for and received a vocational grant. In January 1952, Marion and Harry formally divorced after 21 years of marriage, the last few years in name only. She remarried soon thereafter, becoming Marion Kiss and she died in New York in 1992.[549]

---

547   Czada, p. 127

548   Biberti Estate, letter dated May 13, 1951. The letter also mentions that Frohman had been in recent contact with Theodor Steiner.

549   The interview of Kiss for the Fechner documentary took place in the apartment of the widow of cellist Pablo Casals, Kiss's circumstances being such that her apartment was not suitable.

In 1955, Harry worked on an assembly line for a company that made parts for alarm systems. Erika von Späth described that period: "And sometimes he locked himself in the bathroom and cried, because he simply did not know how to go on. It was very difficult for him to be confined to such a dull work. He was very clumsy with his fingers and it happened that his fingers got stuck in a machine.... He often was sick during that time. But is that a surprise, if a person like him, who has always been working as an artist, is now forced to work in an assembly line?"[550] Harry was earning $60 per week.

Olga Wolff Frohman

Harry also worked in New York as a taxicab driver, a packer at the port, an assistant bookkeeper and a salesman for kitchen fixtures. He had continuing bouts with illness and unemployment. On February 25, 1956, he married a woman named Olga Wolff whom he had met only a few weeks earlier on New Year's Eve. The marriage lasted for four years.[551] After that, the letters between Erika von Späth and Harry became more frequent.

While still in New York, Frohman, after listening to a Harry James record, was inspired to do a recording of "Flight Of The Bumble Bee" (by Rimsky-Korsakov). Harry said: "I worked on something of my own in the USA, a one-man act: Harry Frohman, the one-man orchestra.... This vocal orchestra consists of one little man that imitates shyly, funnily over twenty voices, with himself synchronized on tape in order to have a background for the main melody. This he presents with a microphone and a tape recorder as the only partners in front of an audience while switching from one to the other instrument. So some kind of voice acrobatics. I made a test tape over there [in the U.S.] with machines of inferior quality in order to prove to myself that this was possible to be done by me physically.... I did twelve synchronizations on top of each other, then it was sent through an equalizer in a lab and copied and then copied again through an echo machine. The original tape is partly amazing in its sound, even though there were mistakes in my 'bum-bums' and 'toot-toots' and breathing. Eight hours pass in order to record a three-minute piece with twelve synchronizations. That would mean 84 hours for a program of forty minutes. What did I think I was doing?"[552]

---

550   Erika von Späth in Fechner film

551   Olga Wolff died in 1964 of leukemia. Czada p.131

552   Augustin, Michael and Walter Weber. CD, "This is Harry Frohman speaking." Bremen: Radio Bremen/DLF, 2004

Harry scraped together the money to buy the recording equipment, but he was never able to get a record company interested. By this time, rock and roll had come on the scene and the music world had changed completely. Portions of these experiments, however, can be heard in the Fechner documentary and are available on CD.

Harry was entitled to reparations from the German government and he returned to Germany to claim them at the urging of von Späth. He used an advance on the reparations to pay for his journey, and arrived in Bremen on August 2, 1962. He stayed in a house across the street from von Späth.

A letter written by Harry in January of 1963 to a friend in the U.S. is revealing as to his state of mind at the time,

> In this connection I want to say that it was by sheer luck in 1934 that I heard I was on the Black List of the Nazis also, and was able to leave Berlin over night.[553] Otherwise I would have been perhaps one of the 6 million Jews that have been slaughtered. So they say, God is full of vengeance – Eye for Eye and Tooth for Tooth. If this is really true then my being here is part of it because I make them pay for what I lost in health, in profession and in regards to economical damages!

Harry went on to speak about his stomach troubles, which he believed resulted from "the shocks I suffered when I was derooted by Nazi laws from my job, home and homeland…. I am the last one to excuse the common guilt of the German nation, and generally they try to make good as well as they can. Of course, this doesn't bring back the millions who died, true. But I ask you, would it help anyone to take 6 millions of Germans at random and have them killed in retaliation???" He also mentioned his second wife, Olga, and said that she wanted money but that his lawyer in New York had advised him to "let her wait – as our marriage was entered on a 50-50% basis.[554]

The reparations from the German government came through, and Biberti took the credit: "I succeeded in getting Harry a very high compensation … and a sufficient pension for the rest of his life." As usual, Cycowski saw things differently, saying that all Biberti had done was to provide an affidavit about Harry's former income, which Collin and Cycowski also did.[555] Czada believed that although Biberti did help Frohman with the compensation claim, Biberti "otherwise acted as much to his advantage as possible."[556] In fact, Biberti's affidavit did go beyond a simple statement of income. In connection with the banning by the RMK, Biberti said: "I am certain that Frohman was hit particularly hard by this message, because he was very sensitive and of delicate constitution. I remember him repeatedly not eating, because he constantly thought about the possible future disaster. I am certain that the mental pressures at that time are the reason for Mister Frohman's stomach problems." On the issue of income, Biberti wrote: "I took care of the main business matters of the ensemble and as a part of this task I

---

553   He left Berlin in early 1935 so he may have been confused over the dates.
554   Letter from Frohman to "Bernhard" dated January 17, 1963. Courtesy of Pamela Rosen.
555   Biberti and Cycowski in Fechner film
556   Czada, p.132

also paid the salaries to the individual members. I can therefore confirm that Mister Frohman received an average of RM 40,000 per year out of the income of the Comedian Harmonists."[557]

The disputes about who was the true founder of the Comedian Harmonists and the rights to royalties from recordings do not show Biberti in the best light. For some time Biberti had claimed that he was the *Gründer* or founder of the group, but history has clearly given that honor to Harry Frommermann. The first reprint recording issued listed Biberti as the founder, but after Harry objected, the listing was changed. In an April 4, 1974, letter to Electrola, Biberti, commenting on proposed liner notes for an LP that was about to be issued, pointed out that to call Frommermann the "actual founder of the ensemble" would lead to "very one-sided assumptions in the public eye" and that he did not agree with this "given the history of the foundation of the Comedian Harmonists." Biberti mentioned the "coincidence of goals" between Frommermann and himself and wanted Electrola to make it clear that he had assembled the singers.[558]

During the last years of Harry's life, he engaged in a spirited correspondence with Biberti about who founded the Comedian Harmonists. Biberti was now claiming that he was actually the "co-founder" of the group. A Biberti letter from September 1975 reads (in part):

Dear Harry!

You are of course entitled to your wish to tell the truth about the foundation of the Comedian Harmonists. Part of that is definitely that I have to be accepted as co-founder. I cannot be held responsible for having been named as founder in some publications. My claim to be accepted as co-founder results from facts, which you should really know. One cannot deny the fact that I heard the Revellers already in October 1926, long before you and I came to the very evident conclusion in terms of above-mentioned project. This and the cooperation resulting from your advertisement are a classical case of coincidence....

Who brought – and convinced – the singers, Harry, and who was responsible for the ensemble not breaking apart during the first months of 1928? By the way, your merits for the CH are undisputed. I especially think about your wonderful arrangements,

Yours, Bob

Harry responded, just weeks before he died:

Dear Bob!

Thanks for your answer, to which I would like to say: Don't you think that we old gentlemen should finally bury the battle axe? We would not find an end of the endless 'you did, I did etc.,' so I suggest that we agree to bury the sins of our youth, even if that rankles one or the other of us! . . .

We agree in principle that we want to honor the truth. That includes:

---

557   Biberti Estate, Biberti Affidavit dated October 1, 1962
558   Biberti Estate

The idea to do something like that was in the wind!

Nobody will or wants to deny that you had the same idea, but it was not you, but me, who put the idea into action. The initiative, the weathering through low times, the advertisement etc. – I did that.

As for the question to name you as co-founder:

I cannot agree to that as it does not conform to the facts. You brought Ari, Nussbaum and Roman into the ensemble. Nussbaum was later let go, Ari brought Erwin and Erwin brought Erich. They all could claim to be co-founders, which would not be true.

I however have always stressed your experience and your maturity as special merits – in whatever media – and that is why we selected you to be our official 'mouthpiece'…. But despite your initial help, I am still the founder, the so-called spiritus rector.

In this connection, you surely remember the first months of our rehearsals, during which I worked on the new style of tone emphasis, new to us and the others, which meant to sing the tones softly and to clearly articulate.

Even when Bootz – who was much more knowledgeable than I – took over the musical direction, the path and sound of the group already existed – at least as a skeleton. Bootz, too, who contributed a lot to the group, could call himself co-founder with some right, because he started to tighten the still shaky structure with his often genial accompaniment on the piano. But, however inexperienced in human, musical and business areas, the initiative of the basic style came from my side. I won't deviate from this, because it is a fact, dear Bob. In case you can agree on this basis – very well!

Yours, Harry.[559]

Harry also tried to exert some leverage on Biberti by threatening to revoke his permission to Fechner in connection with the then-planned documentary unless Biberti committed to the "true story of the founding of the Comedian Harmonists." Biberti agreed and kept his word even after Harry died in the interim.[560]

Biberti's comments in the Fechner film and book about his first meeting with Frommermann are revealing. Frommermann played an arrangement on the piano that he had written for the still-to-be-formed group. Biberti said: "It was extraordinary, totally away from all that we had known in this field so far. It had a possible sensation written all over it. And when Harry said, 'If you want, let us start something like this up together' – I was immediately willing to participate without payment."[561]

559   Comedian Harmonists Archive, Theo Niemeyer
560   Biberti Estate, Frohman letters of September 4 and October 13, 1975, to Biberti
561   Fechner book, p. 165

In fact, the December 29, 1927 letter from Frommermann and Steiner, which invites Biberti to appear for an audition, makes the point clear. The letter is signed from the "Melody Makers." A second letter, dated January 9, 1928, to Biberti requests his patience, telling him that they had still not found suitable tenors, while a third letter, dated January 12, 1928, tells Biberti that the first rehearsal will take place on Monday, January 16, 1928, at 3:00 p.m.[562]

Biberti's claim to be the founder seems to stem from several sources. At first, he said that he made the claim to make the Comedian Harmonists' existence more palatable to the Nazis – a group founded by an Aryan might be more acceptable than one started by a Jew. Second, Biberti did supply some of the other group members, either directly or indirectly, and third, Biberti had a fair-sized ego and did not always feel burdened by an obligation to be truthful. Cycowski said: "Bob possessed a certain authority, which none of us others had. He was a strong character, which was not always positive. And he was very egoistical."[563]

The *Constanze* magazine article from 1957 says that when Biberti first heard the Revelers in 1926, he wanted desperately to sing their music and was looking for a way to do that. It said that when Biberti went to Frommermann's apartment for his audition and Frommermann asked Biberti if he knew the Revelers, it hit Biberti like an "electric shock" and he said, "Revelers is my keyword! You do not have to explain anything anymore; I know everything."[564] Of course, the information was supplied by Biberti and the article is replete with stories that show Biberti to have been prescient, again and again, and greatly exaggerates his contributions.

Whatever the reasons for Biberti's claims, there is no doubt that Frommermann conceived the idea for the group and the type of music that they would sing. This is an important point because it was the unique style of the Comedian Harmonists that set them apart. Of course, the individual members were very talented, but that alone cannot explain their extreme popularity, both while they were performing and even today. Of all the vocal groups one could name, there are few that are so easily recognizable just from their sound.

For years, Biberti had been collecting 100 percent of the royalties for the re-issues of the Comedian Harmonists' recordings, even though he was entitled only to a one-sixth share. Electrola had been dealing with the issue for a while – it had been simmering since at least 1959. Biberti wrote a long letter to Electrola, in July 1959, explaining the entire situation (of course, from his perspective) and raising questions about the royalties on several reissues. Biberti complained that Leschnikoff had left him alone with the ensemble and large debts, but now "appears today, after 20 years,

---

562   Biberti Estate. The Fechner book, page 167, states that the first rehearsal was January 5, 1928, but that appears to be incorrect. Czada dates the first rehearsal at January 16, 1928.
563   Cycowski in Fechner book, p. 93
564   *Constanze* magazine, 1957

and suddenly claims his rights...." Biberti also challenged the basis for compensation and raised the issue of the Jewish members registering the Comedian Harmonists name in Paris (in 1935, just after the forced breakup). The reason for Biberti's mentioning this is not clear. He also said that he still had a friendship with Collin and Cycowski (no mention of Frohman) and did "not want to sacrifice these friendships without a pressing reason."[565]

Biberti's lawyers tried to deflect the situation: "If a world company such as Electrola, with a well-working office, can no longer differentiate between the various payments or royalty rights, how can Biberti do the same after all these years?... If Electrola, for whatever reason, can no longer comply with their duty of disclosure (this is also valid for HMV) and if it is mistaken regarding the question of distribution of royalties, then it is only their own fault. The opponents [the non-Aryans] should approach the party with whom they had made a legally valid agreement about their royalties."[566] At one point, in court papers, Biberti even denied receiving certain payments from Electrola but, as Frohman's lawyer said: "The only fact in question now is the fact that he has received money that he was not entitled to. The fact that Electrola did pay money is no longer debated. The defendant should give his clear statement to this." The documentary evidence was clear, and Biberti had to drop that position. Although Leschnikoff was not a party to this case, letters from his attorneys, demanding his share of the royalties, were cited as proof of Biberti's improper dealings. Biberti even accepted royalties from Electrola on recordings made by the Vienna group (in which he had no part) and then disputed his obligation to pay those over to the members of that group![567]

The disputes continued for many years – both in and out of court. On March 21, 1975, Electrola wrote to Biberti:

> However a new situation has come up, in that Mister Bootz now also asks us directly for his claim for remuneration for his part of the royalties. You repeatedly stated that Mister Bootz does not have any claims towards us, because you had already compensated him. The question of compensation for Mister Bootz forces us to re-think again. Please do help us with this, in order to find a clear solution in this case for the past and the future with and between all members.[568]

A May 1975, letter from Bootz to Electrola reads (in part):

> Your company has settled accounts with just Mister Biberti, because of later information given by him that all members of the Comedian Harmonists other than him have already been 'compensated,' and without Mister Biberti having to give any kind of lawful documentation to prove his claim. As I have already assured your Doctor Schorn verbally, there are no such proofs in this case, as no compensation of

565 Biberti Estate, letter dated July 24, 1959
566 Biberti Estate, letter dated August 12, 1969
567 Biberti Estate, paper filed by Frohman's lawyer in court, February 26, 1970
568 Biberti Estate

any kind existed in this case and Mister Biberti does not possess my authorization to collect compensation on my behalf. I therefore kindly ask you:

1. to ensure that my part of the royalties for the newly distributed titles of the Comedian Harmonists will be settled with myself,

2. to let me know the amount of the royalties so far paid to Mister Biberti without consideration of my part of them. I would like to stress that these payments are not binding to me....[569]

Biberti had written to Electrola to say that when Bootz left the Meistersextett, there was debt that Bootz owed and that Bootz had given up all his rights in the ensemble in exchange for the forgiveness of the debt.[570] But, as the above letter from Bootz shows, this was certainly not Bootz's position in the matter. Electrola finally resolved the situation by paying the other members what was owed them, but allowing Biberti to keep what he had already been paid.

Harry's relationship with Erika von Späth was a fortuitous one: It gave him some stability – something that had been lacking in his life for many years. He told Cycowski, "I thank God for every minute that I can spend with this woman."[571] When von Späth's father died in 1968, Harry moved into her house where she made an apartment for him on the second floor. The house is in the middle of a nicely kept street of row houses off a main road in Bremen, and von Späth's son, Eric, and his wife, Beate, still live there. Harry spent the last years of his life with von Späth, who comes across in the Fechner

Erika and Harry

569   Biberti Estate, letter dated May 28, 1975
570   Biberti Estate, letter of April 15, 1975, from Biberti to Electrola.
571   Cycowski in Fechner book, p. 360

film as a very nice and warm person. Her daughter-in-law described her as a "grand dame," an educated, polite woman who loved people.[572] Harry maintained some of his habits from his show-business days. He ate dinner at about 11:00 p.m. (in the old days that would have been after a performance) and went to bed at 2:00 a.m. He then got up at six and made breakfast for Erika and went back to bed. Eric von Späth referred to Harry as his "father" and said that he was a sensitive man who was very good to him.[573]

Harry began to work with instrument imitation again – on his own – using tape recorders. In November 1974, Cycowski, who was returning from a trip to Israel, stopped in Bremen expressly to see Harry. Roman said that they had a wonderful time together and that they talked about the past until one o'clock in the morning.[574]

In October, 1975, Harry and Erika spent two weeks at a health spa and returned to Bremen on a Saturday. Von Späth later recalled something that a priest said at a funeral she attended just after they returned: "the priest there prayed that the next person to die should have a merciful death. I never heard anybody say that....

I thought who knows who will be the next? And I went home and there is Harry in the kitchen making coffee. And I hugged him and said: 'Do you know that I love you more and more?' And Harry said, 'How lucky we are to have each other and to be leading a good life, that we get along so well, and that we have a roof over our heads. I think we have to be very thankful.'"[575]

The next evening, Tuesday, October 29, Harry was in his upstairs room, listening to a program on the radio from London about a Jewish writer. Von Späth said: "We had installed an intercom system in the house during the time that I had been very sick. And suddenly there was a call, 'Please come upstairs real quick.' I had already fallen asleep and did not know what time it was. I went upstairs. He sat in his chair in his pajamas and just repeated, 'No

The staircase in the von Späth house in 2007

---

572   Interview with Beate von Späth, May 12, 2007, Bremen, Germany
573   Interview, Eric von Späth, May 7, 2007
574   Cycowski in Fechner film
575   Erika von Späth in Fechner book, p. 361

air, no air.' I had forgotten my glasses and had to go downstairs to get them – without them I could not read the number of the doctor. Finally I called the doctor and she told me Harry should lie down and put a cold towel on his heart – she would come immediately. I did what she told me and went downstairs to unlock the door. When we both came back upstairs he already lay very still. I held him up a little and the doctor checked his blood pressure and made a worried face. He was already falling asleep and just told me, 'Be very calm.' And I said, 'I am very calm.' And that is how he fell asleep, without any pain."[576] Harry's death came just weeks before a scheduled interview with Eberhard Fechner for the documentary.

Eric von Späth described Frohman's state of mind about living in Germany: "He was scared that what happened in this country in 1933 would come back. That's why he kept a packed suitcase under his bed, for 14 years, so that he could get away from here at any time." Erika said, "[Harry] was a brave man; only rarely did I see him depressed. He was a disciplined man, finding peace within himself. He never complained. He covered everything up and really never showed his deepest emotions."[577] However, Cycowski summed it up: "Harry's life was bitter. The Comedian Harmonists caused him a lot of anguish."[578] Von Späth died in 1998.

Frommermann's arrangements still hold up as masterpieces – intricate, yet appearing simple. Biberti said: "Frommermann had something special and the records show that even today – he was very musical…. He made very good arrangements and worked very hard on them. How he learned that, I don't really know. He did not have an academic education, but his arrangements were – and still are today – excellent."[579]

Frohman grave in Bremen

576   Erika von Späth in Fechner film
577   Erika von Späth in Fechner book, p. 140
578   Cycowski in Fechner film
579   Biberti in Fechner book, p. 141

"So ist das Leben"* (Such is Life)

The Men Behind The Harmony:
Who Were The Comedian Harmonists?

by Pamela Rosen

As a group, the Comedian Harmonists sang in flawless harmony. When the music stopped, however, the Comedian Harmonists were a group of unique individuals whose personalities were as varied as their repertoire. Who these men were as people helped shape the group. But when their shared world started to fall apart, their group mentality also deteriorated. As "every man for himself" became the rule, the best and worst of who they were determined their fates as much as did the tides of history.

So who were the Comedian Harmonists? Besides being musicians, they all shared one common feature: they were all larger-than-life personalities. Ari Leschnikoff, the smallest member of the group, was toughened by his years spent in a Bulgarian military academy, on the front lines of the First World War and by rigorous vocal training. He grew up with a deeply religious Bulgarian Orthodox background. But his sense of honor and morality was highly dualistic. Though there is some evidence that he handled and dispatched injustices and social slights with swift severity, he is known to have been a womanizer, even after marriage. Yet he fought hard for monetary injustices he perceived among members of the Meistersextett, even though correction of those injustices would have left less money in his own pocket.

At the other end of the vocal scale, Robert Biberti represented everything that Ari wanted to achieve. From Ari's immigrant perspective, Bob Biberti, who lived with his mother in the fashionable Charlottenburg district of Berlin and always kept a house servant, represented success and wealth. In truth, the Bibertis were not wealthy at all. In contrast to the stark poverty that gripped Germany in the 1920s, the Biberti family put on a good show, but Bob's mother worked as a pianist in a cinema, and Bob worked on and off as a day laborer to supplement his earnings in the chorus of musicals. When the Biberti patriarch, Georg Biberti, died, he had long since been unable to sing and had supported his family by carving intricate wooden furniture piecework. Both Bob and his mother became very adept at scrimping, hiding money and looking far better off than they were. Bob later put this skill to practice when he took over the management of the Comedian Harmonists.

As the Comedian Harmonists grew richer, all of them flaunted their newfound wealth, but again, Ari had a dualistic nature about money. He was, according to Erna Frommermann, the richest of the Comedian Harmonists. But Ari was also frugal and saved a great deal, and there is no indication that Ari was ever dishonest about money. Ari's years of classical vocal training meant nothing to Biberti, who, in his bravado, felt his own singing was so good, training was unnecessary.

That is not to say that Biberti did not appreciate Ari's talents: it was, after all, Biberti who brought Ari into the Comedian Harmonists in the first place.

Social class also played a role in the dynamics inside the Comedian Harmonists. The two group members who grew up, pre WWI, in wealthier families, Erich Collin and Erwin Bootz, did not find themselves as surprised as the others when the Comedian Harmonists began to earn unprecedented sums of money.

Erich had been a forgetful, dreamy child with a tendency towards impulsivity. As an adult, his inattention became the stuff of legend. Though all the Harmonists remembered Erich fondly for his "absent-minded professor" tendencies – forgetfulness mixed with a strong intellectual curiosity – his widow Fernande remembered it with much less humor than did his friends.

In 1935, Erich made a trip to Paris while the rest of the emigrants escaped Germany, and quietly obtained a copyright for the name "Comedian Harmonists." This move may have been without the other group members' knowledge or consent. Back in Berlin, Bob Biberti's rage was unstoppable. Whether he got any support from pianist Erwin Bootz in this matter is unknown; however, Bootz always seemed to have even bigger fish to fry than being a member of a group.

It wasn't that Bootz was disinterested; in fact he and his lyricist partner Gerd Karlick produced some of the Comedian Harmonists' biggest hits. But Erwin had bigger dreams than being a member of a singing group. In spite of this, his contribution played an enormous role in the group's success, although the group played a lesser role in Erwin's life than it did in the others'. As Fechner noted, for Erwin Bootz, the Comedian Harmonists was just one episode.

When the Reichsmusikkammer made its ruling against the Comedian Harmonists, Erwin's response is the only one that was never recorded for posterity. However, in fairness to Bootz, who had always been sheltered from the realities of the world, first by his mother and then by the management of Biberti, he simply may not have recognized the seriousness of the situation.

As Bootz matured, so did his view on Biberti and the future of the Meistersextett. In the early years, however, Bootz did exert some power in the original group. As the Comedian Harmonists' only fully trained and qualified arranger, he jockeyed for position as the group's musical director with Harry Frommermann.

Frommermann, the founder of the original group, was a home-schooled musician, and was exceptionally gifted. In many respects he was years ahead of his time. This gift worked against Frommermann when he tried to apply the scores in his head to practical use. It is no wonder, then, that in the latter half of the twentieth century, Frommermann turned his interests to music recording and production: he had discovered that his talent lay beyond the technologies that were available in his youth. In the late 1920's and early '30s, however, the professional relationship between Frommermann and Bootz was a symbiotic one: Classically trained Bootz was able to clean up and shorten Frommermann's complicated and overly-long arrangements to fit the technical confines of a 78 r.p.m. record, and from him Frommermann improved his own style. But Bootz, opportunistic, and by his own admission, lazy and overindulged, allowed Frommermann only the less interesting arrangements.

Frommermann quickly found himself in second place, acutely aware that his homespun musical training did not compare with the formal education of his colleagues. He was in constant fear that the group would push him out altogether. This was not an unfounded paranoia – the fact is there was talk by some of trying to oust him early on. Frommermann responded by staying up nights churning out arrangement after arrangement, hoping that the group would find his value in sheer volume.

It is to our benefit that Frommermann overcompensated for his lack of professional training, a fact that Bootz was fond of pointing out. Frommermann arrangements made up the bulk of the Comedian Harmonists' catalogue; it was his drive and determination that gave the group birth; and it was he who made this drive so infectious that the group survived its rocky infancy. Biberti knew this, and he also realized that Harry Frommermann was the essential glue that held the group together.

Between the cultured educated group members, the displaced immigrants and the bullying prima donnas stood Roman Cycowski. The gifted baritone of the Comedian Harmonists was sharply intelligent, intuitive and street-smart. As with Erwin Bootz, being a Comedian Harmonist was a serious detour from his original intent in coming to Berlin; in fact, he was quite vocal about not caring for jazz music at all. He figured that any money he earned with the group could go to pay for his further training as an operatic baritone.

Cycowski shared a friendship with Ari Leschnikoff that went back to their days in the late '20s when they were in the chorus of a series of shows with producer Eric Charell, for whom they would eventually work again as featured players as Comedian Harmonists. Both Russian-speaking immigrants who had a love of discipline, education and classical music, the Eastern Orthodox Leschnikoff and the Hasidic Jew Cycowski understood each other well. Both of them endured the German xenophobia that was endemic to the difficult economic times.

Unlike Leschnikoff, who tried, but never could conform to German expectations, Cycowski was a master of it. Cycowski had spent his life in Poland assimilating with the Hasidic culture in which he grew up, but never completely connected with it, and assimilating into a musical, secular and decidedly non-Kosher world outside the protective walls of his village. So he was no stranger to learning how to fit in quickly.

Cycowski also felt a kinship with Harry Frommermann because Frommermann was the son of a Jewish cantor and trainer of cantors, and Cycowski was himself a trained cantor. Artistically they often butted heads because their musical tastes, humor and religious views were so different, but they had a deep respect for each other's convictions that lasted a lifetime. When the Nazis came to power, it was Cycowski who reminded Harry, who had ceased to be an observant Jew, what Roman's own father had advised him when he left Poland: *Remember who you are.*

However, Cycowski was just as hypnotized by the money and fame of being a Comedian Harmonist as the rest of them, and Cycowski enjoyed the privileges and suffered the pitfalls of great fame and fortune. Far from his provincial home and orthodox upbringing, "remembering who he was" was not easy for Cycowski, and his travels and experiences took him ever further from his deeply religious roots.

Publicly, each Comedian Harmonist spoke in only the most superlative terms about Roman Cycowski, but private letters between Harry and Erich expressed that they were sometimes frustrated by him. Erich Collin found him artistically difficult, stubborn and volatile, and later in life commented that he was glad that the years had "mellowed" Roman.

In the end, when the Reichsmusikkammer (RMK) revoked the right of Jewish performers to work, all of them, including the Protestant-raised Collin, chose to embrace the religion for which they were being persecuted. Cycowski, who responded to the RMK's decision with a renewed sense of pride in his own Judaism, had to have served as the inspiration for that kind of bravery and a religious reckoning for Frommermann and Collin that would last for the rest of their lives.

Cycowski outlived the rest of the Comedian Harmonists by thirteen years, and for many years, particularly in America, much of the group's history was told mainly through his perspective. Roman's point of view alone inspired the 1999 Broadway musical "Band in Berlin" about the group, and because Roman was the only one left alive to talk to writer/performer Barry Manilow for his own musical "Harmony," Roman emerges as the protagonist in the story.

But it was Roman who flew to Fernande Collin's side at Erich's untimely death, and Roman visited with Frommermann a year before Frommermann's death in 1975 and reunited with Bob Biberti in 1977. Cycowski never forgot who he was, even when the terror of the Holocaust caused each of them to act in their own interests – and part of who he was, was a Comedian Harmonist.

~ Pamela Rosen is a Comedian Harmonists enthusiast from California who has studied the group and Weimar-era German show business extensively.

*Recorded by the Comedian Harmonists in 1930.

The Comedian Harmonists have had an unusually enthusiastic following over the years. Here is the story of one German fan's journey:

"Ich bin so furchtbar glücklich"*
(I Am So Awfully Lucky)

by Uwe Berger

My name is Uwe Berger. I was born at the beginning of the Fifties – at a time when the Comedian Harmonists and their unforgettable songs were unfortunately not very popular. The people had more important things to worry about after the horrible Nazi regime and the devastating war. But, while visiting friends of the family in Berlin, at the age of six, I had an experience that was key in shaping my relationship to the Comedian Harmonists. It was there that, for the first time, I listened to original Schellack-records [78 rpm records] of many of the wonderfully sung melodies of the Comedian Harmonists.

From that day on, I became an avowed fan of this music. In the years to follow, my luck persisted, and I was able to meet three of the members in person. The first was in October 1975, while visiting a family member who was staying at a spa in Badenweiler, Germany. There I met the founder of the Comedian Harmonists, Harry Frohman (Frommermann) in the Hotel Ritter – just three weeks prior to Harry's death.

Then, during the semester vacation in 1976, at the Baltic seashore, I met Erwin Bootz and his wife, Helli, in the beautiful spa town, Groemitz. I am still good friends with his wife today.

In the year 1979, I met Roman Cycowski and his wife Mary while they were vacationing in Baden-Baden. Unfortunately I was not fully aware of the significance of this encounter at that time, maybe because I was too busy with my studies and my young family.

For the past seven years, I have been partly responsible for the largest world-wide Comedian Harmonists web site. I feel a duty to do anything I can to conserve this wonderful music for following generations. Because of that, some years back I visited the family of Ari Leschnikoff, the group's first tenor, in Sofia, Bulgaria. I even took an interpreter with me to overcome the language barrier. Ari's son, Anri, welcomed me very cordially, showed me many interesting places in Sofia and told me about the difficult life that his father Ari had under the Communist regime, until his death in 1978. On this visit I was once again reminded how important it is for people to live in peace and freedom, and how important it is to keep fighting for it.

I wish good luck to the author with this book and I wish you, dear reader, interesting and entertaining reading, as well as moments of silence during some parts of the story.

~ Uwe Berger is a Comedian Harmonists enthusiast who lives in the northwest of Germany.

*Appears only in the 1932 film, *Spione im Savoy-Hotel*

CHAPTER TEN

"Auf Wiederseh'n"

(Farewell)

"Too Good To Be Forgotten" [580]

N one of the Comedian Harmonists met with any great financial success after their breakup. Of the Aryans, Bootz and Biberti drifted along and kept some connection with the world of music – especially Bootz – while Leschnikoff led a life of desperate poverty.

Of the Jews, Frommermann also drifted. Collin led a stable but routine lower middle-class American life. Cycowski had the greatest success, becoming one of the foremost cantors in the United States. Neither Frommermann nor Cycowski had any children.

Bootz described the original group: "In my view, it was astonishing, that something like the Comedian Harmonists existed in the first place. If you consider who belonged: Ari Leschnikoff, a tenor with tremendous upper range, but who does not sing falsetto; then a second tenor, Erich Collin, who hardly had any individual timbre, but his voice mixed well with the others; Frommermann, a musical genius mixed with idealism, who in addition to his many nice arrangements, suddenly developed the ability to imitate musical instruments – even though he did not possess any particular vocal resources and who made sure all sounds were harmonious; Cycowski, this wonderful noble voice with enormous range, he could sing as high as a tenor; and finally Biberti, a velvety light, but harmonious bass. Add to all this the personal harmony of these six persons with each other, which was balanced to the extent that there was no danger of our ensemble simply falling apart, which would have meant the end of the career of such an ensemble. Had there not been an intervention from the outside, the group would have stayed together and would have made the people happy.... Even if I did not see it that way at the time, today, looking back, I think that we fulfilled a big task by bringing happiness to the people. I think it is the highest of all wisdoms, to bring happiness and love to the world. I think we did that, and that is why I am very happy to have been a part of it." [581]

Of the later groups in which they participated, the uncomplicated Leschnikoff said it best: "But it didn't sound the same." [582]

Each member viewed his time with the Comedian Harmonists differently. Bootz apparently saw it as just one step in his music career. Leschnikoff had no ongoing connection to that part of his life, but he looked back on it wistfully. Biberti "dined out" on

---

580   Interview with Roman Cycowski, *Musikwoche* magazine, March 23, 1998
581   Fechner book, p. 275
582   Leschnikoff in Fechner film

it for the rest of his life: he was a gregarious person, lived in Berlin and was dedicated to preserving the memory of the Comedian Harmonists. Collin rarely spoke about the group after he gave up on his efforts to form a new ensemble. Frommermann never gave up hope of getting back to the level of success and fame that they had achieved. Cycowski had such a fulfilling life after the group disbanded that he did not appear to give his old life much thought.

The Comedian Harmonists were not forgotten, at least not permanently. For a while they faded into obscurity, but the 1960s and 1970s saw a revival of their music. Beginning in 1974, many of their recordings were re-issued on LPs.

Then came the Fechner documentary, which was shown on German television in 1976 over two nights. The documentary was called, *Die Comedian Harmonists: Sechs Lebensläufe (The Comedian Harmonists: Six Life Stories)*. It is available on both video tape and DVD, but, unfortunately, only in European format (PAL) and only in German, without English subtitles. In my research for this book, it took a great deal of detective work to find what is likely the only copy of the film with English subtitles. And when I found that copy, it existed only in 16mm and was on four large reels of film.[583]

The Fechner documentary is an interesting work for people with varied interests: the Comedian Harmonists, Berlin cabaret culture, the Weimar period, vocal groups, how Nazi programs affected the arts, life in Germany after the war, etc. The film gives us the opportunity to see and hear extensive interviews with the then four surviving members (Collin and Frommermann had died), and spouses of the other two. Fechner followed up in 1988 with a book – with the same name as the film – that included the interviews that he had conducted for the film, including many parts that did not make it to the screen, as well as some "fictional dialogue." The book is in German and there is no English translation available.

In 1993, *Comedian Harmonists: Ein Vokalensemble erobert die Welt (Comedian Harmonists, A Vocal Group Conquers The World)*, a book by Peter Czada and Günter Grosse was released. There was a second edition in 1998. This book, also available only in German, is a basic biography of the Comedian Harmonists. Czada was the heir to Biberti's Estate relating to the Comedian Harmonists and also the owner of the Frohman and Bootz Comedian Harmonists documents.

A two-part musical about the group was staged in Berlin. The first part, performed in 1997, was called *Veronika, der Lenz ist da* after one of the Comedian Harmonists' most popular songs. The play, by Gottfried Greiffenhagen and Franz Wittenbrink and directed by Martin Woelffer, was extremely successful. Some have attributed this success to nostalgia;[584] a more likely explanation is that the group's story is compelling and

---

583 With special thanks to the people at the Goethe Institut in New York and Washington, D.C. for their help with this.

584 Meyer-Dinkgrafe, Daniel. *Boulevard Comedy Theatre in Germany*. Newcastle upon Tyne: Cambridge Scholars Press, 2005, p. 76

their music is great. Part two of the play, called *Now or Never* (one of the song titles of the Meistersextett), told the story of the disbanding of the group, and played in 2005 at the same theater.

In 1997, the Comedian Harmonists' music and their story traveled across the Atlantic when a play called *Harmony*, with music by Barry Manilow and book and lyrics by Bruce Sussman, was presented at the La Jolla Playhouse in California. There was talk of a New York staging, but it has not yet happened.

Many English-speakers were first exposed to the Comedian Harmonists through *The Harmonists*, a film directed by Joseph Vilsmaier and released in 1997. The film was tremendously successful in Germany and met with a fair amount of success in the U.S.[585] One writer said, "The immense conflicts between the Jewish and non-Jewish members of this group at the time of the Nazis' rise to power are smoothed down and polished for the sake of an idealized German-Jewish past."[586] Great dramatic license was taken in this film which includes several unpardonable inventions, the worst being a fictional love triangle among Frommermann, Biberti and Erna Eggstein. No such triangle ever existed and it is difficult to fathom why Vilsmaier found it necessary to fabricate drama and tension when dealing with a real-life story that provided more than enough of both. Bootz's widow was told at a reception in Berlin for the release of the movie, "This is a movie and it is supposed to entertain – it is not bound to the truth."[587] The film triggered another revival of the Comedian Harmonists' music and brought their story to many more people worldwide.

In 1998, the Comedian Harmonists posthumously received the German Echo award given each year by the Deutsche Phono-Akademie (an association of recording companies).

A multi-media presentation called *Band in Berlin* – with slides, puppets, film and live singing by the group Hudson Shad – played at the Helen Hayes Theatre in New York in 1999. The play was directed by Susan Feldman, who said that the music of the Comedian Harmonists is "intoxicating" and that once you heard them sing, "you really don't want to listen to anything else."[588]

There are several web sites dedicated to the Comedian Harmonists. Chief among them is: http://www.comedian-harmonists.com/. Another good one is: http://userpage. fu-berlin.de/~sese/Barbershop_Boys/ComedHrm/Comedian_Harmonists_Story.htm

A June 5, 2008, Google™ search of "Comedian Harmonists," with quotes around the name in order to narrow the search, resulted in over 300,000 hits!

---

585 German viewers made the film the most successful German film of 1998. See, Koepnick, Prof. Lutz. *The Dark Mirror, German Cinema Between Hitler And Hollywood*. Berkeley: University of California Press, 2002, p. 307

586 Stern, Frank. *Facing the Past. Representations of the Holocaust in German Cinema Since 1945*. Washington, D.C.: United States Holocaust Memorial Museum, Center For Advanced Holocaust Studies

587 Letter from Helli Bootz to the author, September 27, 2007

588 "A Musical 'Recapturing': The Comedian Harmonists is recreated for a new generation." The Foundation for Jewish Culture, http://www2.jewishculture.org/theater/theater_band.html (Accessed November 5, 2007)

Noted music critic Lester Bangs, in unpublished 1981 album-liner notes (the album was never issued) that eventually appeared in modified form in the *New York Times* in 1999, said of the Comedian Harmonists and their music:

Now, the more I listen to this record [the planned LP], the more I'm impressed by two qualities it has in abundance: one is soul, and nobody has to tell you how hard that is to find in *anything* new being put out these days: the other is that, near as I can tell, *this record does not fit into the territory*. It creates its own turf and holds it masterfully.

Bangs told potential listeners that he would guarantee them that they would "have a listening experience like unto you never previously suspected existed in this galaxy at least.... This music sounds like it was recorded in the ballrooms of Heaven."[589]

In all, a fair amount of attention for a group that was together for only seven years and disbanded in early 1935.

If you go on the Internet and look on web sites that sell music, there are only three pre-1935 popular music vocal groups whose work is available in any significant numbers: the Boswell Sisters, the Mills Brothers and the Comedian Harmonists. Pretty good company.

Irgendwo auf der Welt

"Irgendwo auf der Welt" (Somewhere In The World), a song recorded by the Comedian Harmonists in 1932, with music by Werner Richard Heymann and words by Robert Gilbert, expresses a sentiment that captures perfectly what the members – particularly the Jewish ones – must have felt as their world began to fall apart:

Somewhere in the world there is a little piece of happiness
And I dream of it every moment
Somewhere in the world
There is a little piece of salvation
And I have been dreaming of it for a long time
If I knew where that is
I would go out in the world,
Because for once I would love to
Be happy with all my heart
Somewhere in the world
My road to heaven begins.

How improbable was their story? In his 1999 *New York Times* review of the movie, *The Harmonists*, Peter Gay said that one scene in the movie was "as likely to happen as Hitler taking spiritual advice from a rabbi." Gay was writing about the scene where a performance in Stuttgart is interrupted by some hecklers. Some SS officers in front

---

589   Rockwell, John. *An Instant Fan's Inspired Notes: You Gotta Listen*. Previously unpublished liner notes on the Comedian Harmonists (written in 1981). *The New York Times*, September 5, 1999.

quiet the hecklers, and then invite the group to dinner – including the Jewish members. In fact, it actually happened. The movie combines two separate incidents and then over-dramatizes them a bit, but the scene in the movie is reasonably close to the truth. Gay had also cited the scene depicting the group's final German concert as being "improbable."[590] Again, it was mostly accurate.[591]

Biberti, Collin, Cycowski, Bootz, Leschnikoff and Frommermann

Auf Liebesleid folgt Liebesfreud [592]

There are two memorable scenes in the Fechner documentary where each of the four surviving members is listening to a recording of their music that some of them have not heard in many years. The first scene shows Leschnikoff – and then Biberti, Cycowski and Bootz – listening to "Gitarren spielt auf," recorded in December 1934. It is moving to see Leschnikoff and Cycowski, listening to this recording 40 years after it was made, sitting thousands of miles apart, and having an almost identical reaction – "schön" – beautiful. The second scene shows Bootz playing the piano and then, in turn, Leschnikoff, Cycowski and Biberti, listening to "Die Liebe kommt, die Liebe geht" (Love Comes, Love Goes) from 1933.

There is a line in the song, "auf Liebesleid folgt Liebesfreud": "From love's sorrow, follows love's joy." While not all of the Comedian Harmonists managed to achieve joy after the sorrow of their forced breakup, the music they created remains a source of delight for all of us – forever, forever.

---

590   Gay, Peter. *New York Times*, January 10, 1999
591   As stated before, fairly recent research has revealed that the Munich concert was not their last German appearance, but that is irrelevant to the point being made here.
592   "Liebesleid" was recorded by the Comedian Harmonists in 1933 on Electrola.

MY FAVORITE COMEDIAN HARMONISTS SONG

As I asked people to write a short paragraph about their favorite Comedian Harmonists song, I was invariably greeted with, "How can I pick just one? There are so many great ones!" Using my author's privilege, I will cheat a little and tell you some of the ones I considered. Of the up-tempo songs, I could have chosen "Mein lieber Schatz, bist Du aus Spanien?," "Schone Isabella aus Kastilien," "Schone Lisa," "So ein Kuss kommt von allein" or "Wie wär's mit Lissabon?" Of the slower numbers, I thought of "Night and Day," "Guter Mond, du gehst so stille," "Heut' Nacht hab ich geträumt von Dir" and "Schade, kleine Frau, ich hatte Dich geliebt." But finally I selected one of my earliest favorites, "Ein bisschen Leichtsinn kann nicht schaden" (A Little Foolishness Can't Hurt), recorded by the Comedian Harmonists on August 21, 1934. I like the way the opening builds and the understated way they show the joy inherent in the song. I liked it before I had any idea what the lyrics meant. You also get to hear a nice solo by Collin and another by Biberti. It's just one of those songs that makes you feel good when you hear it. And, after all, a little bit of foolishness can't hurt.

~ Douglas E. Friedman is the author of this book.

181

Appendix A

Comedian Harmonists Timeline
with contributions from Jan Grübler

1897 to 1924

July 16, 1897	Asparuch David Leschnikoff born – Haskovo, Bulgaria
August 26, 1899	Erich Abraham (Collin) born - Berlin
January 24, 1901	Josef Roman Cycowski born – Tuszyn, Poland
June 5, 1902	Robert Edgar Biberti born – Berlin
October 12, 1906	Harry Maxim Frommermann born – Berlin
June 30, 1907	Erwin Werner Wilhelm Bootz born – Stettin, Germany
1917	The Revelers begin, as the Shannon Four
1919	*Beginning of Weimar Republic*
1920	Cycowski leaves Poland for Germany
1922	Leschnikoff goes to Berlin to study
1923	*Hitler's failed Munich Beer Hall Putsch*
1924	Collin enrolls at the Hochschule für Musik
1924	Bootz goes to Berlin to study
1926	Cycowski goes to Berlin to study
January	Revelers have their first U.S. hit, "Dinah"
February	Peerless Quartet has its last hit

1927

	Biberti joins the chorus at the Grosses Schauspielhaus in Berlin
July	Paul Whiteman, together with the Rhythm Boys, hits the pop chart
December 18	Frommermann places ad in the *Berliner Lokal-Anzeiger*
December 29	Letter from Melody Makers (Frommermann/Theodor Steiner) to Biberti, inviting him to audition on January 3, 1928

1928

January 3	First audition (with Biberti) – Frommermann's apartment
January 16	First rehearsal – Frommermann's apartment
January	Victor Colani and Louis Kaliger rehearse with the group
January	Leschnikoff and Walter Nussbaum join group
May 10	First time for Melody Makers in studio – test recordings
May	Theodor Steiner leaves the Melody Makers
May	Cycowski joins the Melody Makers
May	Bootz joins the Melody Makers
	Failed audition at the Scala
August	Successful audition with Charell – Name change to Comedian Harmonists
August 18	First actual recordings for issuance – Odeon (now with Frommermann, Biberti, Leschnikoff, Nussbaum, Cycowski and Bootz)
September 1	Rehearsals begin for Charell Revue – *Casanova*
September 3	Debut in *Casanova* with a gala performance
October	Appear at the Kabarett der Komiker
October 22	Recording contract signed with Odeon

1929

February 28	Leave Charell
February	Appear in their first short film *Spanisches Intermezzo*
February 28	Walter Nussbaum leaves the Comedian Harmonists
March	Concerts in Hamburg (first ones outside of Berlin)
	Willi Steiner sings with the Comedian Harmonists
April	Collin joins the Comedian Harmonists
May	After rehearsals with Collin, begin performing again – also outside of Berlin – Cologne. Most famous photo of the group taken there by Biberti's brother, Leopold
May	Cycowski meets Mary Panzram in Cologne
June	Perform in Berlin at the Scala
July	Appear at the cabaret Der blaue Vogel
August	Revelers come to Berlin. The Comedian Harmonists and the Revelers meet at a cabaret and have singing "duel"
September 5	Appear in the revue *Zwei Krawatten* with Marlene Dietrich
October 22	Odeon cancels recording contract with the Comedian Harmonists
October 29	*Black Tuesday – The Great Depression begins*
October 31	Comedian Harmonists sign recording contract with Electrola
October	First radio appearance
November 11	First releases on Electrola (now with Frommermann, Biberti, Leschnikoff, Cycowski, Collin and Bootz)
Late 1929	Fred Colman-Jaretzki becomes first manager of the Comedian Harmonists

1930

	Collin meets Fernande Holzamer in Frankfurt
	Bootz meets Ursula Elkan in Frankfurt
	The subtitle "The German Revellers" disappears from the Comedian Harmonists name
January 20	Stettin – first concert on their own
January 26	Perform at the Leipziger Schauspielhaus in the revue *Tempo-Varieté* and get enthusiastic reception
April	Appear in first film, *Das Nachtgespenst von Berlin*
May	Revelers have last chart hit, "A Cottage For Sale"
June	Appear in film – *Die Drei von der Tankstelle*
July	Colman-Jaretzki is fired as Manager
August	Appear in film *Zwei Krawatten*
August 22	Record the classics "Veronika, der Lenz ist da," "Wochenend und Sonnenschein," "Ein Freund, ein guter Freund" and "Liebling, mein Herz läßt Dich grüßen" in a single day!
September 21	Last performance in a revue, *Wie werde ich reich und glücklich?* Frommermann's future wife, Erna also in the revue, listed as Erna Eggstein-Frommermann, even though they were not yet married
November 1-6	Concerts in Amsterdam. First outside of Germany.
December	Bootz leaves group. Replaced by Walter Joseph.
	Fried Walter auditions but is not hired.

1931

	Collin marries Fernande Holzamer
March	Attempt to oust Frommermann from group
April	Boswell Sisters first chart hit, "When I Take My Sugar to Tea"
May 12	Frommermann marries Marie Erna Eggstein

July	Walter Joseph leaves the Comedian Harmonists and Bootz returns
November	Mills Brothers first chart hit, "Tiger Rag"

1932

	Leschnikoff marries Delphine David
	Biberti meets Hilde Longino at Potsdam-Babelsberg Studio
January 21	First appearance at Berlin Philharmonic
March 31	Collin's daughter, Suzanne, is born

1933

	In this year, the Holocaust begins
	Bootz and Ursula Elkan are married
January 30	*Hitler becomes German Chancellor*
February 27	*Reichstag burned*
March	*Enabling Act passed giving Hitler dictatorial powers*
March 22	*First concentration camp opens at Dachau*
April 1	*One-day boycott of Jewish shops and businesses*
April 7	*Law For The Restoration Of The Professional Civil Service passed, barring Jews and political opponents from positions in the government and in universities*
April 11	*Decree issued defining non-Aryans*
June	CH hire Rudolph Fischer-Maretzki as their business manager
Fall/Winter	Tour Switzerland, France, Belgium, the Netherlands, Norway, Denmark and Luxemburg
September	*Reichskulturkammer and Reichsmusikkammer (RMK) established*
November	*Rule put into place that only RMK members can practice their music profession*
November 24	Second appearance at the Berlin Philharmonic – first as sole attraction
December 8	Comedian Harmonists apply for membership in RMK

1934

	Leschnikoff's son Simeon born
Spring	Radio stops broadcasting Comedian Harmonists songs – Comedian Harmonists are the last prominent Jewish artists still performing in Germany
March 13	Munich concert – previously thought to be the last one in Germany
March 16	Unofficial indication that applications by Jewish members for inclusion in the RMK have been denied
March 25	Last German concert, held in Hanover
April 4	Mediation between Aryan and Jewish members of the Comedian Harmonists
April	Concerts in Denmark and Norway
May 1	Expiration of permission from the RMK to perform concerts in Germany
May 8	Sail to U.S. on SS Europa
June 12	Concert on USS Saratoga in New York Harbor for the U.S. Navy
June 30	*Night of the Long Knives – Hitler and the SS purge the SA leadership*
August 2	*President von Hindenburg dies and Hitler becomes both President and Chancellor*
August	Comedian Harmonists return to Germany
September/October	Comedian Harmonists have engagement in Paris
November	Comedian Harmonists tour Italy

1935

January 23	Last Comedian Harmonists concert – Fredrikstad, Norway
February 22	Letter from RMK – Only Aryan members admitted
February 28	Secret last recordings by the group
March 3	Ad in *Berliner Lokal-Anzeiger* by Biberti
March 10	Frommermann to Vienna
March	Collin to Paris
April	Cycowski to Vienna
June 27	RMK gives Meistersextett informal permission to use Comedian Harmonists name along with Meistersextett name
July	Vienna group changes name to Comedy Harmonists and makes first recordings (Frommermann, Collin, Cycowski, Engel, Rexeis and Mayreder)
August	Fred Kassen joins the Meistersextett
Summer	Comedy Harmonists rehearse in Vienna
Summer	Janos Kerekes rehearses with Meistersextett as pianist and arranger. Walter Gorges rehearses with the Meistersextett
August 20	Meistersextett makes first test recording for Electrola (Biberti, Bootz, Leschnikoff, Kassen, Blanke and Sengeleitner)
August	Letter from RMK to Jewish members – denial of admittance to RMK
August	First Comedy Harmonists appearances (Geneva and in France)
September 10	First concerts of Meistersextett (Dresden)
September 15	*Enactment of the Nuremberg Laws*
September 29	Comedy Harmonists record in Paris with Josephine Baker
November	Comedy Harmonists appear in a revue in Vienna at Ronacher
November 21	RMK formally agrees to allow Meistersextett to refer to Comedian Harmonists in their name
Late 1935	Hans-Adolf Grafe becomes the Secretary of Meistersextett
December 26	Comedy Harmonists' first concert on their own (not in a revue) in Brünn, Czechoslovakia

1936

January/February	Comedy Harmonists in Scandinavia (Norway, Denmark and Sweden)
February	Comedy Harmonists record in Copenhagen for HMV
March	Comedy Harmonists in Italy, France and Netherlands,
March 7	*Germany invades the Rhineland*
April	Biberti files suit in Berlin against Frommermann, et al. over their use of the Comedian Harmonists name
April	Comedy Harmonists in Paris, London and Vienna
May	Comedy Harmonists begin tour of Russia. While there, sign contract with S. Hurok to appear in the U.S. in 1939
Summer	Changes in Meistersextett personnel. Zeno Costa sings with them for a short while. Herbert Imlau and Alfred Grunert join group, replacing Blanke and Sengeleitner
July 12	*First Gypsies sent to Dachau*
August 1-16	*Summer Olympics held in Berlin*
Late August	Comedy Harmonists sail from Russia to London
August/Fall	Comedy Harmonists in London, then Belgium, Holland, Luxemburg, Denmark, Norway, Sweden
October 25	*Hitler and Mussolini sign Axis agreement*
December	Both the Meistersextett and the Comedy Harmonists appear in The Hague at about the same time

1937

January – March	Comedy Harmonists in Netherlands, England, France, Austria, Czechoslovakia
April	Comedy Harmonists in Italy then Paris where Ernst Engel is fired and is replaced by Fritz Kramer. Cycowski and Mary are married in England
July	First Comedy Harmonists tour of Australia
November 8	Name Meistersextett temporarily forbidden by RMK
December 17	Electrola must purge catalog of old records by Comedian Harmonists because of Jewish members

1938

February	Comedy Harmonists tour of Italy interrupted because of new Aryan rules - *leggi antiebraiche*
March 12	*German Army crosses into Austria*
March 12	Comedy Harmonists' wives return to Vienna only to flee immediately to Zurich and then on to London
April 10	*Anschluss confirmed by plebiscite in Austria*
May 9	RMK rescinds directive that would have prohibited use of Meistersextett name. Comedy Harmonists tour South America. Bootz leaves Meistersextett. Rudolph Zeller replaces Bootz as pianist of the Meistersextett. Bootz and Ursula divorce
November 9	*Kristallnacht*
November	Comedy Harmonists perform at the London Coliseum

1939

January 4	Last recordings of the Comedy Harmonists – in London
February/March	US and Canadian tour for Comedy Harmonists
March	Meistersextett tour of Italy
April/May	South Africa stop for Comedy Harmonists
April – September	Dispute among members of Meistersextett over partnership for new members and lack of discipline in the group
April 29	Biberti files suit against Leschnikoff
May 3	Last recordings for Meistersextett (not issued)
May 23	Four members of Meistersextett sign letter of intent to sever relations with Biberti
May 23	Electrola declines to issue last two Meistersextett recordings
June	Comedy Harmonists begin second tour of Australia
September 1	*German troops invade Poland marking the beginning of WWII*
September 3	*Britain and France declare war on Germany*
September	Leschnikoff goes to Bulgaria – leaves Meistersextett
September	Biberti dissolves Meistersextett
December	Leschnikoff returns to Germany and lawsuit with Biberti

1940

January	Biberti drafted for Berlin civil air defense
February	Comedy Harmonists in Hawaii
February	Leschnikoff goes back to Bulgaria
March/April	Comedy Harmonists tour U.S.
April 30	*Jewish ghetto established in Lodz, Poland*
May 1	Last concert of the Comedy Harmonists – Richmond, Indiana
May 20	*Auschwitz concentration camp established near Oswiecim, Poland*
July	Biberti rebuilds Meistersextett (now with Biberti, Grunert, Hermann, Sachse-Steuernagel, Vosmendes and Taverne)

July 9	*London blitz begins*
Summer	Siegfried Muchow and Bruno Seidler-Winkler become arrangers for and lead rehearsals of Meistersextett
August 16	Bootz marries Ruth Sametzki (they divorce in 1945)
September 17	Letter from Goebbels' assistant postponing case against Biberti until "after the victory"
November 15	*Warsaw ghetto sealed off*

1941

January	Anton Krenn rehearses with the Meistersextett
January/February	Last appearances of the Meistersextett – Magdeburg and Schweinfurt, Germany
March	Günter Schroeder replaces Sachse-Steuernagel in the Meistersextett
June 22	*Germany invades Soviet Union*
Summer	Cycowski leaves Comedy Harmonists; later that year becomes cantor in Los Angeles. Comedy Harmonists disband
November 24	Meistersextett officially banned by RMK
December 7	*Japan attacks Pearl Harbor*
December 11	*Germany and Italy declare war on U.S.*

1942

	Bootz drafted into German army
January 20	*Nazis meet at the Wannsee Conference to discuss the "Final Solution"*

1943

January	Biberti drafted into German army
February	Frommermann group performs once at the Waldorf Astoria hotel in New York
May	Frommermann joins U.S. Army

1943-1944

	Bootz performance for German Troops Care; Biberti gets exempted from the Army and works as an assistant at technical laboratory in Zoppot

1944

	Bootz' son, Michael, is born
January 10	Leschnikoff's apartment house in Sofia is bombed
February	Frommermann becomes U.S. citizen; changes name to Frohman
June 6	*D-Day*
June 17	Biberti marries Hilde Longino
August 23	*Paris liberated*

1945

March	Biberti flees from Zoppot to Thuringia
May 8	*V-E Day*
September 2	*Japan surrenders*

1946

	Frohman works at Nuremberg trials
	Frohman joins RIAS

1947

Leschnikoff's wife and son return to England
Cycowski becomes cantor in San Francisco
Fernande and Suzanne come to U.S. from France

1948

Frohman leaves RIAS
Frohman meets Erika von Späth
Collin forms new Comedian Harmonists ("American Group")

September   Frohman joins American Group in Denmark

1949

February   American Group records in Switzerland
March   American Group disbands
Frohman joins R.A.I. and forms Italian group, "Harry Frohman and
his Harmonists – Sei Voci e un Piano"

1950

Frohman goes to Switzerland

1951

Court in Munich finds that Kassen was not a Nazi

1952

Frohman returns to NY
Erna (now Marion) and Frohman divorce
Leschnikoff has marriage to Delphine annulled and marries Saschka Siderova.

1955

Collin makes final attempt to re-form the group
Collin gets job at Northrop

1956

February 25   Frohman marries Olga Bertha Wolff

1957/1958

A series of three Extended Play recordings of the Comedian Harmonists
is published by Electrola called, Unvergänglich Unvergessen (Everlasting,
Unforgettable)

1958

Leschnikoff's son, Anri, is born

1959

Bootz goes to Canada

1960

Frohman and Olga divorce

1960s

April 29, 1961	Collin dies in Los Angeles
July 23, 1961	Bootz marries Helli Gade
August 1962	Frohman moves to Bremen and at first lives across the street from, and then with Erika von Späth
1964	First Comedian Harmonists LP is issued, *Liebling, mein Herz lässt Dich grüssen*
February 15, 1968	Biberti's wife Hilde dies
1968	Leschnikoff honored in East Berlin

1970s

	Start of revival of Comedian Harmonists' music
1971	Bootz and his wife return to Germany
1971	Cycowski and Mary move to Palm Springs
1974	The first in a series of five Comedian Harmonists double LP's is issued
November 1974	Cycowski and Frohman meet in Bremen
October 29, 1975	Frohman dies in Bremen
1976	Fechner documentary is aired on regional German TV
1977	Fechner documentary is aired on German TV nationwide
July 31, 1978	Leschnikoff dies in Sofia, Bulgaria

1980s

December 27, 1982	Bootz dies in Hamburg
November 2, 1985	Biberti dies in Berlin
1988	Fechner book is published

1990s

August 1992	Marion Kiss (Erna Frommermann) dies
1993	Czada book is published
December 17, 1994	Collin's daughter, Suzanne, dies
August 17, 1995	Fernande dies in Los Angeles
1997	Play *Veronika, der Lenz ist da* opens in Berlin
1997	Play *Harmony* is presented in La Jolla, California
1997	Vilsmaier movie opens in Germany
1997	Paperback edition of Fechner book is published
1998	Second edition of Czada book is published
August 1998	Erika von Späth dies
November 9, 1998	Cycowski dies in Palm Springs, California
1999	Vilsmaier film opens in U.S.
1999	Play *Band in Berlin* opens in New York
1999	Delphine dies in England

2000s

2003	Saschka Leschnikova dies
2004	Ursula Elkan-Hammil dies in California
2005	Play *Now or Never* opens in Berlin
January 18, 2006	Mary Cycowski dies in Palm Springs

Appendix B
Biographical Information

COMEDIAN HARMONISTS

Harry Maxim Frommermann/Frohman:

    Founder, buffo tenor, arranger. Born in Berlin on October 12, 1906.
    Jewish. Died in Bremen, Germany, on October 29, 1975.

    Married:
    Marie Erna Eggstein (1905-1992) – 1931; divorced – 1952
    Olga Bertha Wolff (1925 – 1964) – 1956, divorced – 1960
    Significant Other: Erika von Späth (1915-1998) – together 1961-1975
    No children.

Robert Edgar Biberti:

    Bass, manager. Born in Berlin on June 5, 1902. Not Jewish.
    Died in Berlin on November 2, 1985.

    Married:
    Hildegard ("Hilde") Liesbeth Longino (1907-1968) – 1944
    No children.

Asparuch "Ari" David Leschnikoff:

    First tenor. Born in Haskovo, Bulgaria on July 16, 1897. Not Jewish.
    Died in Sofia, Bulgaria on July 31, 1978.

    Married:
    Delphine David – (? – 1994). 1932-1947 (?).
    Son – Simeon
    Grandchildren – Jessica, Nancy

    Married:
    Saschka Andrejeva Siderova (1928-2003) – 1952
    Son – Anri

Josef Roman Cycowski:

    Baritone. Born in Tuszyn, Poland on January 24, 1901. Jewish.
    Died in Palm Springs, California, USA on November 9, 1998.

    Married:
    Maria/Mary Panzram (1907-2006) – 1937
    No children.

Erich Abraham-Collin:

    Second tenor, manager. Born in Berlin on August 26, 1899.
    Of Jewish heritage but not raised as a Jew. Died in Los Angeles,
    California USA on April 29, 1961.

    Married:
    Fernande Holzamer (later Currie) (1909-1995) – 1931
    Daughter – Suzanne (1932-1994)
    Grandchildren – Marc Alexander, Deborah Tint

Erwin Werner Wilhelm Bootz:
>   Pianist and musical director. Born in Stettin, Germany on June 30, 1907.
>   Not Jewish. Died in Hamburg, Germany on December 27, 1982.

>   Married:
>   Ursula Elkan (later Hammil) (1910-2004) – 1933; divorced – 1938
>   Married:
>   Ruth Sametzki (1910 - 1996?) – August 16, 1940; divorced – 1945
>   Son – Michael 1944
>   Married:
>   Helli Gade (1933- __) 1961

OTHER MEMBERS

Theodor Steiner   He died in the early 1970s.

Walter Nussbaum

Walter Joseph

OTHERS

Willi Steiner

Victor Max Colani   Born in Zittau, Germany on October 30, 1895.
                                   Died in The Hague on November 25, 1957.

Louis Kaliger   Died in 1944.

COMEDY HARMONISTS

Ernst Engel   Born in Berlin on February 20, 1901. Died in Paris in 1958.

Fritz Kramer   Born in Vienna on November 12, 1904.
                                   Died in New York on February 14, 1988.

Rudolf Mayreder   Born in Mariazell, Austria on October 25, 1902. Died in St.
                                   Pölten, Austria on October 28, 1978.

Johann ("Hans") Rexeis   Born in Lannach, Austria on December 30, 1901.
                                   Died in Birkfeld, Austria on June 6, 1980.

                                   Married:
                                   Theresia Parfuhs (?? – 1983) 1923

MEISTERSEXTETT

Walter Blanke   Born in Hamburg Germany on April 18, 1902. Died - ?

Zeno Coste   Born May 30, 1907 in Ciacova, Romania.
                                   Stage name: Zeno Costa. Died -?

Alfred Fritz Grunert	Born in Güldendorf, Germany on October 21, 1900. Died in Hamburg on January 21, 1982.
Willy Hermann	Born in Rheinsberg on July 3, 1901. Died - ?
Herbert Imlau	Born in Deutsch Eylau on October 18, 1904. Died in Refrath on October 23, 1983
Friedrich ("Fred") Kassen	Born in Langendreer on August 7, 1903. Died in Köln on April 7, 1972.
Janos Kerekes	Born in Budapest in 1913.
Günter Schroeder	Born around 1908.
Richard Sengeleitner	Born in Fürth on July 18, 1903. Died in Berlin in July 1980.
Erwin Sachse-Steuernagel	Born in Frankfurt am Main in 1905.
Bernard Taverne	(Bernard Diamant) Born in Rotterdam on October 11, 1912. Died in Amsterdam on August 25, 1999.
Willy Vosmendes	Born in The Hague on September 23, 1894. Died - ?
Fried Walter	Born in Ottendorf-Okrilla on December 19, 1907. Died in Berlin on April 8, 1966.
Rudolf Zeller	Born in Gelsenkirchen on February 9, 1911. Died in Freiburg on March 11, 1940.

Appendix C

Complete Discography

Information courtesy of Andreas Schmauder
www.phonopassion.de

Song Title	Date Recorded	Group	Label*	Composers	Notes	English Translation
Ach wie ist's möglich dann	January 9, 1933	CH	EG-2724	Traditional	German folk song	Oh How It's Possible
Ach wie ist's möglich dann	November 26, 1936	MS	---	Traditional	German folk song. In "Volkslieder-Potpourri, Teil 1" (Folk Song Medley, Part I)	Oh How It's Possible
Ach wie ist's möglich dann	May 23, 1938	MS	EG-6487	Traditional	German folk song	Oh How It's Possible
Ah Maria Mari	November 13, 1931	CH	EG-2458	W: Vincenzo Rusco/M: Ernesto di Capua	In Italian	Ah Maria Mari
Ali Baba	October 28, 1933	CH	K-7093	W: E. Lecuona, A. Tabetc/M: R. Chamfleury, E. Leusner		
Allein kann man nicht glücklich sein	August 31, 1933	CH	EG-2847	W & /M: Willy Engel-Berger	In film *Das Lied vom Glück*	One Cannot Be Lucky Alone
Alles für Dich	October 26, 1934	CH	EG-3180	W: Ralph Maria Siegel/M: Harold M. Kirchstein		Everything For You
Als der Großvater die Großmutter nahm	January 22, 1929	CH	---	Traditional	In medley "Anno dazumal" Part I	When The Grandfather Married The Grandmother
Als wir jüngst in Regensburg waren	December 15, 1936	MS	---	M: Carl Robrecht	In medley "Studentenlieder," Part II	When We Were Recently In Regensburg
Am Brunnen vor dem Tore	February 13, 1935	CH	EG-3282	W: Wilhelm Müller/M: Franz Schubert		At The Well Before The Gate
Am Brunnen vor dem Tore	November 26, 1936	MS	---	W: Wilhelm Müller/M: Franz Schubert	In medley "Volkslieder-Potpourri" Part II	At The Well Before The Gate

Song Title	Date Recorded	Group	Label*	Composers	Notes	English Translation
Am Brunnen vor dem Tore	May 12, 1938	MS	EG-6684	W: Wilhelm Müller/M: Franz Schubert		At The Well Before The Gate
Amapola	November 23, 1938	MS	EG-6585	W: Joseph M. Lacalle/M: E. Lecuona		Amapola
Amusez-vous	October 4, 1934	CH	K-7341	W: A. Willemetz/M: Werner Richard Heymann	From the operetta *Florestan 1st, Prince Of Monaco*	Have Fun
An der schönen blauen Donau	September 26, 1933	CH	EG-2870	W: Erich Collin/M: Johann Strauss		At The Beautiful Blue Danube
An der schönen blauen Donau	May 5, 1938	MS	EG-6683	M: Johann Strauss		At The Beautiful Blue Danube
Anno dazumal Medley, Part I	January 22,1929	CH	O-2860	Traditional. A: Camillo Morena	Medley: "Als der Großvater die Großmutter nahm," "Komm in meine Liebeslaube," "Und dann schleich' ich still und leise" and "Schaukellied"	Years Ago (Part 1)
Anno dazumal Medley, Part II	January 22,1929	CH	O-2860	Traditional. A: Camillo Morena	Medley: "Siehst du wohl, da kimmt er," "Auf dem Baume da hängt 'ne Pflaume," "Wir brauchen keine Schwiegermama," Ha'm se nicht den kleinen Cohn jeseh'n?" and "Halleluja"	Years Ago (Part 2)
Argentinisches Intermezzo	October 12, 1937	MS	EG-6206	W & M: Fred Kassen		Argentine Intermezzo
Armes kleines Mädel vom Chor	December 16, 1929	CH	---	Traditional	In medley "Hallo 1930" Part I	Poor Little Girl Of The Choir
Au revoir, bon voyage	November 9, 1934	CH	K-7433	W: Louis Poterat/M: Bert Reisfeld, Rolf Marbot	German: "Lebe wohl, gute Reise"	Goodbye, Good Trip
Auch ein Liebeslied	November 4, 1937	MS	EG-6143	M: H. Brasch		Also A Love Song
Auf dem Baume da hängt 'ne Pflaume	January 22,1929	CH	---		In medley "Anno dazumal," Part II	The Plum Hangs On The Tree

Song Title	Date Recorded	Group	Label*	Composers	Notes	English Translation
Auf dem Heuboden	September 10, 1934	CH	EG-3132	W: Petermann/M: Emil Palm		In The Hayloft
Auf einem persischen Markt	December 9, 1936	VG	B-8575	M: Ketelby	Fr. - "Sur un Marché Persan," without lyrics	In A Persian Market
Auf einem persischen Markt	April 28, 1937	VG	K-7906	M: Ketelby	Fr. - "Sur un Marché Persan," without lyrics	In A Persian Market
Auf Wieder-sehen mein Fräulein, auf Wiedersehen mein Herr	February 5, 1936	VG	K-7676	W: Fritz Rotter/M: Nicholas Brodszky	Also: "Auf Wiederseh'n young lady." From film *Katharina die Letzte*	Goodbye Lady, Goodbye Sir
Auf Wieder-sehen, my Dear	September 6, 1932	CH	EG-2606	W: Charles Amberg/M: A. Hoffmann, G. Nelson, A. Goodhart, Milton Ager	Not their "goodbye" song. That was "Auf Wiederseh'n" by Spoliansky which was never recorded by the CH.	Goodbye My Dear
Ausgerechnet Donnerstag	December 17, 1928	CH	O-2745	W: Fritz Rotter/M: Walter Jurmann		Thursday Of All Days
Avec les pompiers	October 4, 1934	CH	K-7341	W: Charlys, Couvé/M: H. Himmel		With The Firemen
Baby	February 13, 1931	CH	EG-2238	W: Walter Mehring/M: Friedrich Hol-länder	From film *Das Lied vom Leben*. Piano, Walter Joseph	Baby
Baby, Du hast Dich verändert	February 21, 1929	CH	O-2870	W: Fritz Rotter/M: Harry Ralton	With Dajos Béla Orchestra	Baby, You Have Changed
Baby, hast Du kein Bubi	February 21, 1929	CH	---	A: Fred Ralph	In medley "Bitte recht freundlich," Part I	Baby, If You Have No Sweetie
Barber of Seville - Over-ture - Part I	November 14, 1936	VG	B-8582	M: Giacchino Rossini A: Harry From-mermann		Overture To The Barber Of Seville
Barber of Seville - Over-ture - Part II	November 14, 1936	VG	B-8582	M: Giacchino Rossini A: Harry From-mermann		Overture To The Barber Of Seville
Barber of Seville - Over-ture - Part I	April 26, 1937	VG	K-7925	M: Giacchino Rossini A: Harry From-mermann		Overture To The Barber Of Seville

195

Song Title	Date Recorded	Group	Label*	Composers	Notes	English Translation
Barber of Seville - Overture - Part II	April 26, 1937	VG	K-7925	M: Giacchino Rossini A: Harry Frommermann		Overture To The Barber Of Seville
Overtüre zu "Der Barbier von Sevilla" Part I	May 30. 1938	MS	EG-6430	M: Giacchino Rossini/A: Erwin Bootz		Overture To The Barber Of Seville
Overtüre zu "Der Barbier von Sevilla" Part II	May 30. 1938	MS	EG-6430	M: Giacchino Rossini/A: Erwin Bootz		Overture To The Barber Of Seville
Barcarole	February 28, 1935	CH	EG-3303	W: Barbier/M: Jaques Offenbach	From operetta *Hoffmanns Erzählungen*. One of the last two recordings of the Comedian Harmonists.	Barcarole
Bei der Feuerwehr	November 25, 1930	CH	EG-2149	W: Gerd Karlick, Erich Collin/M: Ernie Golden		At The Fire Brigade
Benjamin, ich hab' nichts anzuzieh'n	February 21, 1929	CH	---		In medley "Was Euch gefällt" Part I	Benjamin, I Have Nothing To Wear
Bier her	December 15, 1936	MS	---	W: Charles Amberg/M: Carl Robrecht	In medley "Studentenlieder" Part I	Beer Here
Bimbambulla	August 22, 1929	CH	O-11099	M: Karl M. May		
Bin kein Hauptmann, bin kein großes Tier	February 26, 1930	CH	EG-1807	W: Hans Szekely /M: Paul Abraham		I'm No Captain, I'm No Big Shot
Birch Tree, The	February 8, 1949	AG	CduM-S-29024		Russian folk song	
Bitte recht freundlich - Part I	February 21, 1929	CH	O-2861	A: Fred Ralph	Medley: "Wenn der weiße Flieder wieder blüht," "Ich will von der Lilli nichts wissen," "Baby, hast Du kein Bubi" and "Leila, heute Nacht muß ich Dich wiederseh'n"	Please Smile Nicely (Part 1)

Song Title	Date Recorded	Group	Label*	Composers	Notes	English Translation
Bitte recht freundlich - Part II	February 21, 1929	CH	O-2861	A: Fred Ralph	Medley: "Ich bin die Marie von der Haller-Revue," "Noch 'ne Lage Cognac her," "Ich hab' Ihnen viel zu sagen, sehr verehrte gnädige Frau" and "Eilali, eilali, eilala"	Please Smile Nicely (Part 2)
Blau	October 9, 1928	CH	---	A: Walter Kollo	In medley "Wir flüstern," Part II	Blue
Blume von Hawaii	August 14, 1931	CH	EG-2381	W: Alfred Grünwald, Fritz Löhner-Beda/M: Paul Abraham	From operetta *Die Blume von Hawaii*. With Lewis Ruth Orchestra.	Flower Of Hawaii
Blume von Hawaii	September 4, 1931	CH	---	W: Alfred Grünwald, Fritz Löhner-Beda/M: Paul Abraham	In medley "Blume von Hawaii," Part I	Flower Of Hawaii
Blume von Hawaii-Potpourri, Medley, Part I	September 4, 1931	CH	EH-723	W: Alfred Grünwald, Fritz Löhner-Beda/M: Paul Abraham	Medley from operetta *Die Blume von Hawaii* with "Blume von Hawaii" and "Du traumschöne Perle der Südsee." With Marek Weber Orchestra.	Flower Of Hawaii
Blume von Hawaii-Potpourri, Medley, Part II	September 4, 1931	CH	EH-723	W: Alfred Grünwald, Fritz Löhner-Beda/M: Paul Abraham	Medley from operetta *Die Blume von Hawaii* with "Wo es Mädels gibt, Kameraden" and "My golden baby." With Marek Weber Orchestra.	Flower Of Hawaii
Böhmische Musikanten	December 9, 1936	VG	X-4766	M: R. Pehm		Bohemian Musicians
Caspar Blume	January 1936	MS	T-2282	W: A. Limberg	Advertising record for a kitchen range from the company "Caspar Blume," also as a commercial spot	
Chiquita	May 13, 1929		O-11404	W: Fritz Rotter/M: L.W. Gilbert, Mabel Wayne	Also in short film *Der Durchschnittsmann*	
Congo Lullaby	June 18, 1937	VG	B-8602	W: A. Wimperis/M: Mischa Spoliansky	From movie, *Sanders Of The River*	

Song Title	Date Recorded	Group	Label*	Composers	Notes	English Translation
Continental	July 19, 1935	VG	K-7584	W: Marcel Silver/M: Con Conrad	From the film *Joyeuse Divorcée*. This is the first release of the Comedy Harmonists.	
Creole Love Call	September 15, 1933 (Berlin). October 28, 1933 (Paris)	CH	EG-2929	M: Duke Ellington, Bubber Miley, Rudy Jackson	Also in a private film of the Comedy Harmonists from 1938	
Czardas	November 2, 1936	MS	EG-998	M: Franz Lehar	Hungarian folk dances	
D'Ajaccio a Bonifacio	November 14, 1935 (?)/April 7, 1936	VG	K-7602	W: Jean Rodor, R. Chamfleury (?) /M: Roger Dumas, Henry Himmel (?)	"Corsican Boatsong"	From Ajaccio To Bonifacio
Das alte Spinnrad	May 5, 1934	CH	EG-3047	W: Franz L. Berthold /M: Billie Hill		The Old Spinning Wheel
Das Heidenröslein	May 23, 1938	MS	EG-6509		See, "Heidenröslein"	The Heath Rose
Das ist die Liebe der Matrosen	August 14, 1931	CH	EG-2382	W: Robert Gilbert/M: Werner Richard Heymann,	Engl. "The Way With Every Sailor" Fr. "Les gars de la marine." From film *Bomben auf Monte Carlo* (*Monte Carlo Madness*) (*Le Capitaine Craddock*)	This Is The Love Of The Sailors
Das Lieben bringt groß' Freud	November 26, 1936	MS	---	Traditional	German folk song, in medley "Volkslieder-Potpourri" Part II	Love Brings Great Joy
Das Lieben bringt groß' Freud	September 22, 1937	MS	EG-6103	Traditional	German folk song	Love Brings Great Joy
Das Lied der Liebe	October 9, 1928	Ch	---	A: Walter Kollo	In medley "Wir flüstern" Part I	The Song Of Love
Das Wirtshaus an der Lahn	October 3, 1933	CH	EG-2875	W: Comedian Harmonists/M: Carl Robrecht	Also called, "Es steht ein Wirtshaus an der Lahn." The Lahn is a river in Germany.	The Pub At The Lahn
Das Wirtshaus an der Lahn	December 15, 1936	MS	---	M: Carl Robrecht	In medley "Studentenlieder-Potpourri" Part I. Also called "Es steht ein Wirtshaus an der Lahn."	The Pub At The Lahn

Song Title	Date Recorded	Group	Label*	Composers	Notes	English Translation
Denk an mich, oh Creola	February 21, 1929	CH	---	A: Walter Borchert	In medley "Was Euch gefällt" Part I	Think Of Me, Oh Creola
Der alte Cowboy	April 19, 1934	CH	EG-3038	W: E. Walter/M: Billie Hill	"The Last Roundup"	The Old Cowboy
Der kleine Finkenhahn	November 6, 1936	MS	EG-3806	W: Steidl, Hardt-Waren/M: Walter Kollo		The Small Finch
Der Onkel Bumba aus Kalumba tanzt nur Rumba	June 1, 1932	CH	EG-2554	W: Fritz Rotter, A. Robinson/M: Hermann Hupfeld		Uncle Bumba From Kalumba Dances Only The Rumba
Der Onkel Doktor hat gesagt	January 11, 1939	MS	EG-6590	W: Klaus S. Richter/M: Peter Igelhoff		The Uncle Doctor Said
Der Piccolino	October 9, 1936	MS	EG-3763	W: H. Honer/M: Irving Berlin	"The Piccolino" from the film *Top Hat*	The Little Boy
Der Wind hat mir ein Lied erzählt	May 30, 1938	MS	EG-6377	W: Bruno Balz/M: Lothar Brühne, Theo Mackeben ?	From film *La Habanera*	The Wind Told Me A Song
Die Dorfmusik	February 7, 1933	CH	EG-2744	W: P. von Donop, P. Kirsten/M: Marb Fryberg		The Village Music
Die Juliska aus Budapest	September 15, 1937	MS	EG-6072	W: Günther Schwenn/M: Fred Raymond	From operetta *Maske in blau*. Juliska is a Hungarian girl's name.	Juliska From Budapest
Die Liebe kommt, die Liebe geht	September 12, 1933	CH	EG-2856	W: Ernst Marsichka/M: Fritz Kreisler	Also called "Liebe-sleid"	Love Comes, Love Goes
Die Nacht ist nicht allein zum Schlafen da	January 11, 1939	MS	EG-6662	W: H. Robinger, Otto Ernst Hesse (?)/M: Theo Mackeben	From film *Tanz auf dem Vulkan*	The Night Is Not Just For Sleeping
Donkey Serenade	November 23, 1938	MS	EG-6585	W: R. Friml, H. Stothart, Franz Baumann/M: Rudolf Friml	From film *The Firefly*	
Donkey Serenade, The	December 15, 1938	VG	B-8835	W: H. Stothart, Harbach, Wright, Forrest/W: Rudolf Friml	From film *The Firefly*	

Song Title	Date Recorded	Group	Label*	Composers	Notes	English Translation
Donkey Serenade, The	February 8, 1949	AG	CduM-S-29025	W: H. Stothart/M: Rudolf Friml	From film *The Firefly*	
Drei Musketiere			NA		In medley "Hallo 1930" Part II. It is the refrain from "Musketiermarsch."	Three Musketeers
Drüben in der Heimat	September 16, 1935	MS	EG-3417	W: Max Bertuch, Kurt Schwabach/M: Eduard Künneke	From operetta *Glückliche Reise*	In My Homeland
Drunt' in der Lobau	November 12, 1936	MS	EG-3768	W: Eckardt, Fritz Löhner-Beda/M: Heinrich Strecker	Lobau is an area east of Vienna where the Danube flows.	Down There In The Lobau
Du armes Girl vom Chor	February 26, 1930	CH	EG-1807	W: Arthur Rebner, A. Robinson/M: Don Daugharthy, Milton Ager		You Poor Girl Of The Choir
Du bist mein Baby	May 13, 1937	VG	K-8150	W: Gerd Karlick/M: Joe Hajos		You Are My Baby
Du bist nicht die Erste	February 13, 1931	CH	EG-2238	W: R. Bernauer, R. Österreicher /M: Walter Jurmann	With Paul Mania, Wurlitzer-Organ. From film *Ihre Majestät die Liebe*. Piano: Walter Joseph	You Are Not The First
Du hast mich betrogen	August 18, 1928	CH	O-11451	W: Fritz Rotter/M: Erwin Bootz		You Have Betrayed Me
Du passt so gut zu mir wie Zucker zum Kaffee	February 5, 1936	VG	K-7676	W: Fritz Rotter/M: Nicholas Brodsky	From film *Katharina die Letzte*	You Suit Me As Well As Sugar With Coffee
Du traumschöne Perle der Südsee	September 4, 1931	CH	---	W: Alfred Grünwald, Fritz Löhner-Beda/M: Paul Abraham	In medley "Blume von Hawaii" Part I	You Beautiful Pearl Of The South Sea
Du, du bist so wundervoll	December 22, 1936	MS	EG-3796	W: Berthold/M: Walter Donaldson		You, You Are So Wonderful
Dwarf's Yodel Song (Hi-Ho)	December 15, 1938	VG	B-8850	W: Larry Morey/M: Frank Churchill	From Disney's *Snow White And The Seven Dwarfs*	

Song Title	Date Recorded	Group	Label*	Composers	Notes	English Translation
Eilai, eilali, eilala	February 21, 1929	CH	O-2861	W: Hans Pflanzer/M: Hans May	In medley "Bitte recht freundlich" Part II	
Eilali, eilali, eilala	February 23, 1929	CH	O-2826	W: Hans Pflanzer/M: Hans May	With Dajos Béla Orchestra	
Ein bißchen Leichtsinn kann nicht schaden	August 21, 1934	CH	EG-3110	Friedrich W. Rust	From film *Freut Euch des Lebens*	A Little Foolishness Can't Hurt
Ein bißchen Seligleit	August 18, 1928	CH	O-2586	W: Fritz Rotter/M: Horatio Nichols	"Souvenirs." First released recording of the Comedian Harmonists	A Little Bliss
Ein Freund, ein guter Freund	August 22, 1930	CH	EG-2032	W: Robert Gilbert/M: Werner Richard Heymann	In the film *Die drei von der Tankstelle* (The Three from the Gasoline Station) (*Three Good Friends/ Le Chemin du Paradis*)	A Friend, A Good Friend
Ein Lied geht um die Welt	August 31, 1933	CH	EG-2847	/M: Hans MayW: Ernst Neubach	From film *Ein Lied geht um die Welt*	A Song Goes Around The World
Ein Männlein steht im Walde, Part I	May 2, 1938	MS	EG-6350	Traditional	Ernste und heitere Variationen über (Serious and happy variations on) "Ein Männlein steht im Walde, Part I"	A Little Man Is Standing In The Forest
Ein Männlein steht im Walde, Part II	May 2, 1938	MS	EG-6350	Traditional	Ernste und heitere Variationen über (Serious and happy variations on) "Ein Männlein steht im Walde, Part II"	A Little Man Is Standing In The Forest
Ein neuer Frühling wird in die Heimat kommen	September 29, 1933	CH	EG-2874	W: Peter Schaeffers (?)/M: Willy Engel-Berger, Willi Meisel	Bootz said in the Fechner film that the lyricist was Fritz Rotter	A New Spring Will Come Into The Homeland
Eine Insel aus Träumen geboren	January 11, 1939	MS	EG-6662	W: Hans Fritz Beckmann/M: Peter Kreuder, Fritz Schröder	From film *Eine Nacht im Mai*	An Island Born From Dreams
Eine kleine Frühlingsweise	September 29, 1933	CH	EG-2874	W: Hans Lengsfelder/M: Antonin Dvorak	"Humoreske"	A Little Maytime Song

Song Title	Date Recorded	Group	Label*	Composers	Notes	English Translation
Einmal im Leben erblüht uns die Liebe	December 16, 1929	CH	---	A: Walter Borchert	In medley "Hallo 1930" Part I	Once In A Lifetime Love Comes Into Bloom
Einmal schafft's jeder	September 8, 1932	CH	EG-2607	W: Walter Reisch/M: Werner Richard Heymann	From film *Der blonde Traum*	Everyone Can Finally Make It
Eins, zwei, drei, vier	October 17, 1932	CH	EG-2642	W: Robert Gilbert/M: Paul Abraham	From film *Zigeuner der Nacht*. The EMI archive shows a date of September 17, 1932, but Biberti 's diaries list the date as October 17.	One Two Three Four
Es führt kein and'rer Weg zur Seligkeit	March 18, 1932	CH	EG-2516	W: Robert Gilbert/M: Werner Richard Heymann	Also in film *Der Sieger* (Fr. *Le Vainqueur*) See, "La Route de Bonheur" (French version).	There Is No Other Way To Bliss
Es ist eine tiefe Sehnsucht in mir	February 21, 1929	CH	---		In medley "Was Euch gefällt" Part I	It Is A Deep Longing In Me
Es steht ein Wirtshaus an der Lahn		MS	---		In medley "Studentenlieder-Potpourri" by MS. It's only the refrain of "Das Wirtshaus an der Lahn," which was a CH release. See, "Das Wirtshaus an der Lahn"	There Is A Pub On The Lahn
Espabilate	September 29, 1935	VG	Columbia DF 1814	W: Riancho/M: Grenet	With Josephine Baker, from film *La Virgen Morena*	
Fünf-Uhr-Tee bei Familie Kraus	January 30, 1931	CH	EG-2245	W: Artur Rebner, A. Robinson/M: Nacio Herb Brown	"The Woman In The Shoe"	Five O'Clock Tea At The Kraus Family
Gitarren, spielt auf	December 10, 1934	CH	EG-3224	W: Ralph Maria Siegel/M: Ludwig Schmidseder		Guitars Play On
Grüß Euch Gott, alle miteinander	January 22, 1929	CH	---	A: Camillo Morena	In medley "Hallo, hallo hier Wien" Part I	Hello Everyone
G'schichten aus dem Wienerwald	December 3, 1929	CH	EH-432	W: L. Herzer/M: Johann Strauß		Tales From The Vienna Woods

Song Title	Date Recorded	Group	Label*	Composers	Notes	English Translation
Guitarre d' amour	July 19, 1935	VG	K-7584	W: Louis Poterat/M: Ludwig Schmidseder	Ger. "Gitarren, spielt auf"	Guitar Of Love
Guten Tag, gnädige Frau	October 30, 1930	CH	EG-2127	W: Gerd Karlick/M: Erwin Bootz		Good Day Dear Madam
Guter Mond, du gehst so stille	September 21, 1933	CH	EG-2865	Traditional	German folk song	Good Moon, You Go So Quietly
Guter Mond, du gehst so stille	May 23, 1938	MS	EG-6487	Traditional	German folk song	Good Moon, You Go So Quietly
Hallelujah	January 22, 1929	CH	---		In medley "Anno dazumal" Part II	Hallelujah
Hallo 1930 - Medley Part I	December 16, 1929	CH	EG-1685	A: Walter Borchert	Medley: "Armes kleines Mädel vom Chor," "Schöner Gigolo," "Einmal im Leben erblüht uns die Liebe" and "Ich hab' kein Auto"	Hello 1930, Medley Part I
Hallo 1930 - Medley Part II	December 16, 1929	CH	EG-1685	A: Walter Borchert	Medley: "Drei Musketiere" (refrain from "Musketiermarsch"), "Leutnant warst du einst bei den Husaren" and "Puppenhochzeit"	Hello 1930, Medley Part II
Hallo, hallo hier Wien - Medley Part I	January 22, 1929	CH	O-2809	A: Camillo Morena	Medley: "Grüß Euch Gott, alle miteinander," "Wenn zwei sich lieben," "Vogerl, fliegst in die Welt hinaus" and "O komm mit mir, ich tanz' mit dir"	Hello, Hello This Is Vienna - Part I
Hallo, hallo hier Wien - Medley Part II	January 22, 1929	CH	O-2809	A: Camillo Morena	Medley: "Lieber Himmelsvater, sei nicht bös," "Noch amal, noch amal, noch amal" and "Wien, Wien nur du allein"	Hello, Hello This Is Vienna - Part II
Hallo, was machst Du heut', Daisy?	October 19, 1931	CH	EG-2435	W: Charles Amberg, Eugen Till/M: Walter Donaldson	"You're Driving Me Crazy"	Hello, What's Doing Today Daisy
Halt Dich an mich	January 30, 1931	CH	EG-2245	W: Artur Rebner/M: Jesse Greer		Stick With Me

Song Title	Date Recorded	Group	Label*	Composers	Notes	English Translation
Ham se nicht den kleinen Cohn geseh'n?	January 22, 1929	CH	---		In medley "Anno dazumal" Part II	Have You Seen The Little Mr. Cohn?
Hand in Hand	October 9, 1936	MS	EG-3763	W: H. Honer/M: Irving Berlin	"Cheek To Cheek" from film *Top Hat*	
Heidenröslein	April 28, 1937 (?)	VG	B-8742	W: J.W. von Goethe/M: Franz Schubert	Also, "Sah ein Knab ein Röslein steh'n"	Rose Bush
Heidenröslein, Das	May 23, 1938	MS	EG-6509	W: J.W. von Goethe/M: Franz Schubert	Also, "Sah ein Knab ein Röslein steh'n"	The Rose Bush
Hein spielt abends so schön auf dem Schifferklavier	November 8, 1934	CH	EG-3132	W: P. Kirsten/M: Willy Richartz	"Heinie's Sing-Song" (on HMV). "Hein" is a first name.	Hein Plays Beautifully In The Evening On The Accordion
Heinie's Sing-Song					See, "Hein spielt abends so schön auf dem Schifferklavier"	
Heut' fahr ich mit Dir in die Natur	November 25, 1930	CH	EG-2149	W: Erwin Bootz, Gerd Karlick/M: Leslie Sarony	"Jollity Farm"	Today I Drive With You To The Country
Heut' gehen wir morgen erst ins Bett	February 21, 1929	CH	---		In medley "Was Euch gefällt" Part II	We Won't Go To Bed Until Tomorrow
Heut' Nacht hab ich geträumt von dir	October 30, 1930	CH	EG-2127	M: Emmerich Kálmán		Last Night I Dreamt Of You
Heute Nacht oder nie	September 6, 1932	CH	EG-2606	W: Marcellus Fischer (Schiffer?)/M: Mischa Spoliansky	From film *Das Lied einer Nacht*	Tonight Or Never
Hof-Serenade (also: Hofsänger-Serenade)	January 19, 1931	CH	EG-2204	W: Comedian Harmonists/M: Marc Roland	In film *Gassenhauer*	Courtyard Singer Serenade
Holla Lady	February 27, 1939	MS	EG-6785	W: Sepp Weidacher, C.M. Cremrer/M: Giuseppe Becce	From film *Liebesbriefe aus dem Engadin*. Last release of the Meistersextett.	Hello Lady
Holzhackerlied	February 6, 1935	CH	EG-3273	W: Hedy Knorr/M: Giuseppe Becce	"Woodcutter's Song" (when released on HMV). From the film *Der verlorene Sohn*.	The Woodcutter's Song

Song Title	Date Recorded	Group	Label*	Composers	Notes	English Translation
Hoppla, jetzt komm' ich	March 18, 1932	CH	EG-2516	W: Robert Gilbert /M: Werner Richard Heymann	Also in film *Der Sieger* (Fr. *Le Vainqueur*)	Okay, Here I Come
Hundert-tausendmal	September 18, 1931	CH	EG-2405	W: Artur Rebner, Steiner /M: John W. Green		A Hundred Thousand Times
Ich bin die Marie von der Haller-Revue	February 21, 1929	CH	---		In medley "Bitte recht freundlich" Part II	I Am Marie From The Haller Revue
Ich freu' mich so	October 14, 1937	MS	EG-6206	W: Klaus S. Richter/M: Peter Igelhoff		It Makes Me Happy
Ich hab' Dich lieb, braune Madonna	October 19, 1931	CH	EG-2435	W: Fritz Rotter/M: Santiago Lopez		I Have You Dear, Brown Madonna
Ich hab' ein Zimmer, goldige Frau	August 18, 1928	CH	O-2585	W: Fritz Rotter/M: Jim Cowler	From revue *Zieh Dich aus*	I Have A Room, Cute Lady
Ich hab' eine kleine braune Mandoline	August 22, 1929	CH	O-11099	W: Peter Herz, Ernst Wengraf/M: Karl M. May		I Have A Small Brown Mandolin
Ich hab' eine tiefe Sehnsucht nach dir	September 6, 1937	MS	EG-6074	W & M: Ralph Benatzky	From the film *Zu neuen Ufern*	I Have A Deep Longing For You
Ich hab' für Dich 'nen Blumentopf bestellt	May 23, 1930	CH	EG-1911	W: Gerd Karlick/M: Erwin Bootz		I Ordered A Flowerpot For You
Ich hab' für dich 'nen Blumentopf bestellt	May 5, 1938	MS	EG-6431	W: Gerd Karlick/M: Erwin Bootz		I Ordered A Flowerpot For You
Ich hab' ihnen viel zu sagen, sehr verehrte gnädige Frau	February 21, 1929	CH	O-2826	W: Fritz Rotter/M: Hermann Krome	In medley "Bitte recht freundlich" Part II	I Have A Lot To Tell You, Dear Lady
Ich hab' kein Auto	December 16, 1929	CH	---		In medley "Hallo 1930" Part I	I Don't Have A Car
Ich hol' Dir vom Himmel das Blau	December 3, 1929	CH	EH-432	W: Rudolf Schanzer, Ernst Welisch /M: Franz Lehar	From the operetta *Die lustige Witwe*	I'll Get The Blue Down From Heaven For You

Song Title	Date Recorded	Group	Label*	Composers	Notes	English Translation
Ich küsse Ihre Hand, Madame	October 9, 1928	CH	---	W: Fritz Rotter/M: Ralph Erwin	In medley "Wir flüstern," Part II	I Kiss Your Hand Madam
Ich küsse Ihre Hand, Madame	September 14, 1928, November 20, 1928	CH	O-2585	W: Fritz Rotter/M: Ralph Erwin		I Kiss Your Hand Madam
Ich muß heute singen	June 16, 1937	VG	K-8150	W: Rolf Marbot, Fritz Joachim/M: Bert Reisfeld,	Fr. "Les Fenetres Chantent"	I Must Sing Today
Ich sing' mein Lied heut' nur für Dich	November 12, 1936	MS	EG-3768	W: Ernst Marischka/M: Robert Stolz		I Sing My Song Today Only For You
Ich steh' mit Ruth gut	October 9, 1928	CH	---		In medley "Wir flüstern" Part I	I Stand Well With Ruth
Ich träum' von einer Märch- ennacht	October 30, 1930	CH	EG-2125	W: Gerd Karlick/M: Friedrich W. Rust	With Marcel Wittrisch	I Dream Of A Fairy Tale Night
Ich will von der Lilly nichts wissen	February 21, 1929	CH	---		In medley "Bitte recht freundlich" Part I	I Don't Want To Know Anything From The Lily
Ich wollt', ich wär' ein Huhn	August 28, 1936	MS	EG-3723	W: Hans Fritz Beckmann/M: Peter Kreuder	From film *Glückskinder*	I Wish I Could Be A Chicken
Il ne faut pas briser un reve	May 24, 1937	VG	K-7974	M: Jean Jalbr		A Dream Should Not Be Broken
Il pleut sur la route	December 12, 1935	VG	K-7602	W: Himmel/M: R. Chamfleury	French	The Rain On The Road
Im Krug zum grünen Kranze	December 15, 1936	MS	---	M: Carl Ro- brecht	In medley "Studenten- lieder – Potpourri" Part I	In The Green Wreath Tavern
Im tiefen Keller sitz' ich hier	December 15, 1936	MS	---	M: Carl Ro- brecht	In medley "Studen- tenlieder - Potpourri" Part I	Here I Sit In The Deep Cellar
Immer an der Wand lang	January 22, 1929	CH	---	W: Hermann Frey/M: Walter Kollo	In medley "Anno dazumal" Part I (it is the same song as "Und dann schleich' ich still und leise")	Always Along The Wall
Immer an der Wand lang	November 17, 1936	MS	EG-3806	W: Hermann Frey/M: Walter Kollo	It is the same song as "Und dann schleich' ich still und leise"	Always Along The Wall
In A Persian Market			---		See, "Auf einem persischen Markt"	

Song Title	Date Recorded	Group	Label*	Composers	Notes	English Translation
In der Bar zum Krokodil	August 28, 1934, November 9, 1934	CH	EG-3117	W: Fritz Löhner-Beda/M: Willy Engel-Berger		In The Crocodile Bar
In einem kühlen Grunde	January 7, 1932	CH	EG-2483	W: Joseph von Eichendorff/M: F. Glück		In A Cool Dell
In einem kühlen Grunde	May 12, 1938	MS	EG-6682	W: Joseph von Eichendorff/M: F. Glück		In A Cool Dell
In meinem Herzen, Schatz	May 29, 1936	MS	EG-3666	W: Hans Fritz Beckmann/M: Walter Gronostay	"Bubliczki," from the film *Savoy Hotel 217*	In My Heart, Dear
In Mexico	August 28, 1936	MS	EG-3723	W: Erich Meder/M: Peter Igelhoff		In Mexico
In My Solitude					See, "Solitude"	
In stiller Nacht	April 1, 1936	VG	B-8882	M: Johannes Brahms		In The Quiet Night
Irgendwo auf der Welt	September 8, 1932	CH	NA	W: Robert Gilbert/M: Werner Richard Heymann	From the film *Der blonde Traum*	Somewhere In The World
Italienisches Intermezzo	August 22, 1928	CH	EG-960	Johann Strauß	With Grete Waller, from the operetta *Casanova*	Italian Intermezzo
J' aime une Tyrolienne	November 9, 1934	CH	K-7433	W: Louis Poterat/M: Bert Reisfeld, Rolf Marbot	French version of "Mein kleiner grüner Kaktus"	I Love A Tyrolean
Ja der Ozean ist groß	September 21, 1936	MS	EG-3743	W: Charles Amberg/M: Franz Doelle	From film *Und Du, mein Schatz, fährst mit*	Yes The Ocean Is Large
Ja, ja, die Frau'n	October 9, 1928	CH	---	A: Walter Kollo	In the medley "Wir flüstern," Part I (look there)	Yes, Yes, The Women
Jede Stunde ohne Dich ist eine Ewigkeit für mich	September 15, 1937	MS	EG-6074	W: Gerd Karlick/M: Erwin Bootz		Each Hour Without You Is An Eternity For Me
Jeden Tag, jede Nacht	November 8, 1935	MS	EG-3502	W: A. Dubin/M: H. Warren	From the operetta *Ball der Nationen*. Known in the U.S. as "I Only Have Eyes For You."	Every Day, Every Night

Song Title	Date Recorded	Group	Label*	Composers	Notes	English Translation
Jetzt gang i ans Brünnele	November 26, 1936	MS	---	Traditional	German folk song, in medley "Volks- lieder-Potpourri" Part II	I Went To The Well
Jetzt gang i ans Brünnele	September 22, 1937	MS	EG-6103	Traditional	German folk song	I Went To The Well
Jetzt oder nie	March 8, 1939	MS	EG-6785	W: Robert Biberti/M: Sieg-fried Muchow		Now Or Never
Jetzt trinken wir noch eins	February 7, 1933	CH	EG-2744	W: Willy Rosen, Kurt Schwabach /M: Willy Rosen		Now We'll Have Another Drink
Kannst Du pfeifen, Johanna?	April 12, 1934	CH	EG-3032	W: Hans Joachim Bach/M: Sten Axelson		Can You Whistle, Johanna?
Kennst Du das kleine Haus am Michigan-see?	February 21, 1929	CH	---	A: Walter Borchert	In medley "Was Euch gefällt" Part II	Do You Know The Little House At Lake Michigan
Kleine verträumte Madonna	June 18, 1937	VG	K-8049	W & M: Bert Reisfeld, Rolf Marbot	French – "Dans le jardin de mes reves"	Small Dreamy Madonna
Kleiner Mann, was nun?	May 11, 1933	CH	EG-2830	W: R. Busch/M: Harald Böhmelt	In film *Kleiner Mann – was nun?*	Little Man, What Now?
Komm im Traum	May 5, 1934	CH	EG-3047	W: Comedian Harmonists/M: B. Petkere		Come Into My Dream
Komm in meine Liebe-slaube	February 22, 1929	CH	---	A: Camillo Morena	In medley "Anno dazumal," Part I	Come Into My Arbor Of Love
Künstlerleben	November 24, 1936		EG-998	M: Johann Strauß		Artist's Life
La Danza	February 8, 1949	AG	CDuM-S-29024	/M: Giacchino Rossini	Italian	The Dance
La Mia Bella Napoli			---		See, "Mia bella Napoli"	My Beautiful Naples
La Paloma	March 8. 1939	MS	EG-6591	S. de Yradier		The Dove
La Route de Bonheur	May 25, 1932	CH	K-6586	M: Werner Rich-ard Heymann W: Jean Boyer	See, "Es führt kein andrer Weg zur Seligkeit"	The Road Of Happiness
Lach-Foxtrott	January 11, 1939	MS	EG-6590	W: Hans Robin-ger /M: Peter Igelhoff		Fox Trot Of Laughter

Song Title	Date Recorded	Group	Label*	Composers	Notes	English Translation
Lebe wohl, gute Reise	November 15, 1934	CH	EG-3204	W: Comedian Harmonists/M: Bert Reisfeld, Rolf Marbot	French - "Au Revoir, Bon Voyage"	Goodbye, Good Trip
Legende d' amour	December 6, 1928	CH	O-11296	W: Hedy Knorr/M: Guiseppe Becce		Legend Of Love
Leichte Kavallerie	June 11, 1931	CH	EG-2328	W: Charles Amberg /M: Noel Gay, H. Graham	"The King's Horses"	Light Cavalry
Leila, heute Nacht muß ich Dich wieder sehen	February 21, 1929	CH	---	A: Fred Ralph	In medley "Bitte recht freundlich" Part I	Leila, Tonight I Must See You
Les fenetres chantent	May 26, 1937	VG	K-7939	W: H. Varna, Marc-Cab/M: Bert Reisfeld, Rolf Marbot	Ger. "Ich muß heute singen"	The Windows Are Singing
Les gars de la marine	August 24, 1931	CH	K-6375	W: Jean Boyer/M: Werner Richard Heymann	Ger. "Das ist die Liebe der Matrosen." In film *Le Capitaine Craddock* (*Bomben auf Monte Carlo*) (*Monte Carlo Madness*)	The Boys Of The Navy
Leutnant warst Du einst bei den Husaren	December 16, 1929	CH	---	A: Walter Borchert	In medley "Hallo 1930" Part II	You Were Once A Lieutenant In The Hussars
Lieber Himmelvater, sei nicht bös'	January 22, 1929	CH	---	A: Camillo Morena	In medley "Hallo, hallo hier Wien" Part II	Dear God, Don't Be Angry
Liebesleid					See, "Die Liebe kommt, die Liebe geht"	Love's Sorrow
Liebesträume	October 14, 1937	MS	EG-6683	W: Ferdinand Freiligrath/M: Franz Liszt		Love's Dream
Liebling, mein Herz läßt Dich grüßen	August 22, 1930	CH	EG-2032	W: Robert Gilbert/M: Werner Richard Heymann	"Darling;" also in the film *Die Drei von der Tankstelle* (The Three From The Gasoline Station) (*Three Good Friends*) (Fr. *Le chemin du paradis*)	Darling, My Heart Greets You
Little Sandman			---		See, "Sandmännchen"	

Song Title	Date Recorded	Group	Label*	Composers	Notes	English Translation
Love Me A Little Today	June 15, 1937		B-8602	W: Alan Herbert/M: Nicholas Brodszky	Fr. "Si vous m' aimez en secret"	
Mach mir's nicht so schwer	1932	CH	NA	M: Otto Stransky	In film *Spione im Savoy-Hotel* (also: *Die Galavorstellung der Fratellinis*)	Don't Make It So Difficult For Me
Marechiare	May 24, 1937	MS	EG-3965	W: S. di Giacomo/M: Paolo Tosti	Neapolitan song about the moon over the town of Marechiare (now Marechiaro)	
Marie, Marie	January 19, 1931	CH	EG-2204	W: Johannes Brandt/M: Marc Roland	From the film *Gassenhauer*	
Maskenball im Gänsestall	October 17, 1932	CH	EG-2642	W: Kurt Schwabach /M: Hans May	The EMI archive shows a date of September 17, 1932, but Biberti 's diaries list the date as October 17.	Masked Ball In A Goose Stable
Mein blauer Himmel	November 6, 1928	CH	O-2737	W: Fritz Löhner-Beda /M: Walter Donaldson, R. Whiting		My Blue Heaven
Mein Herz ruft immer nur nach Dir	April 19, 1934	CH	EG-3038	W: Ernst Marischka /M: Robert Stolz	From film *Mein Herz ruft nach Dir*	My Heart Always Calls Only For You
Mein kleiner grüner Kaktus	November 15, 1934	CH	EG-3204	W & M: Bert Reisfeld, Rolf Marbot (as "Dorian/ Herda")		My Little Green Cactus
Mein lieber Schatz, bist Du aus Spanien?	September 18, 1931	CH	EG-2405	W: Fritz Rotter /M: Henri Santengini		My Dear Darling, Are You From Spain?
Menuett	September 21, 1933	CH	EG-2856	M: Luigi Boccherini		Minuet
Mia Bella Napoli	January 4, 1939	VG	K-8271	W: Louis Poterat/M: Gerhard Winkler	Also, "La Mia Bella Napoli" and "O Mia Bella Napoli."	My Beautiful Naples
Moment musical	April 27, 1937	VG	B-8742	M: Franz Schubert		Musical Moment
Morgen muß ich fort von hier	February 13, 1935	CH	EG-3282	W: Friedrich Silcher/ M:Traditional	German folk song; also in film *Die Comedian Harmonists singen Volkslieder*	Tomorrow I Must Leave Here

Song Title	Date Recorded	Group	Label*	Composers	Notes	English Translation
Morgen muß ich fort von hier	November 26, 1936	MS	---	Traditional	German folk song. In medley "Volkslieder-Potpourri" Part I	
Morgen muß ich fort von hier	May 12, 1938	MS	EG-6682	Traditional	German folk song	
Musketier-marsch	November 11, 1929	CH	EG-1647	W: Rudolf Schanzer, Ernst Welisch/M: H. Riesenfeld, Ralph Benatzky	Also, "Drei Muske-tiere." From revue *Drei Musketiere*	Musketeer March
Musketier-marsch	December 16, 1929	CH	---	A: Walter Borchert	In medley "Hallo 1930" Part II	
Muß i denn, muß i denn zum Städtele hinaus	January 9, 1933	CH	EG-2724	Traditional	German folk song	Now I Have To Leave The Town
Muß i denn, muß i denn zum Städtele hinaus	November 26, 1936	MS	---	Traditional	German folk song; in medley "Volkslieder-Potpourri" Part I	Now I Have To Leave The Town
Muß i denn, muß i denn zum Städtele hinaus	May 12, 1938	MS	EG-6684	Traditional	German folk song	Now I Have To Leave The Town
My Golden Baby	September 4, 1931	CH	---	W: Alfred Grünwald, Fritz Löhner-Beda/M: Paul Abraham	In medley "Blume von Hawaii" Part II	
Natacha	October 16, 1934	CH	K-7398	W: André de Badet /M: Bronislaw Kaper, Walter Jurmann	From film *Nuits Moscovites*	Natasha
Night And Day	September 15, 1933	CH	EG-2929	Cole Porter	From film *Gay Divorcee*. (Ger. "Tag und Nacht")	
Ninna-nanna a liana	May 11, 1937	VG	K-7959	W: Pio di Flaviis/M: Renato Bellini		
Ninon, du süße Frau	August 18, 1928	CH	O-2586	W: Fritz Löhner-Beda /M: G.B. de Sylva, R. Brown, R. Henderson	"So Blue." Unreleased on Gramophone.	Ninon, You Sweet Lady
Noch amal, noch amal, noch amal	January 22, 1929	CH	---		In medley "Hallo, hallo hier Wien" Part II	Once More, Once More, Once More

Song Title	Date Recorded	Group	Label*	Composers	Notes	English Translation
Noch 'ne Lage Cognac her	February 21, 1929	CH	---		In medley "Bitte recht freundlich" Part II	Bring Another Round Of Brandy
O alte Burschenher-rlichkeit	December 15, 1936	MS	---	M: Carl Ro-brecht	In "Studentenlieder-Potpourri" Part II	Oh Old Students' Glory
O komm mit mir, ich tanz' mit Dir	January 22, 1929	CH	---		In medley "Hallo, hallo hier Wien" Part I	Oh Come With Me, I'll Dance With You
O sole mio	October 12, 1937	MS	EG-3965	W: G. Capurro, A. Bock/M: Ernesto di Capua		My Sun
Öffne Dein Herz der Musik	February 22, 1937	MS	EG-3796	W: H. Honer/M: Irving Berlin		Open Your Heart To The Music
Oh, ich glaub' ich hab' mich verliebt	May 5, 1938	MS	EG-6431	W: Hans Fritz Beckmann/M: Erwin Bootz		Oh, I Believe I Have Fallen In Love
Ohne Dich	September 4, 1933	CH	EG-2848	W: Reinhardt/M: Harold Arlen	"Stormy Weather"	Without You
Ol' Man River	February 23, 1929	CH	O-2870	W: Oscar Hammerstein/M: Jerome Kern,	Without lyrics, C.H. with Dajos Béla Orchestra	
Orientalische Suite	March 8, 1939	MS	EG-6591	M: Popy		Oriental Suite
Perpetuum mobile	September 26, 1933	CH	EG-2870	M: Johann Strauß		Perpetual Motion
Perpetuum mobile	May 23, 1938	MS	EG-6496	M: Johann Strauß		Perpetual Motion
Pojaukenho-chzeit	November 4, 1937	MS	EG-6143	W: Rees/ M:Traditional		Polish Peasants' Wedding
Puppenho-chzeit	November 11, 1929	CH	EG-1647	W: Fritz Rotter/M: Nacio Herb Brown, A. Robinson	"Wedding Of The Painted Doll"	Doll Wedding
Puppenho-chzeit	December 16, 1929	CH	---		In medley "Hallo 1930" Part II	Doll Wedding
Qu' importe si tu pars	May 26, 1937	VG	K-7939	W: André de Badet/M: José Rivada		What Matters If You Leave
Quand il pleut	September 7, 1933	CH	K-7084	W: T. Koehler, André de Badet/M: Harold Arlen	"Ohne Dich" (English - "Stormy Weather")	When It Rains

Song Title	Date Recorded	Group	Label*	Composers	Notes	English Translation
Quand la brise vagabonde	August 24, 1931	CH	K-6375	W: Jean Boyer/M: Werner Richard Heymann	See, "Wenn der Wind weht über das Meer"	When The Breeze Blows
Raffaela	June 15, 1937	VG	K-8049	W: Fritz Joachim/M: José Rivada	Qu' importe si tu pars	
Regentropfen	January 23, 1936	MS	EG-3555	W: Josef Hochleitner /M: Emil Palm		Raindrops
Rhythmus der Freude	May 13, 1937	MS	EG-6117	W: Kurt Feltz/M: J. Kennedy, M. Carr, Klaus S. Richter	"There's A New World"	Rhythm Of Joy
Rosenstock, Holderblüt'	November 26, 1936	MS	---	Traditional	In medley "Volkslie-der-Potpourri" Part I	Rose Tree And Elders Blossom
Rumbah Tambah	February 25, 1936	VG	K-7709	W: R. Hernandez/M: R. Chamfleury		
Sah ein Knab' ein Röslein steh'n	January 7, 1932	CH	EG-2483	W: J.W. von Goethe/M: Franz Schubert	See also "Heiden-röslein"	A Boy Saw A Rose Bush
Sandmän-nchen	April 23, 1936	VG	B-8882	M: Johannes Brahms		Little Sandman
Schade kleine Frau (ich hätte Dich geliebt)	September 10, 1934	CH	EG-3180	W: Rudolf Ber-tram, A. Kaps/M: Bruno Uher		It's A Shame Little Mrs., I Would Have Loved You
Schaukellied	January 22, 1929	CH	---		In medley "Anno dazumal" Part I	Swing Song
Scheinbar liebst Du mich	May 13, 1929	CH	O-11404	W: Roxy/M: Bud Green, Sam H. Stept	"That's My Weakness Now"	Apparently You Love Me
Schlaf wohl, Du Himmelsk-nabe	September 12, 1932	CH	EG-2613	W: Christian Daniel Schubart/M: K. Nenner	German Christmas song (with string orchestra)	Sleep Well, Heaven's Boy
Schlaf, mein Liebling	January 8, 1932	CH	EG-2484	W: Fritz Löhner-Beda/M: Ray Noble	"Goodnight, Sweet-heart." With Marek Weber Orchestra	Sleep, My Dear
Schlafe, mein Prinzchen, schlaf ein	May 23, 1938	MS	EG-6509	M: Wolfgang Amadeus Mozart	Also: "Wiegenlied" (Lullaby).	Sleep My Little Prince, Sleep

Song Title	Date Recorded	Group	Label*	Composers	Notes	English Translation
Schlafe, mein Prinzchen, schlaf ein	September 21, 1933	CH	EG-2865	M: Wolfgang Amadeus Mozart	Also: "Wiegenlied" (Lullaby). Also in private film of the Comedy Harmonists - 1938	Sleep My Little Prince, Sleep
Schöne Isabella aus Kastilien	June 1, 1932	CH	EG-2554	W: Gerd Karlick/M: Erwin Bootz		Pretty Isabella From Castile
Schöne Lisa	December 10, 1934	CH	EG-3224	W: Günther Schwenn/M: Fred Raymond	From *Lauf ins Glück* (revue?)	Pretty Lisa
Schöner Gigolo	December 16, 1929	CH	---		In medley "Hallo 1930" Part I	Beautiful Gigolo
Schreit alle hurra	September 21, 1936	MS	EG-3745	W: Robert Biberti/M: Horatio Nicholls	"Ten Thousand Hoorays"	Everyone Shout Hooray!
Si vous m'aimez en secret	June 15, 1937	VG	K-7974	W: Madelaine Robert-Perrier /M: Nicholas Brodszky	"Love Me A Little Today"	If You Like Me In Secret
Sie trägt ein kleines Jäckchen in blau	January 23, 1936	MS	EG-3555	W: Heuser/M: Fred Fisher, McConnell		She Wears A Small Blue Jacket
Siehst Du wohl, da kimmt er	January 22, 1929	CH	---	A: Camillo Morena	In medley "Anno dazumal" Part II	See, Here He Comes
So ein Kuß kommt von allein	October 5, 1933	CH	EG-2875	W: Willy Dehmel/M: Franz Grothe	From film *Keine Angst vor Liebe*	A Kiss Comes On Its Own
So ist das Leben	May 23, 1930/ June 4, 1930 (?)	CH	EG-1935	W: Felix Joachimson/M: Mischa Spoliansky	From revue *Wie werde ich reich und glücklich?*	Such Is Life
Solimah	September 20, 1935	MS	EG-3462	W: Ralph Maria Siegel /M: Erwin Bootz		
Solitude	February 25, 1936	VG	B-8575	W: E. de Lang, Irving Mills/M: Duke Ellington		
Sonia	October 16, 1934	CH	K-7398	W: Chamfleury/M: Erik Plessow, Edmund Kötscher	Ger. "Wenn die Sonja russisch tanzt"	

Song Title	Date Recorded	Group	Label*	Composers	Notes	English Translation
Sous le ciel d' Afrique	September 29, 1935	VG	Col DF 1814	W: André de Badet/M: Jaques Dallin	With Josephine Baker, from film *Princess Tam Tam*	Under The African Sky
Spanische Intermezzo	August 22, 1928	CH	EG-960	M: Johann Strauß A: Ralf Benatzky, Harry Frommermann	With Grete Waller, from the operetta *Casanova*	Spanish Intermezzo
Spanische Moritat	April 12, 1934	CH	EG-3032	W: Comedian Harmonists/M: Marc Roland		Spanish Fable
Stille Nacht, heilige Nacht	September 12, 1932	CH	EG-2613	W: J. Mohr/M: Franz Gruber	German Christmas song (with string orchestra)	Silent Night, Holy Night
Studentenlie- der-Potpourri Medley, Part I	December 15, 1936	MS	EG-3973	M: Carl Robrecht/A: Erwin Bootz	Medley: "Im Krug zum grünen Kranze," "Im tiefen Keller sitz'ich hier," "Bier her" and "Es steht ein Wirtshaus an der Lahn"	Student Songs Medley
Studentenlie- der-Potpourri Medley, Part II	December 15, 1936	MS	EG-3973	M: Carl Robrecht/A: Erwin Bootz	Medley: "O alte Burschenherrlich - keit," "Wohl auf, noch getrunken" and "Als wir jüngst in Regensburg waren"	Student Songs Medley
Sündig und süß	October 9, 1928	CH	---	A: Walter Kollo	In medley "Wir flüstern," Part I	Sinful And Sweet
Sur un marché Persan			---		See, "Auf einem persischen Markt"	In A Persian Market
Süßes Baby	November 6, 1928	CH	O-2737	W: Fritz Rotter/M: August Egen		Sweet Baby
Tabou	April 28, 1937	VG	K-7906	M: E. Lecuona		
Tag und Nacht	September 4, 1933	CH	EG-2848	W: R. Busch/M: Cole Porter	"Night and Day" (Fr. "Tout le jour, toute la nuit")	Day And Night
Tango de l' Orage	January 3, 1939	VG	K-8271	W: Louis Sauvat/M: Henry Himmel	French, last release of the Comedy Har- monists	Tango Of The Storm
Tante, bleib hier	February 6, 1935	CH	EG-3273	W & M: Peter Kirsten		Aunt, Stay Here
Tarantella sincera	November 13, 1931	CH	EG-2458	W: Eduardo Migliaccio/M: Vincenco de Crescenzo		

Song Title	Date Recorded	Group	Label*	Composers	Notes	English Translation
Tausendmal war ich im Traum bei Dir	August 20, 1935	MS	EG-3417	W: Aldo von Pinelli, Charles Amberg (?)/M: Franz Doelle	From film *Amphitryon*. First release of the Meistersextett.	In My Dream I Was With You A Thousand Times
Tea For Two	December 17, 1934	CH	B-8274	W: Irving Caesar/M: Vincent Youmans	From the show *No, No Nanette*	
Ti voglio bene	May 24, 1937	VG	K-7959	W: Enzo Fusco/M: Rod, Falvo		I Wish You Well
Ti-Pi-Tin	December 15, 1938	VG	B-8850	W: R. Leveen/M: Maria Grever		
Toselli-Serenade	December 6, 1928	CH	O-11296	W: Fritz Rotter (C. Böhm ?)/M: E. Toselli		
Tout le long des rues	February 8, 1949	AG	CDuM-S-29023	M: N. Glanzberg		All Along The Streets
Träume, die nur um Deine Liebe sich dreh'n	October 30, 1930	CH	EG-2125	W: Marcel Lion/M: Friedrich W. Rust	With Marcel Wittrisch	Dreams That Involve Your Love Only
Und dann schleich' ich still und leise			---		See, "Immer an der Wand lang"	And Then I Creep, Silently And Still
Und so weiter	December 22, 1936	MS	EG-3866	W: Wilhelm Krug/M: Hans Barring		And So On
Ungarischer Tanz Nr. 5	February 28, 1935	CH	EG-3303	W: Comedian Harmonists/M: Johannes Brahms	One of the last two recordings of the Comedian Harmonists.	Hungarian Dance No. 5
Ungarischer Tanz Nr. 5	May 23, 1938	MS	EG-6496	W: Robert Biberti/M: Johannes Brahms		Hungarian Dance No. 5
Vagabond King Waltz, The	February 21, 1929	CH	O-11451	W & /M: Rudolf Friml	From film *The Vagabond King*	
Veronika, der Lenz ist da	August 22, 1930	CH	EG-2033	W: Fritz Rotter/M: Walter Jurmann	Also in short film *Kreuzworträtsel*	Veronica, Spring Is Here
Veronique, le printemps est la	October 28, 1933	CH	K-7113	W: André Mauprey/M: Walter Jurmann	Ger. "Veronika, der Lenz ist da"	Veronica, Spring Is Here
Vieni, vieni	May 30, 1938	MS	EG-6377	W: K. Nachmann/M: Vincent Scotto		Come, Come

Song Title	Date Recorded	Group	Label*	Composers	Notes	English Translation
Vogerl, fliegst in die Welt hinaus	January 22, 1929	CH	---		In medley "Hallo, hallo hier Wien" Part I	Little Bird You Fly To The World
Voilà l' travail	May 25, 1932	CH	K-6586	W: Jean Boyer/M: Werner Richard Heymann	See, "Hoppla, jetzt komm' ich."	Here Is Work
Volkslieder-Potpourri - Medley, Part I	November 26, 1936	MS	EG-3954	German folk songs	Medley: "Morgen muß ich fort von hier," "Rosenstock, Holderblüt'," "Ach, wie ist's möglich dann" and "Muß i denn zum Städtele hinaus"	Folk Song Medley
Volkslieder-Potpourri - Medley, Part II	December 15, 1936	MS	EG-3954	German folk songs	Medley: "Das Lieben bringt groß' Freud," "Jetzt gang i ans Brünnele" and "Am Brunnen vor dem Tore"	Folk Song Medley
Was Dein roter Mund im Frühling sagt	May 11, 1933	CH	EG-2830	W: R. Busch/M: Harald Böhmelt	Also in film *Kleiner Mann – was nun?*	What Your Red Mouth Says In Springtime
Was Euch ge-fällt - Medley, Part I	February 21, 1929	CH	O-2862	A: Walter Borchert	Medley: "Benjamin, ich hab' nichts anzuzieh'n," "Es ist eine tiefe Sehnsucht in mir" and "Denk' an mich, oh Creola"	What Pleases You (Medley, Part 1)
Was Euch ge-fällt - Medley, Part II	February 21, 1929	CH	O-2862	A: Walter Borchert	Medley: "Kennst Du das kleine Haus am Michigansee," "Heut' geh'n wir morgen erst ins Bett" and "Was weißt denn Du, was ahnst denn Du"	What Pleases You (Medley, Part 2)
Was mit Dir heut' bloß los ist	September 20, 1935	MS	EG-3462	W: Robert Biberti/M: S. Wood		What Is Wrong With You Today
Was nicht ist, kann noch werden	September 15, 1937	MS	EG-6072	W: Günther Schwenn/M: Fred Raymond	From operetta *Maske in blau*	What Is Not, Still Can Become
Was schenkst Du mir dann?	June 11, 1931	CH	EG-2328	W: Kurt Schwabach/M: Gay, Graham, Franz Grothe	Also in film *Der un-getreue Eckehart*	What Do You Give Me Then?

Song Title	Date Recorded	Group	Label*	Composers	Notes	English Translation
Was weißt denn Du, was ahnst denn Du?	February 21, 1929	CH	---	A: Walter Borchert	In medley "Was Euch gefällt" Part II	What Do You Know, What Do You Suspect?
Way With Every Sailor, The	August 21, 1931	CH	B-3972	W: Leigh//M: Werner Richard Heymann	Ger. "Das ist die Liebe der Matrosen" Fr. "Les gars de la marine." From the film *Monte Carlo Madness* (Ger. *Bomben auf Monte Carlo*) (Fr. *Le Capitain Craddock*)	
Way You Look Tonight, The	April 22, 1937	VG	EA-1988	W: D. Fields/M: Jerome Kern	From film *Swing Time*	
Wenn der weiße Flieder wieder blüht	December 17, 1928	CH	O-2745	W: Fritz Rotter/M: Franz Doelle	From revue *Donnerwetter, 1000 Frauen*	When The White Elderberry Flowers Again
Wenn der weiße Flieder wieder blüht	February 21, 1929	CH	O-2861		In medley "Bitte recht freundlich" Part I	When The White Elderberry Flowers Again
Wenn der Wind weht über das Meer	August 14, 1931	CH	EG-2382	W: Robert Gilbert/M: Werner Richard Heymann	"Over the blue" (Fr. "Quand la brise vagabonde"). Also in film *Bomben auf Monte Carlo* (Fr. *Le Capitain Craddock*).	When The Wind Blows Over The Sea
Wenn die Sonja russisch tanzt	August 21, 1934	CH	EG-3110	W: Gerd Karlick/M: Erik Plessow Edmund Kötscher		When Sonya Does The Russian Dance
Wenn die Vergißmeinnicht blüh'n	May 29, 1936	MS	EG-3666	W: Rudolf Perak/M: Victor Corzilius		When The Forget-Me-Nots Bloom
Wenn ich vergnügt bin, muß ich singen	November 12, 1936	MS	EG-3866	W: Hans Fritz Beckmann/M: Peter Igelhoff		When I Am Happy, I Have To Sing
Wenn Matrosen mal an Land geh'n	June 28, 1937	MS	EG-6117	W: Hans Fritz Beckmann/M: Anton Profes	Also in film *Fremdenheim Filoda*	When Sailors Once Go On Land
Wenn wir beide Hochzeit machen	December 4, 1935	MS	EG-3502	W: Günther Schwenn/M: Fred Raymond	From operetta *Ball der Nationen*	If We Get Married
Wenn zwei sich lieben	January 22, 1929	CH	---	A: Camillo Morena	In medley "Hallo, hallo hier Wien" Part I	When Two People Love

Song Title	Date Recorded	Group	Label*	Composers	Notes	English Translation
When The Sun Says Good- night To The Mountain	April 22, 1937	VG	EA-1988	W: Harry Pease /M: Larry Vincent		When The Sun Says "Goodnight" To The Mountain
Whispering	December 17, 1934	CH	B-8274	W: Vincent Youmans, John Schoenberger /M: Vincent Youmans		Whispering
Whistle While You Work	December 8, 1938	VG	B-8835	W: Larry Morey /M: Frank Churchill	From *Snow White And The Seven Dwarfs*	Whistle While You Work
Wie wär's mit Lissabon?	August 28, 1934	CH	EG-3117	W: E. Lehnow /M: Werner Bochmann	From film *Seine beste Erfindung*	How About Lisbon?
Wie werde ich glücklich?	May 23, 1930	CH	EG-1935	W: Felix Joachimson /M: Mischa Spoliansky	From revue *Wie werde ich reich und glücklich?*	How Can I Become Lucky?
Wiegenlied			---		See, "Schlafe, mein Prinzchen, schlaf ein"	Cradle Song
Wien, Wien, nur du allein	January 22, 1929	CH	---		In medley "Hallo, hallo hier Wien" Part II	Vienna, Vienna, Only You Alone
Wir brauchen keine Schwieger- mama	January 22, 1929	CH	---		In medley "Anno dazumal" Part II	We Do Not Need A Mother-In-Law
Wir flüstern Medley, Part I	October 9, 1928	CH	O-2658	A: Walter Kollo	Medley: "Das Lied der Liebe," "Sündig und süß" and "Ich steh' mit Ruth gut"	We Whisper Medley (Part 1)
Wir flüstern Medley, Part II	October 9, 1928	CH	O-2658	A: Walter Kollo	Medley: "Ja, ja, die Frau'n," "Blau" and "Ich küsse ihre Hand, Madame"	We Whisper Medley (Part 2)
Wir sind von Kopf bis Fuß auf Liebe eingestellt	May 23, 1930	CH	EG-1911	W: Robert Liebmann /M: Friedrich Hol- länder	From revue *Der blaue Engel*	We Are In Love From Head To Foot
Wo es Mädels gibt, Kam- eraden	September 4, 1931	CH	---	W: Alfred Grünwald, Fritz Löhner-Beda/M: Paul Abraham	In medley "Blume von Hawaii" Part II	Where There Are Girls, Comrades
Wochenend' und Sonnen- schein	August 22, 1930	CH	EG-2033	W: Charles Amberg /M: Milton Ager	"Happy Days Are Here Again"	Weekend And Sunshine

Song Title	Date Recorded	Group	Label*	Composers	Notes	English Translation
Wohl auf, noch get-runken	December 15, 1936	MS	---	M: Carl Robrecht	In "Studentenlieder-Potpourri" Part II	Well Now, Drink Another One
Woodcutter's Song			---		See, "Holzhackerlied"	Woodcutter's Song
Y'a d'la joie	February 8, 1949	AG	CDuM-S-29023	M: Charles Trenet		There Is Joy
You And The Night And The Music	February 8, 1949	AG	CduM-S-29025	W & M: A. Schwartz H. Dietz		

Recorded But Not Released

Song Title	Date Recorded	Group	Label*	Composers	Notes	English Translation
A Little May-time Song	January 4, 1939	VG	HMV-Test		Not released	
Anna hat Geld	August 22, 1929	CH	EG-Test	W: Fritz Löhner-Beda/M: B.G. de Sylva, L. Brown, R. Henderson	"The Varsity Drag" – Test Recording	Anna Has Money
Ausgerechnet Du (gehst an mir vorbei)	January 22,1929	CH	O-Test	W: Rosay/M: Irving Berlin	"Sunshine"	You Of All People
Bel Ami	May 3, 1939	MS	EG-Test		Not released. Last recording of the Meistersextett.	Dear Friend
Böhmisches Intermezzo	September 13, 1928	CH	NA	W: Rudolf Schanzer, Ernst Welisch/M: Johannn Strauß	From operetta *Casanova*. Not released.	Bohemian Intermezzo
Dans le jardin de mes Reves	June 18, 1937	VG	---	W: Louis Poterat/M: Bert Reisfeld, Rolf Marbot	Ger. "Kleine verträumte Madonna." French version not released.	In The Garden Of My Dreams
Eine kleine Frühlings-weise	February 27, 1939	MS	EG-Test	W: Hans Lengsfelder/M: Antonin Dvorak	"Humoreske," only test recording	A Little Spring Song
Es gibt nur eine Frau, die dich niemals vergißt	May 13, 1929	CH	O-Test	W: Kurt Schwabach/M: Jim Cowler	Not released	There Is Only One Woman Who Never Forgets You
Guten Abend, gut' Nacht	January 4, 1939	VG	---	M: Johannes Brahms	Not released	Good Evening, Good Night
Jig Walk	May 10, 1928	CH	G-Test	M: Duke Ellington	Not released	
La Chanson des Rues	May 11, 1937	VG	---		In French. Test recording	The Song Of The Streets

220

Song Title	Date Recorded	Group	Label*	Composers	Notes	English Translation
Morgenstim-mung	February 27. 1939	MS	EG-Test	W: Robert Reisfeld /M: Edvard Grieg	From *Peer Gynt*	Morning Mood
Ninon, du süße Frau	August 18, 1928	CH	G-Test	W: Fritz Löhner-Beda /M: G.B. de Sylva,R. Brown, R. Henderson	"So Blue." Unreleased on Gramophone. Released on Odeon.	Ninon, You Sweet Woman
Over The Blue	August 21, 1931	CH	EG-Test	W: Leigh/M: Werner Richard Heymann	See, "Wenn der Wind weht über das Meer"	
Penny Ser-enade	May 3, 1939	MS	EG-Test	W: Günther Schwenn, Paul Scheffers/M: M. Weersmann	Not released	
So Blue	May 10, 1928	CH	---	M: G.B. de Silva, R. Brown, R. Henderson	Test recording	So Blue
Souvenirs	September 13, 1928	CH	---	Horatio Nichols, Edgar Leslie	Not released	Souvenirs
Spiel mir mein Liebeslied (.... Lieblingslied?)	May 13, 1929	CH	O-Test	W: Roxy/M: Irving Berlin	"Roses Of Yesterday"	Play My Love Song For Me
Wie wun-dervoll küßt Annemarie	May 13, 1929	CH	O-Test	W: Fritz Rotter/M: C. Clare, L. Pollack	"Miss Annabelle Lee"	Annemarie Kisses Wonderfully

Appear Only In Films - Never Recorded						
Bißchen dies und bißchen das	December 3, 1930; February 11, 1931	CH	NA	W: Robert Gilbert/M: Werner Richard Heymann	Only in film *Ihre Hoheit befiehlt.* (Fr. *Princesse, à vos Ordres!)*	A Little Of This and Of That
Das Lieben bringt groß' Freud	1932	CH	NA	Traditional	German folk song, in film *Die Comedian Harmonists singen Volkslieder*	Love Brings Great Joy
Es geht bei gedämpftem Trommelklang	1932			?	In film *Die Comedian Harmonists singen Volkslieder*	It Goes With A Muffled Drum Sound
Hasch mich, mein Liebling, hasch mich	1931	CH	NA	W: Gerd Karlick/M: Nor-bert Glanzberg	Only in film *Der falsche Ehemann*	Catch Me, My Darling, Catch Me
Ich bin so furchtbar glücklich	1932	CH	NA	M: Otto Stransky	Only in the film *Spione im Savoy-Hotel* (also: *Die Galavorstellung der Fratellinis)*	I Am So Awfully Lucky

Song Title	Date Recorded	Group	Label*	Composers	Notes	English Translation
Appear Only In Films - Never Recorded						
O Straßburg	April 15, 1932		NA	?	In film *Die Comedian Harmonists singen Volkslieder*	Oh Strasbourg
St. Pauli	1931	CH	NA	?	In short film *Kabarett-Revue Nr. 6*. St. Pauli is a section of Hamburg.	
Wenn ich Sonntags in mein Kino geh'	August 15, 1932	CH	NA	W: Robert Gilbert/M: Werner Richard Heymann	Only in film *Ich bei Tag und Du bei Nacht* (I By Day And You By Night) (Fr: *A moi le jour, a toi la nuit*)	When I Go To The Cinema On Sundays
Zu Straßburg auf der Schanz'	April 15, 1932	CH	NA	?	In film *Die Comedian Harmonists singen Volkslieder*	In Strasbourg At The Rampart
Other						
Spiel mir ein Lied aus meiner Heimat	January 8, 1932	CH	---	?	CH with Marek Weber orchestra. The only reference is in Fechner's discography. There is no known 78rpm record.	Play Me A Song From My Homeland

Group Abbreviations

CH = Comedian Harmonists, the original group

VG = Vienna Group or the Comedy Harmonists

MS = Meistersextett

AG = American Group

Label Abbreviations:

B = HMV B
CduM = Chant du Monde
Col = Columbia
EA = HMV EA
EG = Electrola

EH = Electrola
G = Grammophon
HMV = HMV
K = HMV K (Disque Gramophone)

O = Odeon
T = Tonographie
X = HMV X

In the Label column, only the first release mentioned in the Schmauder book is listed.

Full information is available in Schmauder, Andreas: *Irgendwo auf der Welt – Die Schallplatten der Comedian Harmonists und ihrer Nachfolgegruppen.* Freiburg/Germany, 1999. See, www.phonopassion.de.

Appendix D
Comedian Harmonists

List of Concerts
Courtesy of Jan Grübler and Theo Niemeyer

Date	City	Venue	Notes
September 3 to December 31, 1928	Berlin	Großes Schauspielhaus, Charell Revue *Casanova*	Weekly fee - 600 Marks
October 9-31, 1928	Berlin	Kabarett der Komiker (KaDeKo)	Daily fee - 90 Marks
October 19, 1928	Berlin	Großes Schauspielhaus	"Brigitten-Tag," Ullstein-Verlag
November 1-30, 1928	Berlin	Barberina/Valencia	
November 16, 1928	Berlin	Großes Schauspielhaus	"Brigitten-Tag," Ullstein-Verlag
January 1-February 28, 1929	Berlin	Großes Schauspielhaus	Charell-Revue *Casanova*
January 30, 1929	Berlin	Kaiserhof	25th Anniversary of Lindström Company
February 17, 1929	Berlin	Zoo, Kaisersaal	
March 1-31, 1929	Hamburg	Hansa-Theater	With Willi Steiner
April 27, 1929	Berlin	Atrium-Beba-Palast, Kaiseralle 178/179	Deutscher Bühnen-Klub
May 16-31, 1929	Cologne	Revue theatre Groß-Köln	Five songs daily + encore (25 min.) Total – 2200 Marks
June 1-30, 1929	Berlin	Scala	Theft of tailcoats
July 12-15, 1929	Berlin	Elysium-Kino-Palast	
July 22-31, 1929	Berlin	Kabarett "Der blaue Vogel"	
July 31, 1929	Berlin	?	"Jockey"/ "Zuck…"?
August 1–16, 1929	Berlin	Plaza	
August 16–November 27, 1929	Berlin	Berliner Theater	Spoliansky-Revue, *Zwei Krawatten* (Two Ties), with Hans Albers and Marlene Dietrich. Daily fee – 150 Marks (Rehearsals; premiere September 5, 1929)
September 11, 1929	Berlin	?	"Brigitten-Tag," Ullstein-Verlag, 10 minutes, 200 Marks
October 1-31, 1929	Hamburg	Hansa-Theater	
October 1929	Berlin	Frolics-Restaurant	Two performances
October 12, 1929	Berlin	Bial (?)	
November 9, 1929	Berlin	Titania-Palast	
November 28, 1929	Berlin	Kabarett der Komiker (KaDeKo)	

November 28, 1929 to December 4, 1929	Berlin	Atrium-Beba-Filmpalast (Cinema)	Two performances daily. Altogether 12 performances
December 1, 1929	Berlin	Großes Schauspielhaus	Telefunken-Matinee With Marguerita Perras and Max Hansen
December 7, 1929	Berlin	Universum Filmpalast; Lehniner Platz	
October 10-15, 1929	Berlin	Titania Palast	
from December 23, 1929	Leipzig	Schauspielhaus	Start of rehearsals for *Zwei Krawatten*
from December 25, 1929	Leipzig	Schauspielhaus	Performances of *Zwei Krawatten*
January 2–4, 1930	Leipzig	Schauspielhaus	
January 4, 1930	Leipzig	House of Electrola Company	Reception for Countess Esterhazy
January 8-17, 1930	Leipzig	Schauspielhaus	Extension of contract for *Zwei Krawatten*
January 15, 1930	Leipzig	Schauspielhaus	*Künstler-Redoute*, formal with raffle
January 18, 1930	Berlin	Colosseum (Cinema)	
January 20, 1930	Stettin	Preußenhof Halls	With the solo dancer Dorothea Albu. (Considered to be the first full-evening concert of the Comedian Harmonists). 950 Marks.
January 26, 1930	Leipzig	Schauspielhaus	*Tempo-Varieté*, matinee with Lu Basler and others
February 2, 1930	Leipzig	Schauspielhaus	*Tempo-Varieté* 18 songs, 1324 Marks.
February 7-10, 1930	Berlin	Filmeck Skalitzer Str. 94 (cinema, theatre and varieté)	
February 22, 1930	Leipzig	Private party at Carl-Tauchnitz-Str. 11	Private performance for Geheimrat (Privy Councilor) Edgar Herfurth
March 1, 1930	Dresden	Harmonie/Die Komödie	With Berty Spielmann.
March 2-9, 1930	Leipzig	Schauspielhaus	*Tempo-Varieté* With Blandine Ebinger and others
March 11-15, 1930	Erfurt	Stadttheater	*Tempo-Varieté* With Blandine Ebinger and Curt von Wolowsky
March 29, 1930?	Jena		
March 30, 1930	Apolda	Kristall-Palast	
March 30-31, 1930	Gera	Gesellschaftshaus "Heinrichsbrücke"	Night show with Lu Basler, Ingeborg Lotti
April 1-2, 1930	Weimar	Zentral-Palast	*Tempo-Varieté*. Night show with Lu Basler, Ingeborg Lotti
April 3, 1930	Plauen	Feldschlösschen	*Tempo-Varieté*. Night show with Lu Basler, Ingeborg Lotti
April 4, 1930	Plauen	Zentralhalle	*Tempo-Varieté*. Night show with Lu Basler, Ingeborg Lotti

April 5, 1930	Weimar	Zentral-Palast	*Tempo-Varieté*. Night show with Lu Basler, Ingeborg Lotti
April 10-15, 1930	Mannheim	Apollo-Theater	*Tempo-Varieté*. Night show with Lu Basler, Ingeborg Lotti
April 19, 20, 21, 23, 24, 26, 27, 1930	Frankfurt a. M.	Neues Theater	*Tempo-Varieté*. Night show with Blandine Ebinger and Curt von Wolowsky
May 1, 1930	Baden-Baden	Städtisches Schauspiel-haus	*Tempo-Varieté*. Same program, with Erich Kuttner for the sick Curt von Wolowsky
May 2-4, 1930	Darmstadt	Orpheum	*Tempo-Varieté*
August 23, 1930	Berlin Leipzig	Pariser Hof Schauspielhaus	Start of rehearsals for the revue *Wie werde ich reich und glücklich?*
August 30-31, September 1-6, 1930	Leipzig	Schauspielhaus	Premiere of the revue *Wie werde ich reich und glücklich?* Approximately 500 Mk. per night.
September 7, 1930	Leipzig	Schauspielhaus	Matinee with the conférencier Rudolf Schaffganz and Blandine Ebinger, additional night show
September 8-13, 1930	Leipzig	Schauspielhaus	Revue *Wie werde ich reich und glücklich?*
September 14, 1930	Leipzig	Schauspielhaus	Revue *Wie werde ich reich und glücklich?* Two performances; with Lu Basler.
September 15-16, 1930	Leipzig	Schauspielhaus	Revue *Wie werde ich reich und glücklich?*
September 17, 1930	Leipzig	Schauspielhaus	Revue *Wie werde ich reich und glücklich?* Two performances (one at Brigittenburg)
September 18, 1930	Leipzig	Schauspielhaus	Revue *Wie werde ich reich und glücklich?*
September 21, 1930	Leipzig	Schauspielhaus	Revue *Wie werde ich reich und glücklich?* Matinee with the conférencier Rudolf Schaffganz and Blandine Ebinger; additional night show
November 1-4, 1930	Amsterdam (NL)	Cabaret La Gaité	Two performances. (Additional radio transmission at night November 4 – A.V.R.O. Hilversum.) First foreign concert of the Comedian Harmonists. 150 Guilders per night.
November 5-6, 1930	Amsterdam (NL)	Tuschinski Theater	
November 8, 1930	Berlin	Atrium-Beba-Palast	Night show of the society Deutscher Bühnen-Klub
November 11, 1930	Breslau	Großer Konzerthaussaal	with Marcel Wittrisch, Musikhaus Kayser, Breslau. (Originally planned for November 7.)
November 18, 20-22, 24-27, 1930	Berlin	Atrium-Beba-Palast, Kaiseralle 178/179	Berliner Lichtspiel-Theater-AG.

November 27-December 1, 1930	Berlin	Titania-Palast, Steglitz	
December 4, 1930	Breslau	Großer Konzerthaussaal	Musikhaus Kayser
January 16-18, 1931	Leipzig	Schauspielhaus	
January 22, 1931	Breslau	Konzerthaus	1200 Marks
January 1931?	Glogau (Schlesien)		
February 4, 1931	Leipzig	Funkball at Zoo	Four performances
February 7, 1931	Berlin	Atrium-Beba-Palast	
February 21, 1931	Berlin	Admiralspalast	
February 22, 1931	Berlin	UFA-Palace at Zoo	
February 22, 1931	Stettin	Preußenhof-Säle	
February 28, 1931-March 8, 1931	Leipzig	Altes Theater	Evening gala with Robert Meyn as conférencier and R.A. Sievers and Lina Carstens
March 12, 1931	Magdeburg	Fürstencafé	
March 13-14, 1931	Magdeburg	Fürstencafé	"
March 15, 1931	Leipzig	Neues Theater	Matinee, with Blandine Ebinger, among others
March 19, 1931	Dessau	Kristallpalast	
March 28, 1931	Magdeburg	Kristallpalast	
March 29-30, 1931	Amsterdam (NLD)	Party for Mengelberg	
April 6, 1931	Berlin	Titania-Palace	Matinee with Willi Schaeffers
April 6, 1931	Görlitz		
April 7, 1931	Dresden	Künstlerhaus	
April 8, 1931	Beuthen	Gemeindehaus	
April 9, 1931	Gleiwitz		
April 12, 1931	Marienburg		
April 14, 1931	Elbing	Great Hall of Holiday Home	
April 15, 1931	Tilsit		
April 17, 1931	Insterburg		
April 19, 1931	Königsberg		
April 22, 1931	Danzig		
April 24, 1931	Bremen		625 Marks
April 25, 1931	Hannover	Konzerthaus an der Goethebrücke	
April 26, 1931	Leipzig	Neues Stadttheater	
April 26, 1931	Dresden	Künstlerhaus	
April 27, 1931	Göttingen		
April 29, 1931	Dresden	Vereinshaus	
April 30, 1931	Breslau		
May 1, 1931	Liegnitz	Schießhaus	

May 2, 1931	Hirschberg/Riesen-gebirge		
May 3, 1931	Görlitz	Vereinshaus	
May 4, 1931	Zittau		
May 8, 1931	Frankfurt//Oder		
May 11, 1931	Halle	Thalia-Theater	
May 12, 1931	Hannover	Konzerthaus an der Goethebrücke	
May 14, 1931	Darmstadt	Orpheum	
May 15, 1931	Marburg	Stadtsäle	
May 17, 1931	Worms	Kasinosaal	
May 18, 1931	Hanau		
May 20, 1931	Worms		
May 21, 1931	Darmstadt	Orpheum	
May 22, 1931	Darmstadt		
May 23, 1931	Wiesbaden	Movie palace	
May 27-28, 1931	Mainz	Liedertafel	
May 29, 1931	Heidelberg		600 Marks
May 30, 1931	Mannheim		
June 4, 1931	Copenhagen DK	Tivoli	Plus night show at the cabaret Arena (Tivoli)
July 8, 1931?	Bad Orb ?		
July 30–August 1, 1931	Scheveningen (NLD)		
August 10, 1931	Bad Pyrmont		
August 21-31, 1931	Berlin	Universum, UFA-theatre at Lehniner Platz	
August 29, 1931	Berlin	Funkhalle Kaiserdamm	
September 5, 1931	Copenhagen	Tivoli	1500 DKr.
September 10, 1931	Oslo	Universitetes Aula	
September 12, 1931	Oslo	Universitetes Aula	
September 13, 1931	Oslo	Universitetes Aula	
September 15, 1931	Copenhagen	Odd Fellow Palais	
September 16, 1931	Leipzig	Zoo-Halls	Afternoon and night (for the gazette "Freund der Hausfrau" and the Leipzig Housewives Association)
September 17, 1931	Mockern	Society "Pleissenaue"	
September 18, 1931	Halle/Saale	Thalia-Theater	
September 29, 1931?	Dresden		
September 30, 1931?	Chemnitz		
October 1, 1931	Rössen	Leuna-Works	
October 6-7, 1931	Kassel	City park	

October 9 -15, 1931	Leipzig	Altes Theater	
October 16, 1931	Breslau	Konzerthaussaal	
October 17, 1931	Coburg	Verein d. Musikfreunde	
October 20-21, 1931	Stockholm	Auditorium in Konzert-bolaget	
October 23-24, 1931	Oslo	Nationaltheatret	
October 25, 1931	Oslo	Assembly hall	
October 26-27, 1931	Copenhagen	Odd Fellow Palais	
October 28, 1931	Kiel	Reichshallen	
October 29, 1931	Hamburg	Musikhalle	1252 Marks
October 30, 1931	Stettin	Konzerthaussaal	
November 3, 1931	Zittau	Cancelled	Cancelled. Nov. 2 - Beuthen; Nov. 3 - Gleiwitz
November 4, 1931	Breslau	Konzerthaussaal	
November 5, 1931	Liegnitz	Schützenhaussaal	
November 6, 1931	Waldenburg		
November 7, 1931	Leipzig-Plagwitz	Felsenkeller	
November 8-9, 1931	Glogau	Weißer Saal	
November 10, 1931	Erfurt	Stadthaussaal	
November 11, 1931	Marburg	Stadthalle	
November 14, 1931	Hanover	Konzerthaus an der Goethebrücke	1620 Mk.
November 16, 1931	Amsterdam (NL)	Muziek-Lyceum	
November 17, 1931	Rotterdam (NL)	Gebouw vor Kunst en Wetenschapen	
November 19, 1931	Arnheim (NL)	Musis Sacrum	
November 20, 1931	Leiden (NL)	Stadsgehoorzaal	
November 21, 1931	Amsterdam (NL)	Carlton-Hotel	Wagner-Souper
November 22, 1931	The Hague (NL)	Diligentia	
November 23, 1931	Haarlem (NL)	Stadsschouwburg	
November 24, 1931	Amsterdam (NL)	Muziek-Lyceum	
November 25, 1931	Rotterdam (NL)	Gebouw vor K. en W.	
November 26, 1931	Zeist (NL)	Figi	
November 28, 1931	Halmand (NL)	Zaal Geenen	
November 29, 1931	The Hague (NL)	Diligentia	
December 1, 1931	Amsterdam (NL)	Concertgebouw	
December 3, 1931	Waldenburg/Silesia	Capitol	
December 4, 1931	Zittau	Lindenhof	600 Mk.
December 5, 1931	Görlitz	Evangelisches Vereinshaus	
December 6, 1931	Prague (CS)	Bursa	
December 7, 1931	Vienna (AT)	Mittlerer Konzerthaus-Saal	

December 13, 1931	Berlin	Admiralspalast	"Mixed afternoon"
December 25, 1931	Amsterdam (NL)	Musik-Lyceum	
December 26, 1931	The Hague (NL)	Diligentia	
December 27, 1931	Rotterdam (NL)	Gebouw vor K. en W.	Afternoon performance
December 27, 1931	The Hague (NL)	Diligentia	Night performance
December 28, 1931	Haarlem (NL)		
December 29, 1931	Arnheim (NL)		
January 10, 1932	Prague (CS)	Bursa	
January 11, 1932	Vienna (AT)	Musikvereinssaal	
January 12, 1932	Liegnitz	Schützenhaus	
January 13, 1932	Breslau	Großer Konzerthaussaal	
January 14, 1932	Schweidnitz	Braukommune	
January 15, 1932	Sprottau	Konzerthaus	
January 16, 1932	Glogau/Silesia	Weißer Saal	
January 17, 1932	Neusalz/Oder	Volksbühne/Reichshallen	
January 18, 1932	Waldenburg	Capitol	
January 21, 1932	Berlin	Philharmonie	Winter aid and artists pension aid, with Marek Weber
January 22, 1932	Hanover	Konzerthaus an der Goethebrücke	
January 23, 1932	Göttingen	Stadtpark	
January 24, 1932	Wiesbaden	Kurhaus	
January 26 – 27, 1932	Kassel	Stadtpark	Two performances
January 28, 1932	Karlsruhe	Festhalle	
January 29-30, 1932	Darmstadt	Orpheum	
January 31, 1932	Stuttgart	Liederhalle	
February 1, 1932	Heidelberg	Stadthalle	
February 2, 1932	Frankfurt a. M.	Saalbau	2315 Mk.
February 3, 1932	Erfurt	Stadthaussaal	
February 4, 1932	Weimar	Saal Armbrust	
February 5, 1932	Chemnitz	Kaufmännisches Verein-shaus	
February 7, 1932	Dresden	Evangelisches Vereinshaus	
February 8, 1932	Halle/Saale	Stadtschützenhaus	
February 9, 1932	Hamburg	Musikhalle	2000 Mk.
February 10, 1932	Kiel	Reichshallen	1200 Mk.
February 12, 1932	Danzig	Friedrich-Wilhelm-Schüt-zenhaus	
February 13, 1932	Tilsit/East Prussia	Stadttheater	
February 14, 1932	Elbing/East Prussia	Pädagogische Akademie	
February 15, 1932	Königsberg/ East Prussia	Opernhaus	

February 16, 1932	Potsdam	Konzerthaus	
March 5-8, 1932	Leipzig	Schauspielhaus.	Night shows at the Leipzig Fair
March 9-10, 1932	Leipzig	Schauspielhaus	Rehearsals for *Artisten*
March 11, 1932	Leipzig	Schauspielhaus	Premiere of *Artisten*
March 12-16, 1932 (possibly longer?)	Leipzig	Schauspielhaus	Daily, two performances of *Artisten*
March 19, 1932	Jena	Volkshaus	
March 20, 1932	Dresden	Evangelisches Vereinshaus	
March 21, 1932	Halle	Stadtschützenhaus	
March 22, 1932	Gera	Heinrichsbrücke	
March 23, 1932	Halberstadt	Stadtpark	
March 24, 26-31, April 1, 1932	Berlin	Gloria-Palast	
April 2, 1932	Ilmenau	Turnhalle	
April 3, 1932	Mühlhausen	Konzerthaus	
April 4, 1932	Würzburg	Huttensaal	
April 6, 1932	Munich	Tonhalle	
April 7, 1932	Nuremberg	Kulturverein	
April 8, 1932	Augsburg	Ludwigssbau	
April 9, 1932	Munich	Tonhalle	2353 Mk.
April 10, 1932	Karlsruhe	Festhalle	660 Mk.
April 11, 1932	Stuttgart	Liederhalle	
April 12, 1932	Pforzheim	Saalbau	
April 13, 1932	Ludwigshafen		
April 14, 1932	Frankfurt a. M.	Saalbau	
April 15, 1932	Mainz	Liedertafel	
April 16, 1932	Wiesbaden	Großer Kurhaussaal	
April 17, 1932	Saarbrücken	Wartburg	
April 18, 1932	Offenbach	Turnhalle	
April 19, 1932	Düsseldorf	Kaisersaal in der Tonhalle	
April 20, 1932	Cologne	Bürgersaal	
April 21, 1932	Dortmund	Goldsaal der Westfalen-halle	
April 28, 1932	Berlin	Orpheum Hasenheide	Charity concert
May 6, 1932	Elberfeld	Stadthalle	
May 7, 1932	Cologne	Bürgersaal	
May 8, 1932	Bonn	Beethovensaal	
May 9, 1932	Krefeld	Stadthalle	
May 10, 1932	Essen	Saalbau	
May 11, 1932	Düsseldorf	Tonhalle	
May 12-13, 1932	Basel (CH)	Küchlin-Theater	

May 16, 1932	Bad Kreuznach	Kurhaussaal	
May 17, 1932	Koblenz	Stadthalle	
May 18, 1932	Dortmund	Goldsaal der Westfalen-halle	600 Mk.
May 19, 1932	Worms	Festhalle "12 Apostel"	
May 21, 1932	Aschaffenburg	Festsaal "Frohsinn"	
June 2, 1932	Eisenach	Fürstenhof	
June 3, 1932	Pößneck	Schützenhaus	
June 6, 1932	Gotha	Schießhaus	
June 7, 1932	Meiningen	Casino-Lichtspiele	
August 16, 1932	Scheveningen (NL)		
August 18, 1932	The Hague (NL)	Kurhaus	
September 13, 1932	Copenhagen (DK)	Odd Fellow Palaets	
September 14, 1932	Holbaek (DK)	Musikverein	
September 15, 1932	Copenhagen (DK)	Odd Fellow Palaets	
September 16, 1932	Slagelse (DK)	Casino Musikverein	
September 18, 1932	Odense (DK)	Großer Saal	
September 19-20, 1932	Aarhus (DK)		
September 21, 1932	Vejle (DK)	Saal des Handwerksv-ereins	
September 30, 1932	Danzig	Sporthalle	
October 1, 1932	Königsberg/ East Prussia	Stadthalle	981 Mk.
October 3, 1932	Elbing/ East Prussia	Weltbühne	
October 1932	Essen	Saalbau	
October 8, 1932	Dresden	Ev. Vereinshaus	
October 9, 1932	Chemnitz	Kaufmännisches Verein-shaus	
October 10, 1932	Plauen		
October 11, 1932	Zwickau	Schwanenschloss	
October 16, 1932	Berlin	Theater am Bülowplatz/ Volksbühne	
October 17, 1932	Halle	Stadtschützenhaus	
October 18, 1932	Weimar	Saal Armbrust	
October 19, 1932	Erfurt	Kaisersaal	
October 20, 1932	Apolda	Bürgerverein	
October 21, 1932	Quedlinburg	Kaiserhof	
October 23, 1932	Zürich (CH)	Kleiner Tonhallensaal	
October 24, 1932	Basel (CH)	Großer Musiksaal	
October 26, 1932	Bern (CH)	Großer Kasino-Saal	
October 27, 1932	Zurich (CH)	Kleiner Tonhallensaal	

October 31, 1932	Prenzlau		
November 1, 1932	Stettin	Konzerthaus	1200 Mk.
November 2, 1932	Hamburg	Conventgarten	
November 5, 1932	Munich	Tonhalle	
November 6, 1932	Ulm	Saalbau	First planned for November 4. Postponed for a speech of Adolf Hitler.
November 7, 1932	Augsburg	Ludwigsbau	
November 8, 1932	Regensburg	Neuhaussaal	
November 9, 1932	Nuremberg	Kulturverein	
November 10, 1932	Bamberg	Zentralsaal	
November 11, 1932	Würzburg	Huttensäale	
November 12, 1932	Gießen	Stadttheater	
November 13, 1932	Darmstadt	Städt. Saalbau	
November 14, 1932	Frankfurt a. M.	Saalbau	
November 15, 1932	Göttingen	Stadtpark	
November 17, 1932	Hanover	Konzerthaus an der Goethebrücke	
November 18, 1932	Berlin	Philharmonie	
November 23, 1932	Darmstadt	Saalbau	
November 26, 1932	Prague (CS)	Bursa	
December 4, 1932	Magdeburg	Kristallpalast	
December 5, 1932	Brandenburg	Schweizergarten	
December 7, 1932	Gouda (NL)	Schauburg	
December 8, 1932	Breda (NL)	Concordia	
December 9, 1932	Veisringen (NL)	Hotel Briflania	
December 10, 1932	Dortrecht (NL)	Kunstverein	
December 12, 1932	Arnheim (NL)	Musis Sacrium	
December 13, 1932	Nymvegen (NL)	Muziekverenigung	
December 14, 1932	Hilversum	Casino	
December 15, 1932	Enschede (NL)	Große Societeit	
December 16, 1932	Rotterdam (NL)	Gebouw vor K. en W.	
December 17, 1932	Amsterdam (NL)	Muziek Lyceum	
December 18, 1932	The Hague (NL)	Konzertsaal Diligentia	
December 19, 1932	Utrecht (NL)	Tivoli	
December 20, 1932	Venlo (NL)	Konzerthaussaal "Prins v. Oranje"	
December 25, 1932	The Hague (NL)	Diligentia	
December 26, 1932	Amsterdam (NL)	Concertgebouw	
January 9, 1933	Potsdam	Konzerthaus	930 Mk.
January 10, 1933	Bonn	Bürger-Verein	
January 11, 1933	Cologne	Großer Lesesaal	

Date	City	Venue	Notes
January 12, 1933	Essen	Saalbau	
January 13, 1933	Münster	Stadthalle	
January 14, 1933	Dortmund	Goldsaal der Westfalen-halle	
January 15, 1933	Düsseldorf	Apollo-Theater	
January 16, 1933	Saarbrücken	Wartburg-Saal	
January 17, 1933	Strasbourg (FR)	Palais des Fetes	
January 18, 1933	Karlsruhe	Eintrachtsaal	
January 19, 1933	Kaiserslautern	Fruchthallensaal	
January 20, 1933	Höchst	Volksbildungs-verein	
January 21, 1933	Mannheim	Musensaal	
January 22, 1933	Wiesbaden	Kursaal	
January 23, 1933	Freiburg in Breisgau	Paulussaal	
January 24, 1933	Heidelberg	Festhalle	
January 29, 1933	Berlin	Theater am Bülow-platz/ Volksbühne	Cabaret-matinee. 600 Mk.
February 8, 1933	Flensburg	Deutsches Haus	
February 9, 1933	Kiel	Gewerkschaftshaus	
February 10, 1933	Schwerin	Staatstheater	
February 11, 1933	Lübeck	Verein der Lübecker Presse	Pressefest
February 13, 1933	Copenhagen	Odd Fellow Palaets	
February 14, 1933	Odense	Fyns Versammlungshaus	
February 15, 1933	Rostock	Philharmonie	900 Mk.
February 16, 1933	Hildesheim	Stadthalle	
February 17, 1933	Aachen		
February 19, 1933	Plauen	Pratersaal	
February 20, 1933	Zwickau	Schwanenschloß	
February 21, 1933	Gera	Heinrichsbrücke	
February 22, 1933	Zittau	Lindenhof	
February 23, 1933	Görlitz	Tivoli	
February 24, 1933	Liegnitz	Schützenhaus	
February 26, 1933	Dresden	Ev. Vereinshaus	
March 3, 1933	Hamburg	Conventgarten	
March 9, 1933	Großenhain/ Saxonia	Sachsenhof	
March 10, 1933	Freiberg/Sa.		
March 11, 1933	Eger (CS)		
March 12, 1933	Karlsbad (CS)	Schützenhaus	
March 13, 1933	Teplitz (CS)	Stadttheater	
March 14, 1933	Gablonz (CS)	Turnhalle	

March 15, 1933	Reichenberg (CS)	Turnhalle	
March 16, 1933	Leitmeritz (CS)	Turnhalle	
March 17, 1933	Bodenbach (CS)	Kinovarieté	.
March 18, 1933	Prague (CS)	Luzerna	
March 21, 1933	Sonneberg/ Thuringia	Stadttheater	
March 22, 1933	Schweinfurt	Evangelisches Vereinshaus	
March 23, 1933	Nuremberg	Kulturverein	
March 24, 1933	Würzburg	Huttensäle	
March 25, 1933	Munich	Tonhalle	1740 Mk.
March 26, 1933	Regensburg	Neuhaussaal	
March 27, 1933	Ulm	Saalbau	
March 28, 1933	Bayreuth	Evangelischer Gemeinde- haussaal	
April 1, 1933	Berlin	UFA-Palace at zoo	Night performance for Berlin winter aid
April 7, 1933	Bremen	Zentralhallen	
April 8, 1933	Wilhelmshaven		
April 9, 1933?	Bremerhaven		Probably cancelled
April 10, 1933?	Oldenburg		Probably cancelled
April 11, 1933	Braunschweig	Hofjägersaal	
April 12, 1933?	Celle		
April 13, 1933?	Aschersleben		
April 26, 28-30, 1933	Oslo (NO)	Universitetes Aula	
April 27, 1933	Drammen (NO)	Stadttheater	
May 10, 1933	Cottbus	Staebnersaal	
May 11, 1933	Frankfurt / Oder	Bellevue-Saal	
May 12, 1933	Dessau	Kristallpalast	
May 13, 1933	Magdeburg	Kristallpalast	
May 15, 1933	Meißen	Kronensaal	
May 16, 1933	Bautzen	Hotel zur Krone	
May 20, 1933	Troppau (CS)	Stadttheater	
May 21, 1933	Mährisch-Ostrau (CS)	Deutsches Haus	
May 22, 1933	Brünn (CS)	Stadion	
May 23, 1933	Olmütz (CS)		
May 24, 1933	Frankenau (CS)		.
May 25, 1933	Gablonz (CS)	Turnhalle	
May 26, 1933	Böhmisch Leipa (CS)		
May 28, 1933	Teplitz (CS)	Turnhalle	
May 29, 1933	Schlenkenau (CS)	Lichtspielhaus	

May 30, 1933	Wansdorf (CS)	Kino	
May 31, 1933	Bryx (CS)		
June 1, 1933	Komotau (CS)		Tour was stopped on June 2 in Bodenbach
June 9-18, 1933	Genf (CH)	Kursaal	
October 12, 1933	Braunschweig	Hofjäger-Saal	
October 13, 1933	Hanover	Konzerthaus an der Goethebrücke	1180 Mk.
October 14, 1933	Hildesheim	Stadthalle	
October 16, 1933	Strasbourg (FR)	Palais de Fétes	
October 17, 1933	Genf (CH)	Victoria-Hall	
October 18, 1933	Lyon (FR)	Salle Ruseau	
October 19, 1933	Paris (FR)	Maison Gaveau	
October 24, 1933	Brussels (BE)	Palais des Beaux Arts	
October 27, 1933	Paris (FR)	Maison Gaveau	
November 3, 1933	Copenhagen (DK)	Odd Fellow Palaets	
November 5, 1933	Oslo (NO)	Universitetes Aula	
November 6, 1933	Drammen (NO)	Stadttheater	
November 7, 1933	Oslo (NO)	Logens Store Sal	
November 8, 1933	Oslo (NO)	Universitetes Aula	
November 9, 1933	Copenhagen (DK)	Tivolis Concertsal	
November 10, 1933	Rostock		
November 12-18, 1933	Czechia		
November 19, 1933	Hamburg	Covent Garten	
November 24, 1933	Berlin	Philharmonie	2000 Mk for winter aid. 2600 persons.
November 28, 1933	Plauen	Pratersaal	
November 29, 1933	Zwickau	Schwanenschloß	
November 30, 1933	Freiberg	Tivoli-Saal	
December 1, 1933	Zittau	Lindenhof	600 Mk.
December 2, 1933	Bautzen	Hotel zur Krone	
December 3, 1933	Dresden	Ev. Vereinshaus	
December 4, 1933	Leipzig	Alberthalle	
December 5, 1933	Dessau	Kristallpalast	
December 9, 1933	Halle	Stadtschützenhaus	
December 10, 1933	Frankfurt a. M.	Saalbau	
December 11, 1933	Mannheim	Musensaal des Rosengartens	
December 12, 1933	Heidelberg	Stadthalle	
December 13, 1933	Wiesbaden	Kurhaus	
December 14, 1933	Darmstadt	Orpheum	

December 15, 1933	Luxemburg (L)	Centre municipal "Cercle"	
December 16, 1933	The Hague (NL)	Diligentia	
December 17, 1933	Amsterdam (NL)	Muziek-Lyceum	
December 18, 1933	Harlem (NL)	Konzertsaal	
December 19, 1933	Utrecht (NL)	Tivoli	
December 20, 1933	Eindhoven (NL)	Philipps Gebouw	
December 21, 1933	Deventer (NL)	Buitensozieteit	
December 22, 1933	Nymwegen (NL)	Vereenigung	
December 25, 1933	The Hague (NL)	Diligentia	
December 26, 1933	Rotterdam (NL)	Doelenzaal	Afternoon
December 26, 1933	Amsterdam (NL)	Muziek-Lyceum	Night
December 27, 1933	Venlo (NL)	Konzerthaussaal Prins v. Oranje	
January 3, 1934	Stettin		
January 5, 1934	Berlin	Philharmonie	2100 Mk.
January 10, 1934	Breslau	Gr. Konzerthaussaal	
January 11, 1934	Gleiwitz	Stadttheater	
January 12, 1934	Waldenburg	Helmuth-Brückner-Halle	
January 13, 1934	Breslau	Südparksaal	
January 14, 1934	Liegnitz	Schießhaus	
January 15, 1934	Görlitz	Tivoli	
January 16, 1934	Chemnitz	Kaufmännisches Verein-shaus	
January 17, 1934	Dresden	Ev. Vereinshaus	
January 18, 1934	Leipzig	Großer Festsaal des Zentraltheaters	
January 19, 1934	Vienna (AT)	Großer Konzerthaussaal	
January 20, 1934	Brünn (CS)?		
January 21, 1934	Budapest (HUN)	Vigado-Bau, Großer Saal	
February 1, 1934	Rostock	Philharmonie	
February 2, 1934	Schwerin	Stadthalle	
February 3, 1934	Kiel	Haus der Arbeit	
February 4, 1934	Hamburg	Conventgarten	
February 5, 1934	Wilhelmshaven		
February 6, 1934	Lübeck	Kolosseum	
February 7, 1934	Bremerhaven	Stadthalle, Großer Saal	First forbidden by district head of N.S.D.A.P.
February 8, 1934	Bremen	Großer Saal der Union "Die Glocke"	1487 Mk.
February 9, 1934	Berlin	Philharmonie	2100 Mk.
February 17, 1934	Bielefeld	Tonhalle auf dem Johan-nisberg	

February 18, 1934	Düsseldorf	Tonhalle, Kaisersaal	
February 19, 1934	Rheydt	Stadthalle	
February 20, 1934	Krefeld	Stadthalle	
February 21, 1934	Cologne	Großer Saal der Bürgerge-sellschaft	
February 22, 1934	Dortmund	Goldsaal der Westfalen-halle	
February 23, 1934	Essen	Saalbau, Großer Saal	
February 25, 1934?	Freiburg i. Brsg.		
February 26, 1934	Strasbourg (FR)	Palais des Fétes	
February 27, 1934	Mulhouse (FR)	Grand Salle de la Bourse	
March 1, 1934	Paris (FR)	Théatre des Champs-Elysées	
March 2, 1934	Lüttich (BE)	Théatre Royal	
March 3, 1934	Antwerp (BE)	St. Augustinus Kring	
March 4, 1934	Brussels (BE)	Palais des Beaux Arts	
March 10, 1934	Hof		Forbidden
March 11, 1934	Bamberg	Zentralsaal	
March 12, 1934	Schweinfurt	Ev. Vereinshaus	
March 13, 1934	Munich	Tonhalle	At first forbidden. Previously thought to be last German concert.
March 14, 1934	Augsburg	Ludwigsbau	1200 Mk.
March 15, 1934	Ulm	Saalbau	724 Mk.
March 16, 1934	Worms	Zum Karpfen	600 Mk.
March 17, 1934	Darmstadt	Saalbau	724 Mk.
March 19, 1934	Offenbach	Turnhalle	732 Mk.
March 20, 1934	Stuttgart	Festsaal der Liederhalle	Probably with the reported disturbances. 1909 Mk.
March 21, 1934	Frankfurt a. M.	Saalbau	1978 Mk.
March 22, 1934	Mainz	Liedertafel	784 Mk.
March 23, 1934	Kassel	Vereinshaus	802 Mk.
March 24, 1934	Trier	Treviris	930 Mk.
March 25, 1934	Hanover	Konzerthaus an der Goethebrücke	Last concert in Germany. 1111 Mk.
March 26, 1934	Strasbourg (FR)		
April 21, 1934	Copenhagen (DK)	Odd Fellow Palaets	
April 22, 1934	Oslo (NO)	Universitetes Aula	
April 24, 1934	Oslo (NO)	Logens Store Sal	
April 25, 1934	Oslo (NO)	Universitetes Aula	
May 8, 1934	New York (USA)	Radio broadcasts May 29, 30, 31, June 1, 4, 5, 7, 8, 10, 1934	Departure for New York. Arrival – May 14, 1934.
June 12, 1934	New York (USA)	U.S.S. Saratoga	

June 13-16, 1934	New York (USA)	June 13-16 – radio broadcasting	June 18 – travel to Bremerhaven – arriving June 25, 1934.
August 4, 1934	Scheveningen (NL)		
September 14 to October 4, 1934	Paris (FR)	Theatre A.B.C.	Two revue performances daily.
October 31, 1934	Siena (ITA) (?)		
November 16, 1934	Mailand (ITA)	Theatro del Popolo	
November 18, 1934	Perugia (ITA)	Academia dei Filedoni	
November 19, 1934	Rome (ITA)	Philharmonie	
November 21, 1934	Bologna (ITA)	Liceo Musica	
November 22, 1934	Genoa (ITA)	Giordino d'Italia	
November 24, 1934	Turin (ITA)	Universitae Musicale	
November 25, 1934	Padua (ITA)		
November 26, 1934	Trieste (ITA)	Societa Romerti	
November 27, 1934	Fiume (ITA)		
November 28, 1934	Innsbruck (T)		
December 25, 1934	The Hague (NL)	Diligentia	With radio transmission
December 26, 1934	Rotterdam (NL) Amsterdam (NL)	Doelenzaal (afternoon) Concertgebouw (night)	
January 15, 1935	Copenhagen (DK)	Odd Fellow Palaets	
January 18, 1935	Sarpsborg (DK)		
January 19, 1935	Oslo (NO)		
January 20, 1935	Oslo (NO)		
January 21, 1935	Tönsberg (NO)		
January 22, 1935	Skien (NO) Sarvik (NO)	(afternoon) (night)	
January 23, 1935	Fredrikstad (NO)		The last concert of the Comedian Harmonists.

Sources: Comedian Harmonists Archiv, Theo Niemeyer
Estate Robert Biberti, State Library, Berlin
Czada/Große, *Comedian Harmonists – ein Vokalensemble erobert die Welt*.

* Amounts received for performances are listed occasionally to give the reader some idea of the earnings.

Comedy Harmonists ("Vienna Group")

Complete Concert List

Courtesy of Theo Niemeyer, Comedian Harmonists Archive, Hamburg;
Michael Hortig, Graz, Austria; Jan Grübler, Oranienburg, Germany

Date	City	Venue	Notes
August 1935	Geneva (CH)	Cure Hall	
August 1935	Nice (FR)	Casino de Juan-les-Pins	
September 1935	Lausanne (CH)		
from September 6, 1935	Paris (FR)	Theater A.B.C.	
November 1-30, 1935	Vienna (AT)	Varieté Ronacher	
November 30, 1935	Vienna (AT)	Radio station	Radio concert
December 25, 1935	Brünn (Brno, CS)	Dopzsaal	
December 26, 1935	Vienna (AT)	Konzerthaus	
December 27, 1935	Salzburg (AT)	Mozarteum	
December 28, 1935	Semmering (AT)	Südbahn-Hotel	
December 29 1935	Judenburg (AT)		
December 30, 1935	Iglau (AT)		
December 31, 1935	Vienna (AT)	Theater an der Wien/Kino Lustspielhaus	
January 1, 1936	Vienna (AT)	Hall of Music Association	
January 12, 1936	Sarpsborg (NO)	Folkethus (Folks House)	
January 13, 1936	Halden (NO)	Workers House	
January 14, 1936	Oslo (NO)	Universitetes Aula	
January 15, 1936	Cristiansand (NO)	Coliseum	
January 16, 1936	Skien (NO)	Coliseum	
January 17, 36	Larvik (NO)		
January 18, 1936	Sandefjord (NO)		
January 19, 1936	Oslo (NO)	Universitetets Aula	
January 20, 1936	Drammen (NO)	Theater	
January 21, 1936	Fredrikstad (NO)		
January 22, 1936	Oslo (NO)	In den Logen	
January 23, 1936	Sarpsborg (NO)		
January 25, 1936	Göteborg (SE)		
January 26, 1936	Malmö (SE)	Secondary School	
January 27, 1936	Lund (SE)		
January 28, 1936	Stockholm (SE)	Concert House	
January 29, 193	Örebro (SE)		
January 30, 1936	Jönköpink (SE)		

January 31, 1936	Norköping (SE)	Old Hall	
February 1, 1936	Stockholm (SE)	?	Incl. radio transmission
February 2, 1936	Malmö (SE)		
February 3, 1936	Svendborg (DK)		
February 4, 1936	Copenhagen		
February 5, 1936	Copenhagen	Radio station	Radio concert
February 6, 1936	Odense (DK)		
February 7, 1936	Copenhagen		
February 8, 1936	Göteborg (SE)	Concert House	
February 9, 1936	Örebro (SE)		
February 10, 1936	Uppsala (SE)	Universitetsaulan	
February 11, 1936	Nyköping (SE)		
February 12, 1936	Linköping (SE)	Universitetsaulan	
February 12, 1936	Linköping (SE)	Radio station	Radio concert
February 13, 1936	Näsiö (SE)		
February 14, 1936	Lund (SE)		
February 15, 1936	Helsingborg (SE)	Concert Hall	
February 16, 196	Boras (SE)		
February 17, 1936	Göteborg (SE)		
February 27, 1936	Napoli (IT)	Society "Amici di Musica"	
February 29, 1936	Palermo (IT)	Theater	
March 2, 1936	Rome (IT)	Filharmonica	
March 3, 1936	Forli (IT)	Theatro Communale	
March 4, 1936	Padua (IT)		
March 5, 1936	Fiume (IT)	Theater	
March 7, 1936	Florence (IT)	Theatro Communale	
March 9, 1936	Chiavari (IT)		
March 10, 1936	Mailand (IT)		
March 13-19, 1936	Paris (FR)	Theater Bobino	
March 21, 1936	Amsterdam (NL)	Muziek-Lyceum	
March 22, 1936	Rotterdam (NL)	Doele Zaal	
March 25, 1936	Paris (FR)	Sports Association	
March 26, 1936	Paris (FR)	Salle Gaveau	
March 27, 1936	Paris (FR)	A.B.C.-Theater	Varieté program with Cora Madou, Saint-Granier, Raymond Baird and others
March 27, 1936	Paris (FR)	Conferencia (Université des Annales)	Music gala, with Jean Tranchant
March 28 – April 6, 8, 9, 1936	Paris (FR)	A.B.C.-Theater	

April 11, 1936	London (GB)	Radio station	Three songs in a varieté radio program
April 12 1936	London (GB)	Radio station	Radio concert
May 3-5, 1936	Tiflis (RU)		
May 6, 8, 1936	Batumi (RU)		
May 11-12, 1936	Tiflis (RU)		
May 18-19, 1936	Rostow (RU)		
May 23-29, June 2-18, 1936	Moscow (RU)	Summer Theater	
June 19, 1936	Leningrad (RU) (St. Petersburg)	Thaurian Park	
June 21- July 1, 1936	Leningrad (RU) (St. Petersburg)	Valodarsky Park	
July 6, 1936	Leningrad (RU) (St. Petersburg)	Radio station	Radio concert
July 7, 1936	Leningrad (RU) (St. Petersburg)	Former Duma (statehouse)	
July 8, 10-14, 16-18, 1936	Leningrad (RU) (St. Petersburg)	Volodarsky Park	
July 21, 1936	Leningrad (RU) (St. Petersburg)	Club plus Gorki-Theater	2 performances
July 22, 1936	Leningrad (RU) (St. Petersburg)	Radio station	Radio concert
August 1-2, 1936	London (GB)	Radio station	Radio concert
August 4, 1936	Ostende (BE)	Casino	Incl. radio transmission
August 6-11, 1936	Knokke (BE)		Gala Show
August 18, 1936	Scheveningen (NL)		
August 21-26, 1936	Bruxelles (BE)	Palais d' Eté	
September 10-23, 1936	Knocke (BE)		Probably rehearsals only
September 25 - October 1, 1936	Antwerpen (BE)	Skala	
October 4, 1936	Bruxelles (BE)	Radio station	Radio concert
October 5–12, 1936	Antwerpen (BE)		Only rehearsals
October 13, 1936	Luxemburg (LU)	Grand Dukes Theater	
October 17, 1936	Copenhagen (DK)	Radio station	Radio concert
October 18, 1936	Aalborg (DK)	Aalborg-Hall	
October 19, 1936	Horsens (DK)		
October 21, 1936	Nyköbing (DK)		
October 22, 1936	Copenhagen (DK)		
October 23, 1936	Odense (DK)		
October 26, 1936	Oslo (NO)	Universitetets Aula	
October 27, 1936	Bergen (NO)	Movie Palace	
October 28, 1936	Hangesund (NO)	Festividelen Saal	

Date	Place	Venue	Notes
October 29, 1936	Stavanger (NO)	Church	
October 30, 1936	Bergen (NO)		Matinee
October 31, 1936	Oslo (NO)	Universitetes Aula	
November 1, 1936	Christiansund (NO)		
November 2, 1936	Drammen (NO)		
November 3, 1936	Sarpsborg (NO)		
November 4, 1936	Göteborg (SE)	Konserthuset	
November 5, 1936	Malmö (SE)		
November 6, 1936	Helsingborg (SE)	Konserthuset	
November 7, 1936	Jönköping (SE)	Brakesalon	
November 8, 1936	Stockholm		
November 8, 1936	Stockholm	Radio station	Radio concert
November 9, 1936	Eskilstuna (SE)	Läroverkets Aula	
November 10, 1936	Uppsala (SE)		
November 11, 1936	Gärle (SE)		
November 12, 1936	Lundsvall (SE)	Town Hall	
November 13, 1936	Östersund (SE)	Theater	
November 14, 1936	Stockholm (SE)	Konserthuset	
November 15, 1936	Norrköping (SE)	Hörsalen	
November 16, 1936	Linköping (SE)		
November 17, 1936	Örebro (SE)	Konserthuset	
November 18, 1936	Göteborg (SE)		
November 19, 1936	Helsingborg (SE)		
November 20, 1936	Lund (SE)	Universitetsaulan	
November 21, 1936	Malmö (SE)		
November 22, 1936	Oslo (NO)		
November 23, 1936	Kungsringe (NO)		
November 24, 1936	Harten (NO)		
November 25, 1936	Tönsberg (NO)	Theater	
November 26, 1936	Hamar (NO)		
November 27, 1936	Trondheim (NO)	Freemasons Hall	
November 29, 1936	Trondheim (NO)		
November 30, 1936	Oslo (NO)	In den Logen	
November 30, 1936	Oslo	Radio station	Radio concert
December 2, 1936	Copenhagen (DK)		
December 4, 1936	Lund (DK)		
December 5, 1936	Boras (SE)		
December 6, 1936	Trollhättan (DK)		
December 7, 1936	Karlstad (SE)		
December 8, 1936	Stockholm (SE)		

December 12, 1936	Verviers (BE)	Town Theater	
December 13, 1936	Luxemburg (LU)		Two performances
December 31, 1936	Ostende (BE)	Cure Hall	
January 1-15, 1937	Rotterdam (NL)	Arena (Varieté of Scala-Theater)	
January 16-31, 1937	Amsterdam (NL)	Theater Carré	
February 2, 1937	Amsterdam	Radio station A.V.R.O.	Radio concert
February 6-7, 1937	London (GB)	Music Hall	BBC radio concert
February 8, 1937	London (GB)	Aeolian Hall	
February 10, 1937	Paris (FR)	Salle Gaveau	Incl. radio transmission
February 12, 1937	Colmar (FR)		
February 14, 1937	Paris (FR)	Théatre des Ambassadeurs	Incl. radio transmission
February 15, 1937	Innsbruck (AT)		
February 16, 1937	Salzburg (AT)		
February 17, 1937	Linz (AT)		
February 19, 1937	Gablonz (Jablonec, CS)		Two performances
February 20, 1937	Eger (Cheb, CS)		
February 21, 1937	Karlsbad (Karlovy Vary, CS)	Shooters House	
February 22, 1937	Prag (Prague, CS)		
February 23, 1937	Saaz (Zatek, CS)		
February 24, 1937	Reichenberg (Liberec, CS)		
February 25, 1937	Rumburg (Rumburk, CS)		
February 26, 1937	Trautenau (Trutnov, CS)		
February 27, 1937	Troppau (Opava, CS)		
February 28, 1937	Brünn (Brno, CS)		
March 1, 1937	Teplitz-Schönau (Teplice, CS)		
March 19, 1937	Paris (FR)	Alhambra	Probably for several days
March 24-31, 1937	Vienna (AT)	Margaretner Orpheum	
April 7, 1937	Turin (IT)	Teatro Vittoria	
April 11, 1937	Teramo (IT)	Teatro Comunale	
April 13, 1937	Rome (IT)	Filharmonica	
April 16-29, 1937	Paris (FR)	A.B.C.-Theater	
May 1-5, 1937	Cannes (FR)	Palm Beach Casino	
May 27-June 07, 1937	Paris (FR)	Theatre Paramount (Cinema)	
June 8-10, 1937	Evian-les-Bains (FR)		
June 12-14, 1937	London (GB)	BBC radio station	Radio concerts

July 22, 1937	Perth (AU)	His Majesty's Theatre	First Concert with Kramer as pianist. With partial radio transmission
July 24, 1937	Perth (AU)	His Majesty's Theatre	
July 27, 1937	Kalgoorlie (AU)	Town Hall	
July 28, 1937	Kalgoorlie (AU)	Great Boulder Mine	
August 5, 1937	Canberra (AU)	Albert Hall	
August 8, 1937	Sydney (AU)	Radio station	Radio concert
August 10, 12, 1937	Newcastle (AU)	Town Hall	
August 15, 1937	Newcastle (AU)	Radio station 2FC	Radio concert
August 16, 1937	Newcastle (AU)	Town Hall	
August 19-20, 25-26, 1937	Brisbane (AU)	City Hall	
August 28, 1937	Sydney (AU)	Town Hall	
August 29, 1937	Sydney (AU)	Radio station	Radio concert
August 30-31, September 1, 3, 1937	Sydney (AU)	Town Hall	
September 5, 1937	Sydney (AU)	Radio station	Radio concert
September 8, 1937	Melbourne (AU)	Town Hall	
September 9, 1937	Melbourne (AU)	Princess Theatre	
September 11, 1937	Melbourne (AU)	Town Hall	
September 14, 1937	Melbourne (AU)	Princess Theatre	
September 15-17, 1937	Melbourne (AU)	Town Hall	
September 18-20, 1937	Launceston (AU)	National Theatre	
September 21, 1937	Devonport (AU)	Town Hall	
September 23-25, 1937	Hobart (AU)	Theatre Royal	
September 28, 1937	Geelong (AU)	Plaza Theatre	
September 29-30, 1937	Bendigo (AU)	Town Hall	
October 1-2, 1937	Melbourne (AU)	Apollo Theatre	
October 5, 7-9, 1937	Adelaide (AU)	Town Hall	
October 13, 1937	Kalgoorlie (AU)	Town Hall	
October 15-16, 1937	Perth (AU)	His Majesty's Theatre	
October 18, 1937	Perth (AU)	Government House Ballroom	
October 23, 1937	Broken Hill (AU)	Tivoli Theatre	
October 25-26, 1937	Broken Hill (AU)	Town Hall	
October 27, 1937	Adelaide (AU)	West's	
October 29, 1937	Melbourne (AU)	Town Hall	
October 30, 1937	Melbourne (AU)	"	Matinee
November 1, 1937	Canberra (AU)	Albert Hall	
November 3, 1937	Newcastle (AU)	Town Hall	

November 4-6, 8,9, 1937	Sydney (AU)	Town Hall	Probably Melbourne, Apollo Theatre
November 16, 1937	Auckland (NZ)	Radio station 1YA	Radio concert
November 17, 20, 1937	Auckland (NZ)	Town Hall	
November 23, 25, 1937	Wellington (NZ)	Town Hall	
November 25, 1937	Wellington (NZ)	Town Hall	
November 28, 1937	Wellington (NZ)	Radio station 2YA	Radio concert
December 1, 1937	Christchurch (NZ)	Radio station 3YA	Radio concert
December 2, 1937	Christchurch (NZ)	Civic Theatre	
December 4, 1937	Christchurch (NZ)	Radio station 3YA	Radio concert
December 7, 1937	Christchurch (NZ)	Civic Theatre	
December 9, 1937	Dunedin (NZ)	Radio station 4YA	Radio concert
December 11, 1937	Dunedin (NZ)	Town Hall	Incl. radio transmission
December 13, 1937	Dunedin (NZ)	Radio station 4YA	Radio concert
December 14, 1937	Dunedin (NZ)	Town Hall	Incl. radio transmission
December 16, 1937	Dunedin (NZ)	Radio station 4YA	Radio concert
December 19, 1937	Christchurch (NZ)	Radio station 3YA	Radio concert
December 21, 1937	Wellington (NZ)	Radio station 2 YA	Radio concert
December 24, 26, 1937	Auckland (NZ)	Radio station 1YA	Radio concert
January 4, 1938	Australia?	Radio station	Radio concert
February 4, 1938	Cairo (EG)		
February 9, 11-12, 1938	Athens (GR)		
February 15, 1938	Belgrad (YU)		Cancelled?
February 16, 1938	Zagreb (YU)		Cancelled?
February 17, 1938	Fiume (IT)		Italian tour planned until March 1. Discontinued because of the ban on non-Aryan artists in Italy.
March 14, 1938	Malmö (SE)	Universitetsaulan	
March 15, 1938	Lund (SE)		
March 16, 1938	Jönköping (SE)		
March 17, 1938	Örebro (SE)		
March 18, 1938	Norrköping (SE)		
March 19, 1938	Stockholm (SE)		
March 20, 1938	Göteborg (SE)	Konserthuset	
March 21, 1938	Boras (SE)		
March 22, 1938	Karlstad (SE)		
March 23, 1938	Sarpsborg (NO)		
March 24, 1938	Drammen (NO)		
March 25, 1938	Oslo (NO)		
March 26, 1938	Hamar (NO)		

March 27, 1938	Trondheim (NO)	Freemasons Lodge	
March 28, 1938	Lachsen (NO)		
March 29, 1938	Trondheim (NO)		
March 30, 1938	Loken (NO)		
March 31, 1938	Lillehammer (NO)		
April 1, 1938	Oslo (NO)		
April 3, 1938	Aalborg (DK)		
April 4, 1938	Aarhus (DK)		
April 5, 1938	Copenhagen (DK)		
April 6, 1938	Odense (DK)		
April 7, 1938	Nyköping (DK)		
April 8, 1938	Copenhagen (DK)		
April 12, 1938	Stockholm (SE)	Radio station	Radio concert
April 12, 1938	Göteborg (SE)		
April 13, 1938	Örebro (SE)		
April 14, 1938	Stockholm (SE)		
April 15, 1938	Uppsala (SE)		
April 17, 1938	Gävle (SE)		
April 18, 1938	Stockholm (SE)		
April 20, 1938	Malmö (SE)		
May 10, 1938	Rio de Janeiro (BR)	Theatre Municipal	
May 11, 1938	Sao Paulo (BR)		
May 23, 27, 1938	Buenos Aires (AR)	Teatro Odéon	
June 23, 1938	Buenos Aires (AR)	Belfast	
June 24, 26, 1938	Montevideo (UY)	Teatro Solis	
June 27, 1938	Buenos Aires (AR)	Teatro San Martin	
July 16, 18-19, 21, 1938	Santiago de Chile (CL)	Teatro Municipal	
July 25, 1938	Valparaiso (CL)	Teatro Victoria	
September 20, 1938	Buenos Aires (AR)		Performance for General Motors
October 24, 1938	Rio de Janeiro (BR)		
November 14, 1938	London (GB)	Coliseum	
November 15, 1938	London (GB)	Radio station BBC	Radio concert
November 15-16, 1938	London (GB)	Coliseum	
November 17, 1938	London (GB)	Radio station BBC	Radio concert
November 17-27, 1938	London (GB)	Coliseum	
November 28, December 3-4, 1938	London (GB)	BBC Broadcasting House	Radio concert
December 09, 1938	Lyon (FR)	Salle Rameau	
December 11, 1938	Monte Carlo (MC)		
December 12, 1938	London (GB)		

December 16, 1938	London (GB)	Scala Theatre	Incl. radio transmission
January 6-19, 1939	Brussels (BE)	MGM Cinema	Cinema Varieté
January 10, 1939	Brussels (BE)	Radio station	
January 20-26, 1939	Liege (BE)	Forum Cinema	
January 28, 1939	Brussels (BE)		
January 29, 1939	Brussels (BE)	Radio station IENR	Radio concert
February 10, 1939	New York (US)	Town Hall	
February 13, 1939	Winnipeg (CA)	Auditorium	
February 15, 1939	Edmonton (CA)	Empire Theatre	
February 20, 1939	Lewistown (ID)	High School Auditorium	
February 22, 1939	Baker (OR)	High School Auditorium	
February 24, 1939	Seattle (WA)	Chamber of Commerce	
February 27, 1939	Seattle (WA)	Moore Theatre	
February 28, 1939	Corvallis (OR)	Men's Gymnasium	
March 3, 5, 1939	San Francisco (CA)	Curran Theatre	
March 6, 1939	Los Angeles (CA)	Redlands University Auditorium	
March 8, 1939	Tucson (AZ)	College of Fine Arts	
March 14, 1939	Jefferson City (MO)		
April 24, 1939	Johannesburg (ZA)	Radio station	Radio concert
April 24, 1939	Johannesburg (ZA)		Meeting with A. Rubinstein
April 26, 1939	Johannesburg (ZA)	Radio station	Radio concert
April 26, 1939	Johannesburg (ZA)		
April 28, May 2, 1939	Durban (ZA)		
May 3, 1939	Durban (ZA)	Criterion Theatre	
May 5, 1939	Johannesburg (ZA)		
May 7-8, 1939	Johannesburg (ZA)	Colosseum Theatre	
May 12, 1939	Cape Town (ZA)	Radio station	Radio concert
May 15, 1939	Cape Town (ZA)	Alhambra Theatre	
May 19, 1939	Cape Town (ZA)		
May 20, 1939	Johannesburg (ZA)	Colosseum Theater	
June 13, 17-18, 20, 22, 24, 1939	Perth (AU)	Capitol Theatre	
June 27, 1939	Merredin (AU)		Perhaps June 26 or 28
June 29, 1939	Kalgoorlie (AU)	Town Hall	
July 3-8, 11, 14, 19-20, 1939	Adelaide (AU)	Town Hall	
July 26, 1939	Launceston (AU)	National Theatre	
July 27, 1939	Devonport (AU)		
July 29, August 1-3, 1939	Hobart (AU)	Theatre Royal	
August 5-6, 1939	Melbourne (AU)	Town Hall	

August 8, 1939	Adelaide (AU)	Radio station	Radio concert
August 10, 12-14, 16-17, 1939	Melbourne (AU)	Town Hall	
August 21, 1939	Ballarat (AU)	Alfred Hall	
August 22, 1939	Geelong (AU)	Plaza Theatre	
August 28, 1939	Canberra (AU)		
August 31, September 1, 1939	Sydney (AU)	Town Hall	
September 2, 1939	Sydney (AU)	Town Hall	Matinee
September 5-7, 9, 1939	Sydney (AU)	Town Hall	
September 18, 1939	Toowoomba (AU)	Town Hall	
September 23, 25-26, 28, 30, October 2, 1939	Brisbane (AU)	City Hall	
October 3, 1939	Ipswich (AU)	Winter Garden Theatre	
October 6, 1939	Sydney (AU)	Town Hall	
October 12-14, 16, 1939	Perth (AU)	Capitol Theatre	
October 17, 1939	Merredin (AU)		
October 18, 1939	Kalgorlie (AU)		
October 19, 1939	Boulder (AU)		
October 23-25, 1939	Adelaide (AU)	Centennial Hall	
October 27-28, 30, 1939	Broken Hill (AU)	Tivoli Theatre	
November 14-16, 18, 24, 1939	Sydney (AU)	Town Hall	
November 28, 1939	?	Town Hall	
December 3-4, 1939	Launceston (AU)	Town Hall	
December 9, 11-13, 1939	Brisbane (AU)	City Hall	
February 15-17, 20, 1940	Honolulu (HI)	McKinley Auditorium	
March 12, 1940	Ottumwa (IA)	High School Auditorium	
March 14, 1940	St. Joseph	High School Auditorium	
March 15, 1940	Quincy	High School Auditorium	
March 25, 1940	Findlay (OH)	High School Auditorium	
March 26, 1940	Port Huron (MI)	First Methodist Church	
March 27, 1940	Sandusky (OH)	Auditorium	
March 29, 1940	Philadelphia (PA)	Academy of Music	
April 1, 1940	Chapel Hill (NC)	Memorial Hall	
April 3, 1940	Greenville (NC)	Wright Auditorium	
April 5, 1940	Columbus (MS)	Whitfield Auditorium	
April 8, 1940	Winfield (KS)	Richardson Hall	
April 9, 1940	Oklahoma City (OK)	Shrine Auditorium	
April 10, 1940	Wichita (KS)	High School East	
April 12, 1940	Tylor (TX)	Gary Auditorium	

April 13, 1940	Longview (TX)	Junior High School	
April 15, 1940	Laredo (TX	Martin High School	
April 20, 1940	Seattle (WA)	Moore Theater	
April 22, 1940	Bellingham (WA)	High School Auditorium	
April 23, 1940	Everett (WA)	Elks Auditorium	
April 27, 1940	Aberdeen (SD)	Civic School Auditorium	
April 29, 1940	Oshkosh (WI)	Grand Opera House	
May 1, 1940	Richmond (IN)	Tivoli Theater	Last concert of the Comedy Harmonists

Sources:
Frommermann estate
Cycowski estate
Mayreder estate
Biberti estate
Czada, Peter/Große, Günter: *Comedian Harmonists -
Ein Vokalensemble erobert die Welt*, Quadriga, Berlin 1998
Primavera Gruber: "And zo – all that time we earn no money …"
– Die Comedian Harmonists und der Opernsänger Arthur Fleischer in Wien,
in: Ursula Seeber (Hg.): "Asyl wider Willen – Exil in Österreich 1933 – 1938,"
Picus Verlag Wien, 2003

Meistersextett

List of Concerts

Courtesy of Jan Grübler and Theo Niemeyer

Date	City	Venue	Notes
June 2, 1935	"Ausland" - ?		1410 Mk. (perhaps only receipt of payment?) No evidence that concert took place on this date.
September 10, 1935	Dresden		First verified concert of the Meistersextett. 1437 Mk.
October 18, 1935	Freiberg	Tivoli	300 Mk.
October 19, 1935	Kamenz	Hotel Stadt Dresden	375 Mk.
October 20, 1935	Löbau	Hotel Wettiner Hof	
October 21, 1935	Großenhain	Sachsenhof	
October 22, 1935	Cottbus	Konzerthaus Altmann	
October 23, 1935	Dresden	Seinckesches Bad (?)	
October 24, 1935	Pirna	Haus Tanne	
October 25, 1935	Bautzen	Hotel "Krone"	
October 26, 1935	Bischofswerda	Schützenhaus	
October 27, 1935	Sebnitz	Hotel Stadt Dresden	
October 28, 1935	Meißen	Hamburger Hof	
October 29, 1935	Werdau	Theater-Lichtspiele	
October 30, 1935	Radebeul	"Goldene Weintraube"	
October 31, 1935	Limbach	Schweizerhaus	
November 10, 1935	Halle/Saale	Stadtschützenhaus	
November 11, 1935	Plauen/Vogtland	Prater	
November 12, 1935	Zwickau	Schwanenschloß	
November 13, 1935	Glauchau	Kammerlichtspiele	
November 16-17, 1935	Darmstadt	Orpheum	615 Mk.
November 19, 1935	Mainz	Liedertafel	
November 21, 1935	Offenbach	Turnhalle	
November 22, 1935	Solingen	Stadthalle	
November 23, 1935	Wiesbaden	Kursaal	
November 25, 1935	Koblenz	Stadthalle	
November 26, 1935	Höchst	Kulturverein	
November 27-28, 1935	Kassel	Stadtpark	
November 29, 1935	Göttingen	Stadtpark	995 Mk.
December 6, 1935	Munich	Deutsches Theater	Originally cancelled because of using the old name.

December 8, 1935	Leipzig	Zentraltheater	1512 Mk.
December 9, 1935	Chemnitz		
December 10, 1935	Dresden	Vereinshaus	
December 11, 1935	Hof	Vereinssaal	
December 12, 1935	Nuremberg	Kulturvereinssaal	
December 13, 1935	Ulm	Saalbau	
December 14, 1935	Kempten [original: Ingolstadt]	Haus der Käsebörse	
December 15, 1935	Regensburg	Neuhaus-Saal	400 Mk.
December 16, 1935	Munich	Tonhalle	2350 Mk.
December 25-26, 1935	Breslau (Lower Silesia, today Wrocław, PL)	Großer Konzerthaussaal	1500 Mk.
December 31, 1935	Frankfurt a. M.	Saalbau	2020 Mk.
January 1, 1936	Stuttgart	Festsaal der Liederhalle	970 Mk.
January 3, 1936	Karlsruhe	Festhalle	
January 4, 1936	Essen	Saalbau	
January 6, 1936	Elberfeld	Stadthalle Johannisberg	
January 7, 1936	Düsseldorf	Kaisersaal	1321 Mk.
January 8, 1936	Krefeld	Stadthalle	
January 10, 1936	Köln	Bürgersaal	
January 15, 1936	Stettin (West Pomerania; today Szczecin, PL)	Konzerthaussaal	
January 23, 1936	Brandenburg	Schweizergarten	
January 26, 1936	Guben	Schützenhaus	212 Mk.
January 28, 1936	Frankfurt / Oder	Konzerthaus Bellevue	
January 31, 1936	Meerane	Härtels Hotel	
February 1, 1936	Dresden	Vereinshaus	1079 Mk.
February 2, 1936	Görlitz	Stadthalle	
February 3, 1936	Zittau	Lindenhof	
February 4, 1936	Leipzig	C.T. Saal	
February 5, 1936	Magdeburg	Haus der Arbeit	
February 6, 1936	Erfurt	Reichshallentheater	
February 9, 1936	Kiel	Haus der Arbeit	Two performances
February 10, 1936	Hanover	Konzerthaus an der Goethebrücke	
February 11, 1936	Dessau	Kristallpalast	
February 12, 1936	Braunschweig	Hofjägersaal	
February 13, 1936	Bremen	Union	

February 14, 1936	Schwerin	Stadtsäale	330 Mk.
February 16, 1936	Hamburg	Conventgarten	2149 Mk.
February 29 - March 3, 1936	Leipzig	Operettentheater	Night shows – total 4600 Mk.
March 3, 1936?	Falkenstein		
March 4, 1936?	Meerane		
March 15, 1936	Frankfurt a. M.	Saalbau	
March 21, 1936	Hartha	Gasthof Flenningen	
March 22, 1936	Falkenstein	Neues Konzerthaus	
March 23, 1936	Berlin	Philharmonie	
March 24, 1936	Rostock	Philharmonie	
April 1, 1936	Aschaffenburg	Saal "Frohsinn"	
April 2, 1936	Bamberg	Zentralsaal	
April 3, 1936	Würzburg	Saal im Platzschen Garten	
April 4, 1936	Munich	Tonhalle	1050 Mk.
April 5, 1936	Augsburg	Ludwigsbau	570 Mk.
April 12-13, 1936	Breslau	Gr. Konzerthaus-saal	
April 14, 1936	Liegnitz (Lower Silesia, today Legnica, PL)	Schützenhaus	
April 15, 1936	Waldenburg (Lower Silesia, today Wałbrzych, PL)	Lichtspieltheater Capitol	
April 20, 1936	The Hague (NL)	Gebouw voor Kunsten en Wetenschappen	
April 22, 1936	Oldenburg	Unionssaal	
April 23, 1936	Wilhelmshaven	Kurhaus im Park	192 Mk.
April 24, 1936	Lübeck	Kolosseum	
April 26, 1936	Neubrandenburg	Konzerthaus	360 Mk.
May 3, 1936	Berlin	Hotel Esplanade	In honor of the Comité Exécutif de la Alliance Internationale de L'Hotellerie. In presence of State Secretary Funk.
May 5, 1936	Stettin	Konzerthaussal	
May 6, 1936	Stralsund		
May 7, 1936	Kolberg (West Pomerania, today Kołobrzeg, PL)		
May 8, 1936	Köslin (West Pomerania, today Koscalin, PL)		
May 9, 1936	Anklam		
May 10, 1936	Stettin	Zentralhallen	Cancelled by newspaper notice.

May 12, 1936	Göttingen	Stadtpark	
May 13, 1936	Bad Kreuznach	Kursaal	600 Mk.
May 14, 1936	Bad Nauheim	Kursaal	
May 21, 1936	Baden-Baden	Großer Kursaal	
May 23, 1936	Wiesbaden	Großer Kurhaussaal	
May 24, 1936	Freiburg i. Br. (or Erlangen?)	Stadthalle	
May 27, 1936	Freiburg i. Br.		
November 21, 1936	Zeitz	Preußischer Hof,	K.d.F. concert. 290 Mk. [First concert of the new cast with Kassen, Imlau and Grunert]
November 27, 1936	Stargard (West Pomerania, today Stargard Szczeciski, PL)		For benefit of the K.d.F., Gau Pommern, for its 3rd anniversary
November 28, 1936	Dresden	Circus Sarrasani	
November 29, 1936	Breslau	Konzerthaussaal	
November 30, 1936	Oppeln (Upper Silesia, today Opole, PL)	Saal der Handwerkskammer	
December 1, 1936	Ratibor (Upper Silesia, today Racibórz, PL)	Deutsches Haus	
December 2, 1936	Beuthen (Upper Silesia, today Bytom, PL)	Schützenhaus	
December 3, 1936	Hindenburg (Upper Silesia, today Zabrze, PL)	Casino	
December 4, 1936	Gleiwitz (Upper Silesia, today Gliwice, PL)	Stadttheater	
December 12, 1936	Dresden	Circus Sarrasani + Linckesches Bad	
December 26, 1936	The Hague (NL)		
December 27, 1936	Venlo (NL)	Venlona	
December 28, 1936	Krefeld	Stadthalle	
December 31, 1936	Frankfurt a. M.		1789 Mk.
January 1, 1937	Gießen	Stadttheater	
January 2-3, 1937	Darmstadt	Orpheum	
January 4, 1937	Karlsruhe	Eintrachtsaal	
January 5, 1937	Wiesbaden	Residenztheater	
January 6, 1937	Rüsselsheim	Saal der Opelwerke	
January 7, 1937	Hanau	Stadthalle	
January 8, 1937	Frankfurt a. M.	I.G. Farben-Hochhaus	
January 9, 1937	Höchst	I. G. Farben	
January 10, 1937	Offenbach	Stadthalle	

January 11, 1937	Dessau	Kristallpalast	
January 15, 1937	Hanover	Konzerthaus an der Goethebrücke	1062 Mk.
January 17, 1937	Kiel	Haus der Arbeit	
January 18, 1937	Bremerhaven	Stadthalle	
January 19, 1937	Bremen	Union	
January 20, 1937	Hamburg	Konvent Garten	
January 21, 1937	Stettin (West Pomerania, today Szczecin, PL)	Großer Konzerthaussaal	
January 27, 1937	Berlin	Philharmonie	2549 Mk.
February 2, 1937	Zerbst	Saal im Hotel "Goldener Löwe"	400 Mk.
February 6, 1937	Dresden	1. Kristallpalast, 2. Wilder Mann 3. Vereinshaus	K.d.F. concert – total 2168 Mk.
February 7, 1937	Dresden	Vereinshaus	2257 MK.
February 8, 1937	Leipzig	Alberthalle	
February 9, 1937	Zittau	Lindenhof	165 Mk.
February 12, 1937	Chemnitz	Wagnersaal im kaufm. Vereinshaus	
February 13, 1937	Dresden	Großer Saal im Ausstellungspalast	K.d.F. concert. 891 Mk.
February 14, 1937	Reichenbach	Kaiserhof	
February 15, 1937	Potsdam	Konzerthaus	406 Mk.
February 16, 1937	Berlin	Beethovensaal	890 Mk. - (Plus radio transmission?)
February 23, 1937	Köthen	Stadthalle	
February 24, 1937	Mühlhausen	Schützenberg	
February 25, 1937	Erfurt	Reichshallensaal	
March 2, 1937	Magdeburg	Haus der Arbeit	
March 3, 1937	Hanau	Stadthalle	
March 4, 1937	Duisburg	Städt. Tonhalle	
March 5, 1937	Wuppertal	Gelber Saal	
March 6, 1937	Köln	Bürgersaal	
March 7, 1937	Düsseldorf	Tonhalle	
March 16, 1937	Hagen	Stadthalle	
March 17, 1937	Münster	Schützenhofsaal	
March 18, 1937	Dortmund	Capitol	
March 19, 1937	Essen	Saalbau	With Barnabas von Geczy
March 20, 1937	Osnabrück	Stadthalle	
March 21, 1937	Hamburg	Conventgarten	

Date	City	Venue	Notes
March 30, 1937	Regensburg	Neuhaussaal	
March 31, 1937	Augsburg	Ludwigsbau	
April 1, 1937	Munich	Tonhalle, Türken-straße	
April 2, 1937	Hof	Städt. Vereinshalle	
April 3, 1937	Coburg	Festsaal der Hofbräugaststätten	790 Mk. (Originally forbidden by local N.S.D.A.P authority, but approved after intervention at the RMK, then the mayor returned his two tickets!)
April 4, 1937	Schweinfurt	Ev. Gemeindehaus	
April 5, 1937	Bamberg	Zentralsaal	
April 6, 1937	Plauen	Pratersaal	212 Mk.
April 7, 1937	Zwickau	Schwanenschloß	
April 10, 1937	Greiz	Turnhalle	500 Mk.
April 11, 1937	Stuttgart		
April 12, 1937	Nuremberg	Apollo-Theater	Julius Streicher in the audience.
April 13, 1937	Heidelberg	Stadthalle	
April 15, 1937	Mannheim		
April 16, 1937	Freiburg		
April 18, 1937	Bonn	Beethovenhalle	
April 23, 1937	Dresden	Verein Volkswohl	
April 25, 1937	Leipzig	Central Theater Festsaal	
April 26, 1937	Görlitz	Vereinshaus	
April 27, 1937	Halle	Thaliasaal	
April 28, 1937	Braunschweig	Hofjägersaal	
May 1, 1937	Berlin	May Day party of the Ministry of Folks Education and Propaganda	Sang in front of Goebbels.
May 1 to May 31, 1937	Berlin	Scala	15,000 Mk.
June 1, 1937	Berlin	Hotel Adlon	600 Mk. (For the German Tourists Agency)
June 2, 1937	Bad Wildungen	Kursaal	
June 4, 1937	Bad Nauheim	Kursaal	
June 5, 1937	Baden Baden	Kursaal	"In front of a half empty hall."
June 6, 1937	Nuremberg	Apollotheater	
June 7, 1937	Bad Kissingen	Kursaal	
June 8, 1937	Bad Homburg	Theater	
June 9, 1937	Bad Wörishofen	Kasino	
June 10, 1937	Memmingen	Burgsaal	

June 11, 1937	Bad Tölz	Städt. Kursaal	
June 13, 1937	Traunstein	Turnhalle	
June 14, 1937	Sachsenburg		"Cancelled because of the RMK "
June 15, 1937	Bad Reichenhall	Staatl. Kurhaus	
June 16, 1937	Garmisch	Park-Kasino "Alpenhof"	
June 17, 1937	Bad Wiessee	Konzertsaal. Wandelhalle	
June 18, 1937	Aschau	Festhalle Hohenaschau	
June 19, 1937	Bad Aibling	Kursaal	
September 30, 1937	Guben	Zentraltheater	
October 1, 1937	Frankfurt / Oder	Bellevue	
October 4, 1937	Brandenburg	Schweizergarten	
October 10, 1937	Falkenstein / Vgtl.	Neues Schützenhaus	
November 6, 1937?	Trier		
November 10, 1937	Straubing	Stadttheater	
(November 11, 1937)	Passau	Schmeroldkeller-saal	Forbidden
November 12, 1937	Augsburg	Ludwigsbau	
November 13, 1937	Munich	Tonhalle	
November 14, 1937	Rosenheim	Hofbräusaal	
November 15, 1937	Traunstein	Wochinger, Rokokosaal	
November 16, 1937	Landshut	Kolpingsaal	
November 17, 1937	Ulm	Saalbau	
November 18, 1937	Würzburg	Platz'scher Gartensaal	
November 19, 1937	Schweinfurt	Evangelisches Gemeindehaus	
November 22,1937	Osterode (Silesia, today Ostróda, PL)	Deutsches Theater	
November 23, 1937	Elbing (Silesia, today Eblg, PL)	Bürgerressource	
November 24, 1937	Königsberg (East Prussia, today Kaliningrad, RU)	Stadthalle	
November 25, 1937	Allenstein (Silesia, today Olsztyn, PL)	Capitol	
November 26, 1937	Insterburg (East Prussia, today Tschernja-chowsk, RU)	Stadthalle	
November 27, 1937	Forst	Lindengarten	Cancelled - refusal by K.d. F.
November 28, 1937	Breslau	Großer Konzerthaussaal	1500 Mk.

November 29, 1937	Schweidnitz (Lower Silesia, today Wałbrzych, PL)	Stadttheater	
November 30, 1937	Waldenburg	Capitol	800 Mk.
December 3, 1937	Hanover	Stadthalle	
December 5, 1937	Dresden	Vereinshaus	
December 6, 1937	Leipzig	Alberthalle	
December 7, 1937	Chemnitz	Kaufm. Vereinshaus	208 Mk.
December 8, 1937	Halle	Thaliatheater	
December 10-11, 1937	Lübeck	Collosseum	
December 12, 1937	Hamburg	Conventgarten	
December 26, 1937	Munich	Odeonsaal	
December 27, 1937	Munich	Radio - Station Reichssender	
December 29, 1937	Straubing		Cancelled
December 31, 1937	Frankfurt a. M.	Saalbau	2619 Mk.
January 1, 1938	Worms	Städtisches Spiel- und Festhaus	Two performances, K.d.F.-concerts, 1000 Mk.
January 2, 1938	Darmstadt	Saalbau	
January 3, 1938	Hanau	Stadthalle	
January 4, 1938	Wetzlar	Schützengarten	
January 5, 1938	Offenbach	Turnhalle	
January 6, 1938	Limburg	St. Georgshof	
January 7, 1938	Bensheim	Hotel Deutsches Haus	
January 8, 1938	Weinheim	Stadthalle	1000 Mk.
January 9, 1938	Hoechst	Casino I.G. Farben	Two performances, K.d.F.-concerts. 600 Mk.
January 10-12, 1938	Ludwigshafen	I.G.-Farben-Casino	
January 13, 1938	Gießen	Stadttheater	
January 14, 1938	Köln	Bürgersaal	
January 15, 1938	Dortmund	Goldsaal	
January 16, 1938	Düsseldorf	Tonhalle	
January 17, 1938	Mainkur	Kaiser Friedrich Kasino, I.G. Farben	K.d.F. concert
January 18, 1938	Grießheim	Neue Turnhalle, I.G. Farben	K.d.F. concert
January 29, 1938	Amsterdam (NL)	Konzert Gebouw	Gala-Ball, 200 Gld.
January 31, 1938	Amsterdam (NL)	Concertgebouw	
February 2, 1938	Hengelo (NL)		
February 6, 1938	Schwerin	Stadthalle	K.d.F. concert
February 7, 1938	Rostock	Philharmonie	
February 12, 1938	Kiel	Haus der Arbeit	

Date	City	Venue	Notes
February 13, 1938	Heide	Stadttheater	
February 14, 1938	Erfurt	Reichshallen	
February 15, 1938	Dessau	Kristallpalast	
February 16, 1938	Dresden	Verein Volkswohl	
February 18, 1938	Berlin	Philharmonie	
February 19, 1938	Glogau (Lower Silesia, today Głogów, PL)		
February 20, 1938	Breslau	Großer Konzerthaussaal	
February 21, 1938	Glogau		Cancelled because of the death of Emilie Biberti.
February 24, 1938	Göttingen		
February 25, 1938	Bremen	Großer Unionsaal	
March 1, 1938 to March 31, 1938	Hamburg	Hansa-Theater	15,000 Mk.
March 20, 1938	Hamburg	Alster-Pavillon	Matinee for the benefit of winter aid.
April 3, 1938	Essen	Haus der Technik	
April 4, 1938	Trier	Stadttheater	
April 5, 1938	Koblenz	Stadthalle	
April 6, 1938	Mannheim	Musensaal	
April 7, 1938	Stuttgart	Tonhalle	
April 8, 1938	Nuremberg	Apollo-Saal	
April 9, 1938	Frankfurt a. M.	Saalbau	
April 11, 1938	Saarbrücken	Wartburg	
April 12, 1938	Darmstadt	Orpheum	
April 18, 1938	Dresden	Vereinshaus	1200 Mk.
April 19, 1938	Glogau (Lower Silesia, today Głogów, PL)	Stadttheater	600 Mk.
April 20, 1938	Görlitz	Vereinshaus	288 Mk.
April 25, 1938	Hanover	Konzerthaus an der Goethebrücke	
April 26, 1938	Peine	Peiner Festsäale	
April 27, 1938	Braunschweig	Konzerthaus	
April 28, 1938	Wittenberg	Vereinigte Lichtspiele	
April 30, 1938	Berlin	Kroll-Oper	
May 1, 1938	Dresden	1. Gitterau (?) 2. Bühlau 3. Circus Sarasani	600 Mk.
May 6, 1938	Erlangen	Studentenwerk	
June 8, 1938	Bad Pyrmont	Kurverein	
June 9, 1938	Bad Hersfeld	Kulturverein	
June 10, 1938	Wiesbaden	Kurhaus	

June 11, 1938	Bad Nauheim	Kursaal	
June 12, 1938	Baden-Baden	Großer Konzertsaal	
June 14, 1938	Kissingen	Kurhaus, Großer Saal	
June 15, 1938	Bad Mergentheim	Kurverwaltung	
June 17, 1938	Bad Wörishofen	Kurkasino	
June 20, 1938	Garmisch	Hotel Alpenhof	
June 22, 1938	Salzburg (AT)	Mozarteum, großer Saal	
June 24,1938	Bad Gastein	Kurhaus	
June 25,1938	Bad Hofgastein	Kursaal	
June 27,1938	Bad Reichenhall	Staatl. Kurhaus	
June 28, 1938	Bad Tölz	Kursaal	
June 29, 1938	Bad Aibling		
June 30, 1938	Bad Wiessee	Konzertsaal der Wandelhalle	
December 11, 1938	Berlin	Festsäle der Kroll-Oper	Event of the company Stock & Co. 600 Mk.
December 25-26, 1938	Breslau	Konzerthaussaal	1250 Mk.
December 27, 1938	Liegnitz	Konzerthaus	K.d.F. concert. 600 Mk.
December 31, 1938	Frankfurt a. M.	Konzerthaussaal	2640 Mk.
January 1, 1939	Cologne	Kongresssaal der Messehallen Köln-Deutz,	Program "Wie es Euch gefällt." 700 Mk.
January 4, 1939	Offenbach	Turngesellschaft	
January 5, 1939	Gießen	Stadttheater	
January 6, 1939	Darmstadt	Saalbau	
January 7, 1939	Heppenheim	Halber Mond	
January 8, 1939	Eppstein	Turnhalle	
January 9, 1939	Trier	Stadttheater	
January 12, 1939	Hanover	Kuppelsaal der Stadthalle	Event of the company Continental Gummi-Werke AG. 800 Mk.
January 15, 1939	Mannheim	Nibelungensaal	1835 Mk.
January 16, 1939	Kassel	Stadthalle	With the Heinz Wehner Dance Orchestra, the dancer Sazarina and the child star Carmencita.
January 18, 1939	Marne	Holsteinisches Haus	K.d.F. concert. 600 Mk.
January 19, 1939	Itzehoe	Freudenthal	
January 20, 1939	Kiel	Haus der Arbeit	
January 21, 1939	Rendsburg	Conventgarten	
January 22, 1939	Plön	Turnhalle	
January 24, 1939	Hanover	Konzerthaus an der Goethebrücke	

January 25, 1939	Braunschweig	Hofjäger	
January 26-27, 1939	Hameln	Hotel Monopol	K.d.F. concert
February 1, 1939	Neubrandenburg	Konzerthaus	
February 4, 1939	Magdeburg	Stadthalle	K.d.F. concert
February 5, 1939	Dresden	Evangelisches Vereinshaus	
February 6, 1939	Leipzig	Alberthalle	2749 Mk.
February 7, 1939	Dessau	Kristallpalast	594 Mk.
February 8, 1939	Zeitz		Cancelled because of illness
February 9, 1939	Stassfurt		Cancelled because of illness
February 11, 1939	Bremen	Glocke, großer Saal	
February 13, 1939	Venlo (NL)	Venlona	450 Gld.
February 14, 1939	Hamburg	Conventgarten	2240 Mk.
February 23, 1939	Staßfurt	Stadtschänke	K.d.F. concert. 600 Mk.
February 24, 1939	Zeitz	Preußischer Hof	
February 25, 1939	Magdeburg	Stadthalle	
February 26, 1939	Halle	Stadtschützenhaus	K.d.F. concert
February 28, 1939	Dresden	Vereinshaus	
March 1-4, 1939	Lübeck		K.d.F. concert for the company Lübecker Maschinenbau-Gesellschaft. 2400 Mk.
March 11, 1939	Frankfurt	Großer Konzerthaussaal	
March 12, 1939	Stuttgart	Tonhalle	
March 13, 1939	Milan (IT)	Sala del Condervatorio	5500 Lire. Start of Italian tour
March 14, 1939	Trieste (IT)	Sala del Littorio	3000 Lire
March 15, 1939	Fiume (IT)	Teatro Comunale "Giuseppe Verdi"	4700 Lire
March 17, 1939	Naples (IT)	Sala della Compagnia degli Artisti	
March 20, 1939	Rome (IT)	Sala Pichetti	
March 21, 1939	Turin (IT)	Sala del Conservatori	
March 22, 1939	Freiburg	Stadthalle	
March 23, 1939	Oberursel	Taunussaal	K.d.F. concert
March 24, 1939	Schwäbisch Gmünd	Festhalle	
March 25, 1939	Nuremberg	Apollotheater	
March 26, 1939	Bamberg	Luitpoldsaal	
March 27, 1939	Schweinfurt	Ev. Gemeindehaus	
March 28, 1939	Straubing	Stadttheater	
March 29, 1939	Augsburg	Ludwigsbau	
March 30, 1939	Regensburg	Neuhaussaal	
March 31, 1939	Rosenheim	Hofbräusaal	

April 1, 1939	Munich	Tonhalle	
April 2, 1939	Landshut	Turnhalle Wittstr.	
April 5, 1939	Berlin	Philharmonie	
April 15, 1939	Neu Isenburg	Turngesellschaft	K.d.F.-concert
April 16, 1939	Offenbach	Turnhalle	601 Mk.
April 17, 1939	Köln	Weißer Saal	"Minus. 272.14 Mk."
April 18, 1939	Dortmund	Goldsaal	
April 19, 1939	Düsseldorf	Tonhalle	"Minus"
April 21, 1939	Görlitz	Ev. Vereinshaus, Kleiner Saal	
April 22, 1939	Hirschberg (Lower Silesia, today Jelenia Gora, PL)	Stadttheater	
April 24, 1939	Waldenburg	Capitol	
April 25, 1939	Dresden	Ev. Vereinshaus	
April 26, 1939	Chemnitz	Kaufm. Vereinshaus	
April 27, 1939	Leipzig	Kristallpalast	
April 30, 1939	Dresden	Kristallpalast	K.d.F. concert
May 1, 1939	Oederan	Schützenhaus	
May 2, 1939	Freiberg		
May 5-10, 1939	?		K.d.F. concerts
From May 11, 1939	Norway tour		
May 22, 1939	Freiburg		
June 1, 1939 to July 11, 1939	Munich	Theater am Gärtnerplatz	Participation in the revue/ operetta *Glückliche Reise*. "In total 20,500 Mk." [Last appearance of the cast with Kassen, Imlau and Leschnikoff]
August 3, 1939?	Berchtesgaden		Only planned or cancelled
August 4, 1939?	Bad Reichenhall		Only planned or cancelled
August 8, 1939?	Bad Tölz		Only planned or cancelled
August 9, 1939?	Garmisch	Hotel Alpenhof	Only planned or cancelled
August 10, 1939?	Wiessee		Only planned or cancelled
August 11, 1939?	Wörishofen		Only planned or cancelled
August 22, 1939?	Bad Nauheim		
August 26, 1939?	Wiesbaden		
December 5-10, 1939?	Schlesien		
December 25-26, 1939?	Breslau		
January 24, 1940?	Halle		
February 14, 1940?	Schweinfurt		
March 1-10, 1940?	Ostpreußen		

April 3, 1940?	Stettin		Cancelled
December 13, 1940	Brandenburg a. d. Havel	Neue Stadthalle (former Schweizer-garten)	First concert with the new cast of Biberti, Willy Hermann, Alfred Grunert, Erwin Sachse-Steuernagel, Willy Vosmendes and Bernard Taverne
December 14, 1940	Freiberg i. Sa.		248 Mk.
December 15, 1940	Cottbus		
December 16, 1940	Weißenfels		
December 17, 1940	Halle / Saale		566 Mk.
December 1940	Dresden		
December 25, 1940	Pirna	Tannensäle	
December 26, 1940	Breslau		
December 27, 1940	Forst (Lausitz)	Lindengarten	
December 28, 1940	Radebeul		
December 29, 1940	Großenhain	Gesellschaftshaus	
December 30, 1940	Leipzig	Alberthalle	
December 31, 1940	Frankfurt a. M.	Saalbau, gr. Saal	Traditional New Year's Eve concert. 1632 Mk.
January 1, 1941	Karlsruhe -		Cancelled
January 2, 1941	Gießen		
January 6, 1941	Kassel	Stadthalle, großer Saal	1759 Mk. (Originally planned for Munich)
January 11, 1941	Munich	Tonhalle	Originally planned as concert for the Wehrmacht. Cancelled.
January 12, 1941	Augsburg	Ludwigsbau	K.d.F.-concert. Cancelled, rescheduled on February 11.
January 13, 1941	Nuremberg	Kulturverein	Cancelled, rescheduled on February 04
January 14, 1941	Schweinfurt	Ev. Gemeindehaus	900 Mk.
January 16-31, 1941	Magdeburg	Haus der Deutschen Arbeit	K.d.F.-Varieté, daily fee 600 Mk., sum 8379 Mk. net
February 6, 1941	Munich		Cancelled
February 11, 1941	Augsburg		Cancelled
February 1941	Schweinfurt		[All further dates cancelled]
February 13, 1941?	Villach (AT)		Concert for the Gauleitung Kärnten of N.S.D.A.P. Cancelled.
February 14-15, 1941	Klagenfurt (AT)		Concert for the Wehrmacht. Cancelled.
February 23, 1941?	Falkenstein (Vogtland)		Cancelled.

March to May or May to July, 1941	Norway tour		Planned 3 month tour for the Wehrmacht. Cancelled due to a Directive from the Ministry of Folks Education and Propaganda.
December 16-21, 1941	Tour through Silesia		Planned but did not occur.
February 1-6, 1942	Danzig		Planned but did not occur.

Numbers in the "Notes" column are the amounts paid to the group (in Reichsmarks (Mk.), the name of German currency during this time. Only a few are listed to give some idea of the amounts they were receiving and how that changed.

K.d.F. was the "Kraft durch Freude" (Power by Joy): a department of the organization Deutsche Arbeitsfront (DAF). It was responsible for leisure activities of Germans and organized concerts, travel, sports competitions and training.

Sources:
The book *Irgendwo auf der Welt – Die Schallplatten der Comedian Harmonists und ihrer Nachfolgegruppen* by Andreas Schmauder

Estate of Robert Biberti, State Library Berlin; Sign. N.Mus.Nachl. 86 (CD-ROM Fot. 39 927-1 and 2)

The book *Comedian Harmonists – ein Vokalensemble erobert die Welt* by Peter Czada/Günter Große, Edition Hentrich, 1998

Appendix E
Typical Concert Programs
Courtesy of Jan Grübler

Comedian Harmonists

Early 1929 Repertoire

Chiquita
Sonny Boy
Ol' Man River
Blue River
Varsity Drag (Anna hat Geld)
Es gibt eine Frau, die Dich niemals vergißt (Mutterlied)
Bimbambulla
Ausgerechnet Donnerstag
Ich küsse Ihre Hand, Madame (Parody)
G'schichten aus dem Wiener Wald
Toselli-Serenade
Legende d'amour
Railway Song from the Revue *Zwei Krawatten*
Sing Hallelujah
Jig Walk
(In preparation - Overture to the Barber of Seville)

Leipzig, Schauspielhaus – January 1 and 2, 1930

Anna hat Geld
Wie wundervoll küsst Annemarie
Bimbambullah
Scheinbar liebst Du mich
Chiquita
Jig Walk
Puppenhochzeit
Ol' Man River
Sing Hallelujah

(Note: Would sing four of these songs, changing choices daily)

Dessau, Kristallpalast – March 19, 1931

Veronika, der Lenz ist da
Du bist nicht die Erste
Heut fahr ich mit Dir in die Natur
G'schichten aus dem Wiener Wald
Bin kein Hauptmann, bin kein großes Tier
Ich hab' für Dich 'nen Blumentopf bestellt
Wie wundervoll küßt Annemarie
Halt Dich an mich
Wochenend und Sonnenschein
Baby
Marie, Marie
Hofserenade
Liebling, mein Herz läßt Dich grüßen

Heut Nacht hab ich geträumt von Dir
Puppenhochzeit

Radio Transmission from Copenhagen, September 17, 1932

Einmal schafft's jeder
Irgendwo auf der Welt
Es führt kein anderer Weg zur Seligkeit
Hallo Daisy
Hunderttausendmal
Heute Nacht oder nie
Der Onkel Bumba aus Kalumba
Ich hab' eine kleine braune Mandoline
A Maria, Mari
Sah ein Knab' ein Röslein steh'n
In einem kühlen Grunde
Schöne Isabella aus Kastilien
Auf Wiedersehen, my Dear
Mein lieber Schatz, bist du aus Spanien

October 1933, Tour of France

Veronique, le printemps est la
Quand la brise vagabonde
Halloh Daisy
Schöne Isabella aus Kastilien
La route du Bonheur
Der Onkel Bumba aus Kalumba
Les gars de la marine
Tarantella Sincera
Heut' Nacht hab' ich geträumt von Dir
G'schichten aus dem Wiener Wald
Perpetuum mobile
Quand il Pleut
Tout le Jour, Toute la Nuit
Hofserenade
Mein lieber Schatz, bist Du aus Spanien?

November 24, 1933, Berlin, Philharmonic, Concert for Winter Aid - 1933-34

Schöne Isabella aus Kastilien
Allein kann man nicht glücklich sein
Ein neuer Frühling wird in die Heimat kommen
So ein Kuss kommt von allein
Eine kleine Frühlingsweise (Humoreske)
Tag und Nacht
Der Onkel Bumba aus Kalumba
Guter Monde, du gehst so stille
In einem kühlen Grunde
Schlafe, mein Prinzchen, schlaf ein (Wiegenlied)
An der schönen blauen Donau
Perpetuum mobile
Heut' Nacht hab ich geträumt von dir
Liebesleid

Mein lieber Schatz, bist du aus Spanien
Die Dorfmusik

Oslo, Norway – April 22 and 25, 1934

Ein neuer Frühling wird in die Heimat kommen
Ohne Dich
So ein Kuss kommt von allein
Eine kleine Frühlingsweise (Humoreske)
Tag und Nacht
Kannst Du pfeifen Johanna?
Ali Baba
Guter Mond du gehst so stille
In einem kühlen Grunde
Wiegenlied
An der schönen blauen Donau
Perpetuum Mobile
Spanische Moritat
Liebesleid
Creole Love Call
Die Dorfmusik

Comedy Harmonists

Amsterdam, Muziek-Lyceum, March 21, 1936
and Rotterdam, March 22, 1936

Mein kleiner grüner Kaktus
Wenn der alte Brunnen rauscht
Lebe wohl, gute Reise
Wenn die Sonja russisch tanzt
Der Onkel Bumba aus Kalumba
Music Makes Me
In My Solitude
Barcarole Corse
The Continental
Night and Day
Ungarischer Tanz No. 5
In stiller Nacht
Sandmännchen
Eine kleine Frühlingsweise (Humoreske)
Quand la Brise Vagabonde (Rotterdam: Das alte Spinnrad)
Du passt so gut zu mir wie Zucker zum Kaffee
Guitarre d'Amour
Espabilate
Creole Love Call
Rumbah Tambah
Die Dorfmusik
Auf Wiederseh'n (only Amsterdam)

Repertoire for Australia - 1937

You Are My Lucky Star
Wenn der alte Brunnen rauscht
Wenn die Sonja russisch tanzt

Ali Baba
South American Joe
Il Pleut Sur la Route
Cheek to Cheek
Der Onkel Bumba aus Kalumba
Continental
Love Me A Little Today
Whispering
Liebesleid
The Way You Look Tonight
Du passt so gut zu mir wie Zucker zum Kaffee
Les Gars de la Marine
When The Sun Says Good-Night To The Mountains
Mein kleiner grüner Kaktus
Night and Day
Espabilate
Ungarischer Tanz No. 5
Congo Lullaby
St. Louis Blues
Marechiare
Sandmännchen
Eine kleine Frühlingsweise (Humoreske)
Moment Musical
An der schönen blauen Donau
Heidenröslein
Schlafe, mein Prinzchen, schlaf ein
Tarantella Sincera
D'ajaccio à Bonifacio
In einem kühlen Grunde
Drink To Me Only With Thine Eyes
Overture to the Opera "Barber of Seville"
Guitarre D'Amour
Rumba Tambah
In A Persian Market
Il ne Faut Pas Briser un Rêve
Creole Love Call
Die Dorfmusik
Raffaela
Wie wär's mit Lissabon?
Quand la Brise Vagabonde
Das alte Spinnrad
Vienna, City Of My Dreams

New York, Town Hall – February 10, 1939

Ungarischer Tanz No. 5
Liebesleid (Love's Sorrow)
Eine kleine Frühlingsweise (Humoreske)
An der schönen blauen Donau
Marechiare
Moment Musical
Schlafe, mein Prinzchen, schlaf ein
Overture to "The Barber of Seville"
Pepita

Mia Bella Napoli
Der Onkel Bumba (When Yuba Plays the Rhumba on his Tuba)
Congo Lullaby
Whistle While You Work
No Taboleiro da Bahiana
Night and Day
Rumbah Tambah
In a Persian Market

Encores:
Creole Love Call
Dorfmusik

Philadelphia, Music Academy – March 29, 1940

Les Gars de la Marine
Mia bella Napoli
Ti-Pi-Tin
Whistle While You Work
Liebesleid
Let's Call The Whole Thing Off
Allegre Conga en el Rancho Grande
Creole Love Call
Ungarischer Tanz No. 5 (Brahms)
Guter Mond, du gehst so stille
Danny Boy
Cradle Song (Brahms)
Menuett in G (Beethoven)
No Taboleiro da Bahiana
Il ne Faut Pas Briser un Rêve
Pepita
Overture to *Poet and Peasant*

Meistersextett

Brandenburg at River Havel – January 23, 1936

Ein bißchen Leichtsinn kann nicht schaden
Lebe wohl, gute Reise
Tante bleib' hier
Solima
Drüben in der Heimat
Das alte Spinnrad
In der Bar zum Krokodil
In einem kühlen Grunde
Morgen muß ich fort von hier
Eine kleine Frühlingsweise (Humoreske)
An der schönen blauen Donau
Sie trägt ein kleines Jäckchen in blau
Tausendmal war ich im Traum bei Dir
Die Liebe kommt, die Liebe geht
Regentropfen
Holzhackerlied

Berlin, Philharmonic – February 18, 1938

Ich freu mich so
Jede Stunde ohne Dich
Wenn Matrosen mal an Land geh'n
Und so weiter
Ein Männlein steht im Walde (variations)
Du bist so wundervoll
Ich hab eine tiefe Sehnsucht in mir
Das Lieben bringt groß' Freud
Jetzt gang i ans Brünnele
Liebestraum
Marecchiare
O Sole Mio
Ouverture of "Der Barbier von Sevilla" (The Barber of Seville)
Die Juliska aus Budapest
Der kleine Finkenhahn
Wenn ich vergnügt bin, muß ich singen

Naples (Italy Tour) – March 17, 1939

Jetzt oder nie
La Paloma
Vieni, Vieni
Oh, ich glaub ich hab mich verliebt
Küss mich
Eine Insel aus Träumen geboren
Der Wind hat mir ein Lied erzählt
Donkey-Serenade
Am Brunnen vor dem Tore
Ungarischer Tanz Nr. 5
Morgenstimmung
Orientalische Suite
Der Onkel Doktor hat gesagt
Tag und Nacht
Die Nacht ist nicht allein zum Schlafen da
Amapola

Brandenburg (Havel) – December 13, 1940

Rosamunde
Komm zurück!
Mädel fein, Mädel klein
Penny Serenade
Tango Bolero
Bist Du's, lachendes Glück?
Musik! Musik! Musik!
Liebes Gretelein (Ständchen)
Am Abend auf der Heide
Im schönsten Wiesengrunde (traditional)
Träumerei
Gute Nacht Mutter
Über die Prärie
Wolga-Lied

Walter Kollo Potpourri (Untern Linden; Zwei rote Rosen; Es war in Schöneberg;
Was eine Frau im Frühling träumt; Kind, ich schlafe so schlecht; Warte, warte nur ein Weilchen;
Kleine Mädchen müssen schlafen gehen; So lang noch untern Linden)
Hollah Lady
Weibermarsch from „Die lustige Witwe"
Auf nach Madrid (Spanish March)

Appendix F

Media Appearances of the Comedian Harmonists and Successor Groups

Courtesy of Jan Grübler and Josef Westner

Comedian Harmonists

Short Films and Commercial Spots; Private Movies

- **1928: Silent film of *Spanisches Intermezzo***
  (Company: Tobis Industrie GmbH Berlin)
  Song: "Spanisches Intermezzo" from the revue *Casanova*.
  Director: Eric Charell
  Music: Ralph Benatzky
  Recorded December 27 and 28, 1928 (No known copies exist.)

- **1930: *Besuch um Mitternacht oder Das Nachtgespenst von Berlin*,** Comedy movie
  Song: "Wenn die Sterne mit dem Mond spazieren geh'n"
  Recorded February 7, 1930

- **1931: *Kreuzworträtsel*** (Company: Excelsior Film GmbH),
  Director: Günter Schwenn and Peter Schaeffers
  Song: "Veronika, der Lenz ist da"
  Recorded August 28, 1931

- **1931: *Der Durchschnittsmann*** (Company: Excelsior Film GmbH)
  Director: Günter Schwenn and Peter Schaeffers. Music: L. W. Gilbert, Maybel
  Wayne/Fritz Rotter
  Song: "Chiquita"
  Recorded probably August 28, 1931
  (This film is likely lost.)

- **1931:*Wiener Wald*** (Company: Excelsior-Film GmbH Berlin), with Fritz Grünbaum

- **1931: *Kabarettprogramm Nr. 6***
  Director: Kurt Gerron
  Music: Various
  Song: "St. Pauli" with Maria Ney
  (This film is likely lost.)

- **1932: *Die Comedian Harmonists singen Volkslieder*** (short film)
  Director: Helmut Schreiber
  Music: Various
  Songs: "O Straßburg," "Das Lieben bringt groß' Freud'," "Es geht bei gedämpftem
  Trommelklang," "Morgen muss ich fort von hier," "Zu Straßburg auf der Schanz"

- **1932: Scene in a hotel restaurant:**
  The Comedian Harmonists at dinner (private recording; length: 12 m.)

- **1934: Clips of the appearance on the aircraft carrier "U.S.S. Saratoga"**
  in New York Harbor, mentioned in the book "Comedian Harmonists - Der Film"
  by Josef Vilsmaier, Kiepenheuer Verlag, Leipzig 1997, p. 116. Also, in 1998,
  Joseph Vilsmaier said in an interview that this film exists in the U.S.
  Its location is not known.

- **1934:** *Zu Straßburg auf der Schanz* (Company: Märkische Filmgesellschaft Jofa
  Berlin). Folk song-potpourri: "O, Straßburg," "Das Lieben bringt groß' Freud,"
  "Es geht bei gedämpftem Trommelklang," "Morgen muß ich fort von hier,"
  "Zu Straßburg auf der Schanz." Recorded: February 16, 1934.

Movies

- **1930:** *Die Drei von der Tankstelle* (Company: Universum Film Aktiengesellschaft (Ufa))
  Director: Wilhelm Thiele
  Music: Werner Richard Heymann/Robert Gilbert
  The Comedian Harmonists appear as bartenders. There is also an English
  version: *The Three From The Gas Station*.
  Songs: "Womit kann ich Ihnen dienen?," "Liebling, mein Herz läßt dich grüßen"
  with Leo Monosson, "Ein Freund, ein guter Freund."
  Recorded July 16 and 19, 1930.

- **1930:** *Le chemin du paradis*
  Director: Wilhelm Thiele and Max de Vaucourbeil
  Music: Werner Richard Heymann/Jean Boyer
  Actors: Lilian Harvey, Henri Garat, Heinz Rühmann.
  Song: "Tout est permit quand on rêve"
  (The French version of *Die Drei von der Tankstelle*)

- **1930:** *Zwei Krawatten* (Company: Terra Film AG). Recorded August 9, 1930.

- **1931:** *Ihre Hoheit befiehlt* (Company: Ufa).
  Director: Hanns Schwarz
  Music: Werner Richard Heymann/Robert Gilbert, Ernst Neubach
  The Comedian Harmonists appear as cooks. English version:
  Her Highness Commands.
  Song: "Bisschen dies und bisschen das," recorded December 3, 1930
  and February 11, 1931.

- **1931:** *Princesse à vos Ordres*
  Director: Hanns Schwarz
  Music: Werner Richard Heymann/Jean Boyer (?)
  Actors: Henri Garat, Lilian Harvey, Reinhold Schünzel, Paul Hörbiger.
  Song(s): ??? (French version of *Ihre Hoheit befiehlt*)

- **1931:** *Gassenhauer* (Company: Deutsches Lichtspiel-Syndikat - D.L.S.).
  Director: Lupu Pick
  Music: Marc Roland/Johannes Brandt, Erich Collin
  Songs: "Hof-Serenade" and "Marie, Marie." (The song "Uns kann keiner" is
  questionable.) Recorded December 10, 1930 to January 17, 1931.

- **1931:** *Les Quatres Vagabonds*
  Director: Lupu Pick
  Music: Marc Roland
  Actors: ???
  Song(s): ???
  (The French Version of *Gassenhauer*. The collaboration of the Comedian Harmonists is not certain. The film exists in the Archives Françaises du Film des CNC.)

- **1931:** *Der ungetreue Eckehart* (Company: Lothar Stark Film GmbH),
  The Comedian Harmonists as barkeepers
  Song: "Was schenkst Du mir dann?"
  Recorded June 1 and 9, 1931

- **1931:** *Bomben auf Monte Carlo* (Company: Ufa).
  Director: Hanns Schwarz
  Music: Werner Richard Heymann/Robert Gilbert
  Songs: "Wenn der Wind weht über das Meer," "Das ist die Liebe der Matrosen." Recorded: June 18 and 24, 1931.

- **1931:** *Monte Carlo Madness*
  Director: Hanns Schwarz
  Music: Werner Richard Heymann/Rowland Leigh
  Songs: "Over the Blue" and "The Way With Every Sailor"
  (English Version of *Bomben auf Monte Carlo*)

- **1931:** *Le Capitaine Craddock*
  Songs: "Quand la brise vagabonde" and "Les gars de la marine"
  (French version of *Bomben auf Monte Carlo*.)

- **1931:** *Der falsche Ehemann* (Company: Ufa)
  Director: Johannes Guter
  Music: Norbert Glanzberg/Gerd Karlick
  Song: "Hasch mich, mein Liebling, hasch mich!"

- **1932:** *Der Sieger* (Company: Ufa)
  Director: Hans Hinrich and Paul Martin
  Music: Werner Richard Heymann/Robert Gilbert, Max Kolpe, Robert Liebermann
  Song: "Es führt kein andrer Weg zur Seligkeit"
  Recorded February 16-18 and 22, 1932
  (This film has not been located.)

- **1932:** *Le Vainqueur*
  Director: Hans Hinrich and Paul Martin
  Music: Werner Richard Heymann/Jean Boyer
  Actors: Jean Murat, Käthe von Nagy.
  Song(s): "La route du bonheur"
  (The French version of *Der Sieger* which has not been located.)

- **1932:** *Ich bei Tag und Du bei Nacht* (Company: Ufa)
  Director: Ludwig Berger
  Music: Werner Richard Heymann/Robert Gilbert, Werner Richard Heymann
  Song: "Wenn ich Sonntags in mein Kino geh"
  Recorded August 15, 1932

- 1932: *À Moi le Jour, à Toi la Nuit*
    Director: Ludwig Berger and Claude Heymann
    Music: Werner Richard Heymann/Jean Boyer (?)
    Actors: ???
    Song(s): ???
    (The French version of *Ich bei Tag und du bei Nacht*.)

- 1932: *Early To Bed*
    Director: Ludwig Berger
    Music: Werner Richard Heymann
    Actors: ???
    Song(s): ???
    (The English version of *Ich bei Tag und du bei Nacht*)

- 1932: *Spione im Savoy-Hotel*
    (*Die Galavorstellung der Fratellinis*), (Company: Efzet Film GmbH)
    Director: Friedrich Zelnik
    Music: Otto Stransky
    Songs: "Mach mir's nicht so schwer," "Ich bin so furchtbar glücklich"
    Recorded August 23, 1932

- 1932: *Publikum singt mit*
    This movie and the participation of the Comedian Harmonists were mentioned in
    an exhibition about the composer Fritz Grünbaum in Vienna in 2005.
    No further information. Perhaps it was confused with "Wiener Wald?"

- 1933: *Kleiner Mann, was nun?* (Company: Robert Neppach Filmproduktion)
    Director: F. Wendhausen
    Music: Harald Böhmelt/Ernst Busch
    Songs: "Kleiner Mann, was nun?," "Was dein roter Mund im Frühling sagt"
    Recorded May 6, 1933
    (The appearance of the Comedian Harmonists was deleted by Nazi censorship.
    The scenes with the Comedian Harmonists were removed before the film was
    shown in cinemas and the Comedian Harmonists can only be heard in the
    opening credits with "Kleiner Mann – was nun?") The film exists in the
    Bundesarchiv (Federal Archives) in Berlin.

- 1997: *Comedian Harmonists – Eine Legende kehrt zurück*
    (Movie by Joseph Vilsmaier), the DVD contains a trailer with
    interview pieces with Roman Cycowski
    English version: *The Harmonists* – in German with English subtitles

Note: The often-mentioned appearance in the movie *Die oder – keine* (1932) is not correct.

Comedy Harmonists

- 1935: *Katharina die Letzte*
    (Company: Deutsche Universal-Film GmbH - produced in Austria)
    Director: Hermann Kosterlitz
    Music: Nikolai Brodsky/Fritz Rotter
    The Comedy Harmonists as themselves.
    Songs: "Auf Wiedersehen, mein Fräulen," "Du passt so gut zu mir
    wie Zucker zum Kaffee"

- **1936: *Le grand refrain***
  Directors: Yves Mirande and Robert Siodmak
  Music: Werner Richard Heymann
  Song: "J'ai Quelqu'un dans Mon Coeur"

- **1938 (?): Short concert of the Comedy Harmonists**
  Songs: "Creole Love Call" and "Schlafe, mein Prinzchen, schlaf ein."
  (Eberhard Fechner used parts of the film in his documentary.)

- **1939: Clip of the Arrival of the group in Fremantle, Australia**
  (The film exists in the Australian National Screen Sound Archive.)

- **1940: From, *Pageant of Great Artists* List of artists featured on the radio series**
  Director: John Hickling (?)
  Music: various (?)
  Actors: Louis Armstrong, Richard Tauber, Mills Brothers.
  Song(s): ???
  (An Australian documentary which is in the
  Australian National Screen and Sound Archive.)

- **Various 8/16mm films by Rudolf Mayreder**
  (Silent color films)

- **1939: Clip of the arrival of the Comedy Harmonists in Australia**
  (Australian Movie Archives)

Meistersextett

- **1936: *Caspar Blume*** (Company: Kinemat Film Wuppertal)
  Commercial spot for a kitchen oven
  Music: A. Limberg
  Recorded January 21, 1936
  (Filmed in January 1936 with Sengeleitner and Blanke.
  Parts of the film were used in the Fechner documentary)

- **1936: *Die Entführung*** (Company: Boston-Films Company GmbH, Berlin)
  Director: ???
  Music: Franz Grothe/Hans Fritz Beckmann
  Song: "Die Welt ist schön, Herr Kapitän!"
  Recorded January 13 and 14, 1936
  (First shown in April 1936. First grouping with Sengeleitner and Blanke.)

- **1936: *Schabernack* aka *Wer ist Wer?***
  (Company: Allgemeine Filmaufnahme- und Vertriebs GmbH (Algefa), Berlin)
  Director: E. W. Emo
  Music: Viktor Corzilius
  Song: "Wenn die Vergissmeinnicht blühen"
  (Recorded May 30, 1936, with Zeno Coste)
  (First shown in September 1936. First grouping with Sengeleitner and Blanke.)

- **1937: *Fremdenheim Filoda*** (Pension Filoda)
  (Company: Cine-Allianz Tonfilm Produktion GmbH)
  Director: Hans Hinrich
  Music: Anton Profes/Hans Fritz Beckmann

Song: "Wenn Matrosen mal an Land geh'n"
Recorded: May 27, 1937
(First shown in September 1937. Recorded with Herbert Imlau and Alfred Grunert.)

• **1936:** *Die un-erhörte Frau*
(Company: Hala-Syndikat-Produktion)
(On August 15, 1936, the Meistersextett made a recording of the song "Heut' bin ich glücklicher als glücklich" in a film-studio in Berlin-Johannisthal. This song was written for this movie by the composer Michael Jary (aka Max Jantzen – Real Name: Max Jarczyk.)

• **1936, 1937:** *Und du, mein Schatz, fährst mit* (Company: Ufa)
Director: Georg Jacoby
Music: Franz Doelle/Charles Amberg
Song: "Irgendwo mit Dir ganz allein" and a portion of "Muss i denn zum Städtele hinaus"
(the claimed contribution of Rudi Schuricke is questionable)
Recorded: September 8 and 25, 1936 (First shown in January 1937. Grouping with Zeno Coste and Herbert Imlau.)

Television Broadcasts

Fechner documentary – *Die Comedian Harmonists: Sechs Lebensläufe*. First part: December, 18, 1976; Second part: Dec. 20, 1976. Shown regionally only (German Programs in West, North and Berlin).

Repeated: First part: May 29, 1977; Second part: May 31, 1977
(German Program ARD - nationwide).

Radio Broadcasts

• September 5, 1998: Prof. Dr. Peter Czada, (station: MDR)

• October 26, 2003, *Rudolf Mayreder und die Comedian Harmonists*, with Michael Hortig (station: Radio Steyermark, Austria)

• January 16, 2005 (December 26, 2004): *This is Harry Frohman Speaking*, radio feature with original cuts with Harry Frohman, Eric von Späth and musical experiments of Frohman as "vocal orchestra" (Station: Deutschlandfunk)

Solo Activities

Erwin Bootz
• 1930: Composed the music for the movie *Hans in allen Gassen* (while not with the Comedian Harmonists) in co-operation with Hansom Milde-Meißner (Company: Carl-Froehlich-Film)
Director: Carl Froelich
Main actor: Hans Albers
Songs: "Mensch, Mensch, Mensch, Mensch, werd' bloß nicht erst Reporter,"
"Mädel, reich' mir Deine Lippen," "Mein Auto ist ein feiner Hund."
Lyrics: Rudolf Frank
(Bootz does not appear in the movie.)
(The French version was called *La Folle Aventure*)

• 1930: Erwin Bootz composed the music and appeared as a piano-playing resident of a guest-house in the movie *Abschied* (Company: Ufa).

> Director: Robert Siodmak.
> Music: Erwin Bootz
> Songs: "Reg Dich nicht auf, wenn mal was schief geht" and
> "Wie schnell vergisst man, was einmal war."

• 1931 Compositions: "Ich bin so scharf auf Erika" and Lyrics: Gerd Karlick, published on 78rpm Nr. EG 2259, with Siegfried Arno and the Jack Hilton orchestra (Bootz isn't singing the song on this record) and "Warum lässt Du nichts mehr von Dir hören?"

• 1938: 78rpm records Nr.EG 6527: "Erwin Bootz und sein Orchester" (Erwin Bootz and his orchestra) – as musical director of the Kabarett der Komiker in Berlin:

> 1. "Guten Abend, liebes Publikum" with Olga Rinnebach, Lizzi
> Waldmüller and Peter Igelhoff;
> 2. "Ein kleiner Accord" (Igelhoff/Schwenn)/ "Ein kleiner Roman"
> (Volkner/Brink) with Olga Rinnebach, EG 6528

• 1938: composed the song "Die bezauberndste Nacht der Saison" (The Most Enchanting Night of the Season) and the dance "Ich hab zwei süße Schwestern" (I Have Two Sweet Sisters)

• 1938/39: Composed the music for the revue *Der Apfel ist ab – ein Paradaisspiel* (The Apple Has Come Off – A Paradise Play) by Hellmut Käutner, one-act play in three scenes, based on the Bible, for the Kabarett der Komiker of Willi Schaeffers, lyrics by Hans Fritz Beckmann, director: Arthur Maria Rabenalt.

• 1939: In the first German synchronization of the American cartoon *Gullivers Travels*. Erwin Bootz is the voice of "Pepi".

• 1954: Record Polydor 49156, 25 cm: "Wie das so üblich ist" (swing-foxtrot by Golden & Balz)/ "Kuckuck – rate mal wer ich bin?" (foxtrot by Bootz). Both sung by Evelyn Kunneke, accompaniment: Werner Müller and the RIAS dance orchestra – Berlin.

• ?: Record Philips P44102H: "Kálmán-Melodien/Léhar-Melodien" (Adaptation: Siegfied Muchow), Erwin Bootz at the piano, with small dance orchestra

• ? 78rpm record Telefunken A 10339: "Schattenspiele." Comp. Hermann Flodt (?)/ "Was eine Frau im Frühling träumt" Erwin Bootz at the piano with orchestra accompaniment. Director: Frank Fux

• 1952: In the German dubbing of the American movie *Sons of the Desert* with Stan Laurel and Oliver Hardy; Erwin Bootz dubs his voice for Stan Laurel

• 1956: LP "Märchen aus 1001 Nacht" (Fairy Tales From 1001 Nights): Sindbad der Seefahrer – Aladin und die Wunderlampe – Ali Baba und die 40 Räuber – Kalif Storch; Speakers: Erwin Bootz, (as the Sultan), Willy Wiesgen, Benno Gellenbeck, Henry Vahl, and others

• 1956: Single "Sindbad der Seefahrer" (see above) with Erwin Bootz

• 1956 (December): Radio program about the Comedian Harmonists with the title "Meistersinger der Kleinkunst – die Comedian Harmonists und ihre Zeit" (Master Singers of the Variety Show – The Comedian Harmonists and their Time), repeated February 23, 1957, station: SFB

• 1956/1958: Radio program "Sechs Herren im Frack" (Six Gentlemen in Tailcoats) with Erwin Bootz (station: SWF, Baden-Baden)

• January 25, 1957, 21:45 to 22:00 p.m.:
    1. "Das Magazin" by Erwin Bootz;
    2. "Kitsch im Dreivierteltakt" by Friedrich Hollaender);
    3. "Der Berufsgruseler" by Günter Neumann);
    4. "In der Bar zum Krokodil" by Fritz Beda. Station: UKW Nord

• 1958: 7" single Polydor 55009 "Das tapfere Schneiderlein."
    Music: Franz Josef Breuer. Conductor: Willy Steiner. Speaker:
    Hans Paetsch; the tailor: Hans Irle; the king: Helmut Peine; the
    ambassador: Willy Wiesgen; first giant: Benno Gellenbeck,
    second giant: Erwin Bootz. Director: Sandor Ferenczy.
    Cover Illustration: Irma Seidat

• 1959 - 1971: During his time in Canada Bootz made some radio broadcasts; for instance,
he appeared in a show with his famous variations of "Never on Sunday."

• March 23, 1965: Radio program *Aus der Mottenkiste: Erinnerungen an die Comedian
Harmonists, erzählt von Erwin Bootz* (From the Moth Case: Memories of the Comedian Harmonists, told by Erwin
Bootz); station: SWF Stuttgart; the comments were recorded in Toronto on tape, the music was added at the station;
some repetitions

• 1969: Radio program *Sechs Herren im Frack – Erwin Bootz erzählt über die Comedian Harmonists
und ihre Zeit* (Six Gentlemen in Tailcoats – Erwin Bootz Tells About the Comedian Harmonists and Their Times),
station SWF Baden-Baden

• 1972: Music for the revue *Kleiner Mann was nun?*, directors: Peter Zadek and Tankred Dorat, based on a novel by
Hans Fallada, Bochum theater (also Freiburg 1976/77)

• 1973: Music for *Professor Unrat*, based on the novel by Heinrich Mann, Bochum theater

• 1973: Movie *Die Zärtlichkeit der Wölfe*. Director: Uli Lommel, with Rainer Werner Fassbinder
(the movie represents the story of the German serial killer Fritz Haarmann in 1924): Erwin Bootz appears
and sings "In der Bar zum Krokodil."

• December 29, 1973: Radio program, station SWF (Czada, p. 197)

• July 8, 1977: Radio program *Erinnern Sie sich* (Do You Remember?), station: SWF (same)

• 1980: Music for *Lieber Georg* from Thomas Brasch, Bochum theater

• 1980: Music for *Jeder stirbt für sich allein* from Peter Zadek/Gottfried Greiffenhagen, based on the novel
by Hans Fallada, Schillertheater Berlin

• 1980/81: Composed the film music for the 8-minute animation film *Die vier Jahreszeiten* from Lotte Reiniger

• 1980: Appearance at the Tempodrom Theater Berlin: opening program May 1.-3, 1980 and July 11, 1980,
recording of the première of the program *Von Balkonien bis Feuerland*. Songs: "Mein kleiner grüner Kaktus" and
the refrain of "Heut fahr' ich mit Dir in die Natur." Also, the variations of "Never on Sunday," daily until July 20, 1980.
(A short part with "Heut fahr ich mit Dir ..." in the TV program "Irene Moessinger und das Tempodrom Berlin"
from 1980.)

• 1981: Festival *Theater der Welt* in Köln, 1 ½-hour solo program

Robert Biberti

• 1942: 78rpm record Electrola EH 1322: *Das Ännchen von Tharau*; Robert Biberti sings with Hildegard Erdmann, Hans Schillings and Walter Ecsy, musical potpourri from the operetta (composer: Heinrich Strecker/lyrics: Bruno Hardt-Warden, Berlin Radio Orchestra, conductor: Bruno Seidler-Winkler), Biberti sings among others: "Wer wird auf der Schulbank kleben, schön ist nur das Kriegerleben!"

• ? 78 rpm record Electrola EG 7168: Robert Biberti sings with the orchestra Hans Carste: "Sie will nicht Blumen und nicht Schokolade" (flip side: "Peter, Peter," not with Biberti)

• ? 78 rpm record on Electrola: "Unser Paul Lincke" flip side: part 2, Interpreters: M. Düren, E. Vogel, H. Schillings and Robert Biberti, Orchestra Bruno Seidler-Winkler.

• Between 1954 and 1961 single on Polydor: "Nur für Herrenabende: Es steht ein Wirtshaus an der Lahn" with Will Hoehne, lyrics: Biberti

• March 25, 1963 - Station: SFB: *Singende Musikanten – die Comedian Harmonists und ihre Welt – eine Sendung von und mit Robert Biberti* (Singing Musicians - The Comedian Harmonists and Their World, A Program From and With Robert Biberti), some repetitions until 1966

• Possibly in 1965: Contribution in the dubbing of *Flintstones*

• 1967: Contribution in the movie *Herrliche Zeiten im Spessart* with Lilo Pulver; Biberti as a Bavarian minister, with make-up and a wig, speaks a single sentence, later dubbed by a Bavarian

• Possible contribution in the short film *Mauerblume im Ballhaus Paradox* by Rudolf Lorenzen. Actors are only acquaintances and friends of the writers Annemarie Weber and Rudolf Lorenzen, among them Robert Biberti. The movie came out in Keese's Ballroom, is performed only at the rest room and almost without words.

• 1969: Short film by Rudolf Lorenzen and Karin Hanisch *Die Torte*, recordings in Biberti's apartment, different synchronization versions, the film was broadcast as *Variationen über einen Film* (Variations About a Film) on December 12, 1970, station: ZDF

• 1971: *Wenn auch die Jahre enteilen*, radio program by Rudolf Günter Wagner, station: SFB. Interview with Robert Biberti about the history of the Comedian Harmonists, broadcast May 1, 1971

• Around 1974: Radio program *Weißt Du noch?* with Robert Biberti, station: Deutsche Welle

• August 5, 1975: Repetition of the radio program from SFB in 1971

• September 18, 1975: Radio program from RIAS: *Willkommen - Bienvenue - Welcome* (Comedian Harmonists)

• June 5 and 11, 1977: Radio program *Stunde des Chansons: Schönklingende Stimmen gesucht! Die Comedian Harmonists und ihre Lieder*. Station: SWF Stuttgart

• September 22, 1978: TV-Talk show with Robert Biberti. Station NDR

• November 1978: Radio program *Berliner Fenster*. Station: SFB

• April 19, 1979: Contribution in the TV serial *Ruby Martinson* as a crook. Station: SWF Baden-Baden

• September 2, 1979: Radio program *Erinnerungen an die Comedian Harmonists*. Station: WDR

• January 19, 1981: Appearance in the Swiss TV program *Unbekannte Bekannte* with the Eugster Trio. Recorded in Zürich on January 13-14, 1981

• July 10, 1981: Radio program *Erinnerungs-Star der Woche* ("Fünf-Uhr Tee bei Fam. Krause," "Ah Maria, Mari," "Gitarren spielt auf"). Station: WDR

• January 1984: radio program *A Tribute to the Comedian Harmonists*, King's Singers, interview with Robert Biberti, station: WDR

• 1984: TV-Talk show *III nach 9*, presenter: Alida Gundlach, with Robert Biberti. Station: NDR

• 1985: TV program *Eine kleine Sehnsucht*, with Robert Biberti, Blandine Ebinger, Curt Bois, Humpe Sisters, Udo Lindenberg

• 1985: TV documentary *Ein Berliner Leben: Robert Biberti, Bassist der Comedian Harmonists*, station: HR. (Likely the last appearance of Biberti before his death; see Czada p. 197.)

Harry Frommermann (Frohman)

• October 1960: Radio program about the Comedian Harmonists from Munich

• January 13, 1973: Radio program, *Start 1928* with Harry Frohman. Station: Radio Bremen (RB)

• September 17, 1975: *Pop von einst – Die Comedian Harmonists und ihre Lieder*, with Harry Frohman. Station: Bayrischer Rundfunk (BR)

• June 16, 1984: *Erinnerungen an Harry Frohman und die Comedian Harmonists* with Erika von Späth Station: RB

Roman Cycowski

• April 1998: *Ich war ein Comedian Harmonist* with Roman Cycowski (Station: MDR)

• Spring 1998: Interview with Roman Cycowski (Station: SAT 1)

Erich Collin

• Radio interview in 1999 in California, with Marc Alexander, grandson of Erich Collin.

Ari Leschnikoff

• LP Balkanton BTA 1644 with seven Bulgarian folksongs.
>   Side A: The Abandoned Man's Sorrow, with orchestra Mikrofon; Rosita, Paso Doble, with orchestra Rockstroh; Two Tears, Tango, with orchestra Rockstroh; Love is an Eternal Secret, Tyrolean Walz, with orchestra Mikrofon; Bitter Coffee, M: Asparuch Leschnikoff, orchestra with director A. Owtscharov; The Break of Dawn, Romance; Katjusha, Foxtrot, with orchestra Mikrofon. Side B: songs of another singer.

• LP Balkanton BTA 1645 with six further Bulgarian folksongs.
>   Side A: Parting; White-Stoned Well; I Love Women Passionately; Don't Expect Me; Waves' Whispers; Oh, Gypsy Woman, Dance!. Side B: Comedian Harmonists songs: "Amapola," "O sole Mio," "Gitarren, spielt auf," "Serenade," "Perpetuum Mobile" and "Der Barbier von Sevilla." (Some of the Leschnikoff songs are available on a Bulgarian CD as a mix with Comedian Harmonists songs.)

• 1940: Recording on Patria: The "Ari-Terzett" With Leschnikoff, two unknown female singers and the orchestra Meg Tevelian: "Lili Marleen" and "Tapfere kleine Soldatenfrau"

• January 30, 1965: *Irgendwo auf der Welt* with Ari Leschnikoff. Station: Radio DDR, Dresden

Herbert Imlau
- From 1940: Leader of the group Die 5 Melodisten
- From 1945: Leader of the group Comedien Quartett
- From 1950: Leader of the Hula Hawaiian Quartett
- Later: Herbert-Imlau-Quartett, sometimes: Die sieben Raben
- From 1957: Ponny Boys
- A number of records with each of these groups
- His daughter Margrit started a solo career as singer in 1959 and was a German teenage-star of the 60s.

Fred Kassen
- Some records
- May 2, 1956: Radio program about the Comedian Harmonists

Richard Sengeleitner
- Appears in 1936 and 1937 as tenor in German radio programs (recordings available)
- Some records

Appendix G

Songs Sung By the Comedian Harmonists/Comedy Harmonists/ American Group/Meistersextett But Not Recorded By That Group

Courtesy of Jan Grübler

Comedian Harmonists

Blue River (1929)
Böhmische Polka (1929)
Die Mädis vom Chantant (Leipzig, Feb. 1931)
Es gibt (nur) eine Frau, die Dich niemals vergisst (1929, only test recording)
Heimweh
I Know That You Know (Revelers imitation) (1930)
In der Eisenbahn from *Zwei Krawatten* (railway sound imitation, 1929)
Jig-Walk (only test recording, May 10, 1928)
Miss Annabelle Lee (1929/1939, only test recording)
Scheinbar liebst Du mich (Russian version) (1931)
Sonny Boy (1929)
Spiel mir mein Liebeslied (1929, only test recording)
Spoliansky-Potpourri (1930)
Variationen über verschiedene Wolgalieder (imitation of the Don Cossacks)
Varsity Drag (Anna hat Geld) (1929-1931, only test recording)
Virginia (English)
Walzertraum (Oscar Strauss, 1930)
Warum weinst Du, holde Gärtnersfrau? (1930)
Wenn der Himmel voller schwarzer Wolken hängt (basso-solo by Biberti in the"Funkstunde," Deutschlandsender November 15, 1930)
Wiener Blut (1933)
Zwei rote Rosen

Auf Wiederseh'n (by Mischa Spoliansky)
Letter from Electrola to the C. H. dated January 30, 1932: "Dear Sirs, In the past we have had many requests for a recording of 'Auf Wiederseh'n,' as sung by the Comedian Harmonists. Would you please take into consideration preparing this song for a recording in a complying arrangement and with a suitable pairing." In the 1970s Biberti wrote to an inquiring fan: "This final song of our concerts has never been recorded."

Comedy Harmonists

Ali Baba (1937)
Allegra Conga en el Rancho Grande (1938)
A Marechiare (1937)
An der schönen blauen Donau (Joh. Strauss) (1937)
Annie Laurie (1939)
Barcarole Corse (1936)
Caprice Viennois (1937)
Cheek To Cheek (1936)
Cradle Song (Schlafe, mein Prinzchen, schlaf ein - Brahms) (1939)
Creole Love Call (1937)
Danny Boy (Old Irish Air) (1940)
Das alte Spinnrad (1937)
Dorfmusik (1937)
Drink To Me Only With Thine Eyes (Traditional Air) (1937)
El Rancho Grande (1938)

Guter Mond, Du gehst so stille (1940)
Hen ten Komoden ((1936, Dutch)
Humoresque (Dvorak) (Eine kleine Frühlingsweise) (1936, 1937)
Hungarian Dance No. 5 (Ungarischer Tanz, Brahms) (1937)
In stiller Nacht (1936)
In einem kühlen Grunde (1937)
Lebe wohl, gute Reise (1936)
Les Gars de la Marine – See, "Voila . . . "
Let's Call The Whole Thing Off (1937)
Liebesleid (1936, 1937)
Wie wär's mit Lissabon
Mein kleiner grüner Kaktus (1937)
Mein Onkel Bumba (1937)
Menuett in G (Beethoven) (1940)
Music Makes Me (1936)
Night and Day (1937)
Noches de Paraguay (1938)
No Taboleiro da Bahiana (1940)
Oh! Ma-Ma (1937)
Overture To *Poet and Peasant* (1937)
Pepita (1939)
Quand la Brise Vagabonde (1936)
Sah ein Knab ein Röslein stehn (Heidenröslein) (1937)
Schlafe mein Prinzchen (Mozart; Wiegenlied or Cradle Song) (1937) (appears in a film)
South American Joe (1936)
St. Louis Blues 937
Tarantella Sincera (1937)
Tarantula (1937)
There's A New World (1937)
Toreadors In Madrid (1937)
Torna Piccina (1937)
Tyrekampen (Bullfight) (1936)
Umbrella Man, The (1937)
Vienna, City Of My Dreams (1937)
Voila les Gars de la Marine (1937)
Waltzing Matilda (1937)
Walzertraum (1937)
Wenn der alte Brunnen rauscht (1936)
Wenn die Sonja russisch tanzt (1936, 1937)
When My Dreamboat Comes Home (1937)
Whispering (1937)
Wie wär's mit Lissabon (1937)
You Are My Lucky Star (1936)

American Group (All in 1948)
Aubade from the Opera *Le Roi d'Ys* (E. Lalo)
Bumble Bee (Rimski-Korsakov)
Etude No. 10 (Fr. Chopin)
Granada
Holiday for Strings
In einem kühlen Grunde (folk song)
J'attendrai
Persian Market

Potpourri of Negro Spirituals
Song of the Garden (folk song)
Voila les Gars de la Marine

Meistersextett
Am Abend auf der Heide (1940)
Auf nach Madrid (Spanish March, 1940)
Auf Wiederseh'n (See above)
Bel Ami (only test recording)
Bist Du's, lachendes Glück
Das alte Spinnrad (1935)
Das Fräulein Gerda (1938)
Das Leben ist ein Karussell (1939, from: *Glückliche Reise*)
Das Schiff streicht durch die Wellen (1939, from: *Glückliche Reise*)
Der Käfer und die Blume – (1936/37)
Ein bisschen Leichtsinn kann nicht schaden (1935)
Graf von Luxemburg
Gute Nacht, auf Wiedersehen
Gute Nacht, Mutter
Holzhackerlied (1935)
Im schönsten Wiesengrunde
Im Wald und auf der Heide
In der Bar zum Krokodil (1935)
Indian Love Call
Inseratensong (1939, from: *Glückliche Reise*)
Jede Frau hat ein Geheimnis
Kastanienbaum
Kinder wie die Zeit vergeht
Kollo-Potpourri Parts 1 and 2 (Walter Kollo: Untern Linden; Zwei rote Rosen; Es war in Schöneberg; Was eine Frau im Frühling träumt; Kind, ich schlafe so schlecht; Warte, warte nur ein Weilchen; Kleine Mädchen müssen schlafen gehen; So lang noch untern Linden, 1940)
Komm zurück
Küss mich, bitte bitte küss mich (1938)
Lebe wohl, gute Reise (1935)
Liebes Gretelein
Liebesleid (1935)
Madeira (1939, from: *Glückliche Reise*)
Mädel fein, Mädel klein (Lèhar, 1940)
Mein kleiner grüner Kaktus (1936)
Musik, Musik, Musik
Nacht muss es sein (1939, from: *Glückliche Reise*)
Penny Serenade (only test recording)
Piet Hein (1936, Dutch)
Puppenhochzeit (1936/37)
Rosamunde (1940)
Sarie Marais (1936, Dutch)
Stille Nacht, heilige Nacht (1936)
Tag und Nacht (Night And Day, 1938)
Tango Bolero
Tante bleib hier (1935)
Täumen (Cheek To Cheek, 1936)
Träumerei (Schumann, 1940)
Über die Prärie (Rudolf Friml, from *Rose Marie*)

Walter Kollo-Potpourri, Sides 1 and 2
Weibermarsch (from *The Merry Widow* by Léhar, 1940)
Wenn die Sonja russisch tanzt (1936)
Whispering (1938)
Wie wärs mal mit Lissabon (1935)
Wolgalied (Léhar. 1940)

Appendix H
Resources

Selected CDs

This is Harry Frobman speaking...Die letzten Jahre des Comedian Harmonists (The Last Year of the Comedian Harmonist Harry Frommermann), Radio Bremen NDR Audio (Primarily in German)

Comedian Harmonists

Comedian Harmonists: The International Collection (4 disks – 127 tracks – with booklet in German and English) Membran Music

Comedian Harmonists: Die Grossen Erfolge (The Biggest Hits), Vols. 1, 2, 3, 4 and 5
(91 total tracks – CDs can be purchased individually)
EMI International

Das Allerbeste von Comedian Harmonists (27 tracks of their hit songs)
EMI

Die Schönsten Volkslieder von Comedian Harmonists (22 tracks of traditional songs)
EMI

Süßes Baby 1928 – 1929 (23 tracks of early Comedian Harmonists songs)
Bob's Music

Comedian Harmonists: Bitte recht freundlich! (Please Smile Nicely – the title of one of their early medleys)
(22 tracks of some of the less familiar songs of the group)
Bob's Music

Comedian Harmonists (3 CDs – 41 tracks)
ZYX Music

Stimmen des Jahrhunderts (Voices of the Century) – Comedian Harmonists: Volkslieder (18 tracks)
(Comedian Harmonists and Meistersextett)
Weltbild

The Comedian Harmonists Chantent en Francais (2 disks – 45 tracks – all in French)
Epm

Comedy Harmonists

The Comedy Harmonists
Vienna Group/Exilgruppe, 1936 - 41
Complete Recordings (2 disks and 3 booklets in English and German – also includes song lyrics)
Available at http://www.comedyharmonists.de/

Das Beste der Comedy Harmonists (26 tracks)
EMI

The Comedy Harmonists: Whistle While You Work: Original 1929-1938 Recordings (19 tracks)
Naxos

Meistersextett

Das Meistersextett – Früher Comedian Harmonists (formerly the Comedian Harmonists)
Edition Comedian Harmonists Vol. II: Das Meistersextett (4 disks – 75 tracks - booklet in German –
also contains song lyrics)
RBM

Das Beste Vom Meister-Sextett (28 tracks)
EMI

Other

Rivalen der Comedian Harmonists – Songs by other popular German groups of the era,
including the Kardosch Singers, Fidelios, Humoresk Melodios and Melody Gents
Duophon

Breezin' Along With The Revelers (25 tracks)
Living Era

Films

Die Comedian Harmonists: Sechs Lebensläufe (The Comedian Harmonists: Six Life Stories), a documentary by
Eberhard Fechner first shown on regional German television in 1976 over two nights. Available on both video tape
and DVD, but only in European format (PAL) and only in German, without English subtitles.
Available from Amazon.de.

The Harmonists, directed by Joseph Vilsmaier and released in 1997. Available from Amazon.com and on eBay.
In German and French with English subtitles.

Books

Die Comedian Harmonists: Sechs Lebensläufe
(The Comedian Harmonists: Six Life Stories), by Eberhard Fechner. Published by Quadriga Verlag, Weinheim und
Berlin, 1988. 412 pages. In German only. Primarily interviews, many of which are in the Fechner film (see above),
and a discography.

Comedian Harmonists: Ein Vokalensemble erobert die Welt
(Comedian Harmonists, A Vocal Group Conquers The World), by Peter Czada and Günter Grosse. Published by
Edition Hentrich, Berlin, 1993, 1998. In German only. 201 pages. Biography and includes many photographs and
a discography.

Irgendwo auf der Welt - Die Schallplatten der Comedian Harmonists und ihrer Nachfolgegruppen
(Somewhere In The World – The Records of the Comedian Harmonists and Their Successors).
Self-published by Andreas Schmauder, Horben, 1999. In German only. 100 pages.
The complete discography. See, http://www.phonopassion.de/

Comedian Harmonists
by Tilo Köhler. Published by Gustav Kiepenheuer Verlag, Leipzig, 1997. In German only. 297 pages.
A fictionalized novel about the group, based on the Vilsmaier film.

Comedian Harmonists. Eine Legende kehrt zurück. Der Film
(Comedian Harmonists – A Legend Returns. The Film)
by Joseph Vilsmaier. Published by Gustav Kiepenheuer Verlag, Leipzig, Second Edition (1998) (Paperback).
144 pages. In German only. By the film director. The group's history, film storyboard details, special effects.
Interviews with Roman Cycowski, leading actors, staff and crew.

Die Comedian Harmonists. Phantasie über einen Mythos
(The Comedian Harmonists. A Fantasy About A Myth)
by Pit Holzwarth and Renato Grünig; Libretto for the performance of the Bremer Shakespeare Company in 1997.
Especially about the quarrels within the original group.
Published by Achilla Presse, Stollham, 1997; brochure, 160 pages

Sheet Music

Comedian Harmonists – Das Original 1
Five original arrangements for male chorus with piano: Mein kleiner grüner Kaktus; Eine kleine Frühlingsweise;
Liebling, mein Herz lässt dich grüßen; Guter Mond, du gehst so stille; Das ist die Liebe der Matrosen
by Ulrich Etscheit and Julian Metzger
Publisher: Gustav Bosse Verlag, Kassel, 1997, paperback

Comedian Harmonists – Das Original 2.
Five original arrangements for male chorus with piano: Veronika, der Lenz ist da; Menuett;
Schöne Isabella von Castilien; Mein Onkel Bumba; In einem kühlen Grunde
by Ulrich Etscheit and Julian Metzger
Publisher: Gustav Bosse Verlag, Kassel, 1999, paperback

Comedian Harmonists – Das Original 3.
Five original arrangements for male chorus with piano:
Wochenend und Sonnenschein; Lebe wohl, gute Reise; Creole Love Call; Ungarischer Tanz Nr.5; Barcarole
by Ulrich Etscheit and Julian Metzger
Publisher: Gustav Bosse Verlag, Kassel, 2000, paperback

Comedian Harmonists – Das Original 4.
Five original arrangements for male chorus with piano: Am Brunnen vor dem Tore; Ein Freund, ein guter Freund;
In der Bar zum Krokodil; Träumerei; Wenn die Sonja russisch tanzt
by Ulrich Etscheit and Julian Metzger
Publisher: Gustav Bosse Verlag, Kassel, 2006, paperback

Comedian Harmonists
Five arrangements for mixed chorus (S-A-T-B): Ein Freund, ein guter Freund; Ich wollt' ich wär ein Huhn;
Irgendwo auf der Welt; Mein kleiner grüner Kaktus; Wochenend und Sonnenschein
by Carsten Gerlitz,
Publisher: KDM – Alfred Publishing Verlags GmbH, Neustadt/Wied, 2005; 39 pages, paperback,

Golden Evergreens aus dem Repertoire der Comedian Harmonists - 1
Bel Ami; Das ist die Liebe der Matrosen; Drei Musketiere; Ein Freund, ein guter Freund; Ein Lied geht um die Welt;
Hein spielt abends so schön; Ich hab für Dich 'nen Blumentopf bestellt; In der Bar zum Krokodil; Liebling mein Herz
läßt Dich grüßen; Mein kleiner grüner Kaktus; Veronika, der Lenz ist da; Wenn die Sonja russisch tanzt;
Wochenend und Sonnenschein.
Publisher: Edition Metropol Musikverlage GmbH, Cologne

Golden Evergreens aus dem Repertoire der Comedian Harmonists – 2
Bin kein Hauptmann, bin kein großes Tier; Blume von Hawaii; Du bist nicht die Erste; Heute Nacht oder nie;
Hoppla jetzt komm ich; Ich bin von Kopf bis Fuß auf Liebe eingestellt; Ich küsse Ihre Hand Madame; Ich wollt ich
wär ein Huhn; Puppenhochzeit; Schöne Isabella aus Kastilien, Wenn ich vergnügt bin, muss ich singen.
Publisher: Edition Metropol Musikverlage GmbH, Cologne

Golden Evergreens aus dem Repertoire der Comedian Harmonists – 3 Klavierausgabe. (piano edition).
Piano scores of:
Auf Wiedersehn, my Dear; Barcarole; Ein bißchen Leichtsinn kann nicht schaden; Eine kleine Frühlingsweise;
Guter Mond, du gehst so stille; In einem kühlen Grunde; Irgendwo auf der Welt; Muß i denn zum Städtele hinaus;
Onkel Bumba aus Kalumba; Schöne Isabella aus Kastilien.
Publisher: Edition Metropol Musikverlage GmbH, Cologne

Golden Evergreens aus dem Repertoire der Comedian Harmonists – Folge 1
für Männerstimmen. (for male voices)
Male chorus scores of: Das ist die Liebe der Matrosen; Liebling, mein Herz lässt Dich grüßen;
Mein kleiner grüner Kaktus.
Publisher: Edition Metropol Musikverlage GmbH, Cologne

Golden Evergreens aus dem Repertoire der Comedian Harmonists – Folge 2
für Männerstimmen. (for male voices)
Male chorus scores of: Ein Freund, ein guter Freund; Hein spielt abends so schön; Veronika, der Lenz ist da.
Publisher: Edition Metropol Musikverlage GmbH, Cologne

Golden Evergreens aus dem Repertoire der Comedian Harmonists – Folge 3
für Männerstimmen. (for male voices)
Male chorus scores of: Bel Ami; Ich küsse Ihre Hand, Madame; Ich wollt' ich wär ein Huhn;
Wochenend und Sonnenschein
Publisher: Edition Metropol Musikverlage GmbH, Cologne

Golden Evergreens aus dem Repertoire der Comedian Harmonists – für gemischten Chor. (for mixed chorus)
Bel Ami; Liebling, mein Herz läßt Dich grüßen; Mein kleiner grüner Kaktus; Wochenend und Sonnenschein.
Publisher: Edition Metropol Musikverlage GmbH, Cologne

Golden Evergreens aus dem Repertoire der Comedian Harmonists – für Frauenchor. (for female chorus)
Bel Ami; Liebling, mein Herz läßt Dich grüßen; Mein kleiner grüner Kaktus; Wochenend und Sonnenschein.
Publisher: Edition Metropol Musikverlage GmbH, Cologne

Comedian Harmonists Complete
For male chorus and piano: Bel Ami; Das ist die Liebe der Matrosen; Ein Freund, ein guter Freund; Hein spielt abends
so schön; Ich küsse Ihre Hand, Madame; Ich wollt' ich wär ein Huhn; Liebling, mein Herz läßt Dich grüßen; Mein
kleiner grüner Kaktus; Veronika, der Lenz ist da; Wochenend und Sonnenschein.
Released by Willy Porten
Publisher: Edition Metropol Musikverlage GmbH, Cologne

(Note: There are further editions released by this publisher: Piano scores of single songs, scores for fipple flute,
and so on.)

Comedian Harmonists Erfolge (Comedian Harmonists Greatest Hits)
For piano and keyboard
Released by Steffen: Mein kleiner grüner Kaktus; Veronika, der Lenz ist da; Donkey Serenade.
Publisher: Bothworth Verlag, Vienna-Berlin-London

Plays

Veronika, der Lenz ist da – 1997 in Berlin, by Gottfried Greiffenhagen and Franz Wittenbrink; directed by Martin Woelffer. Part one of two.

Now or Never – 2005 in Berlin. Part two of two.

Harmony – 1997 in La Jolla, California. Music by Barry Manilow and book and lyrics by Bruce Sussman.

Band in Berlin – 1999 in New York at the Helen Hayes Theatre. A multi-media presentation with slides, puppets, film and live singing by the group Hudson Shad – played in New York in 1999. Directed by Susan Feldman.

Web Sites
(All active as of February 2008)

http://www.comedian-harmonists.com/ – the most comprehensive site on the group. Has bios of the members, a list of recordings, films, downloads of music, lyrics, photographs. In German and English.

http://userpage.fu-berlin.de/~sese/Barbershop_Boys/ComedHrm/Comedian_Harmonists_Story.htm – web page by Sebastian Claudius Semler. Basic biographical information on the group and some photos. In German.

http://www.comedian-harmonists.de/ – Extensive information about the group by Simon Umbreit. In German.

http://www.holger-reinhardt.de/english/index.htm – Holger's Page. Contains Midis and lyrics of selected songs. In German and English (lyrics are in German only).

http://www.yodaslair.com/dumboozle/eurojazz/eurodex.html – Brief biography of the group as well as other European groups of the era by Jim Lowe. In English.

http://www.harmonysongs.com/ – My web site that includes information on how to arrange for me to present my Comedian Harmonists program to your organization. There is also a brief biography of the group. In English.

http://www.deutscher-tonfilm.de/ – Biography and filmography in German only.

http://www.cinegraph.de/lexikon/Comedian_Harmonists/biografie.html – Biography in German only.

http://www.geocities.com/caroltraxler/WSB/combar.html – Biography and links by Carol Traxler. In English.

http://www.fb-lueneburg.de/u1/gym03/expo/jonatur/geistesw/zwischen/entartet/musik/comedian.htm – Biography by Projektgruppe Entartete Kunst, Johanneum Lüneburg. In German.

http://www.apencollector.com/palast.html – Downloads and links. In English.

http://www.five-gentlemen.de/main.html?/november.html – Brief information on the group. In German only.

http://www.martinschlu.de/kulturgeschichte/zwanzigstes/comedianharmonists/gruendung.htm – Very brief biography in German.

http://www.radiobremen.de/magazin/kultur/musik/comedian-harmonists/ – Information from Radio Bremen. In German.

http://www.eberhardfechner.de/comedian_harmonist.html – Site about Eberhard Fechner's film. In German.

http://www.phonopassion.de/main.php?key=comedian_en – Web site of Andreas Schmauder, a collector and purveyor of Comedian Harmonists' and other vintage recordings. In German and English.

http://www.heymann-musik.de/xenglish.htm – Web site on the great composer, Werner Richard Heymann, maintained by his daughter Elisabeth. In German and English.

Original 78 rpm Recordings

Phonopassion
Andreas Schmauder
One of Europe's leading trading companies for vintage 78rpm records.
Phonopassion mainly works as a mail-order house but visitors are welcome. A choice of more than 100,000 vintage records from the gramophone era (1890-1960) and a small selection of historic record players and radios.
Friedrichshof
Bohrerstr. 7
D-79289 Horben, Germany
http://www.phonopassion.de/

Historical Musicstore
Andreas Wellen
78rpm records, CDs, 16mm musical film prints (mainly soundies & telescriptions) and high glossy posters on photographic paper showing rare motifs.
http://www.comedianharmonists.de/

Contemporary Groups

GERMANY:

Berlin Comedian Harmonists – http://www.berlin-comedian-harmonists.de/
Die Bornhöved Singers – http://www.bornhoeved-singers.de/home.htm
CHarmonists – http://www.harmonists.org/index.html
Classic Harmonists – http://www.classic-harmonists.de/
Comedian Sixpack – http://www.comedian-sixpack.de/
Comedy Brothers – http://www.comedybrothers.de/
Die Desharmoniker – http://www.desharmoniker.de/index2.html
Disharmoniker – http://www.disharmoniker.de/
Ensemble Espelkamp – http://www.ensemble-espelkamp.de./13822.html
Ensemble Six – http://www.ensemble-six.de/
Five Gentlemen – http://www.five-gentlemen.de/
Die Hofherrn Harmonists – http://www.harmonists.musicpage.de/
Männerwirtschaft – http://www.maennerwirtschaft.de/
Die Mexbrothers – http://www.mexbrothers.de/
Die Pinguin-Singers – http://www.pinguin-singers.de/
Planet Harmony – http://www.planetharmony.net/
Sechs oder Selters – http://www.sechs-oder-selters.de/
Die Singphoniker – http://www.singphoniker.de/
Sixtonics – http://www.the-sixtonics.de/
Die Sweetheartsharks – http://www.sweetheartsharks.de/
Tailed Comedians – http://www.tailed-comedians.de/
Das Vokalkomitee – http://www.vokalkomitee.de/

AUSTRIA:

Comedian Vocalists – http://www.comedian-vocalists.at/
Salzburg Comedian Harmonists – http://www.salzburgcomedianharmonists.at/index.html.html

Vienna Harmonists – http://www.vienna-harmonists.at/

ITALY:

Italian Harmonists – http://www.italianharmonists.it/lang1/index.html

SWITZERLAND:

Six In Harmony – http://www.sixinharmony.ch/

UNITED KINGDOM:

Cantabile – http://www.cantabile.co.uk/
Kings Singers – http://www.kingssingers.com/

UNITED STATES:

Hudson Shad – http://www.hudsonshad.net/

APPENDIX I

Photo Credits

Page	Photo	Permission
Cover	Group at piano	Theo Niemeyer
2	Revelers	Public Domain
3	Lokal-Anzeiger	Theo Niemeyer
5	Stubenrauchstr Plaque	Douglas E. Friedman
6	Stubenrauchstr – Exterior	Douglas E. Friedman
7	Stubenrauchstr – Interior	Douglas E. Friedman
9	Frommermann	Public Domain
10	Frommermann – Bar Mitzvah	Theo Niemeyer
11	Scrapbooks	Theo Niemeyer
11	Biberti	Public Domain
13	Leschnikoff	Theo Niemeyer
15	Cycowski	Theo Niemeyer
17	Bootz	Theo Niemeyer
18	Collin	Public Domain
19	Collin Family	Deborah Tint
20	Hochschule Cover	Theo Niemeyer
21	Nussbaum	Theo Niemeyer
21	W. Steiner	Theo Niemeyer
25	Rehearsal	Theo Niemeyer
31	Odeon Photos – round	Theo Niemeyer
32	Scrapbook/Casanova	Theo Niemeyer
33	Gr. Schauspielhaus – Interior	Theo Niemeyer
35	Knesebeckstrasse	Douglas E. Friedman
36	Group with W. Steiner	Theo Niemeyer
37	Group with Nussbaum	Theo Niemeyer
38	Scala Interior – Postcard	Public Domain
43	Group Photo	Theo Niemeyer
46	Group Photo	Theo Niemeyer
50	Erna Frommermann	Public Domain
51	Wedding Certificate	Theo Niemeyer
52	Passport Photo	Uwe Berger
52	Delphine-Simeon	Jan Grübler

53	Fernande	Deborah Tint
53	Ursula Elkan	Beryn Hammil
54	Bootz-Elkan	Beryn Hammil
55	Mary Panzram	Carolyn Harcourt
55	Hilde Longino	Theo Niemeyer
59	Berlin Philharmonic	Theo Niemeyer
66	April 1 Boycott	Public Domain
70	Caricature – Sax Player	Public Domain
78	Munich concert – 1934	Theo Niemeyer
81	Group on ship Europa	Public Domain
82	Telegram	Biberti Archive (Staatsbibliothek)
83	Tea For Two-Sheet Music	Biberti Archive (Staatsbibliothek)
85	RMK letter – Feb 22, 1935	Biberti Archive (Staatsbibliothek)
91	Group Photo	Public Domain
94	Group Photo	Public Domain
95	Roman and Mary Photo	Theo Niemeyer
97	Mayreder Diary	Jan Grübler
99	Suzanne Collin	Deborah Tint
101	London program	Douglas E. Friedman
103	Frommermann	Public Domain
105	Tivoli Theater – Indiana	Public Domain
111	Group Photo	Public Domain
112	Group Photo	Public Domain
117	Meistersextett – Letter	Josef Westner
126	Collin	Public Domain
127	Fernande Collin	Public Domain
128	Beach Photo	Deborah Tint
129	Group Photo	Public Domain
132	Deborah/Marc	Deborah Tint
134	Collin Grave	Andrea Hollmann
136	Bootz	Public Domain
136	Helli Bootz	Helli Bootz
138	Bootz grave	Andrea Hollmann
140	Cycowski	Carolyn Harcourt
141	Roman and Mary	Public Domain
142	Cycowski Grave	Carolyn Harcourt
145	Leschnikoff	Public Domain

146	Train Station	Uwe Berger
146	Leaflet	Jan Grübler
149	Leschnikoff Letter	Biberti Archive (Staatsbibliothek)
150	Leschnikoff Family	Public Domain
151	Leschnikoff Grave	Jan Grübler
152	Biberti Photo	Public Domain
153	Wedding Announcement	Theo Niemeyer
155	Biberti Grave	Douglas E. Friedman
156	Frohman	Eric von Späth
157	Barber of Seville Sheet Music	Biberti Archive (Staatsbibliothek)
159	RIAS Photo	Public Domain
161	Group Photo	Public Domain
162	Olga Wolff	Public Domain
168	Erika/Harry	Eric von Späth
169	Staircase Photo	Douglas E. Friedman
170	Frohman Grave	Douglas E. Friedman
180	Group Photo	Theo Niemeyer

Note: Any use other than as indicated is inadvertent.

APPENDIX J

Bibliography

Estate of Robert Biberti, Staatsbibliothek, Berlin. A collection of 55,000 documents from the Estate of Biberti

Frohman, Harry M. "The Story Of The Comedian (Comedy) Harmonists." Comedian Harmonists Archive.

Bach, Steven. *Marlene Dietrich: Life And Legend.* New York: William Morrow, 2000.

Czada, Peter and Günter Grosse. *Comedian Harmonists: Ein Vokalensemble erobert die Welt.* Berlin: Edition Hentrich, 1993, 1998.

Fechner, Eberhard. *Die Comedian Harmonists: Sechs Lebensläufe.* Berlin: Quadriga Verlag, 1988 (Fechner book).

Fechner, Eberhard. *Die Comedian Harmonists: Sechs Lebensläufe.* Norddeutscher Rundfunk. Germany, 1976 (Fechner film).

Feuchtwanger, Lion. *The Oppermanns.* New York: Carroll & Graf Publishers, Inc., 1934.

Friedwald, Will. *Stardust Melodies.* New York: Pantheon Books, 2002.

Grunberger, Richard. *The 12-Year Reich: A Social History of Nazi Germany 1933-1945.* Cambridge, New York: Da Capo Press, 1995.

Heskes, Irene. *Passport to Jewish Music: Its History, Traditions, and Culture, Legacy of the Holocaust.* Oxford, Great Britain: Praeger/Greenwood, 1994.

Jelavich, Peter. *Berlin Cabaret.* Cambridge: Harvard University Press, 1996.

Kater, Michael H. *Different Drummers: Jazz In The Culture Of Nazi Germany.* New York: Oxford University Press USA, 1992.

Koepnick, Prof. Lutz. *The Dark Mirror, German Cinema Between Hitler And Hollywood.* Berkeley: University of California Press, 2002.

Meyer-Dinkgrafe, Daniel. *Boulevard Comedy Theatre in Germany.* Newcastle upon Tyne: Cambridge Scholars Press, 2005.

Munz, Lori. *Cabaret Berlin: Revue, Kabarett and Film Music between the Wars.* Hamburg: edel Classics GmbH, 2005.

Nordau, Max. *Degeneration.* New York: D. Appleton and Company, 1895

Niewyk, Donald L. *The Jews in Weimar Germany.* Edison: Transaction Publishers, 2001

Poiger, Uta G. *Jazz, Rock, and Rebels: Cold War Politics and American Culture in a Divided Germany.* Berkeley: University of California Press, 2000.

Ross, Alex. *The Rest Is Noise: Listening To The Twentieth Century.* New York: Farrar, Strauss and Giroux, 2007.

Seeber, Ursula. "Asyl wider Willen. Exil in Österreich 1933-1938." Wien: Picus Verlag, 2003.

Schivelbusch, Wolfgang. *In A Cold Crater: Cultural And Intellectual Life In Berlin, 1945-1948.* Berkeley and Los Angeles: University of California Press, 1998.

Steinweis, Alan E. *Art, Ideology, & Economics in Nazi Germany, The Reich Chambers of Music, Theater, and the Visual Arts.* Chapel Hill and London: The University of North Carolina Press, 1993

Whitburn, Joel. *Joel Whitburn's Pop Memories 1890-1954.* Menomonee Falls, Wisconsin: Record Research, Inc., 1986.

"Musikwoche" Magazine, March 23, 1998, interview with Roman Cycowski,

Stern, Frank. "Facing the Past. Representations of the Holocaust in German Cinema Since 1945." Washington, D.C.: United States Holocaust Memorial Museum, Center For Advanced Holocaust Studies

A Musical 'Recapturing': The Comedian Harmonists is Recreated for a New Generation. The Foundation for Jewish Culture.

Grimes, William. *New York Times*, October 26, 2005, "The Radical Restructuring of a Germany Headed To War."

Rockwell, John. *New York Times*, September 5, 1999, "An Instant Fan's Inspired Notes: You Gotta Listen." Previously unpublished liner notes on the Comedian Harmonists (written in 1981).

Augustin, Michael and Walter Weber. CD, "This is Harry Frohman Speaking." Bremen: Radio Bremen/DLF, 2004

Bootz, Erwin. Radio Bremen Interview, 1957.

Frohman, Harry. Radio Bremen Interview, January 13, 1973.

Numerous web sites.

INDEX

301

LaVergne, TN USA
17 November 2010
205182LV00003B/1/P